You Can't Escape

NANCY BUSH

ZEBRA BOOKS
KENSINGTON PUBLISHING CORP.
http://www.kensingtonbooks.com

A KILLER'S PLAYGROUND

Jordanna walked to the side of the plot. With the toe of her sneaker, she pressed into the deeper brown dirt. Was something there? Carefully, she leaned closer. Reluctantly, wishing she had gloves, she reached a hand forward and lightly scraped at the edge of the soil.

Shoulders tense, she made a hole about six inches deep and started widening it. There was no marker here. No grave. No casket. But somebody had disturbed the earth and then raked over it, trying to make it appear like the rest. At least that's what she thought.

When the hole was about a foot deep and the size and shape of a large book, she stopped. There was nothing here and it was someone's property. Maybe she was disturbing seeds of some kind, flowers planted for the dead.

Sitting back on her haunches, she dusted her hands. It was then she saw the tiny, pearlescent oval. A fingernail. Horror-struck, she nevertheless reached forward and plucked at the nail. Her hand felt a finger and she jerked back on instinct.

The hand that came free was a young woman's, the painted white fingernails, broken.

A scream bubbled up inside her . . .

Books by Nancy Bush

Published by Kensington Publishing Corporation

Prologue

The sleeping girl lay on her back, her hands folded over her chest. She was in her late teens; young to be displaying the affliction, but old enough. She would die soon enough. Peacefully, from the overdose he'd given her. He'd stripped her of her clothes and her unblemished skin shone dove gray in the moonlight filtering through the open barn door.

Glancing outside, he considered how many hours there were till daylight. Not many. He jumped down from the tractor bed and went to the brazier, pulling out the branding iron from white hot coals. The glowing tip drew a bright ribbon of orange through the air as he hurried back and clambered onto the truck bed. Standing above her, he raised up her left hip with the toe of his boot. He wasn't supposed to touch her more than he had to, even though her flesh called to him. As soon as her buttock was exposed, he pressed the searing metal to her skin and smelled the scent of charred flesh.

Had to make sure she had the devil's mark.

Jumping back down, he slammed the back of the truck closed, put the branding iron back in the brazier, then doused the coals with a bucket of water. Steam rose in a hiss, clouding his vision for a moment. Of their own volition, his eyes moved to the door at the back of the barn, the one he'd locked with the wooden bar. For a moment he imagined movement behind it, but he knew that was a lie. The devil, teasing him again. He reminded himself not to think about what he'd had to do, but the enormity of everything overcame him and suddenly he was openly crying. Angrily, he swiped at the tears. Sometimes the hard choices had to be made.

Quickly, he returned to the truck's cab. Firing the engine, he threw the vehicle into gear and it lurched forward. Once outside the barn, he slammed the truck into park, leapt out, then hurried back to pull the barn doors tightly shut before returning to the cab and pressing a toe to the accelerator. The cab jostled and swayed as he bumped over the open field, guided by a path of moonlight that would take her to her final resting place.

Rest in peace, he thought darkly, knowing there was no hope for those Satan had chosen.

Chapter One

The man in the hospital bed came back to consciousness slowly, aware that he'd been cocooned from sensation for some reason, yet also aware that he could feel a heavy weight of worry bearing down on him. *Where is Maxwell? Where am I?* The question had plagued him, circling his brain and disturbing his sleep, though without any meaning he could understand.

There were voices around him. They rose and fell sporadically. People coming and going, he realized at the same moment he understood he was in a hospital. Nurses, doctors, friends . . . ?

Where is Maxwell?

The explosion, he remembered suddenly, then realized at the same moment that he'd lost hearing for a while. His ears still rang a little, but at least the problem had apparently been temporary because he could make out words.

He was injured. Numb and dull-feeling. Painkillers, most likely. He'd gone to find . . . *Maxwell* . . . but his brother-in-law hadn't been there.

The explosion was meant to kill Maxwell, he thought dully, sorting through the flotsam and jetsam left in his shaken brain. Maxwell, his confidant and informant. His friend. Except Max *wasn't there.*

"Mr. Danziger?" A woman's voice. One of the nursing staff?

And then another woman, loudly, "Can you hear me?"

Maxwell hadn't been there because he'd known about the bomb, or whatever it was, and stayed away. It hadn't been meant for Maxwell, he thought with a jolt. It had been meant for *him.*

And Maxwell had known and had purposely been gone.

"You're sure he was waking up?" the first woman asked skeptically.

"Yes. His wife wants to see him."

"Took her long enough to get here."

Wife? *Carmen?* They'd been emotionally separated for years . . . divorced for months . . . though they'd kept the same residence, mainly so that people—people like *Maxwell*—wouldn't know that their marriage had crumbled. Carmen's idea, not his, but he'd been happy to play the charade—anything she wanted—because he just wanted out.

"Mr. Danziger?" the second nurse asked, a bit more urgently. "Your wife's here to see you."

"He's not waking up," the first said in a superior tone.

Jay Danziger felt himself start to fade away again. Good. He didn't want to think too much. *Where's Max?* his mind asked again, but this time he answered himself: *Far away from the accident that was meant to kill you.*

When he resurfaced again—opening his eyes before he was awake enough to remind himself he should keep them closed—he didn't know how much time had passed. A while, for sure. Hazily, he realized a woman was seated beside him, holding his hand. Her palm was sweating.

"Mr. Danziger," a man's voice greeted him. With effort, he zeroed in on the voice, moving his eyes carefully, as there was a dull ache in his head, to take in a man in a white lab coat who stood at the foot of the bed, holding a manila file. "We wondered when you would return."

The man's name tag read DR. WILLIAM COCHRAN. Again, carefully, he swiveled his eyes from the doctor back to the woman seated beside his bed. She was somewhere in her late twenties, he thought, with dark brown hair in a loose bun and tendrils escaping to curl slightly at her temples. It was the same style Carmen wore hers in, most times. No wonder they thought she was his wife. He was pretty sure he'd never laid eyes on her until this moment.

She murmured, "So glad you're okay, Jay. You had us all worried."

He thought about saying something, calling her out as a fraud, but held his tongue. Worry was exactly the emotion filling her hazel eyes just now. She was petrified of something, most likely that he would blow her cover because she sure as hell wasn't Carmen. He didn't know her from Adam, and the fact that she was impersonating his ex-wife was disturbing, though not full-out alarming, which said something about his confused mental state, he supposed. He should have been thoroughly concerned, especially with the new and ugly realization that Max had meant for him to die. Or had he been warned away? Was that why he wasn't there? No . . . it didn't feel like it. Dance sensed he knew something in the deep recesses of his mind, some hidden nugget of truth that escaped him now yet made him question Maxwell's motives. And if the bomb, or whatever had caused the explosion, hadn't been meant for him . . . if it had just been some kind of terrible accident that had gone off and sliced up his leg—

Immediately, he glanced down to his left leg. It was wrapped from hip to below his knee. A thigh injury. He had no sensation of pain, though; the meds must be good.

"Max has been asking about you," the woman holding his hand said, a current of urgency running beneath the words.

Maxwell Saldano. She knows about Max.

Jay "Dance" Danziger had trusted his instincts on numerous occasions and that trust had saved him from all kinds of trauma during the last ten years that he'd worked as an investigative journalist. He trusted them now, so he looked "Carmen" straight in the eye and croaked out, "Take me home."

Her lips parted. Before she could answer, the doctor inserted, "We need to check some tests. Make sure you're all right. Surgery went well. A lot of muscle damage that was repaired. As long as there's nothing unexpected on your MRI, you could get out of here as early as tomorrow."

"Today," Dance muttered.

"Well . . . maybe . . ."

"I'm leaving today," he said positively.

"I'll check the tests." The doctor left them, and as soon as Dance was alone with his hand holder, he slid her a silent look.

"Home might not be the safest place," she said carefully.

She was warning him, in her way, that it wasn't safe to speak freely. Though they were alone in the room, her gaze shifted toward the open doorway. Maybe there were listening ears just outside the door.

"Where should I go?" he forced out with an effort.

She glanced at him, then down at their still-clasped hands, and shot a quick, darting look back at his eyes before letting her gaze wander away. "I know a place . . ."

"Where?"

"Just somewhere I know."

"What do I call you?"

She flicked another look toward the outer hallway. "What do you mean?" she asked cautiously.

The meds were fading a little, he thought. He could feel pain knocking at the door, eager to remind him that his leg was in bad shape and his head could hurt a lot more, too. "Well . . . not . . . Carmen . . ."

He sensed, then, too, that he was fading out himself. Blessed twilight was coming to take him into oblivion for a while longer. So softly he almost missed it, she said, "Jordanna."

"Jordanna," he repeated, unaware that his voice was inaudible as he succumbed to unconsciousness.

Jordanna Winters had always had a healthy disrespect for the police.

At age fourteen, she shot her father with a .22 rifle when he was attempting to have sex with her older sister and learned the hard way that the law enforcement types in Rock Springs, Oregon, were chauvinistic, repellant, and inclined to believe an upstanding citizen like Dr. Dayton Winters over his unstable middle daughter, who, let's face it, was half-wild from growing up on a farm with a mother whose own mental state had always been in question. There was a rogue gene lying in wait in Gayle Treadwell Winters's family that popped up randomly and had brought dubious behavior, suicides, horrific accidents, and even murder over the years to the unlucky Treadwells—or so the people of Rock Springs were wont to believe. Jordanna, they collectively decided after the shooting that grazed her father's shoulder, was clearly an unhappy recipient of that gene, which was undoubtedly the reason for her erratic behavior. The good Dr. Winters was above reproach, so Jordanna's behavior had to be from something else . . . something vile and difficult, maybe impossible, to control . . . the Treadwell Curse.

Bull. Shit. All of it.

From Jordanna's point of view, dear old Dad was a lech, and a pedophile, and a whole host of other things that forced Jordanna to move away from home as soon as possible.

She'd learned from an early age that she couldn't count on anyone other than herself. Even her older sister, Emily, had insisted it was her own fault she had been in their father's bed. Emily had assured her that she was sleepwalking again, and had just wandered into Dad's bedroom. She'd insisted that she'd just been dreaming about their mother and had climbed into the bed, looking for her. When Jordanna had objected, Emily had then accused Jordanna of being just as screwed up as everyone thought she was. *She* was the one who needed help.

Jordanna had stubbornly kept to her story. She'd heard Emily scream out Dayton as if she were scared—but Jordanna's insistence did no good. No one had believed her, and less than a year later Emily had lost her life in an automobile accident along the treacherous switchback roads above Rock Springs on a particularly cold and icy day. Her car slid over a steep ridge and tumbled down a cliff side. Heartbroken, Jordanna had stood as far away from her father and the rest of her family as possible at the funeral. She'd felt like a pariah, and why not? Everyone thought she bore the Treadwell Curse, though they wouldn't say so to her face.

And then while a cold, January rain beat down on them, her younger sister, Kara, had moved up next to her and whispered in a strained voice, "It wasn't an accident."

"What do you mean?" Jordanna demanded.

"Somebody killed Emily," Kara had responded.

"Our father?" Jordanna suggested. But Kara had merely shrugged and shaken her head. They had both gazed across the plot where the pallbearers were laying their sister to rest, and, feeling her father's eyes on her, Jordanna had set her jaw and vowed to get to the truth someday . . . when she was stronger and the time was right.

She'd moved out of the house at seventeen and ended up rooming with a group of students who attended Portland

State. She'd then worked her way through night classes at the university as well, majoring in journalism and communications. She'd also taken courses in criminal investigation and spent her days working at coffee shops and restaurants. Eventually, under a pseudonym, she began a blog that was a newsletter about victims of crimes, what happened to them afterward, and maybe what caused the crime in the first place, and had managed to turn her work into various newspapers. To date, she'd been published in both the *Laurelton Register* and the *Lake Chinook Review*, and it was her dream to hit the big leagues. She'd been working toward that end for ten years, spurred by the ill treatment she'd received in her own hometown, bent on proving herself free of the "crazy" Treadwell Curse. So far, she'd done a fairly decent job of it, ignoring or flouting rules along the way. Her only hiccup had been her own hero worship of another investigative reporter, Jay Danziger, a man she'd literally followed for his insight, acumen, and success in digging into the truth. Tracking him had led to the madness of her current situation: breezing into Laurelton General and passing herself off as his wife. It was the reason for her thumping heart and sweating palms when she'd stated in a low, fast voice to the receptionist, "Tell Officer McDermott that Carmen Danziger is here."

"Ma'am?" the receptionist had asked blankly.

"Jay Danziger's my husband." She'd uttered the lie quick and sharp. No gatekeeper was going to stop her. "One of the bombing victims. I was called." She was amped enough by her charade not to have to manufacture the trembling of her lower jaw.

"Uh . . . yes . . ." The receptionist looked around for help. Chaos surrounded them. Though the bombing had been over twenty-four hours earlier, Laurelton General had received the bulk of the casualties and was swarming with extra medical staff and, of course, the police. Jordanna had made an educated guess that Jay Danziger had been brought here. She'd known he had been at the explosion of the building in downtown Laurelton that had sent the community scrambling while wailing sirens and dust and debris filled the air. She'd known because she'd seen him there, had been across the street when the bomb had blown. The concussion of the blast had knocked her off her feet, but she'd managed to pick herself up. She'd fumbled for her phone, her ears still ringing, poised to call 9-1-1, but then realized she could already hear the wail of distant sirens. Instead, she'd staggered to her Toyota RAV4 and driven to her apartment.

After cleaning herself up, she'd stared into the bathroom mirror and asked herself what had happened. She hoped to God Jay Danziger was still alive. The shudders that racked her body at the thought had brought her to her knees. *Those goddamn Saldanos!* she'd thought, filled with fury. And that's when she'd hatched her crazy plan. If Danziger was still alive, and she fervently hoped to hell he was, she was going to find him, interview him, and convince him of the Saldanos' evil. She'd been casually following . . . okay, half stalking . . . the man around for weeks, catching him outside the gates of his home or tooling after him as he met with members of the Saldano family, the corporate crime family with tendrils in more businesses and government offices than a haystack had pieces of straw. Until Danziger had gotten swept up in the Saldano net of greed, Jordanna had admired the man. Dreamed about him a little, if the truth be known, as he was damned attractive. But his biggest appeal was his freewheeling investigative style and the results he produced. That was number one.

And he was married. Which was just as well, really, because she was not interested in a married man. She only wanted Danziger's story, and by God, she was going to get it if it killed her. She looked enough like Carmen Danziger to bluff her way inside while everything was in a state of flux. Carmen mostly stayed out of the spotlight, but Jordanna knew she wore her long, brunette hair in a messy bun and that when she did go out, she favored tight dresses and the highest heels imaginable for a woman to still be able to walk. In the few hours since the bombing, Jordanna had purchased both at the nearest mall. She'd damn near broken an ankle hurrying into the hospital, but luckily, no one had noticed.

"Call him," Jordanna had urged the receptionist, dabbing at the real tears that formed at the corners of her eyes. Fear. Or excitement. At least it was working for her.

"Do you have ID?"

Shit. "I . . ." She pretended confusion, gazing back through the glass double doors to the parking lot.

At that moment, Officer McDermott himself had stalked through the reception area. She'd seen him on the news earlier and she knew he was part of the investigation. Fully crying, she grabbed his arm. "Please tell me my husband's alive."

He gazed down at her impatiently. "Who is your husband, ma'am?"

"Jay . . . Jay Danziger? Is he here? Please . . ."

If Carmen Danziger had actually already been at the hospital, Jordanna would have probably been arrested. She'd been pretty sure she was safe, though, because she'd seen Carmen with a ton of luggage heading to the airport a few days earlier. Jordanna had hoped she was still far, far away and hadn't returned yet. But Jordanna figured if she was caught in her masquerade, so be it. It was still worth a try. Recklessness had served her well in the past and she wasn't going to play it safe and miss a golden opportunity.

"Mrs. Danziger." McDermott had looked like he wanted to peel her off his arm.

"Is he here? Is he all right?"

"He's still recovering from surgery."

She'd pressed a hand to her mouth and shaken her head, letting emotion overcome her.

"I'm sorry, ma'am. We have a lot of injuries. Check with the hospital staff."

Jordanna had nodded, releasing him. The bombing had taken place at the Saldanos' main company headquarters, where, according to general speculation and Jay Danziger's investigation prior to his being seduced by the family, the Saldanos received and shipped all manner of illegal drugs. Max Saldano and the entire family hotly denied this accusation. They were honest businesspeople involved in importing and exporting commodities from Mexico and Central and South America. They were *not* criminals.

More bullshit.

Danziger was a longtime friend of Max Saldano, the man who had introduced him to his sister, Carmen. Jay and Carmen had already been married by the time Jordanna had begun admiring Danziger's journalistic style. It was only after the Saldanos came under suspicion of criminal activity, all the while being championed by Jay Danziger, that Jordanna had begun to think her idol had feet of clay. *Money involved*, Jordanna had told herself darkly. *Lots of money.* And Jay Danziger had rolled over for it, much like her father had when he'd married into the Markum family after Jordanna's mother's death.

As soon as those thoughts circled her mind again, Jordanna had shut them off, concentrating instead on discovering Danziger's room, which she'd been unsure how to find until she overheard two nurses talking about him and had followed them to the fourth floor. Her tight green dress and heels had gotten her noticed, but the camouflage had helped connect her as Danziger's wife. The nurses had believed her when she'd said Officer McDermott, and a doctor she'd seen mentioned on the news, had sent her to the fourth floor. It had been almost too easy, which had struck her as odd.

That's when she'd first thought that Danziger might be in danger. None of the Saldanos had been at their building when it exploded. It had been virtually empty of family members, though a number of employees had been hurt from the fallout. The initial theory was that a rival group had bombed the Saldanos to send a violent message, though the family patriarch, Victor Saldano, had scoffed at the suggestion.

In her disguise as Carmen, Jordanna had decided to alert Danziger to possible danger. She might not trust his motives any longer, but he'd damn near died because of his association with the Saldanos. That was clear. He'd been the one in the line of fire, not Maxwell, nor his father, nor any other Saldano, for that matter. So, she'd entered his room cautiously, but found him asleep. Uncertain for a moment, she'd decided to sit down and wait to see if he woke up. She'd sat tensely in the chair next to his bed, all the time feeling a ticking clock inside her head, like the countdown to a bomb, warning her that Carmen Saldano Danziger or someone who knew her was bound to show up any time.

But then Jay Danziger had awoken and she'd just started . . . improvising.

And so had he.

She looked at him now. At the handsome face with the two lines of worry etched between his brows even in sleep. She felt an emotional pull inside herself, one she desperately needed to control. Did he understand about the danger? Maybe he knew more about it than she did. He certainly hadn't argued with her. In fact, he'd put himself in the care of a stranger without a qualm, no questions asked, and she'd committed herself to getting him out of here. With her mind on the old farmstead in Rock Springs where she'd grown up—a place she'd avoided for years—she'd told him she would get him somewhere safe.

She just hoped to hell she could deliver on that promise.

Chapter Two

Jordanna stood by the northeast-facing window of Jay Danziger's hospital room, staring through the blinds to the parking lot below. It was actually two separate lots; the one toward the north side was a level lower than the one on the east. The hospital sat on a hillside, and the main entrance and emergency room were on the top level, while most of the parking that surrounded the other three sides of the building step-staired its way down toward the rear of the building.

If I park back here, I can get away without being seen, she thought. There was no way she was getting Danziger through the main entrance without press and questions and all kinds of commotion. But one of the rear entrances might work for the stealth assignment she'd tasked herself with. Were there security cameras around? Possibly. She couldn't see any from this angle, but it was amazing how much of today's world was under surveillance. She would just have to assume cameras were watching, and that their progress to her car would be recorded. If anyone then chose to go so far as to try to find Danziger once he left the hospital, something she sensed could easily happen, the cameras would catch her on video.

She exhaled a long, soft breath. Some Saldano Industries employees had also been hurt, but none of them had suffered the injuries Danziger had. The bomb had been on the other side of the wall from the entrance where Danziger had been standing. Though others had been hit by flying shrapnel, no one else had been close to the explosion's source. Jordanna subscribed to the "there are no coincidences" theory, and in her mind that meant the bomb had been meant for Jay Danziger.

She glanced again toward his unconscious body. He was breathing evenly now, but since she'd been standing vigil, he'd gasped a couple of times in his sleep. Whether this was from an injury or some uncomfortable memory or dream, she couldn't tell. Either way, every time it happened it caused her breath to catch in her throat and her heart to race.

She paced to the other side of the room and cautiously peered around the door and into the hallway. A woman's voice, one of the nurse's, was complaining from the nurse's station around the corner. Someone hadn't done as she'd ordered her and it sounded as if there would be hell to pay. It reminded Jordanna of her aunt Evelyn, who found great joy in recounting every slight and misery she'd been subjected to, whether real or imagined, to anyone with one good ear. She was a grievance collector of the first order.

Needing to use the restroom, Jordanna turned down the hall, teetering a bit on one heel. She had half a mind to take off the shoes. They'd served their purpose and now she needed to walk. Before she could make that decision, however, she heard someone coming from behind and just managed to reach the corner before being seen. Her heart jolted when she looked back and spied two policemen, McDermott and another younger man, entering Jay Danziger's room, and a cold frisson slid down her back as she considered what would have happened if she'd had to speak to them.

She didn't trust that McDermott would continue to think she was Carmen.

A bell went off at the nurse's station up ahead to her left, jarring her nerves further, but Jordanna ducked into the bathroom on the right. Inside, she leaned against the wall beside the door, watching it start to close behind her.

What the hell are you doing?

The complaining nurse suddenly snapped, "You've got to be kidding!" Then footsteps marched toward her. Jordanna moved quickly away from the door and to the sink, sure her charade was about to be unmasked. She pretended to wash her hands, but no one entered the bathroom. Cocking her head, she tried to listen, but the door was firmly shut now and the bathroom walls apparently too insulated to hear through. In that moment she caught sight of her reflection in the mirror and forced herself to clear the lines of anxiety between her brows.

Gathering her courage, she carefully stepped back into the hallway and hurried back to the corner once again. To her right was the nurse's section. If she went left, she would reach the branch of the hallway that led to Danziger's room. Swallowing, she dared a quick look and saw that his door was open. The complaining nurse's voice suddenly sounded from the direction of the nurse's station. It was muffled at this distance, but she was plainly still upset.

"Can I help you?"

Jordanna just managed to keep from leaping out of her skin at the unexpected female voice. She turned to find a young aide behind her. She'd come from farther down the hall. To Jordanna's right, another nurse was approaching the nurse's station with a file in her hands.

"I'm just debating whether to see my husband again, or let him get some rest," Jordanna told her, inclining her head toward the branching corridor.

"There's a waiting area ahead." The aide pointed past the

turn to Danziger's room and toward the opposite end of the hall from the nurse's station. If she chose to go there, Jordanna would have to cross the corridor that led to Danziger's room, and if the policemen were standing outside his door, it was more than possible one of them might see her. Would they think she was just some other visitor, or would they know how Carmen Danziger dressed?

"Thank you," she said to the aide, who smiled and turned toward the nurse's station. Jordanna stood still for a moment, then held her breath and decided to cross to the waiting area. She moved quickly, forcing herself not to turn her head. In her peripheral vision, she caught a glimpse of one of the officers still in the hallway, but she kept her pace even, only breathing a sigh of relief when she was safely down the hall and at the small waiting room, which was really an alcove with several brown faux-leather side chairs and a glass table with metal legs. A row of windows gazed down upon the very parking lot where Jordanna was thinking about leaving her car, and she leaned her chin on one hand and calculated the distance from Danziger's room to the elevator, and then the elevator to the back door. . . .

The woman's voice was full of annoyance. ". . . asleep, and when he's awake, you can question him."

A man's voice answered, implacable and cool. "We'll wait."

"I've paged Dr. Cochran," the woman warned. "Until he arrives, I suggest you wait in the hall."

"Ma'am, we've spoken with Dr. Cochran and he knows we're here."

"Even if that's true, patient health is Laurelton General's first responsibility," she responded crisply, undaunted. "Please wait in the hall until Mr. Danziger awakens."

Silence. Dance pictured a glare-off between the man and

woman. Even in his dull state, he had a pretty good idea
that the man was a police officer. There was just something
authoritative in his tone. And they would be wanting to
question him. They would want to know if he knew anything
about the explosion. Dr. Cochran had basically released him,
so they wouldn't miss this opportunity while he was still at
the hospital.

He toyed with the idea of letting the nurse duke it out
with the officers; there were at least two of them or the man
wouldn't have been speaking in plurals.

But Dance didn't see how that was going to help him. He
sensed he was in trouble, either a target of the bombing or
someone who'd merely gotten in the way. What that meant,
he wasn't sure. His head felt stuffed with cotton; it hurt to
think. Either way, he wanted to get the hell away from the
hospital, where he felt like a sitting duck. If this Jordanna
person could spring him, he was going to go with her.

She could be in on it.

He opened his eyes.

Two people were in the room, and he sensed another
standing just outside the door. The iron-jawed, middle-aged
nurse with the glare was just as he'd expected. The fifty-ish
man with clipped gray hair gazed calmly back at her and
wore a policeman's uniform. The third person was outside
his line of sight.

It was the nurse who saw him first. Her eyes momentarily flicked his way, but returned to the police officer without
letting him know Dance was awake. But then the officer in
the hallway suddenly entered and his gaze collided with
Dance's.

"His eyes are open," he said, effectively breaking the
glare-off between the other two.

"Mr. Danziger," the nurse said, bustling over to his bedside officiously. "How are you feeling? Can you talk? These

policemen wish to speak with you, but you do not have to right now."

"I can talk," Dance rasped.

Her lips tightened. "I've paged Dr. Cochran, and—"

"No, I'll talk," he said again, clearing his throat. "I want to."

She inhaled a breath, hesitated a moment, then said, "If you're sure," in a tone that said there was no way he could be.

"Mr. Danziger," the policeman greeted him, ignoring the nurse and gazing at Dance through flinty eyes. "If you're feeling up to it, we'd like your account of the accident."

"Was it a bombing?" Dance asked him.

The older officer—McDermott, by his name tag—glanced at the nurse, who tried to ignore his pointed stare before bustling out of the room in a flurry of indignation.

Once she was gone, McDermott turned his attention back to Dance. "It appears to have been."

The younger officer, whose name tag read BILLINGS, kept silent, clearly leaving the questions to his more experienced partner.

"We've been waiting to interview you," McDermott explained. "You feel up to it?"

Dance kind of figured the interview was coming at him regardless, but he managed a careful nod.

"Do you mind telling us what you were doing at Saldano Industries?" the older officer asked.

"I was meeting Maxwell Saldano there."

"A business meeting?"

"We were planning to play golf," Dance said, side-stepping the question. "I was meeting Max at his office."

"Maxwell Saldano is your brother-in-law?"

"Yes."

"Your wife was here earlier . . . ?" McDermott frowned and looked back toward the door as if he was wondering what had become of her.

Dance was wondering the same thing, except his thoughts

were on the woman named Jordanna. Was she getting ready to take him out of here? He hoped to hell she stayed away while the police were here, although why he trusted her like a lifelong friend and not the police was a question he couldn't quite answer. He didn't *mis*trust the officers exactly, but he was in something deep that he didn't completely remember at the moment. He understood he was lucky to be alive. And he wanted out of the hospital.

You don't know this Jordanna. She could be part of the setup.

Setup? Was this a setup? His brain suddenly offered up a memory. *The audiotapes . . .*

"Mr. Saldano wasn't at the company building when the explosion happened," McDermott said.

"He was late," Dance said, tired all over. Maybe his injuries were worse than he'd thought, but he didn't care. He was leaving today, no matter what Cochran said.

The drugs were making it impossible to think straight. The bombing couldn't have been about him. No one was after him. No one knew about the tapes except Max.

And Max *wasn't there. . . .*

Dance licked dry lips and asked, "Have you talked to Max?"

"One of our detectives has spoken to Mr. Saldano, and she would like to talk to you, too."

"She?"

"Detective Rafferty."

He sensed underlying disapproval in the man's voice. Because she was a woman? Or because she was a detective? Or both? Deciding to twist the knife a bit, he asked, "This Rafferty's the boss, huh?"

"No," McDermott snapped back, unable to help himself, his lips tight. The younger officer looked uncomfortable. Dance had done enough reports on crime and dealt with enough police to know there was often a wall between the uniformed officer and the detectives. The detective being a "she" was bound to pour salt in the wound, especially since there was something about McDermott, nothing definable . . . call it a reporter's nose . . . that smacked already of misogyny. Or, he supposed it could be simple envy, but whatever it was, Dance was pretty sure McDermott had stepped out of his job description to interview him.

"We like to corroborate people's accounts," McDermott explained.

Read that as he'd taken it upon himself to interview Dance first. Maybe he was stumping for a job promotion.

"Do you remember the explosion?" McDermott asked.

"No . . ." Dance admitted truthfully. He could remember the before and after, but his mind seemed to be skipping the actual event, shying away from it, he supposed. Isn't that what happened to trauma victims? He could recall the plans he'd made in the morning . . . on the cell phone with Max. They'd talked about golf and a little about Carmen, that she was on her way to Europe . . . Italy. . . . He'd kept bigger issues to himself, sensing his time with Max was precious and tenuous. But, for the life of him, he couldn't remember the drive to Saldano Industries' main building. He could recall climbing into his Highlander—the car his ex had always wanted him to replace with a BMW, like that was going to happen—and then putting it into reverse. . . . Or, at least he thought he could. His hand had been on the gear shift, but the feeling of low dread was what he remembered most. . . .

He thought he could remember the explosion. The huge *boom* seemed to still ring in his ears and fill his insides as if at a cellular level. But the only other thing he could recall was that Max hadn't been there.

And he was sick of that line circling his mind.

"What did Max say?" he repeated.

"Detective Rafferty can fill you in," he snipped.

Yep. Misogynistic, professional envy. "You're not going to tell me?" Dance pushed.

"She did the interview of Mr. Saldano."

"Unless she gets here fast, she'll have to catch me at home," Dance warned. "I'm being released." *And I won't be home, either.*

"Today?" McDermott asked, his brows lifting.

"Yes." Dance was certain. "I'd like to help you more, but this bombing is a Saldano problem."

"You know that for certain?" Billings interjected eagerly, earning a scowl from McDermott.

"It's the most likely scenario," Dance said. He didn't really believe what he was saying, but he was tired of their questions, especially since it sounded like he might be going through them again very soon with the female detective.

The officers left a few moments later and Dance collapsed back on his pillows, glad for the reprieve. He was strong enough to leave, and that was what he was going to do. Maybe he was a fool to accept help from this Jordanna person, but he was going to do that, too.

She could be anybody. She already dressed up like your wife to gain access, for Christ's sake.

At that precise moment, the door swung inward and Jordanna appeared again, still in the tight green dress and heels. Her gaze met his and she put a finger to her lips as she slipped inside and closed the door behind her.

"I'm going to go home and get some things," she told him. "When I return, I'll come through a back door, if possible. We'll go out the same way. When do you get released?"

"Soon, I hope. A police detective's planning to interview me. There were two officers here."

"McDermott and that younger man. I saw them leave your room."

"Did they see you?" he asked curiously.

"No, but I've met McDermott already," she admitted.

"As Carmen?" he asked.

"Well, yeah. It was when I was at reception. . . ."

"You don't really want to see him up close and personal again because he could start asking questions."

"You got that right." Her smile was quick and disappeared immediately.

"What's your stake in this?"

She shook her head, hesitated, then shook it again. "I don't trust the Saldanos."

"You know the Saldano family?"

"By reputation, but that's enough." Her tone made her feelings clear on that.

"They're not as bad as you think they are."

"Then why are you here, instead of one of them?"

"Bad timing."

"Very bad, if that's true," she agreed. "Were you working on a story?"

"No," he lied, and he saw her eyes search his face.

"You were working on something on the Saldanos." It was a statement instead of a question.

"What's your interest in them?" he asked.

"I just . . ." She hesitated.

When she didn't finish, he grew impatient and demanded, "Tell me, where do you fit into this?"

"I just want to help you."

"A lie," he stated with certainty. When she turned away, he said with dawning realization, "You know something about the Saldanos and me."

"No."

"Oh, shit. You're a reporter. Channel Seven?" he demanded.

She jerked in surprise. "I'm not on television."

"But you are a reporter. You're looking for a story." He could hear the derision in his voice.

"I'm here to save your hide," she snapped back. Hearing

herself, she whispered harshly, "And yeah, okay, I'm a reporter, and maybe I'd like a story. But there's a reason you're in this hospital bed. Someone put you here. *They* did. The Saldanos."

"What makes you such an expert?"

"I've been following you, Mr. Danziger. I don't know what happened, but something did, and now they need you out of the way."

"That's bullshit conjecture. You're just making up dangerous accusations."

"You want to talk about dangerous?" she challenged. "I was there. Across the street when the explosion happened. If it wasn't a bomb, it was a gas leak, something big. You're damn lucky to be alive."

"You were there? Following me?"

"You know something about the Saldanos, and you're a threat to them."

"You don't know anything," he snarled, dropping back against the pillows.

"Your life's in danger. *You* know why, but I just know it's true."

"And you've come to save me?" He allowed wry disbelief to enter his tone.

"Yeah." She wouldn't back down an inch. "You still with me?"

The truth of it was, she wasn't wrong. He had doubts of his own about the family he'd married into . . . and there was the audiotape . . . the reason for his dread.

"Yeah," he rasped. "I'm still with you."

She gazed at him through sober, hazel eyes fringed with dark lashes, then threw a glance at the closed door to his room. "Then, I'm gonna go now and make plans for us. I'll be back in a couple hours."

"Jordanna . . ." She looked back at him. "Be careful," he

said, and he thought he saw the faintest of smiles touch the corners of her mouth.

"Nothing I do seems to be careful," was her answer.

They assessed each other for a moment. Then Dance exhaled heavily and said, "Park about a half mile away and walk to the hospital, so the license plate doesn't show up on any cameras."

"Half a mile? You can't walk that far."

She was right. "Find a safe place to take off the plates just before you get here. Come back inside and pick me up. We'll head out, and then put the plates back on as soon as we can."

"As long as I don't get stopped by the police," she pointed out.

"Then don't get stopped by the police," he ordered.

She nodded and headed for the door, peering into the hallway, then looking back at him for a moment. "You're just gonna walk out of this place whether you're released or not?"

"Oh, I'm going to get the doctor's release."

"You look like hell. If I were your doctor, I'd keep you in here."

"I'm not a prisoner."

"No, but you're a patient and frankly, I'm not sure you have the strength to get to my car."

"You just bring the car. I'll do the rest."

"Okay."

He closed his eyes, but the vision of her seemed imprinted on his lids. She was a very pretty woman, prettier than Carmen in ways, although his ex was pretty, too. She was also reckless in a way he understood. A reporter . . . damn . . . it made sense.

He must have fallen asleep because when he opened his eyes again, she was gone and a nurse was in his room, checking his vitals. The battle-ax from earlier. When he requested the paperwork to be released, she fell back on her earlier threat to call Dr. Cochran. "Call him all you want," he told the woman. "I'm going, whether you have all the forms you need signed or not."

Jordanna drove with controlled speed back to her apartment. She was only loosely affiliated with the *Laurelton Register* and the *Lake Chinook Review.* They took some of her stories, paid her a pittance, and treated her like she was totally expendable, which she was. Neither was any kind of regular gig, so they weren't going to be looking for her if she dropped out for a while, or maybe even forever. Her apartment was paid up for two months because she paid in advance whenever she had the money, just in case she didn't later. She could do the same with the utilities, guesstimating what they would be and paying online.

Are you really doing this?

"You'd better believe it," she muttered as she took the steps to her second-floor unit two at a time. The place was nothing to write home about, but it served her purposes. She had yet to make a meal or use the range top apart from heating a teapot for hot water when her microwave went on the fritz. She had a new microwave now, purchased at Target, and it was the first thing she grabbed as soon as she entered the front door, unplugging it from the wall. Where they were going, they wouldn't have many conveniences and she wasn't about to give up her morning coffee unless she absolutely, positively had to. After the microwave, she added a blow-up mattress with pump, bedding, and towels.

She made a series of trips to her car, until the ten-year-old Toyota RAV4 was filled to bursting. She had just enough room for a few bags of groceries, and she dug into her Special Emergency Fund account to take along for unforeseen expenditures: Zip-loced stacks of cash that she kept between her mattress and springs. She took out three of the plastic bags, then looked long and hard at the other three before taking them, too. She had her laptop and an iPad and half the clothes she possessed, the only ones she actually wore.

At the grocery store, she bought bread, peanut butter, cheese, salad in a bag, apples, salt, pepper, mayonnaise, sliced pickles, barbecue sauce, and canned chicken. She wasn't certain what she would find at the old farmhouse, so she added plastic forks, knives, and spoons, paper plates and bowls. She hoped to God there was still an operating refrigerator, but she hadn't been there for years. Though she purposely stayed out of contact with her father, her sister, Kara, was in sporadic contact with him and his wife, and kept Jordanna somewhat abreast of what was happening in Rock Springs, whether she wanted to know or not.

"I still can't believe he married Jennie," Kara had said the last time they'd spoken.

"She's the right age for him," Jordanna had clipped back. "And she's Chief Markum's daughter."

"Is that what it's about?" she'd murmured, sounding disappointed. She'd always believed in their father more than Jordanna had.

Jennie Markum, now Winters, was the daughter of the police chief, Greer Markum, and a registered nurse who just happened to be an ex-classmate of Jordanna's older sister, Emily. Jordanna had first learned of their nuptials through the *Rock Springs Pioneer*, which had extolled the much-anticipated wedding, which had taken place the summer before at the outdoor chapel on the bluff above Fool's Falls, with Reverend Miles of the Green Pastures Church in attendance. The weather had been exceptionally beautiful and the backdrop of blue sky and rushing water had only added to the perfection of the scene as Rock Springs' beloved GP and his radiant bride said their vows.

"If Jennie keeps our father away from other young women, they have my blessing," she'd told Kara.

"Dad isn't the problem," Kara had said, like she always did.

"Then what is?" Jordanna had demanded, like she always did.

"If I knew, I'd tell you, but you and I both know there's something rotten in Rock Springs and that's why we left."

"It has a name: Dayton Winters."

"No . . . it's something else. I can feel it like a suffocating shroud whenever I'm there. Makes me claustrophobic."

Kara always spoke in quasi-mystical terms that irked Jordanna, who had a very sensitive bullshit meter. "Like what killed our sister?"

"I don't know. Maybe."

Jordanna had started to argue with her, but she hadn't wanted to alienate the only family member she still cared about, so she'd managed to swallow back further smart comments and settle for "Hmmm" noises instead.

"I'm going to be gone for a while," Kara had said when she'd ended that last conversation. "I've always wanted to see the Himalayas. I think I could mountain climb. Maybe not Everest, but the mountains are the one thing I miss about Rock Springs."

"The Cascades are a far cry from the Himalayas," Jordanna couldn't help pointing out.

"I know. But the mountains are where my soul flies free. Emily felt that, too. But you don't, do you?"

Jordanna had let that go and asked instead, "You have enough funds?"

"Oh, I'll work for a while." Kara waitressed and did odd jobs and just kind of floated. Jordanna made just enough money to get by, and she sometimes wondered how Kara managed it all.

That had been the extent of their last conversation and, as ever, it had left Jordanna feeling like an outsider to her own family. Not that she wanted to be closer to her father, but she would have liked to have Kara more accessible. And Jordanna didn't believe for one minute that her father had given up his sick ways just because he'd married Jennie, but since no one had believed her accusations then, there was little she could do about it now. At the time, Jordanna had been ordered to seek counseling and had managed to sit through ten sessions with a psychologist recommended by her father's good friend, Chief Markum. Anna Eggers had been nice enough, but totally clueless in Jordanna's biased opinion. The only useful thing she'd learned was that Dr. Eggers felt the Treadwells' genetic affliction was a myth.

"Mental function alters with age," she'd told Jordanna toward the end of their sessions, when Jordanna had felt safe enough to bring up the curse. "It happens to a lot of people."

"Young people?" Jordanna asked. "My mother got this in her thirties."

"Sometimes."

"You don't believe in any of it?" Jordanna had pressed.

"I think there's been a gross exaggeration around here of possible genetically linked mental illness. Your family has gotten a bad rap for a long time."

Jordanna had felt immense relief at her words, but it had been short-lived as Dr. Eggers's opinion was not shared by Aunt Evelyn, who'd told her that Anna Eggers's father was a Benchley and Benchleys and Treadwells had intermingled for years, to the detriment of both. "Of course she's going to say that," Aunt Evelyn had sniffed. "She doesn't want to admit she could be afflicted, and she's got ties to both families. I've been so, so lucky myself. God is merciful. You know, I pray every day for you, my dear, just like I pray for your mother's soul."

Aunt Evelyn Treadwell was ten years older than her sister, Jordanna's mother, and had been spared the affliction, apparently, but fear of it was the reason she'd never married nor had children. Jordanna wanted to believe the whole thing was bunk, but she remembered her mother's spells and ravings, and her split with reality.

Aunt Evelyn had added, "I wish you were seeing someone who might actually be able to help you. Your erratic behavior is very concerning. Your father is a wonderful man who put up with an awful lot from Gayle. I don't know another man who would have been as patient."

Jordanna was appalled. "My mother was sick."

"She didn't go to church." The last comment was ripped from Aunt Evelyn's bosom, a scourge against the sister who'd been loved despite her illness. Before Jordanna could defend her mother again, Evelyn had finished with, "Putting yourself in God's hands is the road to salvation. You need to start now, Jordanna, before you really hurt someone." In her aunt's eyes, she was to blame, the ungrateful, possibly mentally unstable daughter who'd tried to blacken the revered Dr. Winters's good name.

Well, fine. She didn't need Aunt Evelyn and she didn't need Kara, and she certainly didn't need her father. She'd learned to live with the way things were, and these years away had helped harden her to the unjust way she'd been treated. Most of the time, she just thought what the hell, it was over. She didn't live in Rock Springs any longer, and never planned to again, so what did it matter?

Except now she was heading back there with Jay Danziger in tow.

Jay Danziger . . .

Her heart fluttered and she snorted out a laugh. What she was doing was crazy, no doubt about it. Maybe all the tongue-waggers and finger-pointers in Rock Springs had reason to worry about her. And though she truly believed he was in danger, a part of her was almost giddy with the rush of being in league with her onetime idol. He was damnably attractive. Even with the bruising and bandages, he made her pulse race a little. She could feel herself shut down around him; a necessary defense mechanism. He already knew she was a reporter, so he could just keep thinking this rescue was all for a story. And yes, it was, but that wasn't the worst of it. She'd chosen him as her unwitting mentor, and then had fallen for him in a very feminine way. Hero worship at its worst.

But it was all an illusion. She wasn't crazy enough to think otherwise, no matter what people thought.

Back at her apartment, Jordanna gave a quick recheck of her Carmen Danziger clothes and makeup then locked up the apartment, got back in the RAV, and turned out of the parking lot. She drove east toward Portland, but took the exit off Sunset onto the access road to Laurelton General, slowing near a series of office buildings that fed into the hospital. She pulled around the back to a near-empty lot, then looked around surreptitiously, her engine still running. There didn't appear to be anyone about, so she pulled out the crescent wrench she'd slipped into her purse, then climbed from the car. Her pulse raced and her hands shook a little as she bent in front of the car and quickly removed the license plate. Then she circled to the back, taking off that one, too. Momentarily, she thought about stealing one from another car, but gave that idea up immediately. No license plate she could maybe explain, if she were unlucky enough in the quarter mile to the hospital to encounter a cop, but if somehow this was all traced back to her, stealing a license plate would be a crime.

Throwing the plates into the backseat, she jumped back in the black SUV and wheeled from the back parking lot and onto the street. Her knuckles ached from the tight grip on the wheel as she drove toward the hospital.

"Please, please, please . . ." she murmured.

She was afraid to let out her breath when she pulled into

the hospital's rear lot without incident. She parked near the back door, then glanced up, counting the windows until she found Danziger's room.

Walking quickly to the rear entrance, she noticed a posted warning that said the doors would be locked to visitors after 7:00 PM. That should give her just enough time. It was May and there would still be hours of light as they headed toward Rock Springs.

Drawing a sharp breath, she reached for the door handle and slipped inside the hospital.

Chapter Three

"Learn anything?" Detective Gretchen Sanders asked, her voice tinny and faraway. September had her on speakerphone while she climbed into the driver's side of her department-issue Jeep.

Setting the phone in the cup holder, September answered, "Not much. Maxwell Saldano acted shell-shocked, disbelieving. He professes to be worried about his brother-in-law."

"Danziger. The guy caught up in the blast," her partner said.

"Yep. I'm heading to Laurelton General now to interview him."

"Head injury . . . looks to be minor, and his leg's messed up?"

"That's what I'm hearing. That, and he's going to be released today."

"Doctor let him out already?" Gretchen asked suspiciously.

"Don't know yet."

"Let me know when you do."

September's partner had been put on administrative leave the previous fall after killing a man who was doing his damndest to kill September. Though Gretchen had been cleared and been back on the job most of this year, their boss, Lieutenant Aubrey D'Annibal, had been very careful about putting her on assignment with September again. Too careful, both Gretchen and September felt, but there had been two separate shootings involving police in a very short period of time, and it had ratcheted up the public anxiety to such a degree that both the Laurelton Police Department and the Winslow County Sheriff's Department were being extremely careful. Both Gretchen and September worked for Laurelton PD, and though Gretchen's shooting had been entirely justified and had undoubtedly saved September's life, D'Annibal wanted to keep it a non-topic in the current turbulent political climate.

Which was a long way of explaining why September was interviewing people affected by the bombing at Saldano Industries by herself and why the whole enterprise was irritating her partner no end.

"Bernstein from Portland PD checked with the Saldanos right after the bombing. They're probably taking over the investigation," September said.

Gretchen answered, "No surprise there. Saldanos have a lot more businesses outside Laurelton than in it. But D'Annibal wants us on the case."

"For follow-up," September reminded her.

"And to keep an oar in the water. Doesn't want Laurelton PD to be pushed around."

"Yeah. Okay, I'm on my way to the hospital."

"Keep me informed."

"You bet."

September clicked off, then turned the Jeep away from Victor Saldano's sprawling Italian-style manor with its flattish roof, wide eaves, and massive, filigreed brackets. Victor was the patriarch of the Saldano family and a true pain in the ass. Autocratic, short-tempered, opinionated, and impatient, he'd had no interest in being cooperative. "You should be looking for whoever bombed us!" he'd yelled at September, waving his right arm around as if he wanted her to saddle up and hit the range. His son, Maxwell Saldano, had tried to rein in his father, apologizing for his behavior at the same time. "My father hasn't been well. We already told the other investigators the same thing."

The other investigators were Detective Dan Bernstein and probably his partner with the Portland PD, who'd muscled in immediately after the bombing was reported. Lieutenant D'Annibal had asked September to reinterview the Saldanos and Jay Danziger as a means of keeping his team on the case, as he'd gotten his feathers ruffled over jurisdiction. ATF investigators were already examining the bomb itself, or what was left of it, so in many ways September's follow-up was superfluous. Still, if she could learn anything, she would.

"I understand you were supposed to be at the site?" September had asked Maxwell.

"I was." He nodded. "But I got a call from Raydeen. Raydeen Abolear," he added. "My father's nurse. Dad was having chest pains and didn't want Raydeen to send for an ambulance."

Victor had snapped his wrist impatiently at the dark-haired woman who hovered nearby. "I was fine! Treats me like I'm going to break."

"They were still arguing about it when I was on the phone, so I turned around and came here," Max said. "We sent for the ambulance."

"And I didn't get in it," Victor said triumphantly, as if it were a contest. "A little oxygen was all I needed. I don't plan to go to that hospital again until I'm at death's door, and I don't plan to be there in this lifetime." He chuckled at his little joke, but his eyes glared at the nurse.

"I'm on a kind of twenty-four-hour alert," Max explained to September, which drew Victor's glare to him, instead of

Raydeen. "I was supposed to meet Dance, but I turned around. I was on the phone. I didn't call him and tell him."

"You could have gone," Victor declared, though September thought he was over-minimizing his condition. His pallor was gray and there was a whiff of the scent September associated with age and illness, something damp and slightly sour overlaid by acrid cleaning substances, floating in the air throughout the first-floor rooms Victor Saldano used as his own personal suite. Though the house was large and rambling, a beautiful addition to the huge stately manors dotting Portland's West Hills, which embraced spectacular views of the city and the Willamette River, September sensed most of the rooms were empty and unused.

"The FBI was here," Victor complained, lifting his hand again and snapping it down. "Bah. Treated us like criminals."

"The ATF. Not like criminals," Max corrected.

"I'm with Laurelton PD," September said.

"You say your name was Rafferty?" Victor queried.

"That's right," she answered.

"That FBI man said you'd be coming," Victor said with a grimace.

"Who?" September asked.

"It was the Portland PD detective," Max corrected again.

"Bernstein?" she inquired.

"Never liked G-men," Victor overrode her, speaking loudly. Max Saldano gave her a quick nod as Victor ran on. "Humorless robots, every one. All they want to do is find some reason to close us down."

"Dad, the ATF was here because of the bomb," Max said with extreme patience.

"'Bomb experts.'" Victor snorted. "You know what their attitude was, miss?" He turned back to September, black eyes glittering. "That we deserved it. We're the goddamn Sopranos, that's what they think."

"Come on, Dad . . ." Max was long-suffering.

"You know I'm right." Victor rounded on him. "Given half a chance they'd throw us all in jail! We couldn't possibly be running a legitimate business. That would be too much for their walnut-sized brains to consider!"

Max ignored his father and gave his attention solely to September. "I'd like to see Dance . . . Jay . . . but I can't get information from the hospital."

"Don't give them any reason to suspect us further!" Victor exclaimed.

"I'll let him know. I'm going there next." She, too, tried to ignore the Saldano patriarch.

"Thanks," Max said.

"Young lady, you need to find who's responsible for this attack on us!" Victor's voice rose as he tried to commandeer the conversation again. He went on about how maybe it was a competitor, reversing his earlier stance on the subject. Raydeen moved closer, clearly worried about what Victor's anger was doing to his health because as his voice rose, his gray pallor took on a red tinge, anger suffusing his face. When one of his hands crawled up his chest to above his heart, Raydeen said, "Please stop, Mr. Victor," her eyes shooting daggers at Max, who called an end to the interview.

September was about ready to call 9-1-1 herself, but the nurse knew what to do. Soon enough Victor's pallor had lost its wild color and subsided back to the pale-gray shade that was apparently its normal shade. With all of them watching Victor tensely, she'd thanked them all for their time, then let Max show her out.

As the door shut behind her, she'd put a call in to Officer McDermott, the testy fifty-two-year-old cop who'd been stationed at Laurelton General in the first crazy hours of the bombing's aftermath, and alerted him that she was on her way to the hospital. He'd answered tersely and she'd inwardly sighed, having run up against him or his ilk enough times to know they felt that there was no way she'd gotten her job out of merit. She was too young and, well, not the right gender.

Ah, well. Such was life.

Directly after the bombing, when everything was crazy and no one knew how many patients there were, officers had been sent to various hospitals around the area. Luckily, only Jay Danziger had been severely hurt, and the half dozen people who'd been close enough to be hit by shrapnel had been treated for their cuts and scrapes as hospital out-patients. D'Annibal wanted September to interview them as well, as a matter of course, but first on the list was Danziger.

She was almost glad to leave the Saldanos to the Portland PD and the ATF. Max seemed fine enough, but dealing with his father was no picnic. "Have at it," she said after hanging up from Gretchen and making her way down from the West Hills to Sunset Highway and back toward Laurelton.

She wasn't sure what she wanted to say to Jay Danziger when she saw him, but it didn't really matter. She was on a routine job that would end today, and then maybe D'Annibal would partner her with Gretchen again. Though September had originally found Gretchen's "take no prisoners" style a bit over the top and aggressive, and she'd certainly enjoyed working with Wes Pelligree, the "black cowboy" as he was affectionately referred to around the department, she was looking forward to being back with her original partner, especially since Pelligree would be re-partnering with George Thompkins, the only other detective at Laurelton PD. George had a tendency to just ride his desk chair and use the phone and Internet rather than interview in person, but he somehow managed to get the job done well enough. Pelligree, though easy to work with, almost preferred investigating on his own.

Now September glanced down at the ring on her finger.

May sunlight was half-blinding her and she lifted her left hand to flip down the visor, the light refracting in flashing slivers off the stone. The previous summer she'd reconnected with a high school hook-up, Jake Westerly, and had never looked back. They'd moved in together last fall and at Christmas he'd gotten down on one knee in front of a yuletide fire and proposed. She'd been blown away, but had managed to nod out a "yes," and now they were on the road to marriage.

"I'm engaged," she said aloud now. "To be married. To the man I love."

Why she found that prospect so alarming, she couldn't say. Her brother had been living with his girlfriend for months. They were talking marriage in a desultory manner but weren't technically engaged yet, and neither of them seemed to be worrying about that. She, on the other hand, was filled with angst. She wanted Jake. No question there. She wanted a life with him. And after the frightening accident that had nearly killed him, she'd been by his side constantly, irrationally afraid of losing him to some other unforeseen calamity that was just waiting to happen.

But now she wondered if they might be rushing things. Her emotions were all over the place and it was their fault that she'd said yes. Two nights earlier, she'd said as much to Jake while they'd been curled up together on the couch, watching television under the warmth of the quilt her grandmother had made for her when she was a girl.

"Cold feet?" he'd asked, looking into her eyes, his blue eyes searching hers.

"No . . ."

"You don't sound sure."

"I'm sure about us. It's marriage I've got a problem with. It doesn't work for everybody. Look at my family. . . ."

"You and I aren't your father and Rosamund."

"God, no," she agreed. Her father had married a much younger woman and they'd just had a baby girl the past

January, naming her, well, January. Her father's penchant for naming his children after the month they were born was well-documented. Her twin brother, August, had been born just before midnight of September first, and she'd been born directly afterward. Hence, they were August and September, though people who knew them called them Auggie and Nine—her nickname, since September was the ninth month.

"My father makes me crazy," September said. Braden Rafferty still tried to direct his grown children's lives, even if they didn't listen to him anymore. She and Auggie had thwarted their father by going into law enforcement against his wishes, but that didn't stop Braden from trying to get her to quit. He'd pretty much given up on Auggie, who kept himself far, far away from Braden's influence, but no matter how hard September tried to stay as aloof and distant as her twin, she seemed to keep getting dragged back into family drama time and time again.

"So, you want to put off the engagement?" Jake's tone had been neutral, but September had felt his tension.

"No," she'd answered quickly. "I want to be engaged."

"But—?"

"Just don't get offended while I work this out, okay?" she cut him off. "It's going to take me a while. You have parents who love each other and their kids. I don't."

"Your father loves you," he argued, but she'd seen the beginnings of a smile lurking around his mouth.

"You're trying not to laugh," she declared, hitting him with a throw pillow.

"Only because you Raffertys make it so goddamn hard. What's wrong with just saying 'I love you'?"

"Blasphemy," she retorted, which elicited a full-scale bark of laughter.

And then he'd thrown her down on the cushions, wrestling and tickling her, all the while crying, "I love you, I love you,

I love you!" over and over again. She'd first tried to escape, then collapsed into gales of laughter and finally succumbed to molten desire as they made love into the wee hours of the morning.

Now, as September wheeled into the hospital parking lot, she purposely pushed thoughts of Jake and her family aside and concentrated on the matter at hand, interviewing Jay Danziger.

Jordanna stood on first one foot and then the other as Danziger looked through mounds of paperwork. "Are you ready yet?" She stepped to the door and risked another glance into the hallway.

"I'm just lucky I got 'em," he muttered. "I've got prescriptions that need to be filled, too." He placed several small papers to one side as he glanced over the spread-out pages on the narrow table that reached across his bed.

"We can fill them on the way." She tried not to crack her knuckles, a bad habit she reverted to in times of stress. "You said a detective's coming."

"Mmm-hmmm. That's what Officer McDermott said."

"I'd rather not wait for him. Let's get going, if we're going."

"Her."

"What?"

"The detective's a 'her.'"

"Oh, okay." She glanced over at him and saw that now he was staring off into space. "You all right?" she asked tensely.

"Yeah . . . I was just . . ." In lieu of answering, he shuffled the papers into a pile and slid the table aside. Then he picked up the prescription slips and held them out to her. Jordanna grabbed them and tucked them into the purse she had slung over one shoulder.

"You were just what?"

"Thinking."

"You're not changing your mind, are you?" she asked, her heart clutching a little. She believed he was in danger, but he seemed to be having second thoughts. Maybe he was relapsing. Maybe he thought the whole thing was crackers. Maybe it was.

His blue eyes were bloodshot, but nevertheless sharp and clear. He looked over at her. "No. Get me out of here, and I mean out of Laurelton and Portland. All of it."

"That's what I'm here for," she said.

Nodding, he flipped back the covers and moved his wrapped leg, straining a little at the effort. Jordanna stepped forward automatically to help him. Were there crutches? A wheelchair nearby?

He glanced toward the closet. "I'm going to need some pants, other clothes."

"Oh." She hesitated. "You want me to try and get you some?"

"Excuse me. . . ."

The female voice arrested them both, and Jordanna threw a tense look in the newcomer's direction. She was slim, young, and her auburn hair was pulled into a ponytail that was loosening from its tie. Her expression was serious and Jordanna got a distinct shock as she realized this was the detective she'd seen on television. Detective . . . she couldn't remember her last name, but she'd been on Channel 7 with Pauline Kirby, heading up a murder investigation.

Holy . . . shit . . .

"I'm Detective Rafferty with the Laurelton PD. Are you leaving, Mr. Danziger?" she asked, pulling out her identification. "Didn't Officer McDermott tell you I was coming to see you?"

Danziger had frozen in place and Jordanna was suddenly very aware of her hands on his torso, helping hold him up.

Beneath the thin hospital gown his muscles were hard and his skin felt hot. It had to look pretty intimate and from the detective's expression, Jordanna realized that she believed she'd interrupted Jay with his wife.

"Yes, he told me. I just was heading to the . . ." His eyes drifted to the bathroom.

Detective Rafferty inclined her head and said, "I can wait in the hall."

As soon as she was gone, Jordanna released him and he sank back onto the bed. He whispered tautly, "Can you go to my house? Get me the clothes, shoes, definitely pants. They must've cut off the ones I had on."

"Okay . . ."

"You know where my house is?"

"Um . . . no," Jordanna lied, keeping silent about all the times she'd spent surveilling him from afar.

He told her the address, then said, "Take my keys. My clothes are upstairs in the master bedroom closet."

"What about your wife?" she asked quietly, throwing a nervous glance toward the door to the corridor.

"I told you. She's in Europe."

"That's not good enough. What about the Saldanos? Surely they've contacted her by now. She has to have heard. I bet she took the first flight back."

"No."

"She's your wife," Jordanna insisted.

"She's my ex. We're divorced. . . . We just haven't moved apart yet."

"Huh." Jordanna thought that over, possibilities flying through her mind that she tamped down. She was going to have to give herself a very stern talking-to about him. "She should still be here. Why isn't she?"

"Lucky for you, she's not," he pointed out.

"I don't care if she's your ex. As soon as she knows, she'll be back. Which could be any minute," she finished, her gut clenching at the thought.

"Well, what the hell do you want to do?"

"I don't know. Give me a minute," Jordanna whispered harshly.

They stared at each other a long moment. *I could get lost in those eyes,* Jordanna thought, so she wrenched her gaze away.

Danziger said, "Look, my bedroom's at the top of the stairs, first door to the right." Jordanna glanced back in time to see him gazing down at his thickly wrapped leg. Then he shook his head and looked out the window, where a watery May sun was half-shadowed by a small, stubborn cloud. "Pants aren't going to work. I've got sweats in a bottom drawer inside the closet."

She nodded in assent. They were still going forward with their plan. She started toward the door, but he gritted out, "Wait," causing her to freeze in place.

"What?" she asked, looking back at him.

He inclined his head toward the bathroom and said reluctantly, "I need some help getting there."

She immediately returned to him and slipped her arm around his torso once more. "We have to get you some crutches," she said. Danziger was naked apart from the hospital gown, but Jordanna made a point of not looking. They moved awkwardly, Danziger barely able to put any weight on his left leg while Jordanna wobbled on her heels. When he was finally at the bathroom door, his head was hanging down and she was afraid to let go. "You're not gonna pass out, are you?" she asked urgently.

"No. Just . . . damn weak . . ." he muttered irritably.

"Where are the keys?"

"Probably in there." He waved a hand in the direction of the tiny closet, then let himself into the bathroom.

Exhaling a deep breath, she quickly ran through the drawers

in the closet and found his meager personal belongings: keys, change, a cell phone, a shirt, a pair of boxers, socks, shoes, remnants of a pair of Dockers.

Picking up the keys and slipping them into her pocket, she waited briefly for him to come out of the bathroom. Then, after a moment's hesitation, she headed back into the hall. She would have to put the license plates back on the car ASAP.

Detective Rafferty was leaning against the opposite wall, staring down at the ring on her left hand. A nice stone, Jordanna thought, though the two lines etched between the detective's brows said she might not feel the same way.

She looked up as soon as Jordanna stepped outside the room. "Mrs. Danziger?"

"Yes . . ." Jordanna's throat was tight.

"I understand Officer McDermott spoke to you earlier."

"Umm, yeah . . . I was looking for . . . Jay. I didn't know which hospital he was brought to. It was all kind of confusing."

She nodded as she straightened from the wall. "I heard he's being released today. That's good. His injuries were the worst from the explosion."

Jordanna was racking her brain for something to say, for something his wife would say, a question to be asked. She was so nervous her palms were sweating, but she tried to merely look concerned. "Jay said it was a bomb?" she asked, playing her part.

The detective nodded. "I just came from speaking with your father and brother. It was definitely a bomb and the ATF, the Bureau of Alcohol, Tobacco, Firearms and Explosives, is investigating the nature of it."

Hearing the words on the detective's tongue chilled Jordanna anew. "Did . . . my brother . . . say what he thought about it?"

"Your father believes it was a competitor, but I don't want

to speculate too much. We don't have enough information yet." Rafferty looked past Jordanna toward the room, where they both heard Danziger bark out a swear word as he stumped from the bathroom back toward the bed.

Jordanna thought about turning back to help him, but already knew he wouldn't appreciate it. She'd been tasked with a job and needed to do it quickly.

"When did you get back from Europe?" Detective Rafferty said, sending Jordanna's pulse shooting sky high.

"Um . . . last night. I turned around as soon as I heard and it took a while to get here."

"You asked what your brother thought. What do you think?"

"Oh, I don't know. I don't want to speculate, either." Jordanna was starting to sweat. When it came to light that she wasn't Carmen Saldano—and it would—this detective was going to be wondering who the hell she'd been talking to. "Maybe it's a disgruntled employee?"

"What about your husband?" she asked her.

"What about him?"

"He was the one directly in the line of fire."

"Well, yeah, but no one knew he was going to be there, except Maxwell. That's a long shot. And anyway, why would it be about Jay? I mean, yes, he's a journalist, and he's made his share of enemies, but they couldn't know he was going to be at Saldano Industries at that exact moment?" Was she talking too fast? She felt like she was talking too fast.

"It's a long shot," Rafferty agreed, but the way she was looking at her, with a kind of intense curiosity, sent Jordanna's pulse racing. "So, you think a disgruntled employee set the bomb."

"I really don't know."

"What about a competitor?"

"You're really talking to the wrong person. I don't work for Saldano Industries, and I don't know that much about what's going on. I do . . . interior design." She glanced down the corridor. "Now, I've really got to get going. Lots to do . . ."

Rafferty nodded. "I'll talk to your husband, but I'll call you if I have any further questions."

"My husband can give you any information you need." She heard the tension in her voice and cleared her throat.

"Don't worry. This is all routine," Detective Rafferty assured her.

Jordanna nodded and hoped the woman didn't notice her shaking hands. She was pretty sure Rafferty could see right through her, and it made her want to run down the hall as fast as she could. With an effort, she kept her feet rooted to the spot and tried on a smile. "I'll maybe talk to you later, then."

"Or someone from Portland PD." She nodded. "It's a joint effort right now. All hands on deck."

"Okay." Jordanna's chest constricted at that news. She only managed to stave off more of a reaction by turning as the remark was made. It took a helluva lot of concentration to walk away on her high heels as if she did it every day. Heart pounding, she forced herself not to look back.

Dance watched the pretty police detective enter his room and kept his expression neutral. He'd seen her before, he realized, but it took him a moment to place where: *Channel 7 News*. With Pauline Kirby. She'd been the Laurelton Police Department's new face last year. Dance had had his own dealings with Kirby, who was a grasping bitch jumped up from fluff reporting to hard news after sleeping with her boss, her coworkers, and anyone else she felt could give her a rung up, or so the story went. She'd certainly been *uber*-friendly to Dance when she'd interviewed him after a long investigation into political fraud, one he'd doggedly chased right up to the state level. Kirby had wanted to put

Dance on camera, but he'd refused. He didn't want to be more recognizable than he already was. Anonymity was the fuel that powered his ability to function in his job. If his face was plastered all over television, he wouldn't be able to move through the shadows of an investigation.

Still, Kirby had managed to get a small clip of him and had aired it a couple of times, though Dance hadn't signed off on it. He'd gone down to the station loaded for bear and only the threat of a lawsuit had gotten Kirby to, reluctantly, and with repressed fury, back down. She wouldn't give him the tape, however, and Dance's paper hadn't wanted a full-scale war with the television station, so she still had control, which pissed him off.

Of course, since that time, other pictures of him had found their way to the Internet, so the question was basically moot, and this bombing would plaster his face on the front-page news. Still, he didn't have to like it.

"All right to come in now?" the young detective asked him, peeking her head back inside the room.

He'd levered himself back into bed, more because he wanted to hang on to what little dignity could be afforded him in the airy hospital gown than because he needed support, though he was damn near immobilized without some kind of crutch.

"I spoke with your wife just now."

"Oh . . . yeah?"

"I asked her a little bit about her family, but she said I should talk to you. We've determined the explosion was caused by a bomb."

"Officer McDermott told me."

She nodded. "Okay. I just came from speaking with Victor and Maxwell Saldano. I understand the reason you were at Saldano Industries was because you were meeting with Maxwell Saldano?"

"Yeah. We were thinking of playing golf, but Max suggested

we meet at the office as it's about halfway between my house and his."

"But Mr. Saldano was called away to be with his ailing father at his home in the West Hills."

"I didn't know that at the time. I thought we were still on."

"He said he never called you because he was on the phone with Raydeen Abolear, your father-in-law's nurse."

"Okay."

"There weren't a lot of employees near the bomb site, which was at the front of the building, on the opposite side of the wall from the building entrance."

"Was it in Max's office?" Dance asked.

"It was against the west wall of the outside entrance. Is Max's office on the other side?" she asked right back.

Yes. Dance could feel his mouth dry as he thought about that meeting with Max at the end of last week and the audiotape he'd handed his friend.

"What?" the detective asked.

"Maybe this bomb was meant for Max." Dance purposely didn't tell her about the tape. "It's lucky he wasn't there."

"Yes," she agreed.

"Do you know anything about the bomb itself?"

"The ATF hasn't given out details yet."

She asked a few more questions about his relationship with the Saldanos, but Dance's attention was drifting away. He didn't recall the explosion, but he remembered getting ready to meet Max. The golf game was just a reason to get together with his friend. He'd wanted to talk to him about Carmen and the truth of their living arrangement. He was tired of the deception. He wanted to be divorced, really divorced; he didn't want to live in the same house with her any longer. He remembered walking out to his Highlander, hitting the remote button, and wishing he could blow up their relationship publicly, so to speak. He'd even experienced a wild moment of longing that he'd had some tawdry affair, or had been stinking drunk at some important social event, or found some other way to humiliate her so that Carmen felt compelled to throw him out, make a permanent end to it. He was sick of being careful, amicable, and polite. That's what he'd been thinking, his last conscious thought before waking up in the hospital.

"Mr. Danziger, you're an investigative journalist. Who or what do you think was the bomb's target?"

"I haven't had time to really think about it."

She gave him a straight look that called him a liar.

"All I know is I was supposed to meet Max, but . . ." He broke off. "I need to talk to him. What's his theory? Did he say?"

"I'll let him tell you," she evaded smoothly. *Tit for tat*, he thought. He wasn't saying anything and neither was she. "Mr. Saldano, Maxwell, said he's tried to get in touch with you, but hasn't been able to. The hospital isn't putting calls through to your room, per our request."

And my cell phone's probably dead.

"We can lift that restriction," she said now.

"Yeah, sure." He was going to be gone soon enough anyway.

She circled around and asked a few of the same questions in other manners, but Dance had nothing more to add. Soon enough, she thanked him and left. He watched her walk away and then leaned back against the pillows, closing his eyes and forcing himself to breathe deeply and evenly. His head felt clear, a bit achy but nothing truly troubling, which was a major relief. But his leg worried him. Cloaked in painkillers, he felt okay for the moment. However, his left thigh was going to hurt like a son of a bitch when the analgesics wore off, and he feared the damage to his muscles was extensive. He thought about Max again. His friend was trying to reach him. Deciding it was time to check his cell, he got up and bumped around, swearing some more, until he found the drawer that held his cell. He clicked the power button, but nothing happened. The battery was dead, as he'd expected. He was lucky the phone had survived the bombing at all, but then he'd had it in his right-hand pocket and all the damage had been to his left side.

He stared at it for a long time, then searched around until he found a hospital-issued plastic bag, which he carried, along with the cell phone, back to the bed. He liberated a paper clip from the pages of the hospital documents strewn across the bedside table, then bent it straight. With the paper clip and his own brute force, he pulled the phone apart and took out the battery and SIM card. Afterward, he put all the pieces in the bag.

Back in the bed again, he gazed at the hospital phone. No reason he couldn't call out. Reaching over, he picked up the receiver, then sat frozen as he searched through his mind for Max's cell number. It finally came to him, which cheered him up a lot as it said that his brain was still working pretty well, even if his cognitive ability had been dulled and slowed by the painkillers.

He pressed the numbers carefully, pausing before the last one. When it was ringing through, he suddenly cut the connection. There was the matter of the audiotape, a private conversation he'd been given by a source inside Saldano Industries. A message that certainly sounded like it implicated Saldano's import/export business in a smuggling operation. He'd given the tape to Max—actually a copy, though he'd lied and told his friend it was the original—and Max had listened to it and said it had to be fake. He'd wanted to know who'd given the tape to Dance, but Dance had answered that he'd received it anonymously. Max had then said he would put the tape in his office safe and he would figure out what the hell it was about. He'd assured Dance the accusations were entirely false.

Were they? Dance had wanted to believe that with all his

heart. He'd been toiling over the issue, and had half-convinced himself it was some kind of setup against his friend.

But the bomb had blown out the east wall of Max's office, the west wall of the building entrance. That was the wall where the safe was—little more than a filing cabinet with a lock—and if Max had put the tape there, then it was probably blown to smithereens.

But there was that copy in a safe deposit box.

Does Max know you well enough to know you would always make a copy? Yes. Is it too much of a stretch to believe he might try to destroy the evidence and you, too? An act of desperation to save his family?

No.

Yes.

"I don't know," he said aloud, his chest hurting.

Whatever the case, until he knew, he was putting himself in Jordanna Winters's hands. He just hoped he wasn't making a bigger mistake.

Chapter Four

The Danziger house was what the locals called Old Portland style with white columns and an imposing porch flanked by dual rectangular windows on either side of the massive front door. Jordanna held the keys in one fist as she pushed open the wrought-iron gate that surrounded the yard, looking around furtively at the sudden shriek of metal upon metal the gate made, as if it were seldom used. She'd parked down the block, where the houses were still stuck in the sixties or seventies with a predominance of split entries. This street, however, was in full gentrification mode. Though the Danzigers' house's style made it look as if it were from another era, it was newer than any of the rest and sprawled over what had once been two or three lots.

Jordanna had changed into jeans and a dark blue T-shirt, her hair up in a ponytail. She was torn about dressing up as Carmen for her last turn at the hospital. She didn't want to anymore. Playing the part for that detective had given her a bad feeling all over. Yet she didn't want to draw attention to herself by dressing down on her final trip to pick up Danziger, either. She wanted anyone who saw "Carmen" to remember that she was dressed the same every time.

But, for now, she was Jordanna Winters.

Hurrying up the porch steps, she slipped the key in the lock and opened the door. A faint bell-like tune greeted her, nearly stopping her heart, the kind of "welcome" music often heard when entering craft shops or candy stores. Jordanna had an instant mental vision of what Carmen Danziger was like and it didn't quite fit the image she'd created for the tight-skirted, CFM-shoe-wearing woman she'd been emulating.

Feeling like a thief, she shut the door behind her, shoved the keys into her front pocket, and tiptoed across the foyer to the stairs, hurrying up the oak stairway with its red, brown, and gold runner in an ornate fleur-de-lis pattern. She discovered the master bedroom at the end of the hall and headed straight to the walk-in closet, where she could see a California Closet-type system. The closet door was slightly ajar and there was a full-length mirror inserted into the front panel. Pushing it open further, she then quickly opened and closed several drawers before finding some sweats and a pair of cargo pants that looked maybe loose enough to fit over his wrapped thigh. Quickly she scanned the overall closet, exhaling in relief when she saw a large duffel bag. She tossed the pants inside, then threw in a short stack of T-shirts. The closet door had begun to swing shut again, and she caught a glimpse of a men's black fleece jacket hanging from the hook on the back side. She grabbed it and added it to the pile. Then she opened and shut several drawers in succession, passing by a junk drawer and one with feminine jewelry before finding one that held boxers and socks, which she grabbed up indiscriminately and stuffed into the bag, too. Lastly, she grabbed a pair of men's Nikes, and carefully arranged them so the soles faced up, away from the clothes.

She was in the process of zipping the bag shut when she heard the downstairs door open and the welcoming trill of the bells.

You didn't lock the door behind you.

Of course not, she thought wildly. She was turning and burning. She was only supposed to be here a few minutes.

Her mouth went dry. Her pulse pounded in her ears like a surf. Carefully, she pulled the duffel bag close to her body and then did her best to hide behind the closet door. She thought she heard measured footsteps on the stairs. Sweat dampened her underarms. God. What the hell was she doing? What if that was his wife? *Holy shit.* Squeezing her eyes closed, she stood still and tense, listening hard.

The footsteps entered the bedroom. She scarcely breathed. If they came into the closet and found her behind the door, what could she say?

Long moments passed. It occurred to Jordanna that this person, whoever he or she was, was acting oddly. Waiting or listening or something.

The tension made her want to jump out and reveal herself, cry out, "He told me to get his clothes!" but she stayed still. She knew better. . . . She knew better. . . .

Abruptly, the person turned and walked out—stalked out, actually, making no effort to disguise the sound. Jordanna sagged against the wall, spent. She heard the steps travel back downstairs, then bells sing at the front door again.

Who was it?

It took all her courage to leave her spot in the closet and enter the bedroom. It was late afternoon and clouds had gathered outside, darkening the room, but it was May, and it stayed light damn near forever these days. She had to get out of here, but she wanted to know who'd come inside the Danziger house. They must have had a key themselves. Carmen? Someone else?

What if this person is waiting for you? What if he saw you go in?

Well, to hell with it. She needed to know who this person was.

Hugging the duffel, she carefully descended the stairs,

keeping her body just inside the windows that flanked the door. At the entrance, she risked a peek through the blinds and saw a dark sedan—maybe an Audi?—pulling out of a spot across the street. She was too far away for a license plate, though she thought she saw an L and a 5. There was no way of knowing if that car had anything to do with whoever had been inside Danziger's house.

But there was no way she was heading out the front now. She would be too exposed, but the surrounding wrought-iron fence ran the length of the property. There was no way out unless it was through the front, the way she'd arrived, or through the garage itself.

Padding softly toward the rear of the house, she passed through the kitchen, barely noticing the gleaming stainless-steel appliances, the hand-painted terra-cotta tiles. It looked Italian country, beautifully done, and it felt more like what she imagined Danziger's wife's style to be than the tinkling door chime.

Outside the back door was a walkway screened by hedges, thank God, and it led directly to the garage main door. She hurried quickly toward it, the duffel banging against her leg, and tested the door handle, relieved to feel it turn beneath her palm.

Inside the double-car garage was one vehicle: a Mercedes sedan.

Carmen's car? Then not the Audi? Danziger's Highlander was probably still at the bomb site unless the authorities had picked it up.

She was going to have to open one of the two garage doors to let herself out. Looking in the Mercedes she spied the electronic remote. Opening the driver's door, she snatched it up then pressed the button. The garage door hummed and rattled upward, and Jordanna hurried outside, re-pressing the remote button, which stopped the door in mid-ascent, then pushing it a final time so the door could churn its way downward once again.

The garage door emptied onto a side road that ran north and south. Clutching the duffel and remote, Jordanna turned south and walked the long way around a wide block to where she'd parked her car. Hitting the keyless lock, she climbed inside, dropped the garage remote on the passenger seat and then placed her hands on the wheel, inhaling several deep breaths. She'd left her purse under the seat, and now she dragged it out and dug inside until she found her car keys, which immediately slipped from her grasp and fell to the floor. Realizing her palms were sweating, she wiped them on her jeans and set her jaw. If she was seriously planning to be an investigative reporter, she was going to have to grow a pair of balls.

Dance was in the golf shirt he'd been wearing when he'd gone to Saldano Industries when Jordanna Winters reappeared in his hospital room. She was dressed once again like Carmen except this dress was gray instead of green and not quite as tight.

"You got in all right," he observed.

She dropped his brown duffel on the bed. "Yeah, but I was nearly caught. Someone came to your house while I was in your bedroom closet."

"Who?"

"I don't know. I thought it could be your wife, but her car was in the garage."

"She went by town car and left the Mercedes. But she wouldn't just go in and go out. I don't think she's back yet."

"I suppose it could've been someone else. I didn't lock the front door after me. Maybe someone followed me in?" She didn't sound like she liked that idea much, either.

"Maybe someone who thought you were Carmen."

"I was in jeans. Does she ever wear 'em?"

He shook his head.

"Then, I don't think they thought I was Carmen."

Dance felt chilled. Had someone been looking for him?

"I followed them downstairs, but I never saw them," she went on. "A dark Audi pulled out from across the street but it could have been anyone. Or, maybe it was just a car that looked like an Audi. I don't know."

He unzipped the duffel, yanked out a pair of sweatpants, then moved awkwardly to a chair to put them on. *Weak as a kitten. Shit.* "Wonder if the Highlander's still where I left it."

"You want to look before we head out?"

He shook his head, sending a wave of dizziness through him that created fresh nausea. He put his head between his knees and took in deep breaths.

"Are you sure you're okay?" Jordanna asked, taking a step nearer to him.

He held up his hand. "Yeah, yeah . . . just give me a minute."

"Okay," she said doubtfully.

She was tense and he felt his own muscles coiled for flight. They'd dinked around too long already. He heard it in her voice, and he felt it himself. Hanging around was dangerous. With an effort, he finished pulling on the sweats; then, without being asked, Jordanna helped him with socks and the Nikes he'd been wearing when the bomb went off. The left one had a gash across the toe but was otherwise still in working order.

They looked at each other. Her hazel eyes stared into his blue ones as if seeking answers. "You ready?"

"Yup."

She reached an arm around him, and Dance levered himself upward, leaning heavily on her. Her shoulders were small, but she felt tough and wiry beneath the weight of his arm.

"I had to put the plates back on, then take them off again. Hopefully no one's paying attention to how many times I'm driving behind that empty strip mall."

He grunted a response. Sweat was beading on his forehead. He hadn't counted on being so miserably weak.

"There's a wheelchair in the hall," she said as they worked their way out the door. He dropped into it gratefully and then Jordanna hurried back in the room. He heard her moving around and realized she was gathering all his meager belongings and putting them into the duffel. She returned a few moments later, dropped the bag in his lap, then began pushing him down the hall.

Two nurses were standing and talking to each other at the end of the corridor, but neither of them gave them more than a cursory glance. "I think I can do the stairs," he said as they approached the bank of elevators at the far end of the hall. He didn't want to be in a closed elevator car.

"We're taking the elevator."

"I don't want to risk being in the elevator with anyone else."

"You can't make the stairs."

"I can. I will."

"Horseshit."

For a moment, he was pissed; then he almost laughed. "Fine. Hell. The elevator."

She slammed her palm on the button, then waited behind the wheelchair, inhaling and exhaling heavily, clearly fighting back her own anxiety. When the elevator doors opened, a man and woman in scrubs broke on either side of them and walked in opposite directions. Jordanna pushed him inside, then turned the chair around. Just before the doors closed, a young aide squeezed into the car. She gave them a smile.

"You're being discharged already?" she asked him, and he wondered if he'd been under her care. He was a little fuzzy about the staff who'd attended him.

"Doctor okayed it," he told her.

She nodded, her eyes sliding toward Jordanna, who suddenly leaned down and kissed him on the side of his cheek, purring, "I'll just be so glad to have you home, darling."

Boo looked through the dirty window to the late-afternoon shadows and longed to be with them. He always wanted to hide in the shadows. It was where he belonged.

He said, pleading, "I want to go to the playground."

"There is no playground," Buddy told him. "Not anymore."

"You promised," Boo cried.

"There is no playground."

But Boo knew Buddy was lying. They were always lying to him. All of them. They said they wanted to protect him, but they just didn't want him to be with his friends. They didn't *trust* him. He could feel the anger building and he wanted to wish it away but it wouldn't be wished away. He could never wish it away. He'd tried so many times before. Bad things happened when he got angry, but sometimes he just couldn't stop the feeling.

"There's a playground," he stated belligerently. Belligerently . . . B . . . e . . . l

"I told you, there's no playground. How many times do I have to say it?"

"Don't be mad." But Boo could feel his own face tighten into its mad look.

"I'm not mad."

"Yes, you are. You're lying. You told me not to lie. You told me God's watching."

"God is watching," Buddy said, turning to stare fully at Boo in the darkening kitchen. "Every minute of every day, so you need to be quiet."

Boo glanced around nervously. Was it really dark outside

now? Or, was he making it dark. He could do that. "I just want to play with my friends."

"They're not your friends, Boo. How many times do I have to tell you? They're not like us. They pretend they're nice, but they're tainted."

"They're what?"

"They're tainted. Inside . . ." Buddy walked up close to Boo and crouched right in front of him. "Deep inside them is a dark place where they hide from the rest of us."

Like me? Boo wanted to shriek, but he kept it inside by chomping down on the insides of his cheek. "No . . ." he finally said. It was scary to argue with Buddy, but he had to. "They climb on the monkey bars and the pirate ship down at—"

"Listen to me, you idiot. They're not your friends and you stay away from them."

"Don't call me names!"

"Then do as I say!" Buddy straightened abruptly and turned away. Boo wanted to hit him. He almost jumped up and punched him in the back, but he knew it wouldn't be enough. But he knew what to do.

"I don't give a gah-gah-*god*damn!" he blurted out triumphantly.

Buddy was on him in a flash, yanking him out of his chair and slapping him hard across the face one, two, three times. Boo's ears rang and he was sobbing by the time Buddy was finished.

"You keep your filthy tongue in your head," Buddy ground out, "or so help me I'll cut it out!"

"Sor-sorree," Boo wailed, his throbbing face in his hands. He just wanted to go to the playground, that was all. "I just"—*hiccup*—"wanna go"—*hiccup*—"to the playground!"

"THERE IS NO PLAYGROUND!" Buddy thundered and stomped out of the room. But Boo knew he was lying again. Buddy just didn't want him to have any friends. He

wanted to lock Boo away forever and ever. He could fee[l] [the]
anger again, knew his mad face was getting madder. A[fter a]
seething moment or two, Boo pulled down his pants an[d] [let]
his fingers find the slightly raised mark on his right butt[ock.]
He could visualize it even though he'd only seen it i[n a]
mirror. A "C," that's what the doctor had said, then, "L[ooks]
like a C. How'd you get it?"

"I don't 'member."

The doc had looked down at him and said, "It look[s] [like]
a branding."

"It's a scar," Boo had answered, feeling proud th[at he]
knew.

The doc had eyed him in a way that had made Boo
uncomfortable, and he'd wanted to say something[,]
something that he maybe remembered . . . maybe . . . b[ut the]
way the doc looked at him had made his stomach
squirmy so he hadn't.

He wondered now if he should tell the doc that B[oo]
was lying.

Boo had trouble thinking things through. His mam[a had]
told him that so many times he accepted it as truth. If [Mama]
were still around, she'd be saying it again, he was prett[y sure,]
so when he wandered closer to the window and looke[d] [out]
at the stretch of farmland that swept toward the moun[tains,]
he thought of his mama, could almost see her in the sha[de]
out by the apple tree that her grandpa had planted. [He could]
almost hear her again . . .

"You be careful, Boo. Be real careful. Sometimes p[eople]
are going to be mean to you. I know you have trouble t[hink]-
ing things through, so I'm gonna tell you something
now and you need to remember it. Think you can do t[hat?"]

"Yes, Mama," he'd answered, even though his hear[t] [sank]
'cause he was afraid he couldn't.

"If they come for you and I'm not here, you ne[ed to]
protect yourself. There's a floorboard in the shed. It's [loose.]

Back by the wall with Old Nickel's leashes. You find it, and there's something inside for you. But don't look unless you have to, you understand?"

"Yes, Mama."

"I mean it. Don't look. Better if you don't know until you have to, okay? Promise."

"P-p-promise," he'd stuttered. "But you won't leave me!"

"No, honey." And she'd hugged him close and he'd clung to her, but she'd lied, too, because she was gone before Santa came that year, and Santa didn't bring Boo any presents so he knew it was his fault.

He hadn't looked for Mama's treasure. She'd told him not to, and he'd sort of forgotten about what she'd really said anyway. It was a big jumble, which Buddy had explained was just the way his "screwed-up brain" worked. But the last few nights he'd woken up and seen Mama by the hawthorn tree and her words were back inside his head.

Buddy was being mean to him, that was for sure. Maybe he was going to come for him and be meaner. Maybe now was the time to find Mama's treasure in the shed beneath Old Nickel's leashes.

Boo's eyes and nose got all hot and burny as he thought about the old, gray mutt with the thumping tail who'd been his friend. Now he was gone and so was Mama and Buddy wouldn't let him go to the playground.

Yep. Maybe now was the time. . . .

Chapter Five

The old, once-white farmhouse looked foreboding in the evening light, its windows balefully watching the car as Jordanna pulled around the back behind the long, long woodshed that connected the house to the listing carport at the far end. "It's a walk from here," she said, "but I don't want anyone seeing us. You can lean on me."

Danziger threw a glance toward the woodshed, which was all you could see from this point as it sheltered the house. "No one's going to see us," he pointed out.

Jordanna nodded, slightly embarrassed. He was right, of course. The house was a quarter mile down a curving lane, and there were fields and rolling hills on either side. The property backed up to the foothills of the Cascades and the nearest neighbor was over a mile away. This was her family home, located on the outskirts of Rock Springs, about three hours southeast of Laurelton. She'd chosen it because it was a helluva hideout for Jay Danziger, though she didn't like the place at all. She'd never felt completely safe here, for reasons burned into her own psyche.

She aided him from the passenger seat and could see how much his helplessness bothered him. "Stop fighting me," she had to tell him as they hitched their way toward the woodshed door and then moved slowly along the planks that had been laid down on dirt, a makeshift walkway to the back door. Chunks of firewood were stacked to the ceiling on both sides and the only illumination was from the series of pane-less windows that ran along the southern exposure. Now there was only darkness beyond so Jordanna used her free hand to hold her cell phone, its flashlight app on.

"Woodstove," she explained as they neared the door to the house.

"I did a story in Rock Springs once," he mused, though his voice was tense from the effort of walking. "Animal cruelty."

"Mr. Purdy's horses," Jordanna said.

"That's right. He was a hoarder. More stupidity than out-and-out cruelty. He didn't realize he was starving them."

"You defending him?" she questioned as she shoved her shoulder against the sticking door. She didn't have keys, but unless her father had changed things, this door only needed an extra hard push for entry.

"Of course not," he said as the door gave. "It was a criminal act and it was lucky the horses were found when they were. But hoarding's a mental disease. Used to be categorized with obsessive/compulsive disorder, but it's a whole 'nother thing."

"You researched it," she said.

"That's what I do."

It was cold in the kitchen, and when she hit the switch nothing happened. "No electricity. Goddamn you, Dayton," she muttered.

"Who's Dayton?"

Jordanna didn't answer as she helped him to the couch. He sank down with a sigh and immediately closed his eyes and laid his head back.

"I'm going to unload the car."

He didn't say anything as she returned to the car and started making the trips through the woodshed to the house and back again. She'd changed back into her Nikes when she'd replaced the plates, and now she yanked out her suitcase, trudged upstairs to her old bedroom, then switched into jeans, a long-sleeved black T-shirt and a light jacket, her arms breaking into gooseflesh at the drop in temperature as night descended. Dressed again, she hauled the rest of the boxes of her belongings inside, making a half dozen trips back to the car, feeling her arms quiver from weariness. No surprise there. She was on an emotional roller coaster herself. The fear and thrill of sneaking through his house and helping him to her car—she'd left the wheelchair in the parking lot—and then sliding the RAV behind the empty building, putting on her plates again, and driving to Rock Springs, all the while keeping one anxious eye on Jay Danziger, was taking its toll.

She'd purposely taken a circuitous route, heading into the heart of Portland and around the city before turning further east and finally south toward Rock Springs. Danziger had roused himself about halfway through the journey and looked out at the countryside as they clipped along the two-lane highway that led to the town, the landscape growing more rural by the minute. They weren't all that far from Portland in distance, but it was a world away in almost every other respect.

"Where are we going?" he'd asked.

"Home," she'd answered after a moment, and though she felt his eyes on her, she hadn't turned to look at him.

"Where is that?"

"Rock Springs."

"It's a pretty small town, right? What's the population?"

Jordanna had had no interest in talking about herself and answered with, "How come your wife hasn't contacted you? Whatever shape your marriage is in, you were hospitalized."

"Why don't you want to talk about Rock Springs?"

"Because I want to talk about the Saldanos, and the bombing."

"Because you want a story."

Jordanna had really, really wanted to deny it, but he wasn't an idiot and, well, there was truth in that. "Maybe. But I think you're in danger, and so do you or you wouldn't be here, so let's lay our cards on the table."

"There's nothing to say I haven't already said. I was in the wrong place at the wrong time."

"And the Saldanos are angels. All suspicion against them is a load of bull, corporate envy, blah, blah, blah." When he didn't respond, she said, "If you're having second thoughts, we can go back."

"You know I can't go back."

"Do I? Tell me, how would I know that?"

"You're the one who came to the hospital wild-eyed and trembling."

"I wasn't trembling," she protested.

"Yeah, you were."

"I was scared for you. I was there," she admitted. "Across the street. I *saw* the explosion." He'd stared at her then, a kind of reassessing that made her want to shrink inside her skin. "I was doing my own research on the Saldanos, and that included you. Sorry. It did. And after the explosion, I was scared out of my mind, running on gut emotion. I wanted to see you, make sure you were okay. So, I dressed up like Carmen. I'd seen her take off in the town car with bags. Figured she was on a trip and I had a window of opportunity. But I wanted to make sure you were safe because something's rotten in Laurelton and it has to do with the Saldanos. You know it, and that's why we're here together now."

Her impassioned speech sent him back into silence. After a few moments Jordanna said, "Tell me more about this arrangement you have with your wife. I don't get it."

He hesitated so long that she thought he wasn't going to answer, but then he finally said, "Carmen brought me divorce papers about three months ago and I signed them, but she wanted me to stay on the premises with her for a while, until she was ready to come forward, tell her family and friends. I said okay. I was working on a story and I didn't much care. Neither one of us really wanted to tell Max and Victor. I told her she could be the lead dog on that. Before she left for Europe, she said she was going to take care of things when she got back."

"You think there's any chance she doesn't know about the bombing?"

"She might know, but it's more likely that if she's heard I'm alive and recovering, there's no need for her to come back. She asked me to sign the papers. She wants it over, too. She said she was living with a ghost, that I wasn't there for her, and that's not something you do to Carmen Saldano."

"Why did you marry her?"

"She was sexy and attractive and she was Max's sister. We were together a lot. It seemed like the right fit." He gave her a look and said, "I see you think that's not enough. I'm guessing you're single."

"People get married for a lot of reasons," she'd answered with asperity.

"Well, those are mine."

"So, you don't think we'll have to worry about her?"

"Max is the one I have to worry about. He's the one who'll wonder where I am."

"If that bomb was meant for you—"

"I'm not going to contact him. I'm off the grid. In your hands. I just need some time to put things back together in my mind." He'd then closed his eyes, making it clear the conversation was over, or at least that's what Jordanna had thought, but after another ten miles he'd asked, "How long were you watching the Saldanos?"

She'd thought about all the days and nights she'd kept tabs on Danziger's whereabouts, how she'd dogged him, her idol, as she'd written her fluff pieces and dreamed of being a true investigative reporter. And a lot of that time had been because she wanted to be the one to break the story on the Saldanos. "A while."

"That's specific."

"Long enough to know that you started out investigating them, but then you got sucked in."

He shifted in the seat. "Sucked in?"

"Did you just start turning a blind eye to their corruption?"

"They're not corrupt."

"You're the only one who seems to think that, and you damn near got yourself blown to kingdom come because of it."

"If they wanted me out of the way, they wouldn't bomb their own building."

"It's exactly what they would do. They've got more money than God, so they can afford to blow some stuff up when they need to misdirect the investigators."

"They didn't do this," he'd insisted.

"They're all guilty as hell," she'd responded recklessly. "I've tracked them . . . and you . . . and whatever they're selling, it's not just benign import/export items. You were investigating them before you married into the family. What happened? Did you finally find them out?"

"You're way off base."

"You need to say that with more conviction."

"It has to be a competitor," he answered. "That's the only thing that makes sense."

"Are you talking to me? Or, are you trying to convince yourself?"

"They're not murderers," he'd flashed. "And they're not

drug dealers, either, no matter what fantasies you want to believe. They're decent, hardworking people."

"Who tried to kill you."

"Someone bombed *them*," he said. "I just got in the way."

"Keep telling yourself that, but I can tell even you don't believe it, not completely."

"I don't know what the hell the bombing was about," he growled.

"There. That's at least honest. If you trusted them like you're trying to make me believe, you'd be with them right now, not some wannabe investigative reporter who's taking you to parts unknown. You're scared for your skin, Mr. Danziger, and I, for one, believe you have every right to be. . . ."

"It's Dance," he'd said through his teeth.

"What?"

"It's what everyone who knows me, calls me."

"Well, I don't know how well we know each other . . . Dance, but okay."

"You kissed me."

"What?" she repeated, surprised.

"When we were getting off the elevator."

"As Carmen! I wanted her to think I was Carmen. You know that."

"We know each other okay. That's what I'm saying."

After that, the conversation had pretty much ended until they'd gotten to the house. Now, Jordanna trudged back a last time from the car, carrying the microwave into the dusty kitchen and placing it on the counter. She thought about kissing him on the cheek and it made her gut tighten a bit. She'd done it so naturally.

Oh, sure, the voice inside her head told her. *You wanted to. You've wanted to do something like that for ages, following him around like a lovesick dog.*

"Shut up," she said aloud.

"What?" she heard him call from the other room.

"Nothing," she yelled back.

Pushing thoughts of him and the kiss aside, she silently vowed to head into town as soon as possible for more cleaning supplies, as what she'd brought wasn't going to fill the bill by any means. She plugged the microwave in even though there was no electricity. She could feel the chill deepen and with a sigh went out to the woodshed and hauled in chunks of oak and maple. There was a stack of old newspapers, a rusted can of lighter fluid, and a box of long wooden matches near the back door. How long any of it had been there was a question she didn't ask herself as she carried the wood to the stove in the living room, where Dance was asleep still in his sitting position, his head thrown back against the cushions. She returned for the other items, then knelt on the floor in front of the stove and loaded it with wood, newspapers, and a spurt of lighter fluid, then touched a lighted match to the whole thing. The lighter fluid would smell for a bit, but she wanted the fire up and running as fast as possible because the nights were still cold.

Dance had surfaced as if pricked by a pin when she brought in the first pile of wood and his face had darkened. "What's wrong?" Jordanna threw over her shoulder as she headed back toward the woodshed.

"We didn't refill my prescriptions," his voice called after her.

"I'll do it tomorrow. Okay?" she yelled back.

"Yep" was the faint reply.

When she finished with the wood, she brought him a blanket, which he ignored, then set about putting the fire together. Once it was going strong, Jordanna carried the blow-up bed into the only downstairs bedroom, the one-time sitting room that had been converted for her mother at the end of her life. Out of habit Jordanna sniffed the air as she had when she was a little girl. She hadn't liked the medicinal scent overlaid with floral aromas that hadn't fooled anyone, least of all her. But apart from a dusty, unused smell, the room was fine. There was no bed any longer; that had been removed years earlier. Now, she pushed back the occasional chairs and a couple of rickety tables that her father hadn't taken with him when he'd remarried, apparently, and laid the mattress on the floor. She plugged in the battery-operated inflation device and waited while the mattress filled. Then she returned for the bag with the bedding, dragging out the mattress pad and sheets, and made up the bed.

It was slightly warmer by the time she returned to the living room. "I've got your bed ready," she said to him, his face all shadows and planes in the orange glow from the woodstove. "The furniture here is only what my father left, so it's a blow-up mattress."

"I heard," he said.

"I know it's going to be hard to get up and down from the floor, but otherwise the bedrooms are upstairs and I haven't looked to even see if there are any beds up there. I'm guessing not."

"Where are you going to sleep?" he asked.

She looked from him to the couch he was sitting on. It wasn't much more than a love seat and its worn velveteen surface was covered with dust. She slid by that and said, "We have well water. The pump's attached to a back-up generator, so I'm hoping for the best. If not, I can call Clancy. He should get us going."

"Who's Clancy?"

"Mike Clancy's a friend." That was reaching a little, as the Clancys had been friends with the Winterses as a family. Jordanna had burned more than a few bridges, and she wasn't certain Mike was in her camp any longer or if he would help her. "His family does all kinds of service repair work and he can figure out how to put things right around here."

"Who's Dayton?" he asked again.

"Dayton's . . . the owner of this house."

"A relative," he guessed.

Jordanna rubbed her nose, getting dirt on its tip. She sensed it immediately but thought, *To hell with it.* "My father," she admitted.

"You're not a close family."

"Not since I shot at him with a .22 rifle."

She could see him straighten to attention. "Did you hit him?" he asked after a tense moment.

"Yep."

"But he's still alive."

"I hit his shoulder. Not for lack of trying. I'm just a so-so shot."

"Why'd you do it?"

"Because he deserved it," she snapped. Now that she'd opened the door, she wanted to close it.

He chuckled and she squinted at him through the darkness.

"What's so funny?"

He shook his head.

"You're amused that I shot my father? That's why you're laughing?"

"Maybe you're cut out for another line of work."

"Okay, fine," she bit out. "Think what you will."

"What'd your father do?"

"NOTHING."

"I just want to make sure you're not going to try to shoot me later," he said, a note of faint amusement in his voice that made her want to throttle him.

"I'm trying to help you. That's all. That's all there is. If there's a story in it for me, great. If not, fine. This'll be over soon enough."

"That sounds kind of ominous," he said slowly.

"Don't worry. I'm not going to go all Kathy Bates on you. Tie you to the bed and smash your ankles. What I want is to bring down the Saldanos with your help. But first we've got to get you on your feet, and if that means a lovely four-day, three-night stay in Rock Springs, or whatever it takes, so be it."

With that, she left him for a trip to the pump house with her phone flashlight to see if she could get the water flowing.

Dance felt weary all over. He'd tried very hard not to let Jordanna know how tired he was. He didn't want her to see how weak he truly felt, which made no sense really, since she knew the extent of his injuries, but it seemed important anyway. Now, while she was away and he was sitting in the dark with just the woodstove throwing out faint orange light, he wondered why he was fighting so hard.

He was cold, despite the fire, so he picked up the blanket and pulled it around his shoulders.

The hell of it was she was right. In his hazy memories, he saw the audiotape and the look of surprise on Max's face. Surprise because of guilt? Or surprise that he'd been duped by his father because Victor Saldano maybe knew about the smuggling? The tape was from an old-school recorder that one of the employees had hidden in his pocket, and on it were three voices chronicling a deal with someone in Mexico. The informant was one of those guys that were on the hustle, so Dance had initially dismissed the tape. But he needed to be sure, so he'd made a copy, put the copy in a safe deposit box, then brought the tape to Max.

"Where did you get this?" his friend had asked him before he even listened to it.

"A source."

Max had looked at him with disappointment. "You're gonna pull that source shit on *your family?*"

"Listen to the tape," Dance had answered.

"Is this the only copy?"

"Yes." The lie had come out automatically, and then he and Max had stared each other down.

That was the only time they'd talked about it, but it had been understood that decisions would be made at the golf game.

He expelled his breath on a long sigh, thinking about his friend. Behind the couch was a window with wispy, once-white lacy curtains. Beneath the light of a three-quarter moon, he could see a portion of the rutted driveway rising to the south before the lane curved around the side of the old house. When they'd approached, he'd stared at the two-story wooden structure, noting its clapboard siding, also once white, and the faded blue shutters that looked gray in the fading light. The house had to be from the turn of the last century, built more farmhouse style than Victorian, and even before Jordanna had helped him inside, he'd known that it was abandoned.

He wanted to ask her about it, but there was something prickly about her that had cropped up during the drive. He'd been so immersed in his own dull world of pain and exhaustion that it had taken him a while to notice. When he had, he'd picked up the way her words grew clipped, seen her white-knuckled grip on the steering wheel and the set expression on her face—all of which had deepened as they'd neared the town of Rock Springs.

"You grow up here?" he'd asked her as they drove down Rock Spring's main street, and he'd glanced at the buildings on both sides of the road. The town was nestled up against the foothills of the Cascade Mountains and there was a small stream running behind the last row of businesses. As they reached the southern end of the district, Dance could see a rushing waterfall that spilled from a plateau high above, poured down a jagged cliff and splashed into a pool below, raising a cloud of mist above the river. The river itself ran behind the buildings on the eastern side of the main street before curving away from town. FOOL'S FALLS, he'd read on the sign posted nearby.

"No one would want to grow up here," she'd answered after a long pause.

"What happened?"

"Nothing happened. I moved away."

Now, of course, he knew about the shooting so he assumed her departure had something to do with that. If he'd felt more like himself, he would have plied her with more questions and/or started a side investigation, just for his own personal reasons. As it was, the mystery would remain a mystery, for the moment, unless Jordanna suddenly decided to unburden herself, which didn't seem likely.

But at least her colorful history had kept his mind off his own problems momentarily. She wanted to poke around about the Saldanos, though, like worrying a sore tooth, which he didn't want to do until he'd had some time to really think things through. Right now, he was too muddled to make any kind of decision. He just wanted time to *be*. He didn't want his friend, or any of the Saldanos, involved in something criminal.

Is Max culpable? his brain posed, even while he was trying to shut down his thoughts.

He rubbed his eyes and then pressed his fingers to his temples, thinking. His friend was cheerful and upbeat and uncomplicated, a far cry from his sister, who was sultry and brooding and full of secrets, though it was just those qualities that had attracted him to Carmen in the first place. Living with the woman, however, had quickly dissipated those feelings. She was too demanding and unsatisfied in who she was, enraged at a deep level that her father had chosen Max as his right-hand man, overlooking her because she was a woman. Dance could have told her that Max was simply the better choice. Besides being easy to be around, he had a quick appreciation of business that Carmen just didn't have. The one time Dance had sought to have a heart-to-heart with his unhappy wife, he'd damn near gotten his head bitten off. She did not take kindly to hearing her faults, even if it was just as a comparison to her brother, whom she loved fiercely though Max was less enamored of her.

Therein lay the problem, he thought. Carmen was devoted to Max and her father, and while they might love her, they didn't really want to deal with her.

If only you'd known that before you tied the knot.

Well, he was out of that now, for better or worse, and he was lucky that she'd been the one to finally see that their marriage wasn't made to last.

He heard a quick shriek, then muttered swearing, as Jordanna stomped back into the house. "Squirrels," she muttered. "And a goddamn raccoon family! They're in the crawl space beneath the house."

"You planning on killing them?" he asked mildly.

She looked at him in horror. He could just make out her expression in the uncertain light from the woodstove. "God, no, but I don't want to live with them, either. Let's hope they move on now that we're here."

"I heard water when we pulled in, somewhere behind the property," he said. "Maybe that's where the raccoons fish?"

"Yeah, there's a stream out back."

"Part of Fool's Falls?"

She shook her head. "That comes from the foothills of the Cascades. Benchley Creek runs behind the house," she added after a moment, as if she wasn't too certain about revealing that fact. "It meanders around and catches up with the Malone River. Malone's the nearest town east of here."

"Benchley Creek."

"Named for the infamous Benchleys, who married Tread-wells, many of whom died from insanity, or so the story goes."

"What story?"

"Never mind."

"Your story?" he pressed. When she didn't answer, he said, "You tantalize me with all these hints from your past. When are you going to tell me the whole tale?"

She was already heading back to the kitchen and he had to raise his voice to make sure she heard him. She yelled over her shoulder, "I've got peanut butter sandwiches for dinner. I don't want to hear that you're allergic."

Dance almost smiled. "I love peanut butter," he called back, and heard sardonic muttering beyond the wall that sounded like "Hallelujah for nothing."

Chapter Six

The generator was working so the pump was pumping and the water was flowing. Jordanna could've cheered. But the hot water heater was being finicky and she didn't know how much propane was left to run the generator. Didn't much matter for the moment, but Jordanna was going to have to take care of things in the morning.

She helped Dance to bed, and by the time he was lying on the clean sheets she'd put on the air mattress, beads of sweat were standing on his forehead. "Maybe you did leave the hospital too soon," she said ruefully.

"Not soon enough" was the taut answer.

She nodded. At least they still agreed that it was better his whereabouts were temporarily unknown.

He'd taken his jacket off but was still in the clothes he'd changed into. "You need anything else?" she asked as she placed a plastic bottle of water on the floor beside him.

"No. See you in the morning," he said, and Jordanna left him and went back to unloading the rest of the items she'd brought from her apartment. By the time she was finished it was after 11 PM, and when she laid another sheet over the back of the couch and across the cushions, she just wanted to fall onto it. She stripped down to her underwear, then pulled on her own sweatpants and a T-shirt that advertised Holcomb's Hardware, a gift from Marty Holcomb after she'd written a piece about the Holcomb family and the family business that was one of the oldest in Laurelton. The logo included a smiling man holding a chain saw. Then she covered herself with one of the extra blankets she'd brought. She'd known, sort of, what she would encounter at the house because since her father's remarriage he'd all but abandoned the place.

Just before she climbed into her makeshift bed, she switched on her cell phone, which she'd turned off to save battery life. There were several e-mails from acquaintances, one from her bank, and a surprise from her sister, Kara, who wanted to know if she was going to be home this weekend. Since a visit from her wanderlust sister was rare, Jordanna quickly e-mailed back that she hoped to be, wondering if she could make that happen. She wasn't sure how long she'd be here with Dance, and she didn't want to explain about him to Kara. Her and Dance's plan was so half-baked that anything could happen.

Switching off the phone, she threw a glance toward the short hallway that led to his room. Now that she'd met her one-time idol up close and personal, she wasn't sure what she thought of him. Maybe she didn't even like him. She wanted to save him from harm, but he put her on edge. The man was handsome, but so what? She'd hoped, dreamed, of maybe working together with him somehow, someway, but those thoughts had dried up and blown away.

Be careful what you wish for.

Yeah, well, when had she ever listened to that old saw?

As she fell into exhausted sleep, her thoughts turned uncomfortably to her father and older sister, Emily, the mess she'd made of things . . . and how she'd become the scourge of Rock Springs.

* * *

Jay Danziger's dreams were full of tattered images of the bombing. He was aware enough to know he was dreaming but couldn't quite wake himself up. There were pieces of information, too, that he sensed were real, but every time he reached for them, they disappeared like fairy dust deeper into his subconscious. He surfaced to wakefulness several times, but then would just fall back into deeper slumber, never able to grab hold of the pieces beyond a sense of flying debris and fear of injury to his head. He could recall throwing his arms over his face. There was also a sensation of weightlessness and an overriding feeling of dread. When his eyes finally popped open into full wakefulness, it was pitch black outside. The moon was undoubtedly obscured by the low-lying clouds that had dogged them all the way to Rock Springs, and without the benefit of streetlights, or any other ambient light, it was damn dark.

He had to go to the bathroom, and with an effort that had him biting back swear words and gritting his teeth, he managed to lever himself upright against the nearest wall. His head throbbed with the effort, which pissed him off. He tried putting weight on his injured leg but felt a rip of pain that had him imagining flayed tissue and permanent damage.

"Son of a bitch," he snarled through clenched teeth.

Knock, knock. Gently done.

"Yeah?" he snapped.

"You need help?"

"No."

"You sound like you need help."

His full bladder was sending a message of discomfort to his brain, reminding him painfully that he'd better get relief soon. "I'm heading to the bathroom," he informed her.

She opened the door and saw him leaning against the

wall. Sliding up to his right side, she said, "Lean on me," and he tried to walk while she half-carried him to the room. She left him standing in front of a toilet that he could just make out from the faintest of gray light that came through a high window in the darker recesses of the bathroom.

"You might want to sit," she said as she left the room.

Another time, he might have been amused by that, but he was too weary and goddamn mad to do more than mutter, "Close the door." He ignored her advice however. There was just so much indignity he could stand. In the darkness, his eyes made out the new package of toilet paper, a towel on the ring and two more on a bar. There was no shower curtain surrounding the tub yet, but she'd done what she could.

When he flushed the toilet, he heard the pipes groan as if in pain.

She appeared without asking a few moments later to find him leaning against the sink. "The bathrooms were added sometime in the forties. There's one upstairs, too."

"Great."

"Just letting you know we don't have to share."

She put her arm around him to help him walk as he asked, "How old is this place?"

"Turn of the last century. Craftsman style. One of those homes you could buy in a package from the Sears catalogue."

"Historic home," he said. "You don't seem to like it much."

"It's a good hideout for you."

"Why'd you shoot your father?" he asked again.

"Like I told you, he—"

"Deserved it, I know. But why? Was he molesting you?"

She made a strangled sound that could have meant any-thing. "Not me" was what finally came out after she'd helped lever him back onto the bed.

"Your . . . sister?"

"You're a good guesser," she said with a trace of bitterness.

"Yes, my sister. Emily. She's gone now. Died about a year after I took the shot at our father."

"What happened to her?"

"Car accident on an icy road." She looked toward the rear of the house. "Up in the hills."

There was a long silence during which he thought maybe that was all she was going to say, but she didn't immediately leave his room. Finally, she said, "Emily swore she was sleepwalking, dreaming about our mother, and that she'd wandered into his bed."

"The night that you . . ."

"That I shot him," she said impatiently. "You can say it. The night I shot my father, I found my sister in bed with him. Emily said it was all a mistake, but I heard her call out 'Dayton!' which is what woke me up. I grabbed the rifle and charged in there. I just kinda knew. Emily was half out of the bed and he was reaching for her and I shot him."

In a distant part of his mind, Dance thought he should be more worried, frightened, even, by this midnight confession, but he only felt curiosity and an empathy he usually reserved for victims of crimes, not perpetrators.

"About a year later she was driving along the ridge back behind the house." She moved her arm in the darkness and waved it in the direction of the long woodshed. "It was icy and Emily lost control and the car went over the edge and into the trees down below."

"I'm sorry," he said.

She shrugged. "It was a long time ago. Nobody wanted to believe me. It was easier to believe in my father . . . and Emily," she added reluctantly. "They put it down to the Treadwell Curse and everyone just backed away and hoped I would get better."

"What is this 'Treadwell Curse'?"

"Nothing I really want to go into." Her tone said, *Ever.*

"What happened when you left this home? Where'd you go?"

"You writing a story?' she asked sardonically.

"You've been following the Saldanos, following me, my work. How long?"

"A while." She moved toward the door. "Call for me if you need any more help."

"You don't like talking about yourself."

"No, and I bet you don't, either, so we're even."

In that, she was right. Dance never wanted to talk about his own life. It wasn't so much that it was something to hide; it was just . . . uninteresting. Unlike Jordanna Winters, it seemed, he had a pretty mundane, middle-class childhood, the only bump coming when his parents divorced. He'd lived with his mother after his father remarried and started another family. He hadn't liked it, and he'd been relieved to go to a junior college and eventually to the University of Washington. After college, he'd left Washington for California, but then had ended up in Oregon. He'd thought about law school but had been interested in reporting and had worked to become a feature writer for *The Oregonian*. His thirst for tougher stories had veered him into investigative work. Now, he stared up at the ceiling, dark as a tomb. Everyone was going to wonder where he was. If Carmen weren't a Saldano herself, she, too, would probably think the Saldanos had fitted him with some concrete shoes, such was the feeling about the family he'd married into. Dance had told himself for years that the world's suspicions were crap, but that was before he'd been given the unsolicited audiotape.

The Saldanos aren't your family. They don't care about you. They maybe aren't even your friends.

Dance's mouth compressed into a thin line and he closed his eyes tightly. He was going to hang out with Jordanna while he got his strength back, but then he was going to face Max and find out where the hell he'd been during the bombing.

And you'd better have a good story, friend, he thought. *A really damn good one.*

In the darkness, Boo's eyes shot open and he strained to see. There *was* a playground. He knew where it was, and it didn't matter what Buddy said, it was there.

But it was a long way away. Could he make it there? By walking?

Carefully, he pulled on the worn jeans that he'd dropped over the side of the bed and cinched his belt. Then he ran a hand over his curly hair and grabbed up the shirt he'd wadded and thrown into the corner of the bedroom. It wasn't really clean. He'd worn it for two days and Buddy sure wanted things clean, but then so did Boo. Still, he didn't think he could risk opening a drawer and finding something new, so he put the shirt on and padded as silently as he could to the back door and the line of coats and shoes that were there.

He slipped his arms through the jacket sleeves, then hesitated, chewing on the inside of his cheek in fear. He had to get outside and the door to the carport was pretty creaky. Buddy had asked Boo to put the WD-40 on it, but Boo had forgotten. And he couldn't put his boots on yet; that'd be for after he got outside . . . but how . . . ?

Boo searched his mind for a plan, but came up empty. That was the problem. Buddy always told him his brain was a bunch of worthless goo, but he said it kind of nice like and rubbed Boo's head.

Then he remembered the window down in the cellar that was pretty easy to open, though kinda high to get to. If he climbed on a box or two, though, he could get outside and then leave the window open for his return.

It took a long time, but he managed to squeeze out the small window. Buddy would have a lot of trouble doing it, but Boo was lots smaller. When he was clear of the house and out in the night, he looked around. Dark forever and ever. He lifted his nose and sniffed and thought they were in for some rain. Boo was good at forecasting the weather. He was hardly ever wrong.

Which meant he needed to zip up the jacket tight and hold the collar close. Shoulda brought a hat, but he didn't really mind rain.

Glancing around, he decided to take the little-used track behind the barn and head toward the mountains. There was a way up, but it was hard. He'd been with Buddy to the shelf of land that looked over the valley and across the river to the town with its lights. "Looks like a necklace," Buddy had said, staring down, and Boo had seen the way the lights curved in at both sides, 'cause that's how the river ran. The falls were on one end, but you couldn't really hear them. Too far away. Couldn't hear the bars where the sinners drank and smoked and fucked. Buddy had told him about that, too, and it had made the hair on Boo's arms lift and given him an embarrassing flagpole that had made Buddy snicker a little.

Boo really wanted to go up on the shelf now and look down at the town, but it was in the opposite direction of the playground, so he went south and walked and walked, across open fields and over fences toward the trees at the edge of the mountains, and walked some more, until he started crying.

He shouldn't have come. Buddy was right. There was no playground.

Boo sank down on a stone and put his face in his hands and sobbed. He'd made a mistake again. Just like last time.

But then he heard Buddy's voice in his ear. "You can't keep coming back here."

Boo shot to his feet, electrified. "Buddy!"

When there was no answer, he crashed through the deepening woods, half running, half stumbling upward until he was almost at a level with the shelf but much farther away from town. And suddenly, there it was—the playground—and Buddy was lying on the ground, next to the teeter-totter.

"Knew you couldn't stay away," he said sadly.

"I just want to be here."

"Why?" Buddy asked.

Boo said, "It's good here."

"You came a damn long way," Buddy said, and Boo shrank back a little, 'cause Buddy didn't swear much.

"Am I in trouble?" Boo asked tearfully.

"Look around."

Buddy had gotten to his feet and now he gazed across the playground, which wasn't really all that good in the dark. Boo needed to be here in the daylight. "I'll come back in the sun."

"You can't come back, Boo. You know you can't come back."

"Why not?"

"LOOK."

So, Boo tore his gaze from Buddy's stern face and gazed across his beloved playground. Except . . .

"What do you see?" Buddy demanded.

"Uh . . ."

"WHAT DO YOU SEE?"

"It's not my playground," he said in a small voice, fighting back another surge of tears.

"It's a cemetery," Buddy told him harshly.

"But we played in the playground . . ."

"It's a cemetery, meathead. It's where I have to put them. They're not your friends. They're not here waiting for you to play with them. You understand?"

Boo saw the faintly rounded mounds of dirt. Buddy had been lying beside one of them. A new one. "They're dead?"

Buddy laid a hand on his shoulder and said in a sad voice,

"I know you'll forget again, but you have to try to remember. They've been cursed. Had to give 'em the devil's mark."

Boo fought hard not to reach a finger to where he knew his own mark was. "They're like me," he said.

"Not like you," Buddy said sternly.

"They're my friends."

"They're aberrations. Abominations. You stay away from them. You're better than they are. You've been cured."

Boo stared up at Buddy as a blast of rain poured down, half-blinding him. He wanted to believe him, he really did. But he knew deep in his soul that he was no better, and cold fear gripped him that Buddy would someday have to put him here, too.

Chapter Seven

Jordanna awoke early and checked her phone. 6:00 AM. She was cold. The blanket she'd thrown over herself hadn't been able to completely dissipate the chill. Her bare feet hit the wood floor and a cold frisson ran up her leg. She was going to have to get the electricity back on one way or another.

She went upstairs to the bathroom and sluiced her face with cold water, then she fumbled for the hand towel she'd put up yesterday and buried her face in it. After that, she went into her old bedroom, the one she'd shared with Kara, and dug in her bag for a fresh pair of jeans and a long-sleeved T-shirt. Faint morning light was piercing the gloom.

Returning to the first floor, she went into the living room and stirred up the embers in the woodstove. She then added more kindling and chunks of fir and oak and worked to get the fire going. Once satisfied it was going to stay lit, she filled a kettle with water, then placed it on the stovetop. She'd brought some instant coffee and tea bags with her, and there was a little bit of cream left in the carton she'd put into a bucket with ice. She was half-proud of herself for bringing in the supplies she had, but she also knew she had to get into Rock Springs and replenish.

And face her father.

She grimaced as she held her hands over the stove, willing its heat to enter her frozen bones. It wasn't that cold, but she couldn't seem to scare up any body heat. Guilt? Fear? Dread?

"You always act too rashly," her father had declared on more than one occasion, long before she'd actually taken out the .22 and proved him right in a spectacular way. "One day, you may pay a heavy price. I don't want that for you."

She snorted. Dayton Winters had never given a damn about any of his three daughters, nor had he cared about his wife. He was only interested in Dr. Dayton Winters, pillar of the community, healer to the sick and ailing, father to three undeserving girls. His marriage to one of the Treadwell women, whose genetic line was impure, had been either a moment of pure insanity, or just proof of his inherent goodness and need to care and help those who truly needed him . . . depending on whom you spoke to.

Jordanna believed her father had married her mother purely because she was so downright beautiful. Maybe he hadn't believed the townspeople's claims that Treadwells were "fucking crazy," or maybe he'd just been young and horny enough to not care. From what Jordanna knew of her Treadwell grandparents, which wasn't much, as they'd both died young, her grandfather had been pretty handy with a gun and had possibly caught young Dayton Winters in the backseat of a Camaro and said it was marriage or the family jewels. Jordanna didn't have the whole truth of that; however, what she did know was that her father had never lacked for female companionship. Marrying Jennie Markum, the chief of police's daughter and an RN who worked at the clinic her father had founded, had been a political move, but Jennie was, well, just what the doctor ordered: young, attractive, uncomplicated. And in one fell swoop, he'd ensured there would be no further speculation or investigation by the police about his certain proclivities.

Kara had apparently attended the wedding, but had again left for parts unknown shortly afterward; therefore Jordanna's information about her father and Rock Springs always tended to be old news.

She dropped a spoonful of coffee crystals into a mug, then poured the tepid water over the top. Couldn't get it to boiling. Had to get that electricity on, even if they were only here a few days. Of course, the bill would be sent to her father, she supposed, unless she could work out a way to pay online.

She tentatively sipped, making a face at the lukewarm coffee, then heard thumping coming from Dance's bedroom. Setting the cup down on a side table, she walked down the short hall to the bedroom, surprised when the door banged open and Dance stood braced in the doorway, most of his weight on his right leg.

"I need crutches," he said.

"Pharmacy is top of my list."

"Do I smell coffee?"

"Sort of. Instant and not exactly hot."

"Close enough," he said.

Jordanna poured him a cup and was going to help him to the couch, but he managed to limp his way to it before sinking down into the cushions. He looked at the neat pile of blankets.

"How'd you sleep?" she asked.

"How'd you?"

Wiggling her hand in a so-so motion, she said, "I'm going to head into town and pick up everything we're missing." She pulled out her cell phone and checked the time. "But first I'm calling the electric company and getting us hooked up."

"Good luck with that."

She eyed him closely. "You think it'll be a problem?"

"Well, who owns this house?"

She hesitated. "My father."

"Yeah, the electric company will probably want him to call and okay it."

"No."

"I'm just warning you."

She eyed him speculatively. "You can call and say you're him."

"That's not going to work."

"Sure it will. I know his Social, birthdate, whatever. You can be him."

"His name's Dayton?"

"Dayton Winters," she said.

"And what's the power company?"

"Pacific Power."

"Hand me your phone," he ordered. "And write that stuff down, so I can just look at it."

She held out the phone to him, then pulled out one of the small notebooks she used on the job. She flipped to the back pages, where she kept her father's information, while Dance Googled the power company's number. He made the call and answered questions easily enough, and without a squawk they accepted that he was Dayton Winters, though they said they would have to send someone out to the property to hook them up as there was apparently some problem with the line. The appointment was for the next morning.

He handed her back the phone and she said, "You're a good liar."

"Yeah?" he asked cautiously.

"No, don't worry. I consider it an asset. I'm not as good at lying, although I'm working at it."

She saw a flash of white from the brief smile he shot her and had to look away. Yep, the man was too damn attractive . . . too damn attractive.

"All right, I'm leaving for a while. I'll bring you back breakfast."

"I'm not all that hungry."

"I'm still going to bring it back. And we've got tuna and peanut butter and bread for sandwiches later. I'll pick up some more ice and we should be good until the power company gets here."

Jordanna started to turn away, but he stopped her with, "How long you planning on being here?"

She glanced back at him. "How long are you?"

"Still working that out."

"Okay."

"What if . . . this takes longer than either one of us think?"

She paused. "Still working that out," she responded, then headed for the door that led through the woodshed and the carport beyond.

Jordanna plugged the phone into the car charger as she drove into Rock Springs. It was a twenty-minute drive; the old homestead was out in the sticks, for sure. Jordanna had resented that, too, when she was growing up, but now she found herself feeling differently about its isolation. She'd been so hell-bent on getting out of Dodge when she was a teenager that she hadn't been able to see one good thing about Rock Springs or the house. Now, she viewed it differently. Not only was it a great place to go to stop the world for a while, but also, she reluctantly allowed, it did have a beauty of its own, a somewhat untamed landscape and a quaint western-themed town that harked back to its Wild West roots. These charms had totally escaped her when she was younger. In her mind, Rock Springs had been backward, unsophisticated, and totally Nowheresville.

The sun was bright and beaming down warmly, expelling the spring chill, as she reached the outskirts of town. She was headed to the diner for a cup of coffee when she saw a blue neon sign that read in script: FOR THE LOVE OF JOE.

"A coffee shop," she said in wonder. Well, it had been years since she'd been back. Even Rock Springs had apparently been touched by the coffee craze. All she could remember from when she'd lived here was the abundance of churches and taverns.

She stepped inside the coffee shop and was hit by the mouthwatering scents of maple, honey, and buttery pastries, and the rich, deep aroma of coffee. She ordered herself a steaming cup with room for cream, then purchased two maple-crusted scones. "Gonna eat both of those?" a male voice asked her, pointing to the small, white sack in her hands that held the scones.

She turned around to see a familiar face . . . though her brain took a few seconds to make the connection. "Ahh . . . Rusty Long," she greeted him as he straightened from the table, where he'd been hunched over a cup of coffee and a couple of doughnuts. Another man sat across from him and he eyed Jordanna with interest, but just sipped on his coffee.

"Jordanna Winters. You look just the same," Rusty said.

"So do you," she lied.

Rusty Long had been a classmate at Rock Springs High, a freckled, strawberry-blond kid who now possessed a paunch and a stringy mustache to go with a receding hairline. But he still grinned like a jack-o'-lantern, his face an open book.

Slapping his growing belly, he fought back a belch. "Hell, no, I don't, but you know . . . what're we doin' around here if we're not drinkin' somethin'?"

"Rusty closed down the Longhorn last night," the other man at the table revealed.

Jordanna automatically looked across the street, where the town's most notable and disreputable bar had stood, and saw it was now a discount furniture store. She tried to place the man who'd spoken. She was pretty sure she didn't know him.

"Longhorn's outta town a ways now," Rusty said, following her gaze across the street. "Gives us all a chance to get home before Markum or Shitface come after us. Sorry, Mr. Shitface," he added, then guffawed and ended up coughing wildly.

"Introduce us, Rusty," the other man said. He was dark-haired and brown-eyed, about five to ten years older than Rusty, and he didn't look nearly as dissolute.

"This here's Todd Douglas," Rusty said.

"Hi." He leaned forward and shook her hand.

"Hi," Jordanna responded.

"Rusty's talkin' about Peter Drummond. You know him?" Douglas asked.

Jordanna shook her head. She didn't know Rusty's companion, either.

"I'm Rusty's better-looking cousin from over in Malone," he said with a quick smile.

Since this was absolutely true, Jordanna didn't know quite how to respond, but Rusty guffawed.

"How does Rusty know such a pretty gal?" Douglas asked.

Jordanna snorted. In jeans and a shirt that needed ironing, with no makeup and her hair scraped back into a ponytail, she knew just what she looked like . . . and "pretty" was a stretch. "We were classmates at Rock Springs High," she said.

"That's right," Rusty agreed. He grinned at Todd and said, "We Bobcats beat your Malone Prairie Dogs every damn year."

Todd shrugged and merely waved Rusty off, as if he were a bothersome gnat. Malone High were the Huskies, not the Prairie Dogs, and they all knew it. Having ribbed his cousin long enough apparently, Rusty turned to Jordanna and asked, "You know Drummond. A couple classes ahead of us. Maybe your sister's? That . . . um . . . Emma . . . ?"

"Emily," Jordanna corrected.

"Yep. That's right. Emily . . . Well, Pete Drummond was an asshole in high school and he's a bigger asshole now. Works for the chief."

"Chief Markum?" Jordanna kept her voice as neutral as she could.

"He was chief of police then, too, wasn't he?" Rusty realized, sounding half astonished. "Jesus. Nothing changes around this town, does it? So, how come you're back?"

It was Jordanna's turn to shrug. "Oh, I don't know. . . ."

"You workin' on a story?" He turned to Todd, said, "She's a reporter." Then his attention swiveled back to Jordanna. "I've read a thing or two of yours. Nice stuff."

"Uh, thank you."

"A reporter, huh?" Douglas sounded interested, but maybe a bit disbelieving.

"I've done a few local stories," Jordanna said, moving toward the area of the counter that held the lids, napkins, and cream.

"You do investigations?" Douglas asked.

"I'd like to do investigative pieces, but I'm kind of working my way to that. Have to prove myself." Because they were looking at her expectantly, she added the lie she'd worked on while she was driving into town, one that would explain what she was doing in Rock Springs. "I'm kind of looking for a place to bring my hiking group, and I thought of the foothills around here."

Douglas straightened up as if she'd goosed him, but it was Rusty who said, "Cuz, here, is a hiker himself. Maybe he can show you some of the trails."

"I've been all over this section of the Cascades," Douglas admitted. "Damn near know it like the back of my hand. There's purity in the mountains."

Rusty groaned. "Don't go there, Todd."

Jordanna immediately backtracked, seeing she'd made a huge mistake. "But work comes first. I've got to get back to the story I'm researching, so I may have to put the hiking on the back burner."

"If you change your mind . . ." Douglas said, looking faintly disappointed. "What story is that?" he asked, then, as a thought struck him: "You here to write about the missing Fread girl?"

"The missing freed girl?" Jordanna queried. "What was she freed from?"

"Fread's their last name," Rusty said, then spelled it aloud. He cocked his head and closed one eye. "I bet you're researching the dead guy who was practically found in your backyard."

"He was found on government land," Douglas argued a bit testily.

"Yeah, but by dead reckoning, the body was found almost straight east of the Winters property, just on the other side of Summit Ridge Road," Rusty insisted.

"What dead guy is this?" Jordanna asked curiously, pausing after she poured cream into her cup. Absently, she reached for a plastic to-go top.

"The homeless guy," Rusty said. "Hey, come on down to the Longhorn tonight and we'll fill you in, right, Todd?"

"Sure," his cousin replied.

"And the missing Fread girl," she said. A lot of news for Rock Springs.

Rusty waved that off. "Todd's just thinking about her 'cause she's pretty, too, but we all know she just ran away from her weird family. One of those super religious ones that are against everything, y'know?"

"You should shut up about stuff you know nothin' about," Douglas suggested congenially.

Rusty snorted. "Me and Todd have differing views on

how to save our sorry souls. He finds God and church in the mountains. I find it in a good lager, y'know?"

"You're goin' straight to hell, cuz," Douglas said.

Rusty started laughing and shot back, "You sound just like Reverend Miles. Good God in heaven, there's someone to stay away from." He retook his seat. "Jordanna, I'm not kiddin'. Come on down to the Longhorn later."

"I'll think about it," she said.

A dead homeless man near her family's homestead? And a missing girl? She'd been looking for a story to present to her editor with that kind of edge, but she'd never expected to find it in Rock Springs. Maybe it was just Rusty and his friend blowing smoke, but she thought she might actually show up at the Longhorn later and see what they had to say.

And it would give her a reason to put some space between herself and Dance, who clearly wanted to be left alone.

As Jordanna walked down the street, sipping her coffee, she wondered where the *Rock Springs Pioneer* had relocated, or if it even existed any longer. It was a biweekly that mostly covered the social happenings around town with a smattering of information about the local businesses, farms, and ranches. She also wondered, if it did still exist, if it printed a police report of any kind. Unless he'd drastically changed, which she highly doubted, she just didn't think Chief Markum would be the kind to work in tandem with the press.

Braxton's Pharmacy was cheek to jowl with the local Thriftway and it sported a long, maroon awning over its front door. As she pushed through one of the double glass doors, she was greeted by country/western music and the scents of vanilla and something fresh and spring-smelling. Dropping her empty cup into a trash receptacle, she made a mental note to pick up candles for the dusty and dry house, then looked above the rows of shelves ahead of her to view the signs that directed her to bandages. While she walked along the ends of the rows, looking down the aisles, she caught glimpses of the dinerlike counter at the back of the store that served breakfast and lunch off a grill. Jordanna had spent many hours there as a kid, living off grilled cheese and hamburgers, especially as her mother grew more ill.

She found the correct aisle and perused the stock of bandages and antibiotics and various and sundry supplies for cuts and sores. She had no desire to change Dance's bandages, but it didn't hurt to be prepared. If, and when, he wanted to make that choice, she would do her best, as she wasn't great with the sight of blood.

She had a vision of her mother staring vacantly out the kitchen window across the empty field while blood ran down her palm and off the tips of her fingers from an accident with a knife, though many had questioned whether it was really accidental. Jordanna had grabbed the roll of paper towels and yanked wads of paper free, wrapping them around her mother's hand, more because she wanted to stop seeing the blood than because she'd been old enough to understand the concept of direct pressure. Didn't matter. Blood had soaked through as quickly as it was sopped up. Jordanna's shrieking had brought her sister, Emily, who'd called 9-1-1 and told Jordanna that she was an imbecile for not immediately making the call herself. Their mother had been sped to Dayton's clinic as the nearest hospital was an hour away in good traffic, and Dayton himself had stitched her back together. The scar on her palm had been thick and jagged, and every time Jordanna had seen it, she'd gotten a sick feeling in the pit of her stomach.

Now, grabbing up the largest cotton bandage pads she could find, a bottle of rubbing alcohol, some Neosporin, and several rolls of elastic bandages as well, she then searched around for a basket, finally finding one by the front doors.

She dumped the armful of items inside, then picked up the black plastic basket and headed toward the prescription counter, where two pharmacists were on duty. She thought she recognized the older woman but couldn't place her. The young man with the big smile who came to see what she wanted was a stranger. "You rent crutches here?" she asked.

"We do. Among other things. What size?"

"Jordanna?" a voice behind her asked in wonder.

She held her breath. She hadn't really counted on running into so many people who knew her. Turning around, she faced a young woman with sleek, straight, brown hair. She had green eyes with too much black eyeliner and wore a white blouse with a prim Peter Pan collar, coupled with a pair of dark denim skinny jeans. The woman was looking back at her expectantly.

"Uh . . . hi . . ." Jordanna mumbled.

"Oh my gosh. You can't say you don't know me!"

The truth hit Jordanna in the gut. It was the straight hair that had thrown her. "Jennie," she said, picturing her father's wife with her normally wildly curly hair.

"What are you doing here?" Hearing herself, she added quickly, "I mean, it's so great to see you, but goodness, I didn't think you'd come home for anything."

It was a dig about missing the wedding, but Jordanna chose to ignore it. "I'm just cruising through."

"Rock Springs? No, you're not. Tell me why you're here. And you've just got to come by and see Dayton. Are you here for a while?" Her gaze dropped to the bandages in Jordanna's basket. "What's this?"

"Oh . . . first aid supplies. . . ." Going back to her earlier lie, she said, "I'm actually with a hiking group and last time we went out, we weren't prepared." She wasn't good at lying unless given a script. Then, she could generally sell it.

She glanced over at the guy at the counter, who'd been listening in to her meeting. She hoped to hell he didn't bring up the crutches, and she hadn't even gotten to Dance's prescriptions yet.

"I'll come back," she told the pharmacist as she turned away, hoping to shut him down. She could feel his eyes on her, but didn't look back, and he stayed mum as she walked toward the diner grill. Jennie, however, was right on her heels.

"Is your group hiking around here, then?" she asked.

"No, this is for the future. I'm just doing reconnaissance."

The only employee at the diner was an older woman who'd spread *The Pioneer* on the counter and was reading it as she stood. Looking up, she folded the paper closed and asked, "You want something, dearie?"

"Um . . . maybe . . ."

At that moment, a door behind the prescription counter opened, and a middle-aged woman in a smock marched through. She looked vaguely familiar, and as Jordanna catalogued that, the woman glanced her way and stopped short.

Jennie was saying, "You have to stop by the clinic, if nothing else. Dayton will be there till six today."

"I'm sorry. I just don't think that's going to happen," Jordanna said.

The newcomer's steel-gray hair was curled to an inch of its life. She looked from Jordanna to Jennie with sharp, assessing eyes, while the employee who'd been reading the paper at the diner casually gathered it up and strolled further behind the counter, moving out of sight.

"How long's it been since you've seen your father?" Jennie appealed to her. "Really, Jordanna. Just a pop-in will do."

The woman behind the prescription counter edged closer and said, "You're one of the Treadwell girls."

Jordanna responded, "It's Winters, actually. I'm Jordanna Winters."

"Your mother was Gayle Treadwell. May God have mercy on her soul." The woman nodded her head gravely.

"Well . . . yes." Jordanna could see down the aisle toward the front of the store and straight through the glass doors to the street beyond. The longing to bolt was nearly overpowering.

"Such a shame," Jennie said, then, "Jordanna, I know you haven't forgotten Margaret Bicknell. She's practically an institution at Braxton's."

"I've been filling Dr. Winters's prescriptions since before either of you were born," the older woman added with a forced smile. Her lips looked like they might crack with the effort. "You have two sisters," she said directly to Jordanna. "What are their names again?"

"Emily . . . and Kara."

"I remember Emily," she muttered. "Sad story, there. And your mother was a lovely woman, even if . . . well . . . end of life can be a challenge. God is merciful, though."

"Yee . . . es . . . ss . . ." Jordanna said.

"He took your mother's pain away," Margaret added.

Jennie interrupted, "Say you'll stop by. Please. It would mean so much to Dayton."

"If I have time."

"I'll give you my number. Put it in your phone." Jennie waved at Jordanna's purse, so Jordanna reluctantly pulled out her cell. Then Jennie carefully listed the digits, hovering over Jordanna to make sure she entered and saved them.

Feeling Margaret Bicknell's sharp gaze still on her, Jordanna flicked the older woman a look and said, "You're wondering if I'm the crazy one with the rifle. Yep, that's me."

"Oh, goodness, don't say that!" Jennie declared.

Margaret Bicknell frowned, as if she found Jordanna's behavior unsavory. Then she said, "We're all susceptible to the devil's influence. Sometimes we win the battles and sometimes we don't."

"Well . . . huh . . ." Jordanna murmured.

"You didn't kill your father," Margaret said. "God has a plan for us all."

"Yes, he does," Jennie agreed, grabbing Jordanna's arm and practically dragging her away. Out of earshot, she said, "You'll have to forgive her. Margaret's had some troubles of her own. A close friend was killed in a drunk-driving accident. He was the drunk driver. No one else was hurt."

"Oh . . ." She wanted to peel Jennie off her arm, but didn't know how to politely.

"I really should be going. I've got stuff to do," she said a bit lamely.

"Oh, so do I. But call me, okay? Really. It would be so nice to get you and your father together."

Jordanna nodded, hearing her anxious tone. Jennie might act like everything was hunky-dory, but she knew about the rift between Jordanna and her father. She gave her a smile that she hoped didn't look too fake, then walked away from the diner counter, heading for the front of the store. Though she'd had some half-baked idea about sitting down at the grill counter and having a moment of reflection, hoping maybe that Jennie would leave her to remember the few good moments from her childhood, that clearly wasn't going to happen.

She placed her basket on the counter next to the cash register. The clerk, a young girl with solemn blue eyes and a bored attitude, took Jordanna's credit card. All of a sudden, Jennie, whom she'd thought had left, popped up beside her.

"Where are you staying?" Jennie tried.

"I'm not. Staying. Like I said, I was just scouting around for hiking places."

"Um . . . you never gave me *your* cell number."

"I . . . never can remember it. You'll get it when I call," Jordanna said.

"You're not putting me off on purpose, are you?"

"No . . ." Jordanna sighed and finally relented with, "I

think you overestimate my father's interest in seeing me. He's not likely to forget I shot him."

"With a gun?" the girl at the register couldn't help bursting out. She ripped off the credit card receipt and slid it and a pen across the counter to Jordanna.

"Yup." Jordanna signed and handed back the merchant receipt while the girl's wide eyes grew wider.

"It was an accident," Jennie told the girl frostily.

Jordanna picked up her sack of purchases and turned toward the door, but Jennie was in front of the double glass doors. "Seriously?" Jordanna asked. "You're not going to let me out?"

"You're not going to call." Jennie looked sad and distressed. "For heaven's sake, am I really asking for so much? Your father hasn't seen you in years and here you are. You picked this area for your hike for a reason. It looks to me like you want to make amends."

Jordanna gazed past her father's wife with longing for the outside street once again. She'd fooled herself into thinking she could get away with hiding out at the homestead for a while. She should have checked Jay Danziger into a motel somewhere under her name and let him work out his problems with the Saldanos on his own.

Except you wanted him for yourself. Lie to others all you want, you've always been more interested in him than you want to believe.

"Jennie, get out of my way, or I'm going to push you through this door and let you fall on your butt."

She whipped her phone out. "Give me your number."

Jordanna started laughing. She couldn't help herself. "Oh, for Christ sake," she muttered, then snapped out the numbers, which Jennie quickly inserted into her phone.

"I never believed everything they said about you," she said, not looking up as she moved out of the way. "I defended you."

"Well, you made a mistake." Jordanna pushed through

one of the glass doors. Heading toward her RAV, she was supremely aware of Jennie, just inside the pharmacy, tracking her progress.

She pulled out of her spot, then drove around the block, taking her time. When she returned, she caught sight of Jennie heading north on Main Street, out of town, ostensibly back to her home. Quickly, Jordanna hurried back inside the pharmacy and ordered the prescriptions. Luckily, she got the younger guy this time, though he warned her he would have to call them in.

"Do it," Jordanna told him. Of course, it would pinpoint their location to Dr. Cochran, but she was pretty sure the doctor couldn't hand out that information indiscriminately so unless the authorities requested the information, they would be left alone. "And I'll take those crutches," she added. "Ones for around a six-foot-two man."

"Hope these work," she told Dance an hour later when she handed him the bag of scones and then lifted up the crutches. She'd made a big show of heading north through town in Jennie's wake, then east toward the nearby town of Malone before circling back and returning along a perimeter road that kept to the outskirts of Rock Springs before finally ending up back on the two-lane road that led to the homestead driveway. The whole time she'd questioned herself, wondering why she hadn't just made up a false number to give to her stepmother.

"Thanks," Dance said. He took a scone and handed the bag back to her, eyeing the crutches. "Those oughta do. What about the prescriptions?"

"I have to go back for those. They're working on 'em."

He nodded. "I did manage to get to the bathroom and back while you were gone."

"Progress. Good." She pulled out the other scone, bit into it, and mumbled, "I shoulda got more coffee. And groceries."

"I thought that's why you went."

"It was. Just didn't work out that way."

"What happened?" he asked, but Jordanna shook her head.

"How's the leg doing?" she asked.

"I think I'll need to change the dressing soon."

"Oh . . . yeah . . ." The last bite of scone seemed to stick in her throat. "Like at a doctor's office?"

"I'd like to avoid that if I could. I've got enough antibiotics, but it'll probably have to be looked at soon."

Jordanna could feel herself growing squeamish and tried to hide it. And what was the alternative anyway? Her father's clinic?

"I just need some time to figure out what's going on," he said.

"You can't go back yet," she agreed, worried that's where his thoughts were heading.

"Well, I'm not leaving today, clearly. You said you have an iPad . . . ?"

"Not charged."

"How about paper and pens, then? Old school. I want to make some notes."

"Yeah. Sure." Jordanna went back to the kitchen, which was the catchall where she'd dumped not only the pharmacy supplies, but everything she'd brought from her apartment as well.

"What happened in town?" he asked again, when she returned with a letter-sized, lined notepad and several pens.

"Nothing."

"You weren't kidding about being a terrible liar." The light from outside the window illuminated his blue eyes and the three days' growth of beard darkening the strong line of his jaw. Jordanna forced herself to look away from his very male attractiveness.

"Okay, I ran into some people I knew," she admitted.

"Not a happy reunion," he guessed.

"Nope."

"When are you going to tell me the whole story?"

"Hopefully never," she said, only half kidding. She had a thing for him. Had for a long time, but had never believed she would have the opportunity to actually be with him in any capacity, especially one-on-one. "I'm going out tonight to a bar to meet some people I know."

"Really? So, the whole town's not against you, huh?"

"Not all of them." She almost told him all about her father, and sister, and mother, but when it came right down to it, her tongue wouldn't form the words. Instead she said, "Apparently the body of a homeless man was found close by here and I wanted to follow up."

"Close by here?" He circled a finger to encompass the house.

"That's the rumor. And there's a missing girl, but it sounds like she's probably just run away from a strict, religious home. There are a lot of churches around Rock Springs and some of them with a lot of rules. Anyway, I'll get some more food while I'm out this time, I promise. And the prescriptions, and tomorrow, fingers crossed, we'll have electricity."

She left him then, and returned to the kitchen with her cell phone, checking on her own e-mails, which were practically nil, but mostly just using the time to be by herself and away from the appeal of Jay Danziger.

Chapter Eight

September was just getting up from her desk when her brother walked into the squad room. "What are you doing here?" she asked.

Detective August "Auggie" Rafferty was her twin and the reason she'd gone into police work in the first place. He'd joined the force several years before her and it had whetted her appetite for law enforcement, much to the horror of their wealthy, overbearing father, who'd basically disowned them for a time. Though Auggie had been working for the Laurelton Police Department when September was hired, he'd since joined a joint task force with the Portland PD that had morphed into a full-time position.

Now, she eyed him with affection and a certain amount of misgiving as his appearance meant he wanted something, probably related to the Saldano case, and she was on her way home. His hair was medium brown to her auburn, but they shared the Rafferty blue eyes. His easy, loping style was strictly his own as she was far more rigid, though she was in constant battle with her own type-A demons.

"Hey, Nine," he greeted her.

"I'm outta here," she informed him as he looped a leg

over the corner of her desk as if he planned to stay awhile. "It's quitting time. Look around. Everybody's gone."

"Hey," George Thompkins objected, swiveling his desk chair around. He was, as ever, buried into the chair's leather cushion. It practically took an act of congress to get him into the field.

September said drily, "My mistake, Detective Thompkins is still here."

"I'm the point man when D'Annibal's gone," George reminded her, referring to their lieutenant, whose corner office had its lights out, shades drawn over the glass walls.

Ignoring him, she said to Auggie, "I don't know why I ask since you never tell me what you're doing. What I should have said was, what do you want?" She swatted at the leg on her desk which didn't move one iota.

"What's got you in such a bad mood?" Auggie asked.

"You came here for a reason," she reminded him.

"She doesn't like being a fiancée," George reported.

September rounded on him. "That is not true." She was shocked that George, who was not known for his social awareness in any way, shape or form, had picked up on her ambivalence. "I do want to marry Jake. I do. It's just . . . I'm having trouble with all the folderol and everyone's happiness for us. It's strangely overbearing."

She would have gone on, but Auggie interrupted, "Yeah, well, I didn't come to worry about your love life."

"Thanks. I figured," she said annoyed. "You want to go over the Saldano bombing, but you came to the wrong place. We're no longer on that case. The feds have taken over."

"I don't give a damn about the feds," he cut in sharply. "They can do whatever they damn please, but it's Laurelton jurisdiction, and I'm going to find out who planted that bomb."

"And you're no longer a part of Laurelton jurisdiction," she pointed out.

"Jesus, Nine. When did you become such an Urlacher?"

September just managed to keep herself from snapping back at him. Guy Urlacher was the seemingly mild-mannered pit bull who manned the Laurelton Police Department's front desk and he was September's personal nemesis. He was a stickler for protocol in a way that made her want to rip out her hair and scream, and he delighted in making her show her ID every time she entered the building, a faint smile touching the corners of his mouth that drove her mad. Her partner, Gretchen, was tough and prickly enough to keep him at bay—a self-proclaimed bitch on wheels—and she frightened Urlacher just enough that he gave her a pass. But September had yet to learn the art to getting him to do what she wanted. She had an innate politeness that kept her from blasting him the way she did in her mind, and her passiveness, rather than out-and-out aggression like her partner, left Guy and her in a kind of low-grade, one-on-one war.

September told Auggie, "I stopped by the hospital and talked to Jay Danziger and his wife, Carmen, who were both singularly unhelpful." She edged toward the hall, hoping he'd get the message. The break room was down to the right and held her locker, which in turn held her messenger bag and coat.

"Hmmm." Auggie nodded, taking that in. "There were fragments of paper and cardboard. Looks like somebody left a box at either the front desk or just outside the main doors. The company security cameras weren't on. Apparently this is par for the course, so there's no record so far."

September stopped short. "I thought the bomb was placed in the office next to the entry."

"That was just a guess by the receptionist. Covering her ass for leaving the box outside. Lucky she did, or she could have been killed."

"Okay, so the box was on the porch and you're saying

there's no video. That's a little convenient," September muttered.

"Yeah. One of the cameras wasn't working and hasn't been for quite a while," he admitted, easing himself to his feet. "But there are cameras across the street on a couple of the buildings. They're mostly small range, only catch the person right at the door and maybe a little further, but not all the way to the Saldanos' property. Still, you never know what you'll catch. We're checking 'em one by one."

"You are, or the feds?"

"I've got Geoffrey working on it. The feds are breathing down our necks, but he's going to come to me first."

"Like I said, it's not our case, and it's definitely not yours."

"Should be," George piped up, sounding put out. Since he didn't do much more than act like a dispatcher, September was half-amused by his proprietary tone.

"Saldano Industries has corporate offices in Portland as well, and since I've got a foot in both departments, my lieutenant's allowed me a few days," Auggie said.

"And the feds?" September asked.

"Don't have to like it, but that's their problem. The bomb was at the front of the building, not the warehouse in the back, so it seems like more of a warning. If they'd wanted to sabotage the inventory, they placed it in a strange position."

"At least no one was killed," September said, heading into the hall.

Auggie followed after her. "That reporter, Danziger, was hurt the worst. What exactly did he say to you when you interviewed him?"

"That he was in the wrong place at the wrong time." She stopped at the break room, conceding, "There really wasn't much more. Both he and the wife were clear that they felt the bombing had nothing to do with him, and that his being there was a matter of unfortunate timing. They were anxious to just get out of the hospital. I thought he looked like he coulda stayed in a day or two longer, but what do I know. Whole thing had to have shaken 'em up."

"Danziger's done some pretty dangerous reporting in the past," Auggie reminded her. "Brought to light some ugly corporate secrets."

"He's never gotten hurt until now," September said.

"What was he working on? Did he say?"

"Nope." She shook her head.

"He's good friends with Maxwell Saldano."

"And Maxwell's sister is his wife."

"Maybe there's something there," he mused.

"Like what?"

"I don't know. The whole thing looks like it's straight against the Saldanos, but Danziger's been a goddamn terrier on this kind of thing with other companies. Gotten a couple of CEOs jailed. I know the Saldanos are his family, but . . ." He frowned, his jaw tightening, giving him a harder, more dangerous look. Her brother had been a chick magnet for years, but had been aloof to most women, that is until last year, when he'd met Liv Dugan.

"What do you know about the Saldanos?" September asked him curiously. Something in Auggie's tone had caught her up.

"Unsubstantiated rumors, mostly. The same you've probably heard."

"You don't think they're into drugs with that import/export business?"

He grimaced. "Supposed to be only art pieces, but how do you know? What was the wife like? Carmen Saldano."

"Eager to get away from me," September said. "I kept thinking she was going to bolt."

"I've seen pictures of her. Tight dresses and long legs." He grinned wolfishly.

"Yeah, right. Like you can see anything past Liv." She

walked to her locker, then hesitated a moment, looking back at Auggie, who was leaning a shoulder against the break room doorjamb. "You know, it's funny. She's not nearly as openly sensual in person. She's actually kind of coltish."

He barked out a laugh. "You gotta be looking at her through a woman's eyes, little sister. That woman sets off heat sensors when she struts by."

"Believe what you want to believe, dear brother," she retorted. "Carmen Saldano is very pretty and she looks great in a tight dress, but she sure as hell doesn't know how to walk in high heels. Not that I do, either, I'm just sayin'." She grabbed up her bag and jacket and messenger bag and slammed the locker shut, which made him choke with amusement.

When she got to the door, he didn't move. Just stood there grinning, which kind of pissed her off. He said, "I've never known you to be jealous, but it's either that or you're blind if you don't think she's smokin' hot."

"Actually, she reminded me a lot of Liv," September said, pushing him in the chest to get him to move out of the doorway. "Sexy enough, but quite a few degrees away from 'smokin' hot,' if you know what I mean. Maybe you're the one blinded by love. Now get the hell out of my way . . . and stop *laughing*."

When Jordanna returned to Braxton's Pharmacy to pick up Dance's prescriptions, she was unlucky enough to get Margaret Bicknell again. Inwardly groaning, she put on a false smile as the older woman pursed her lips and said, "That's a powerful painkiller," as she took Jordanna's credit card.

"Very true," Jordanna answered.

"Remind Mister"—Margaret looked at one of the bottles, though Jordanna suspected she knew the information by heart—"Danziger to take all the antibiotics. Everyone wants to stop early and it just makes the bad bugs more resistant. We gotta kill 'em before they infect the rest of us."

"I'll remind him."

As soon as the transaction was complete, Jordanna quickly walked away from the counter and headed over to the grill. She'd shared peanut butter sandwiches with Dance at noon, and then she'd hung around the house for a few hours with him, but in the end she'd found herself struggling for conversation. Every topic was either one he didn't want to talk about, or one she didn't want to discuss. She'd asked him about his pain, but he'd assured her, rather testily, that he could wait until she returned with the new prescription. It had been almost a relief to finally leave. She wasn't really hungry yet though, and it was too early for a stint at the Longhorn, so she ordered a small basket of fries and a diet cola at the grill counter. The employee who'd been reading the newspaper earlier—Loretta, per her name tag—asked, "That all you want, dearie?" Jordanna nodded and checked the battery life on her phone. If she was lucky, she might just make it until Pacific Power showed up tomorrow.

She dawdled over her fries and cola for nearly an hour, ignoring the two times that Margaret Bicknell came to the end of the pharmacy counter, ostensibly just in the course of working, to stare at Dayton Winters's infamous middle child. Jordanna just kept eating her fries and pretended to be checking her phone. When she was finished, she headed into the Thriftway next door and stood lost in thought for a few moments. In the end she bought a bottle of cabernet, a six-pack of sparkling water, and two limes. Until she had some electricity, there wasn't that much to buy that she hadn't already brought with her. Tomorrow wasn't that far away. She could just come back.

It was just after five when she returned to her SUV, hours before Rusty was likely to be at the Longhorn. Deciding it was best to get Dance the prescriptions, just in case she decided to stay out later than planned, she drove back to the house, a forty-minute trip. Once inside, she realized that Dance was already in his bedroom and the door was closed, so she left the bottles on the kitchen counter, next to the peanut butter jar, which was pressed up to what was left of the loaf of bread. She set the sparkling water and limes next to them, along with the bottle of red, then found the wine cork and placed it in plain sight as well. There were coffee crystals available, too, and she took the time to mix up some tuna with mayonnaise for a future meal. It wasn't gourmet, but it was what they had, and so far he hadn't been complaining. As a last errand, she fed another large chunk of fir into the woodstove.

When she stepped back outside, she could feel a bit of spring warmth in the air and she inhaled deeply. The sky was a dusky blue, just beginning to darken around the edges. She could be gone a while longer, and she supposed Jay Danziger would be just as happy on his own. She'd already suspected he was tired, and he'd practically bitten her head off when she'd tried to help him move around, so she'd given up on that. He was grouchy as a bear with a sore paw, and though she'd heard that was a sign of healing, it sure didn't make it any picnic to be around him.

Climbing into the RAV once again, she drove back into Rock Springs and down the street in the direction Rusty had said the Longhorn now resided. Just outside of town, she saw the place and wheeled into the side lot, parking in front of a hitching post made from a fir tree limb. The bark was peeled away and the wood sanded and lacquered to a soft shine beneath a string of small, round white bulbs that hung from the overhead porch, making the place look surprisingly inviting. There were no horses tied up, though in this town one never knew. However, there was a bicycle chained to the rustic post.

After she parked, she sat for a moment, looking through the windshield at the board-and-batten-sided building with its grayed wood, taking in the whole rustic, western style. Like the hitching post, the trusses that held up the entrance's porch were made from rough-hewn fir limbs.

"Okay," she said aloud, then stepped from the SUV.

The Longhorn's front door was a slab of black oak, and Jordanna shouldered it open with an effort. She then had to push through the saloon doors at the far side of the vestibule. Beyond lay an oblong room divided by two posts in the center, both stripped and lacquered fir tree boles as well. Three wagon-wheel light fixtures hung in a line overhead, and the bar itself was a masterpiece of carved walnut, stained and nicked and lined by bar stools with spoked backs on swivels, the kind that punched you in the kidney when you tried to dismount.

She didn't see Rusty anywhere, but then she was probably still too early for the kind of late-night barfly she suspected he was. She wasn't hungry after the fries, so she bellied up to the bar and ordered only a light beer, which won her a cold look from the bartender, who truly had a handlebar mustache and muttonchops. Had he been wearing suspenders over a loose-fitting white shirt, the image of the old west barkeep would have been complete. As it was, his green golf shirt and Dockers kind of spoiled the effect.

"You don't serve light beer?" she guessed.

"Not unless we have to, missy, and I haven't had to in a long time."

"What would you suggest?"

"A diet cola," he said, taking her measure, which sort of deflated her. She almost asked for sassafras.

"Give me Jack and seven," she responded heedlessly. In response, she got an indifferent shrug and, a few minutes later, an old-fashioned glass with the asked-for drink.

She had the insane desire to knock it back, but managed

to just sip it. There weren't many people in the bar, just two tables were occupied, but the soft click of pool balls said there were more patrons in the far room. As she sipped at her drink, the jukebox suddenly filled the room with Patsy Cline's "Crazy."

The song brought back memories of her father and mother dancing in the living room. She could still see them, moving around in front of the woodstove, swaying and smiling at each other. There had been love between them once, before her mother had gotten sick, but it was a long time ago.

Jordanna drew in a long breath and exhaled it carefully. The illness was supposed to linger, a slow decline like in Alzheimer's. But her mother's progression had been fairly rapid, and Gayle Winters had had a tendency to hike into the hills and wander if she wasn't watched closely. Then came the day that she hadn't been watched closely enough. Her father had had an emergency, and Jordanna and her sisters had been at school, and Gayle had trekked into the hills and gotten lost. They'd found her a day and a half later and taken her to the hospital in Silverton, but she hadn't made it.

The downhill spiral that had begun when Gayle Treadwell Winters had first showed symptoms, a slide Jordanna's father had solemnly told his three daughters would end with her death, had worsened faster than anyone had predicted. After her death Dayton had tried to act like everything would go back to normal as a matter of course, but that sure as hell hadn't happened. Kara had grown ever more distant and spent time in her room alone, or anywhere she could jump onto Wi-Fi once she had a smartphone, and then she'd left for faraway places as soon as she was old enough. Jordanna had written stories and tried to tamp down a seething anger that at first had had no direction, except for her journal, and Emily had begun staying out late and sneaking back into the house in the wee hours of the morning, placing her finger over Jordanna's lips whenever she tried to ask where she'd been.

Emily . . .

Jordanna's thoughts turned back to her older sister, who'd been beautiful and oddly otherworldly. She'd been a sleepwalker, and more than a few times Jordanna had woken up to find Emily wandering in and out of her bedroom, eyes open yet unseeing. It had freaked her out the first time, but then she'd grown used to it—and also impatient with her sister.

"Wake up!" she'd yelled more than a few times when Emily had wandered into her room, clapping her hands or throwing a pillow at her wraithlike sister, who'd slept in long nightgowns while Jordanna wore oversized T-shirts. Sometimes it had worked, sometimes it hadn't, but even when it had, her sister would blink at her in shock and then break down and cry. Jordanna had dragged a pillow over her head even while she felt like a heel.

When Emily started sneaking out, Jordanna had been torn. A part of her had been frightened because that was the way their mother had died: walking on a solo trip into the Cascades. The other part had cheered on her sister's rebel spirit, something she hadn't even known existed. Jordanna had talked to Kara about it, but Kara hadn't really wanted to hear it.

"She's seeing someone," Kara had told her one night, when Jordanna had been in the bedroom she shared with her younger sister and they'd indulged in a tete-a-tete. "She's always been crazy about guys. She's screwing half the high school."

"What! That's not true," Jordanna had sputtered. "You always say stuff like that!" Emily was the prettiest of them and Kara had always suffered jealousy over Emily's looks. It came out in mean ways, and Jordanna refused to listen.

"Well, she's got a boyfriend," Kara had insisted.

"Good. Hope she does." Then, when her younger sister had remained silent: "Who?"

"You think she'd tell me?" Kara had snorted.

"Then how do you know?"

"Because I've seen her sneak out with him. She's not heading off into the mountains like Mom. She's going the other way, down the driveway, bent over like she thinks that'll hide her, or something. But I've seen her, and I've heard his car engine sometimes, too."

"Does Dad know?" Jordanna had asked, seized with fear for her sister. She wasn't sure she totally believed Kara, but she wanted as much information as she could garner, and if it was true, then there would be hell to pay with their father.

"If he did, he'd get the .22 out and shoot the bastard."

"You're nuts. Dad would never shoot anybody. Why do you think he's a bastard?"

"Because he's just using Emily."

"Well, who is he?"

"I told you I don't know," Kara had snapped.

"You act like you know," Jordanna had pointed out.

"Well, I don't! But he's using Emily. That's what I know."

"Can't Emily just have a boyfriend? Someone who really likes her?"

"Maybe, but this one just wants to get into her pants. She's pretty, and she doesn't use her brains. She doesn't have to, and she doesn't. She uses sex, Jordanna. Wake up. You're always so blind to her faults. Haven't you seen the way she walks around? Like she's begging for it?" Kara had then strutted across the room, exaggeratedly swiveling her hips and bending over suggestively.

"That's not how she is," Jordanna had declared witheringly.

"Oh, yes, it is. With my own eyes, I *saw* Martin Lourde stick his hands up her blouse and squeeze her boob."

"You did not!" Jordanna had wanted to clamp her hand

over her little sister's mouth, afraid someone would overhear. "Where? When?"

"At the football game at Malone High last year. He was humping her against the snack shack after everybody was gone."

"You're full of it, Kara!"

"You just don't want to believe me, but I saw them." When Jordanna stood in silence, trying to assess the truth of Kara's words, Kara had added, "You ever done that?"

"What? Let some guy . . ." Jordanna had broken off, staring at her little sister, who had been barely fourteen at the time, in a kind of suspended wonder. "No."

"Well, I bet Emily does it all the time. She had her eyes closed and her mouth open and she was making these noises—"

"Stop!" Jordanna had clapped her hands to her ears, not sure whether to laugh or scream. "I don't care. I don't care!"

"She's kind of a ho. That's what I'm saying, but maybe she can't help herself, y'know? Maybe it's the Treadwell Curse."

That was the first time Jordanna had heard anyone verbalize their family's affliction aloud, and she hadn't liked it. She'd slammed out of Kara's bedroom. She hadn't wanted to hear about her older sister's sexual exploits, but more than that, she hadn't wanted to hear about the disease that ran through their family. And though she'd reminded herself she didn't believe anything Kara had to say, especially about Emily, she'd found herself observing her older sister more closely. Whenever Emily sleepwalked into her room and woke her, Jordanna didn't drive her away any longer. Instead, she followed her around the house, realizing more often than not she would make her way out the front door to stand on the porch, her unseeing gaze focused down the long drive toward the road.

During Emily's waking hours, Jordanna had tried to talk

to her about her sleepwalking . . . and her sneaking out. In no uncertain terms, Emily had told Jordanna to mind her own business. When Jordanna said, "I'm just worried about you," Emily had answered, "Don't be. I've given myself to the Lord."

This had been news, and then Jordanna had understood what she'd meant and said drily, "Oh. *Martin* Lourde?"

"Who?" Emily's blue eyes had been blank.

"Kara saw you and him after a game last year, at the snack shack." When Emily continued to look confused, she'd added, "You were making out and he was . . . all over you."

"That wasn't me. I'm not with him."

"Kara said you were."

"Well . . . oh . . . maybe . . . but not anymore . . ." She'd trailed off for a moment, frowning.

"Who are you with now, then?" Jordanna had pressed.

"I just told you."

"The Lord?"

She'd looked at Jordanna, her eyes glowing as if lit from within. "Yes."

"The Lord isn't the one picking you up in a car," Jordanna had pointed out drily.

"No . . ." And then a faint smile had crossed her lips at that, but she wouldn't say anything more except, "You have to stop worrying about me. I'm on the path, and you and Kara need to be on it, too."

The next day Jordanna had told Kara about what Emily had said, but Kara had shrugged and said, "You expected her to tell you who he is?"

For a while, Jordanna had tried to learn whom Emily was seeing, but then she'd begun having her own high school crush, a friend of Martin Lourde's, Nate Calverson, and she'd lost interest in her sister's romance. She'd been day-dreaming about handsome, wealthy, athletic Nate, and working hard to find ways to "accidentally" run into him. This seemed to be a pattern, Jordanna could admit now with faint amusement, thinking of her behavior with Jay Danziger.

Luckily, nothing had ever come out of her teen obsession. Nate Calverson had ended up marrying Pru Briles, who had been rumored to be pregnant, though that was either small-town gossip or she'd miscarried because she hadn't given birth in the allotted time frame. Nate had taken over the ranch, the biggest around, and that was saying something, as his father's health had begun to decline. Jordanna wasn't sure if Gerald Calverson was still alive or not. Martin Lourde had also followed into his father's business, but they raised dairy cows and it wasn't on the scale as the Calverson Ranch.

Jordanna's crush on Nate had dissipated over time, and no other boys around Rock Springs had ever interested her. Somewhere in her junior year she began using her spare time for other endeavors, one of them being to learn how to shoot a gun. After school she would take the .22 out to the back-yard and blast cans off fence posts. Shooting kind of relaxed her, even while her mind began coming up with stories that she would later write down. One such story, about a girl who was stalked and captured by a killer only to grab up his rifle and aim for him as he was running away, becoming a smaller and smaller dot on the horizon that she dead-eyed and shot squarely, intrigued her English teacher, who'd praised Jordanna's writing style—and then asked if everything was all right at home.

Then came the night that she'd heard noises from her father's bedroom, the kind of noises she imagined Emily and Martin Lourde making as he humped her against the snack shack wall, an image wholly in her mind that wouldn't seem to go away. She picked up the .22 as a matter of course, her heart pounding. Was her father with some woman? Should she care? Maybe it was best to just let it happen. Their mother had been gone for several years and there was nothing wrong with her father wanting some companionship—at least that was what everyone said.

But Jordanna had seen the way he looked at Jennie Markum when he didn't think anyone was watching, and the way Jennie looked back. Rage and injustice bubbled through her blood, and though a cool part of her mind warned her that she was being irrational, that her father didn't have to be true to their mother's memory, that people moved on, the thought of him with Jennie burned into her brain and she was half convinced they were in bed together.

With her father and Jennie Markum's images superimposed over the ones in her mind of Emily and Martin Lourde, Jordanna had quietly used one hand to push open the door to her father's bedroom. In her head, she'd formed the words she was going to say: "Get the hell out of my father's bed, you pious little ho."

But the woman atop her father wasn't Jennie Markum. Jordanna sensed it right away, and for a moment she stood there, blinking, her gun coming up almost of its own accord. The woman somehow sensed someone else was there—a subtle change in air pressure? A noise Jordanna didn't hear?—and she suddenly whipped around, still astride Jordanna's father. *Emily!* Her nightgown was hiked up to her thighs although her father was still in pajama bottoms, a piece Jordanna didn't see in her moment of shock and outrage. "Dayton!" Emily had screamed at the same moment Jordanna, who'd lifted the gun sight to her eye, had aimed and fired.

If Emily hadn't thrown herself sideways, Jordanna might have shot her sister. As it was, Dayton Winters took the bullet wound in his left shoulder.

Now, looking back, Jordanna wondered, as she always did, if she truly had lost her sanity just long enough to pull the trigger. She didn't remember doing it at all. What she remembered was her sister with her father, the *blam* of the rifle, Emily's screams as she awoke from another bout of sleepwalking, and then her fury as she'd realized what Jordanna had done. She'd continued screaming, shrieking bloody murder at Jordanna, while they'd both tried to staunch the flow of blood from their father's wound.

Dayton had been taken to the hospital by ambulance. Though he hadn't blamed Jordanna for the shooting, everyone else had. Before the ambulance arrived, her father had demanded Jordanna and Emily tell the same story: that Jordanna had mistaken her sleepwalking sister's footsteps for those of an intruder, that she'd been certain someone else was in the room, choking her father, that it was all a terrible, terrible accident, and Jordanna had fired the gun to save her only living parent.

Kara had slept through the scene entirely, having taken a heavy dose of her mother's sleeping medication, claiming afterward that she couldn't bear the bad dreams she'd begun to suffer from. Even after Emily and Jordanna had shaken her, she'd barely managed to come to before the EMTs arrived.

Jordanna had struggled to recount her script when she was questioned by Chief Markum, which had left him to wonder about her even though his good friend, Dayton, insisted they were all telling the truth. Because of the two men's friendship, the issue was dropped. When asked later, Jordanna would admit she'd shot her father with a .22. When asked why, she never fully explained because Emily and her father were both invested in the script, so people ended up thinking what they wanted. Some felt Dayton Winters's middle daughter had a screw loose, and most of those whispered about the dread disease that followed their family.

In January of her senior year, Emily drove into the foothills and along the icy, ridge road that doomed her to her death when her car plunged over the edge, down a steep cliff side, rolling over several times. There was talk that she'd killed herself over a bad love affair; there was other talk that she'd inherited Gayle Treadwell's fatal disease and decided to end her life early. Kara told Jordanna she believed foul play was involved, but she only had wild theories that couldn't be proven. Eventually Emily's death had been ruled an accident and labeled an unfortunate tragedy, the latest on a long list involving the Winters family. Over the years Jordanna had often recalled Emily's assertion that she was "giving herself to the Lord," and she still wondered what had really been going on in her sister's life prior to her death. Had her sister lied about Martin *Lourde*? Had he really been her boyfriend, the one Kara had insisted she was involved with? Or, had fear of the Treadwell Curse had some bearing on the accident? Some kind of religious sacrifice to escape the dread disease that ran through their family like slow-acting poison? Or, was it, as it was classified, simply a case of an inexperienced driver on a treacherous ice-covered road?

She was still musing on her sister's death when a couple walked through the swinging saloon doors and the man stopped short and declared, "I heard you were back in town."

Jordanna swiveled around and stared at them. It took her a moment before she realized it was Nate Calverson and his wife, Prudence Briles.

Chapter Nine

Seeing Nate in the flesh, Jordanna couldn't believe she'd ever had a crush on him. Looking over his cold eyes and smirky smile, she thought she must have been blinded by obsession. It sent a frisson down her back and she shivered a bit. And she didn't think she would have recognized the big-busted woman, who clung to one of his arms as if she expected him to run away at the first opportunity, as the Prudence Briles she'd gone to school with, had she not been with him.

He aimed an imaginary rifle at her and made a soft "puh" sound with his lips as he squeezed the trigger. "Gotcha," he said as Pru squeaked in protest.

"Nate," she cried, scandalized.

Jordanna wasn't exactly sure what that meant, but settled on this being Nate's politically incorrect way of connecting. "Want a drink?" she invited calmly, holding up her glass.

"We come for the little burgers and lemonade, I'm afraid," Nate said, his smirk permanently etched on his face, apparently

"Little burgers as in sliders?" Jordanna suggested.

"That's right," Pru said, her gaze still lingering on her

husband's round face. "We all have lemonade as there's no drinking at Green Pastures. Not that we would anyway."

Jordanna met Nate's eyes. There'd been a helluva lot of drinking when they were underage. "You belong to Green Pastures," she said, recalling it was the church where her father and Jennie had married.

"Oh, yes," Pru said eagerly. "You know Reverend Miles, I'm sure. He's good friends with your father and Jennie."

"Ah . . . well . . . I don't keep up with their social life that much," Jordanna admitted.

"Why is that?" Pru asked.

"Pru," Nate admonished, trying to surreptitiously peel her hand from his elbow, which she was having none of. She was clamped on like a vise. "There's bad blood between Jordanna and her father, don't you remember?"

"Of course she remembers," Jordanna said.

Pru looked trapped. "No, I don't."

"Pru, it's okay." Jordanna decided to be magnanimous. There was no escaping her past in Rock Springs. "Everybody remembers that I shot him."

"Well, it was an accident," Pru said, defending her as Jennie had, which was kind of surprising in itself.

Nate kept on smiling and said slowly, "Yeah, an accident."

She didn't remember Nate being such an out-and-out ass in high school, but then, she thought despairingly, she seemed to be continually fooled by good-looking men. Jay Danziger being no exception.

Not that Nate Calverson was so good-looking any longer. He'd definitely gone to seed over the years. The once-hot football player's waist had expanded and his iron jaw was puffy and surrounded by a patchy light brown beard. His eyes had sunken and there was also something about him that made her think he might be tippling something a little stronger than lemonade behind his wife's back.

Pru said, "You really shouldn't talk like that, Jordanna. People will get the wrong impression."

"She knows exactly what she's doing," Nate said, eyes lasered on Jordanna. "She's a reporter now. It's all part of the game, isn't it?"

"What game is that?" Jordanna asked.

"Acting like you don't care. Like you're above everything. You go run off from Rock Springs like we're just small-town jerks out here, all hot to make your way in the newspaper world. How is it getting into other people's lives and ripping 'em apart for a story?"

Pru was looking at Nate like she'd never seen him before.

"Not sure where you got that idea," Jordanna said. "I've written some human interest stories."

"That what you call them?" Nate retorted.

Jordanna wondered where this was coming from, and truthfully, he was really starting to piss her off. She'd steered clear of Rock Springs to avoid exactly these kinds of encounters. Turning to Pru, she said with false interest, "So how are the kids?"

"We've only been blessed with our Joshua," Pru said. There was a touch of bitterness in her voice that she tried to hide by adding, "The Lord has His plan and He's seen fit to enrich our lives with just one child, our sweet boy. You're not married yet?"

"Nope."

"Boyfriend?" she asked hopefully.

"Just an obsession . . . with work," she tagged on, when Pru's brow furrowed.

"You remember Martin Lourde," Pru said, as if she'd just been waiting for a way to insert his name.

Martin Lourde . . . she hadn't thought about him all that much until this afternoon's reflection, but here his name was popping up again. "Ahhh . . . only by reputation. He was older than I was, my sister's grade." Taking a stab in the dark, she added, "Actually, Emily was dating him for a while."

"Martin? Oh, no." Pru drew her head back as if the very thought made her recoil. "That can't be right. Emily was too into herself then to date Martin."

"She was into Martin for a while," Nate snapped impatiently.

"Was she? Well, she wasn't picky, that's for sure." Hearing herself, she added, "I'm sorry. I don't mean to speak ill of the dead."

"That's all right. I just can't quite remember who she was seeing," Jordanna pressed, but Pru shook her head and Nate had grown totally bored by the conversation. Soldiering on, Jordanna added, "She basically told me she'd joined the God squad that last year, I was thinking maybe it was someone—"

"Emily didn't come to any of our prayer meetings," Pru interrupted, as if that were the answer to everything.

"Maybe it was a different religious group," Jordanna suggested.

Pru seemed disconcerted by the idea, and it took her a moment before she said, "Well, your sister was always full of secrets, wasn't she?" She looked at her husband, whose gaze was focused somewhere in the middle distance, as if he were lost in thought. "You remember Emily, Nate? She was the really pretty one?"

"We all knew Emily," he said.

"I think Pete Drummond had a thing for her," Pru recalled.

Mr. Shitface. "Pete Drummond," Jordanna inserted quickly. "He's with the Rock Springs PD now, I heard. The name seems familiar, but I don't think I know him. Think he was her boyfriend?"

Pru looked unsure, but Nate suddenly came back from wherever his thoughts had taken him. "The chief gave him that job with the police," he said, barely hiding a sneer. "And he's no more qualified that Pru is."

"That's not a very nice thing to say," Pru said.

"Wasn't meant to be nice," he said, uncaring.

If he was a member of the Green Pastures Church, Jordanna thought he might have to work on his piety.

Pru, clearly uncomfortable, asked Jordanna, "How's Kara? The last time I saw her was a couple of Christmases ago."

"She was at the wedding," Jordanna said.

"Oh, yes, that's true. I kind of forgot." She tugged at one of her earlobes until Jordanna worried she would pull the silver hoop with the row of small diamonds right off.

"She's traveling," Jordanna said, dragging her gaze away from Pru's tugging hand.

"You Treadwell girls like to stay away," Nate observed. "Surprised you're here. Something happen?"

"I'm following a story," Jordanna improvised. "The homeless man whose body was found near the old homestead."

Pru frowned. "Really? That was years ago. You mean the one found behind your mother's family's place?"

Jordanna didn't immediately answer. She'd always thought of the house as her father's. She also hadn't realized that Rusty's homeless man was old news.

Pru confirmed, "The one that was branded, right?"

Jordanna looked at her. "The body was branded? You mean like, from a branding iron?"

Pru demurred, "Well, I thought so." She glanced at Nate a little desperately.

He rescued her with, "The guy was just a fool hiker. Fell off a cliff on government property off Summit. Maybe some relative of yours that lost his way, huh?"

"Nate, don't be mean," Pru said.

Jordanna ignored his tone. "But the body was branded,"

she repeated. "I never saw that on the news, and a branding is pretty newsworthy."

"You should ask Martin about it," Pru put in quickly. "He's the one that told us about it. He's divorced now, y'know? She wasn't a good woman. So, if you're around for a while, maybe we could all get together? We do a lot of Sunday potlucks after church, and Sunday's just a few days away."

"Yeah, well, I'm not sure I'm going to still be here Sunday, but thanks," Jordanna said.

"If circumstances change . . ." she suggested.

"You'll be the first to know," Jordanna lied to her. Tomorrow was Friday and Kara had said she would be around, meaning Laurelton, for the weekend, so Jordanna was half-planning a quick trip back to her apartment, possibly on Saturday. It wasn't inconceivable that Dance would want to go back with her, if he felt strong enough to face the Saldanos, which she hoped wouldn't be the case yet, but who knew?

There'd been a steady stream of people pushing through the saloon doors, and with relief Jordanna looked over to see that the latest newcomer was Rusty. She waved at him, and Pru and Nate turned around as one to see who it was. Nate immediately swung back to Jordanna and said, "Don't believe everything he tells you. He's a drunk and a liar."

"He's your friend," Pru declared, but she looked at Rusty with distaste.

"Be careful," Nate added, making eye contact with Jordanna before steering his wife away to a table as far from the bar as possible.

Rusty moved up to Jordanna, his strawberry-blond hair catching the light from the overhead wagon-wheel fixture. He dropped his bulk into the seat next to her, but his eyes were following the Calversons' quick exit. "I see Nate's hustling his little lady away from me," he observed.

"She's not a fan?" Jordanna asked.

"He doesn't want her to know that he and I have shared more than a few drinks together."

"Ahhh . . . not lemonade, I take it."

"Brewskies."

"He told me you were a drunk and a liar," Jordanna related.

Rusty nearly choked on his laughter. "Well, now that might be true, but he only knows 'cause of our poker games. And Pru doesn't know about the drinking or the poker."

"I've been questioning Nate's commitment to the church," she said.

He gave her an appreciative look. "You were always smart. Why'd you stay away so long?"

Jordanna shrugged. Rusty had been a big goof-off at school, but he wasn't nearly the redneck hick he seemed to want everyone to believe. "Pru said something about that homeless man being branded. Is that true?"

"Yep." He nodded.

"When was the body found?"

"A couple years ago, maybe?"

"I never saw that anywhere on the news."

"Oh, the chief didn't want the branding let out to the press. I think he mighta thought it would look bad for the town, or that it was something to hold back if it turned out to be a homicide and he wanted to catch the killer. Who knows. But in any case, he kept that out of the news."

"Doesn't seem to be a well-kept secret around here," Jordanna pointed out.

"You can lay the blame on Mr. Shitface for that." Rusty gave several deep nods.

"Pete Drummond. In my sister Emily's class."

"That's the one."

"You think it was a homicide?"

"Probably not. Nobody ever said so."

"Sounds like a story." She thought about her pretty elder sister and said, "Wish my sister was still around to give me an intro, since Pete had a thing for her."

Rusty's brows knit. "Drummond had a thing for your sister . . . Emily? You mean in high school?"

"That's what Pru said."

"I don't remember that." He shot her a sympathetic look. "It was a shame, what happened to her."

Jordanna nodded. Everyone remembered Emily's fatal car accident the spring of her senior year.

"I wouldn't take the Drummond thing seriously. He has a thing for all pretty girls. If you talk to him, be mindful." He held up a finger. "He's not to be trusted."

"Everyone keeps warning me about everyone else," she remarked. "I thought your cousin was coming."

He snorted. "Todd's straddling the fence between church and tavern. You go one way or the other in this town, and he can't make up his mind. His kind of church is more like communing with nature, which I can get behind. Better than a lot of the really strict ones around here. I mean, they are NO FUN."

"I guess that puts us firmly on the tavern side," she said, looking around.

"You got that right." He drummed his palms on the bar like he was playing the bongos and yelled, "Danny, over here. You blind?"

The barkeep gave him a short nod as he served up Budweiser on tap to a young couple who'd just arrived.

"Do you know how it was determined the man was homeless?" Jordanna asked.

"It's been a few years ago. I don't think anyone ever claimed the body, so that was the theory."

"Pru also mentioned that Martin Lourde was the one who told her the man was branded."

"Sounds just like him, but Lourde's a . . ." He searched around at length and then finally came up with "putz."

Jordanna smiled. "And here I thought you were going to say something more colorful."

"Because I call Drummond Mr. Shitface? Hey, I'm not all bad," he assured her. "Lourde's just a putz. If you're really following this thing, you'd probably get more information from Drummond."

"But be careful around him."

"He's dumb as a box of rocks and can't keep his mouth shut, no way, no how, but he thinks he's a player." He drank half his beer down in a couple long swallows, then set the glass on the bar again with a little more force than necessary. "You should really talk to Todd. He was being all closed up this mornin', but he's got information."

"What kind of information?"

"He hikes all over these mountains and talks to people. He pays a helluva lot more attention to things than I do. I get bored."

She smiled. She could believe that.

"You got a cell phone number?" Rusty asked, pulling his own mobile phone from his pocket.

"Um . . . sure . . ."

She was usually far more careful about giving out her digits than she'd been today, but she figured if Jennie had her number, she might as well give it to Rusty, too. She recited her digits, and Rusty, in turn, gave her his.

"I'll have Todd call you," he said.

"You also mentioned the missing Fread girl. A runaway," Jordanna reminded him.

"Well, I don't know for sure she's a runaway, but if I were Bernadette, I'd just hightail it out of there before my crazy religious father locked me up, or hit me again, or something. Old man Fread's a real case. Forbade her from seeing her boyfriend, Chase Sazlow, who's a damn nice kid, actually.

But Fread just lost it when he caught them together. I heard Reverend Miles had to have a little talk with him, as Mr. Fread was bordering on abusive."

"Reverend Miles of the Green Pastures Church."

"That's the one." He finished the rest of his beer, and Jordanna swallowed the last bit of her own drink as well.

"How do you know so much about Bernadette Fread?"

"My mom was good friends with Bernie's. They knew each other from grade school. But then Bernie's mom married Abel Fread just out of high school and they went all religious. But I don't think it took too well, 'cause Bernie and her mom would stop by, kind of sneakily-like, whenever they could." He made a face. "But they're all part of Green Pastures now."

"Is your friend Todd any part of that church?"

"God, no. You have to be fuckin' crazy to go there, and he's not crazy." Hearing himself, he added, "And neither are you, Jordanna Winters. You weren't when you were in high school. You're not now."

"I appreciate that," she said, meaning it.

"Todd takes his religion seriously, but it's a make-it-up-as-you-go kind of thing. Nature, being a good neighbor, getting to your core truth, you know what I mean?"

She nodded. Todd Douglas's unstructured spirituality appealed to her.

Rusty went on, "You gotta be way, way out there to belong with the Green Pastures flock. I'll allow that Reverend Miles did a good thing for Bernadette, but get too close to that kind of religion?" He shook his head. "I'd break out in hives."

"What kind of religion is it, exactly?"

"The kind that makes up all the rules and spends too much time telling you what you shouldn't do or you'll burn in hell."

They talked for a while more, veering off the subject of

missing Bernadette Fread and her apparently Bible-thumping, authoritative father. Jordanna left about an hour later and drove back to the old homestead under a dark sky, watching as raindrops, driven by a strong wind, raced across her windshield in squiggly lines. When she entered the living room once more, she saw that Dance was out of bed and stretched out asleep on the couch, and that the woodstove needed to be fed. The room was toasty, though, so she only added one more chunk of fir, listening to it spit and crackle as she turned away from its heat to look down at him.

Dance's eyes shot open. "You're back."

"Yep."

Catching his sudden wince of pain, she asked, "How's the pain? You need another pill?"

He swore, then said belligerently, "I'm not taking any more pills."

"Okay." She didn't think it was a good idea, but she didn't appreciate him acting like it was her fault somehow.

Hearing himself, he muttered, "Thanks for getting them, but I need a clear head."

"Let me just say, you're supposed to keep ahead of the pain."

"I'm doing just fine," he said shortly, looking up at her.

"Yeah, well . . ." She moved over to the hard wooden bench on the opposite side of the room, the only other piece of furniture she could sit on. "You don't have to be a hero. You just have to heal."

He snorted. "How'd it go with your friends?" he asked shortly, deliberately changing the course of the conversation.

Jordanna said, "I don't have any friends in this town."

"So, you sat alone?"

"There were a few people from high school that I talked to," she allowed. "You know that homeless man I learned was found just east of here? In the foothills? Rumor is that he was branded."

Dance's interest sharpened. "Branded . . . before or after death?"

"A question I don't know the answer to, yet. Let me get you another pill."

"Don't," he said, but she was already on her feet and heading into the kitchen.

She returned with a bottle of plain water and one of the prescription painkillers, which she pressed into his palm. "I really don't care if you take it, or if you'd rather bite on a bullet or scream into a pillow, or just go into frozen shock. Do what you gotta do. But know this, I'm not taking you to the clinic in town unless you're at death's door, and even then, I'll think about it. My father runs the clinic, and I am not going there. So, take the drugs, don't take the drugs, whatever. Just don't count on me."

She sat back down on the bench as she spoke but only looked at him when she finished her speech. She'd scared a smile out of him, she saw, and that made her look away from the attractiveness of the man. It was easy to deal with cold, angry, or clinical Jay Danziger, but with the warm, attractive, sexy Dance, it was not.

"I'm going to do some research on the branded man," she told him. "The chief kept that tidbit out of the papers, but it's an open secret around here. There's a story there."

He nodded, thinking that over. "You giving up on the Saldanos?"

"Nope. Just gonna follow your lead on that one. When you're ready, I'm ready."

"I need a few more days," he said. "I need to walk better, but even if that takes a while, I'll go back next week sometime."

"You going to confront them?"

"I'm going to talk to Max, and see where that takes me."

"You should have the police with you," she said, feeling

a renewed wave of fear, the same sensation that had driven her to pluck him from the hospital.

"That won't really work if I want answers."

"Let me go with you, then. You shouldn't go alone."

"You're going to protect me?" he asked, his mouth curved ever so faintly.

He had her number. At least he knew that she wanted a story, and maybe he'd even guessed she'd suffered feelings of adoration, which was downright embarrassing. "I want the truth to come out about them, and I want to be a part of bringing that truth to light. So, when you're ready, I'm in."

He met her gaze silently, and she suspected he was weighing her worth. She stared right back, but in the end she was the first one to break. "In the meantime, I might as well look into what's going on in Rock Springs."

"I'd like to help," he said.

Surprised, Jordanna realized he was serious. Apparently he'd found her worthy. Or, maybe this was his way of killing time while he worked through the Saldano case and let his body heal. "Okay," she told him happily. "I'll do some leg-work and let you know what I come up with."

Chapter Ten

Randall from Pacific Power came by the next morning at eight and explained that the electrical wires from the property to the road had been unhooked, either by vandalism or by someone's choice, but that he would have everything put together again in a couple of hours. He was as good as his word and at ten he came to the front door and Jordanna stepped out onto the porch to meet him. "Coulda been Mother Nature," he said, forestalling Jordanna's first question before she could even utter it. "If someone purposely undid those wires, they took a big risk." He shook his balding head. "You Mrs. Winters, then?" he asked her.

"Oh. Um . . . no."

"Is Mr. Winters here to sign the paperwork?"

"Can I sign it?"

"He's the one who called."

"I'm here," Dance said from the interior of the house. He thumped his way over and took the pen and clipboard from the lineman's hands, signing in an unrecognizable scrawl.

When Randall was inside his truck, firing the engine, Jordanna followed Dance back inside. "Thank you," she said.

"Not a problem. I've pretended to be a lot of people along the way."

"Guess I'm on that path, too," she said. "Let's turn on the heat and hope the furnace works."

She hurried to do so, flipping on a light on the way. The sudden, bright illumination was almost a surprise; she'd half expected there to be some problem. Heading to the wall just outside the kitchen that held the dial thermostat, she said, "My God, I can make breakfast." She could have cheered, but added immediately when she saw Dance working his way toward her, "Which is a fried egg and some toast under the broiler, so don't get crazy with excitement."

"I'll try to hold myself back." He stopped and leaned on his crutches as Jordanna turned up the temperature. After a hiccuping sound, she heard the rumble of the furnace, and she turned with a brilliant smile toward Dance, damn near wanting to embrace him.

"You hear that?" she asked.

"I do."

They were standing close to one another. The way he was leaning on his crutches dropped his height so he was nearly eye to eye with her. She could see the striations of darker color within his blue eyes and she felt a jolt of awareness that spread through her in a charge of heat. She immediately moved away, muttering that she was going to charge up her phone and iPad, which although the truth, wasn't the real reason that she needed some space.

Oh, brother, she thought, both tantalized by and afraid of how easily he inflamed her senses. What the hell. It felt like she was reliving a schoolgirl crush.

On her way to the kitchen, she called over her shoulder, "I'm almost afraid to ask, but I guess I will. Do you need a pain pill?"

She heard him thump his way into the kitchen behind her, but she kept her attention on the older-model refrigerator, attempting to plug it in. She hoped to hell the damn thing didn't blow up or something. It looked as if it was on its last legs.

"I took one in the middle of the night," he admitted. "But I'm gonna get off 'em."

There was no sound from the refrigerator even though it was plugged into the socket. "Uh-oh," she said, opening the refrigerator door and looking inside its dark interior. She wanted to believe the bulb was out, but there was no humming, no sound at all. "I suppose it was too much to ask to expect it to actually work. I was hoping I wouldn't have to get more ice." She looked over at him. "The pain pills are on the counter."

"I know where they are."

"Okay."

He seemed more relaxed, she realized, so maybe he was right about the pills. Maybe making the decision to confront his old pal and brother-in-law had eased his mind, too. Hiding out like a scared rabbit wasn't his style and didn't sit well with him, even if it was the best course of action.

"You never told me about the branded man," he reminded her now.

They'd gone to their respective beds soon after she'd returned, so they hadn't discussed it further. She'd tried to help him to bed, but he'd made it clear he was through with being an invalid, so she'd gone upstairs and changed, then returned to the living room couch to sleep. Surprisingly, she'd slept pretty well and it was only when she'd heard Dance stirring around in his room about six that she'd risen from the couch. She'd heated up water on the woodstove, and they'd had instant coffee and orange slices, cheese, and crackers for breakfast before Randy had arrived.

"I really didn't learn much, except that he was found somewhere on government property almost straight east of here. If you keep on Wilhoit Road, the way we came in, it just heads south. A lot of this property is still original homesteads. But a couple farms down, Summit Ridge Road branches east into the foothills and winds up past Fool's Falls into the lower hills and Cascades."

"How do they know he was homeless if they don't know who he is?" he asked.

"Good question. He was found several years ago and no one ever claimed the body, so maybe that's why."

"You said the chief didn't want the branding of the body made public?"

"That's the way I heard it."

"Because he wanted to withhold that information, hoping it would aid in making an arrest?" Dance looked dubious.

"Chief Markum does things his own way, and he'll give you a lot of reasons for what he does that are supposed to make sense."

"You know him well?"

She'd told him she hadn't been back in Rock Springs in years, so his skepticism was warranted.

"I know him. He was the chief when I shot my father."

"Ahh."

"Yesterday I learned that there's someone else at the station I might be able to talk to other than the chief—Peter Drummond. Not that he'll want to help—my friend Rusty calls him Mr. Shitface—but he was a classmate of my older sister, Emily. I don't know in what capacity he works for the chief, but it sounds like he has loose lips. I can also check back issues of the *Pioneer* and see when exactly that body was found."

"Wouldn't your father know something about it? This is his property."

"He'd be the last person I'd ask," she stated firmly as she plugged her iPad into a kitchen outlet. Yes, her father ought to know, not only because the body had been found somewhere behind his property, but also because he and Chief Markum were such good friends.

"Father- and son-in-law, too," she muttered.

"What?" Dance asked. He'd turned toward the living room, and she hadn't expected him to hear her.

"Nothing. You ready for those eggs and toast? Kind of a brunch?"

"Sure."

With a glance at the iPad to make sure it was beginning to charge, she next plugged in her cell phone, then pulled out the small skillet she'd brought from her apartment, placed it on the electric burner and added in a pat of margarine. Within seconds, the margarine was sizzling along the bottom of the pan as it spread and melted, and Jordanna settled in to make one of the half dozen meals she'd mastered in the kitchen.

September set her jaw determinedly as she breezed into the station and past Guy Urlacher's desk. Before he could speak, she ordered, "Open the damn door, Guy."

"You haven't signed—"

"And I'm not going to . . . Guy." She wanted to say asshole. Really wanted to. "I'm not going to sign in like a visitor."

"I'm just following protocol."

"Really? That's what it says in the handbook?"

Guy pinched his lips together. "Every officer is required to sign in."

"Does the lieutenant sign in? Does Gretchen? Does *my brother*? Don't answer. I don't care. I'm not going to sign in, and if you don't open the damn door, I'm going to phone every officer in this building and tell them what's going on right here, right now. Believe me, we'll get some action then, and you can explain protocol until you turn blue. Nobody wants to hear it." She yanked out her cell phone and placed a call through to Wes, who would be only too happy to help her if he was on the premises.

Bzzzz.

September pushed through the door before Guy changed his mind, hearing it close with a loud click behind her. She smiled grimly, knowing it was a temporary victory. Guy would seethe for a while, then he would go back to acting like nothing had changed. It was the dumbest war on record, but there it was. Guy and his own need for power. She suspected she could get him fired over his pettiness, but he was just the kind of guy to file a lawsuit for harassment or something, and well, there was the "official handbook," which probably backed him up in some way. She just needed to get stronger and intimidate the hell out of him in a silent stare-down. Then he wouldn't be able to repeat anything she might say that she would regret. It was harder to complain to the powers that be that a woman had intimidated him or bullied him or harassed him just by staring at him.

Three hours later, as she was coming from the break room with her messenger bag, ready to head to an early lunch, her desk phone buzzed and she saw it was from the front desk. Guy. Bracing herself, she picked up the receiver and said coolly, "Detective Rafferty."

"Someone here to see you," he responded tonelessly.

"Do you have a name?"

"Yes."

Counting to five, September said, "I'm on my way out, so you may need to send them to someone else."

"They asked for you specifically."

"All right, then I'll meet them outside." She slammed down the receiver, causing George, the only other person currently in the squad room, to lift his brows.

"The fiancé?" he asked innocently.

"NO."

September headed out of the squad room and pushed through the door to reception, where she was confronted with a woman in a tight, burnt-orange dress and heels, her brown hair artfully pulled into a messy bun, her dark eyes boring into September as if looking for flaws. She seemed vaguely familiar, but September couldn't place her.

"I'm Detective Rafferty," she said. "Did you want to see me?"

She narrowed her eyes and lifted her chin, in a consciously, or maybe unconsciously, arrogant post. "I thought Detective Rafferty was a man."

"Ahh, I believe you're looking for Detective August Rafferty, my brother," September said.

"Oh." A pause. "Yes."

"You might have better luck at Portland PD, as he's affiliated with them now, more than here."

"I called Portland PD. They told me Detective Rafferty was the man I should talk to about the bombing, but the hospital told me Detective Rafferty was with the Laurelton PD."

It was September's turn to pause. "I'm sorry. Who are you?" But she suddenly knew, in that precognitive way, even before the woman said her name.

Her brain made the frizzing leap, at the same moment she introduced herself as, "Carmen Danziger. I'm Victor Saldano's daughter, Maxwell Saldano's sister."

September was momentarily at a loss for words. This woman was a far cry from the fresh-faced, hazel-eyed woman with the almost coltish look, the one who'd been introduced by *Jay Danziger himself,* as Carmen Danziger, his wife.

"Detective?" the woman asked when the moment hung out there a bit too long.

"Yes . . . um . . ." Out of the corner of her eye, September sensed Guy Urlacher's growing interest and it brought her back to the present. "Yes . . . Mrs. Danziger. My brother is the one you should really talk to. But I do know a little bit about the case, so you can come on back to my desk, if you like. I'll hunt down Auggie for you, er, the other Detective Rafferty, in the meantime. I know he'll want to talk to you."

"Thank you," she said, coolly imperious.

September shot Guy a look. If he chose now to play his game and not buzz her back inside . . . but instead he decided to be the picture of helpfulness . . . greeting Carmen Saldano with a brief nod before buzzing them both past security. In front of others—people who mattered—Guy could be a totally different person.

Snake in the grass, September thought as she held the door for Carmen. She followed after Jay Danziger's real wife, watching as she tip-tapped her way quickly and efficiently toward the squad room, moving on extremely high heels with practiced ease. September was given a view of her undulating hips as the orange dress swayed to and fro ahead of her.

You were right, big brother. There was no missing the woman's overt sensuality. She practically sizzled.

So, who the hell was impersonating Carmen Danziger? And why was Jay Danziger playing along?

September led Carmen to the chair on the far side of her desk. While Carmen arranged herself into the seat, September heard the squeak and squeal of George's desk chair. She slid him a look. George was gazing raptly at Carmen. She could practically see the slaver. She held his gaze until George came back to himself. With an annoyed noise, he returned to his computer monitor.

"Let me text Detective Rafferty," September said, pulling out her cell phone.

"I understand a woman managed to fool you all into thinking she was me."

September was in the middle of creating the text for her brother and fumbled a bit over the tiny letters. She hoped her face didn't reflect her dismay. "You . . . were at the hospital?" she guessed.

"That's right." She was clearly seeking to hold in her emotions, but she was doing a piss-poor job of it, as she was seething with rage.

Forced to defend herself, September said, "Mr. Danziger identified the woman as his wife."

"His wife . . ." She clearly wanted to say more, but what came out was, "Well, now *Mr. Danziger* is missing from the hospital, kidnapped by this imposter."

September added, Hurry, may have a situation here to her longer message about the appearance of the real Mrs. Danziger and quickly sent Auggie the text.

"I believe Mr. Danziger was complicit in the deceit and left on his own free will," September answered carefully.

"Complicit." She sniffed. "He had a head injury."

"He signed the release papers."

"Or, were they forged?"

"I'm . . . sure that can be determined." September didn't want to say too much, but neither did she want to act like she was stalling. So far Carmen seemed to be feeling her way, and September didn't want to set her off.

On my way

Thank God. "Detective Rafferty's on his way here now. Would you like a coffee while we wait? Or tea? Water?"

"No, thank you," she said. "How soon will he be here?"

"Twenty minutes, maybe?"

She pursed her lips and shook her head, as if she just couldn't believe their ineptitude, then settled into the chair, recrossing her legs in a manner that had George craning his neck and goggling once again.

* * *

"4G, my ass. I'm getting nothing out here," Jordanna grumbled, staring at her phone. "Must not be a cell tower for a hundred miles."

"Take it into town," Dance suggested.

She gave him a suspicious look as she reached for the handles of her laptop case. "You trying to get rid of me? For the Love of Joe looked like it had Wi-Fi."

"One of us should be doing something we want to."

His earlier good mood had evaporated and she suspected he was in some pain. Better to get the hell out while the getting was good. "If I learn anything, I'll let you know," she said on her way out.

"Good," he answered, and she had the feeling he really meant it.

Carmen Saldano was not a patient waiter. She tapped her foot and gazed over the tops of September and George's heads as if she were mentally sending herself to some distant place, far away from the riffraff and peons before her.

When Auggie appeared, she perked up, her gaze lingering on him in a way that both amused and annoyed September. Yes, her brother was attractive: near black hair, blue-gray eyes, strong chin, the hint of a dimple, and a mouth that quirked with humor. . . . The man had turned more than a few female heads. But August Rafferty had met his waterloo when Liv Dugan crossed his path, leaving the Carmen Saldanos of the world shit out of luck. Not that Jay Danziger wasn't equally attractive, she reminded herself. Beneath the bruising had been a pair of piercing blue eyes and a lantern jaw, and the five-o'clock shadow had added a raffish air.

She was annoyed with herself for fantasizing.

"Detective Rafferty?" Carmen greeted Auggie, unfolding

herself from the chair and slowly rising to the feet. In her high heels, she was only a few inches shorter than he was.

Auggie thrust out a hand. "Mrs. Saldano."

Her mouth tightened momentarily as she shook his hand. "You're the man in charge of the bombing investigation?"

"I'm working the case," he answered easily. Clearly she hadn't connected with the feds yet. "So, I understand you weren't the woman at the hospital with your husband," he said. "You have any idea who she might be?"

"Isn't it your job to find out?" she said, throwing a look around the room to encompass all of them.

"We're investigating the bombing, and to that end, anything your husband can add would be helpful," Auggie countered. "September—Detective September Rafferty—already spoke with him. I'm sure she told you about it?"

"I just want to know what's being done," Carmen said before September could respond.

Her preemptive manner didn't phase Auggie. "Fair enough. Right now we're examining the mechanism that controlled the bomb, and we're checking video footage from different cameras angled toward Saldano Industries. There were several across the street that may give us something, since the cameras inside weren't working."

"I mean about this woman," Carmen said impatiently.

"Mrs. Saldano—" Auggie began.

"Carmen," she corrected.

"Carmen," he began again. "We certainly want to find her and talk to her, but . . ." He took a moment and rubbed the tip of his nose in a gesture September had seen him employ as a means to gather his thoughts a hundred times before. "She's not the focus of the investigation as your husband went with her willingly."

Carmen reared back as if she'd been slapped.

"I spoke with your husband's physician, Dr. William

Cochran, who said your husband was eager to be released. Having this woman impersonate you is unorthodox—"

"Criminal," she hissed.

"—and we certainly want to get to the bottom of it, but our prime focus is to find the parties responsible for the bombing."

"Maybe she's responsible," Carmen said, flushing. "I can't believe you're going to let her get away with this!"

"We're determining if a crime's been committed," Auggie tried to appease her, to which she practically shivered with rage.

"When you figure it out, talk to your superior, because that's who I'm calling next. Thank you for your time," she practically sneered. With that, she moved smartly toward the front exit, no sashaying this time, and Auggie, after lifting his brows at September, followed after her, clearly hoping to ameliorate the situation.

"Whoo," George expelled.

"Glad she's Auggie's problem," September said.

But when her brother returned a few minutes later, she learned that she'd spoken too soon. "Check up on the relationship between Carmen and her husband. I want to know who this impersonator is."

"You acted like she's a low priority," September reminded him.

"Maybe she isn't. I want the hospital camera footage when she left with Danziger."

"You think she's involved in the bombing?" September questioned.

"It's an anomaly, that's all."

September's desk phone rang at that moment. When Auggie turned to leave, she held up a finger. "Wait." Picking up her line, she said, "Rafferty."

The dispatcher said, "Pauline Kirby from Channel Seven called for you."

September swore pungently, and both Auggie and George stared at her in surprise. "I'm not available right now." She slammed down the phone.

"Who was that who got the truck-driver mouth treatment?" Auggie asked.

"Pauline Kirby wants to talk to me."

"Oh. God." Auggie shook his head. "Don't say anything about the bombing."

"Like I would." She snorted. "I'm not going to call her back."

George said fatalistically, "She won't give up."

September made a choking noise and her brother said, "I gotta go. There's a woman on one of the cameras who was across the street at the time of the bombing and was knocked over by the blast. The camera was damaged from the same concussion, so we've only got a small amount of videotape, but it's something."

"Was she injured?" September asked.

"Don't know yet. Maybe she went to an ER, but so far we haven't found her at any hospital. We're checking other cameras, too, even if they're too far away. Just sifting through whatever we can find."

"And you want me to look into the Danziger marriage?" September asked.

"It pisses me off that it's not really our case anymore. I want to get as much as I can before I'm yanked off completely. Let's check Jay Danziger. Find out where he took off to, once he left the hospital, because he clearly didn't go home."

"You think he's involved in the bombing?" George asked.

"Took a pretty big risk to his own health, if he is. I think it's much more likely that he knows something, or at least suspects, and that's why he's gone off the radar."

"And the fake Carmen?" September asked.

"Find out who Danziger's women friends are," Auggie said. "Maybe there's one that's very close."

"Who looks like his wife," September said.

"Except more coltish," Auggie answered with the faintest of smiles.

Chapter Eleven

For the Love of Joe's clientele had slowed down from the morning rush but was still a fairly steady stream by the time Jordanna stepped inside. She found a table toward the far end of the narrow coffee shop and headed for it before someone could sit down. The problem was it was situated right up against the front window. Anyone and everyone in Rock Springs could pass by and see her. Still, she needed Wi-Fi, so she ordered a cup of black coffee, asked for the wireless code, then was able to flip open her laptop and connect to the free service.

She went straight to the *Rock Springs Pioneer* site, which could be accessed for a small fee on her credit card, and searched past stories. There was mention of an unidentified male body found by a nine-year-old boy, Zach Benchley, while he was riding on an ATV three years earlier. The boy's dog had run into the brush and started barking and the boy had gone to see what he'd found, thus discovering the body. This was likely the "homeless" man who'd been branded, because Jordanna was fairly certain her father's property—or mother's, depending on whom you asked, apparently—abutted, or was near, Benchley property. The Benchleys themselves were shirttail relatives of some sort. She recalled her father—or was it her mother?—saying something about them, but it had been a throwaway line. Aunt Evelyn had mentioned that the psychologist Jordanna had seen for a time, Dr. Anna Eggers, was a Benchley, so maybe that's what she was remembering?

She shook her head. It was weird after all this time to actually want to know something about her own heritage. For most of her life, she'd run away from it.

Though she tried different combinations of words in her search for more on the unidentified body, that was all, apparently, that the *Pioneer* had to offer. Closing her laptop, she drummed her fingers on the top of its matte black finish. She'd just decided to head to City Hall and the police department, see if she could scare up Rusty's frenemy, Pete Drummond, Mr. Shitface, when one of the men standing in line for a coffee swept his eyes over her, only to sweep them back, his gaze pinning on her.

Jordanna threw him a sideways glance, not relishing another trip down memory lane with any other town residents. He was tall and slim and looked tough as rawhide. His arms were long and ropy and his face was weathered and wind-burned. She could picture him throwing hay bales onto the back of a wagon beneath a blistering sun. She half expected him to call her name, but he remained silent.

She'd just gotten to her feet and was stowing her laptop into her case when he finished with his order and came up to her. Jordanna instinctively took a step back.

"Sorry, not trying to startle you. You're that reporter, right? Emily's sister."

"Umm, yes . . ." She regarded him curiously.

"Martin Lourde." He thrust out a calloused hand, which she shook tentatively, glad he didn't crush her hand. He just had that look about him, somehow.

"Jordanna Winters," she answered, remembering that Pru had said he ran his father's dairy farm. Hard work, every day.

Nate Calverson did not exude the same appearance even though his father's ranch was many times the size, but then Nate undoubtedly had hired hands.

"You're the one who shot your old man," Lourde said loud enough to make Jordanna want to cringe.

"That would be me."

He grinned suddenly, and it transformed his face. For just a moment, Jordanna caught a glimmer of what must have intrigued her sister enough to indulge in a serious bump-and-grind session against the snack shack. He looked immediately younger and happier, and it dredged up an unbidden memory of him from those high school days: Martin Lourde and Nate Calverson sniggering in the hallways about some girl who'd just come up and tried to talk to them, one of the unpopular ones who were smitten with cool, wealthy Nate. They were polite enough to her while she was there, but she had to have heard their suppressed laughter after she left. If Jordanna could, she would permanently erase the memory of her own crush on Nate. Good God, it was embarrassing, even all these years later.

"I like a girl who can handle whatever's thrown her way," Martin said.

"Well, good." Her memory of him was limited to that moment in the hallway; otherwise, he'd just been a name, a student at Rock Springs High who never moved in her social sphere. "Maybe you can help me with something."

"What?" His tone grew instantly suspicious.

"I just heard about an unidentified body that was found somewhere on Summit Ridge. Thought I might look into it, and Pru Briles, er, Calverson, said you were the one that told her the body'd been branded."

He seemed taken aback. "That was years back."

"I just never heard anything about it."

One of the baristas suddenly sang out his name and he headed back to the counter to pick up his drink. But he came right back and gestured to the seat, silently asking if he could join her. Jordanna nodded and perched back onto her seat across from him. She could smell the scent of cinnamon coming from his latte. She'd expected him to drink black coffee like she did, just by the ranch-tough way he looked.

"Why're you looking into that, so late in the game?" He took a sip and said, "Shitfire. They know how to make 'em hot here. Jesus. I could sue," he called out in a loud voice, turning toward the baristas, but the women who'd handed him his drink never so much as lifted a brow.

"The branding," Jordanna said truthfully. "That's a story. Everybody calls the victim homeless, but it sounds to me like he's just unidentified."

"He wasn't from around here."

"How do you know?" Jordanna asked.

"'Cause no one knew him." He looked at her like, *Duh*. "No one claimed the body. He just wandered up off Summit Ridge and up and died."

"What was the cause of death, do you know?"

"Exposure? Old age?" He leaned in more intimately and another smile flashed across his face. "Evil drink, maybe?"

"How old was he?"

He shrugged and slurped up some of his latte. "Older than us, I'm pretty sure. Didn't pay that much attention. Wasn't that interesting except for he got himself branded."

"I heard the chief didn't want that information to get out."

"Markum?" He snorted. "Damn useless old goat. This why you're back in town? 'Cause of that body? Thought you Treadwell girls skedaddled because you didn't like us anymore."

"Winters. I'm always interested in a possible story. I heard you knew my sister, Emily."

"Emily . . ." He shrugged, as if he could hardly remember her, but his eyes shifted away.

"I actually heard you knew her pretty well," Jordanna added softly.

His eyes were dark brown and now they focused back on her. There was some emotion in there that he was trying to quash. "Yeah?"

"There was that time you were . . . making out . . . against the snack shack, after a game."

"Making out?" He laughed shortly. "Who told you that? Wow."

"Emily," Jordanna lied.

"That surprises me. She sure as hell pretended it didn't happen afterward."

"You weren't her boyfriend, then?"

"It was a long time ago. High school, jeez." He shook his head. "You're the one who's a reporter," he said, as if the shoe had just dropped. "Looking for stories. That make you any money? Your job?"

"Well, I don't do it for my health."

He laughed again, forced heartiness. A few heads turned their way, but Jordanna kept her attention on Martin Lourde. He didn't seem like a truly terrible guy, but, like he'd said, he also didn't seem like Emily's type.

"So, the night at the snack shack was a one-time thing, then?" she probed.

He finished off his latte, tipping back the paper cup to get every last drop, then wiped the back of his hand across his mouth. "Emily got religion, like half the town. All the girls who were hot pants in high school got religion. Made 'em feel better about their misspent youth, maybe. But Emily . . ." He lifted a hand off the table, then dropped it back down. "It happened real quick with her."

"Must've. 'Cause I don't remember her being particularly religious until the very end," Jordanna said.

"Well, that's when it was. She got bit by the bug, she was gone, and I mean gone. She stopped talking to me about

Christmas that year. I had a pretty bad crush on her," he admitted. "Bought her this necklace. Wasn't worth much, but I gave it to her, thinking it was something big. Such a fucking dope." He dolefully shook his head. "It was all wrapped up in a box. She didn't even want to open it, but I made her. Told her I wouldn't be able to live if she didn't accept my gift, blah, blah, blah." He shook his head and ran a palm over the top of his thinning hair, embarrassed at the memory. "When she finally opened it, she just looked at the necklace like it was a snake, or something. Said she couldn't keep it, that she was on a path now. I didn't know what she meant, but she went on to say that she'd wandered for a while . . . which was apparently when she was getting all hot and crazy with me . . . but that she was firmly on the path of the righteous."

"The Lord's path," Jordanna said, remembering what Kara had said.

He hooked a thumb at his chest, grinned and declared, "Not this Lourde," in a way that made it clear he'd done this same play many, many times before. "Thought you were looking into the branded homeless guy. How'd we get on your sister? Oh, right . . ." He answered his own question. "You thought I was her boyfriend."

"Who was her boyfriend back then?"

He grimaced. "She had a lot of 'em. That's all I want to say about that. She really crushed me back then, y'know? I've been married and divorced and had a couple other relationships since then, but . . ." He shrugged. "It's stupid, but I still think about her once in a while."

"*L'amour*," Jordanna said with a smile.

"Huh?"

"Nothing."

He shrugged. "But Emily changed at the end of high

school. She got weird. Not just the religion stuff, but it was like she was going mental, or something."

"Sure you haven't got her confused with me?" Jordanna asked drily.

"People were talking about her. They kept saying how crazy she was, just like the rest of . . ." He cut himself off.

"The Treadwells," Jordanna finished for him. "Yeah. Go on."

"Sorry."

"You were on a track about Emily. What were you going to say?"

"Oh, just that . . . when they were saying those things about her, I kinda ate it up. Because she dumped me, y'know. I acted like it was me who dumped her, but she's the one who did it."

Jordanna nodded. "Those things seem really important in high school."

"Don't they?" He shook his head in disbelief. "Back then, I didn't care if she was mental, or not. I was just stupid in love, or lust . . . both. First love, y'know? Sticks with ya."

Jordanna nodded, though in many ways her own high school experience was a fuzzy blur, a time she'd purposely dropped from her consciousness except for a few sterling moments that she would rather forget.

He sighed heavily. "But then she died. That was the worst. I was sick. Thought I'd never get over it."

Jordanna smiled faintly. It was kind of sweet, and unexpected, his teenaged love for Emily.

"You don't look much like her," he said thoughtfully, his eyes frankly assessing.

"It was quite a few years ago."

"Yeah . . ." The conversation stalled and Jordanna felt like she'd squeezed Martin Lourde dry of information. She wondered if she could sneak away now, or if he was going to try to prolong their friendship, such as it was.

"Well, I'd better get going," she said, rising to her feet again.

"If you're really looking for a story, you should find out what happened to Bernadette Fread. She disappeared over a week ago, and I hope to God she's okay."

"You know Bernadette?" She almost said "too" but managed to keep that back.

"Sure. The Fread ranch is right next to my farm. I've known 'em all my life."

His tone suggested it wasn't always a happy acquaintanceship.

"Someone said they thought she ran away."

He thought that over, then shook his head. "Maybe, though Bernadette's not really the type. The Freads raise cattle mostly, and Bernadette's been right in there, helping out. She did a 4-H project. Raised an orphaned calf. Fed it from a bottle day and night, when it was little. Cried when they sold the steer, after it was full grown. I didn't blame her. It was like part of the family."

"Sounds traumatic," Jordanna agreed.

"Old man Fread's real fire and brimstone, not that I don't believe in the Great Man, myself, but he's definitely of the opinion spare the rod, spoil the child."

"He abused Bernadette?"

Martin backpedaled quickly. "That's the trouble with you reporters. Putting words in our mouths. I mean, he was strict . . . too strict. Bernadette's been on a very short leash, a very long time."

"But you don't think she just ran away, or do you?" Jordanna questioned.

"I don't know. It's just peculiar and it worries me."

"I'm thinking about talking to Chief Markum about the branded man, so I'll ask him about Bernadette, too."

"Don't bother. The chief's a Green Pasturer, and so are the Freads."

And so's my father and Jennie. "I hear an awful lot about that church," Jordanna said. "The Calversons belong, too."

"Not Nate . . . not really," he assured her. "Pru, yeah, but Nate's another story. You remember him."

"I ran into him and Pru at the Longhorn last night."

"No, I mean, *you* remember him." There was a glimmer in his eye.

Jordanna's pulse jolted. Did he know about her secret crush? One that maybe wasn't so secret after all? "What do you mean?" she asked, slipping the strap of her purse over her shoulder and grabbing her laptop case.

"Hey, don't be embarrassed. I told you about me and Emily, didn't I? Every girl in high school was crushin' on Nate. That's just a fact." He spread his hands as he got to his feet, no harm, no foul. "Nate had a posse of 'em after him."

"Well, I wasn't one of them," she lied. "I barely talked to him."

"Emily said you wrote about him in your diary."

"*What?*"

"What I'm saying is, you don't have to cover up to me."

"Well, it wasn't like that." Jordanna was sputtering, still trying to recover from the fact that Emily had apparently read her journal and spilled its secrets.

Ignoring her, Martin went on, "Nate was a goddam god in those days. Hell, we all knew it, and if we didn't, he made sure we did. And the Calversons were about the richest family in three counties, so any girl with brains wanted Nate for their boyfriend."

"I was never interested in the Calverson money," Jordanna got out with an effort. There were so many things wrong with what he was saying, she hardly knew where to begin her defense.

"Don't worry about it. We were kids, right?" He wagged his head dolefully. "Emily shouldn't have gone so soon, but awful things happen."

Jordanna made a sound of agreement, determined not to say anything more that would make things worse. She would have left right then, but Martin was standing in her way.

"Life's here to teach us all lessons, though, huh?" Martin mused. "Nate ended up with Pru, and I guess they're happy. She's sweet and simple, and he sneaks out and plays poker with us now and again. Took over the family business, but then so did I."

Martin finally shifted position, and Jordanna managed to edge around him. "Nice to see you again," she said belatedly, holding out her hand.

"Oh, we'll see each other again." A short bark of laughter. "Pru'll find a way to make that happen, if I know her."

"She mentioned something about that to me," Jordanna admitted.

"Sunday potluck?" He made a sound of disgust. "Hope you don't think I came over here to hit on you. She just said one of the Winters girls was in town, the one who was a reporter, and when I saw you sitting here with your laptop, it just seemed like you might be the one."

He surprised her then, by suddenly grabbing her arm, and Jordanna sucked in a breath. She'd pretty much decided Martin Lourde, whom Rusty had labeled a putz, was harmless, but now she could feel herself tighten. Sensing her tension, he loosened his grip a bit. He looked like he was going to say something serious, but all that came out after a long moment was, "Don't be a stranger." Then he dropped her arm and turned away.

"Huh . . ." September said aloud, staring at her computer screen intently.

"What?" George asked, sitting back and swiveling in his chair to face her.

"Well, I'm looking at a copy of the Danzigers' divorce decree. Finalized three months ago."

"Finalized?"

"That's what it says here."

"She never mentioned that, and you and Auggie both called Danziger her husband."

"Yes, we did," September said reflectively. "So, maybe this woman who was pretending to be Carmen was actually Danziger's girlfriend? That might explain why he didn't tell us who she was." She yanked out her cell, started to text, then made an annoyed sound and hit the "favorite" button to place a call to her brother. Sometimes texting just pissed her off. While she was waiting to be connected, she said, "I gotta remind myself that I can still use a phone instead of texting."

"I never text," George said, swinging back to his desk to face his computer screen.

"Yeah, well, sometimes it's the answer . . . like now . . . that I'm getting Auggie's voice mail." Uttering a sound of frustration, she clipped out, "Call me. I've just been looking at the Danzigers' divorce decree. They haven't been legally married for three months."

She clicked off just as Gretchen came into the station. "Good news," her ex-partner said. "D'Annibal's putting you with me on my case. I had to kiss some ass, which I'm not suited for in any way, shape, or form, but at least I got us together again."

"Good." September was pleased to hear that their lieutenant had finally partnered her with Gretchen again. "Auggie can get someone else to do follow-up for him. Maybe George."

"I live to serve," George muttered, not looking up from the screen.

"Well, since you never get off your ass, you're perfect for

the job," Gretchen said pointedly. Then, to September, "Come on. You gotta see this."

"What?" September pushed her chair back.

"The little domestic dispute I was called to help settle has turned into something more interesting."

"Like what?"

"Skeletons in the closet." She smiled her feral smile and her slanted turquoise eyes glittered. "And I mean that literally. The wife and husband were screaming at each other and wifey suddenly yells, 'Look in the basement closet!' so I did. A whole lot of bones and some human skulls. I arrested 'em both, and hustled 'em out of there. Techs are there now."

"Holy God," September said.

"Yeah, c'mon. You just never know what you're going to find."

September picked up her gun from her desk drawer and carried it to the break room, where she opened her locker and snatched her messenger bag from the hook on the back of the locker door. She placed the gun inside, slammed her locker shut, then came back for the jacket she'd slung over her chair. She followed her partner down the short hall to reception, slid a look toward Guy Urlacher, then nearly ran smack into Pauline Kirby from Channel Seven.

"Detective Rafferty," Pauline greeted her with a fake smile. "I've been calling you."

"Oh, right . . ." September tried to ease past her, but it was Gretchen who came to her rescue.

"You need to talk to Detective August Rafferty," she said coolly to the reporter. "He's on the Saldano bombing."

"I understood it was you," Pauline said to September.

September shook her head. "No."

"Where are you going?" Pauline asked, craning her head around as September swept by her.

"Lunch," September said.

"None of your business," Gretchen said at the same time,

shooting September a look as it was after 3:00 PM and lunch was long over.

"You're on a case together," Pauline said, correctly reading their haste to leave together. "Is this your first since the shooting?"

"Check with *August* Rafferty," Gretchen reminded her. "He's your man." They were on the outside steps when September's cell rang. "Don't answer it," Gretchen warned. "It's probably Kirby. She's got your number and she won't give up."

"It's Auggie." September put the phone to her ear. "Hey, you get my message?"

"Yeah, funny Carmen didn't mention the divorce. But that mystery woman? Maybe Danziger's girlfriend? She's also the woman on the videotape from the camera on the building opposite Saldano Industries."

"What? She was there? At the bombing? Oh, God, that's suspicious." September slowed her steps, but Gretchen made hurry-up motions, so she climbed into the passenger seat of the department-issued Jeep, her cell glued to her ear.

"Yep. And it's the same woman who helped Danziger into a black RAV—no plates—at Laurelton General and drove him away."

"What the hell."

"I checked at the *Oregonian*. Danziger's not working on anything specific for them right now. A coworker said he's taken a leave of absence. I'm going to dive deeper into his friendships there. Somebody knows something."

"Mystery woman has moved from the back burner to the forefront," September observed.

"And the bomb?" Auggie went on as if he hadn't heard her. "It was operated by remote control. Coulda been from across the street, or further."

"Okay . . . but Danziger wasn't afraid of this woman at

the hospital, if you think she set the bomb. He wanted to go with her."

"It doesn't look like she had anything in her hands, any kind of detonator. But it puts her in the forefront of this investigation. Where are you? You sound like you're outside?"

"I'm with Gretchen. We're on a case together."

"Tell Sanders to try not to shoot anybody today."

September relayed the information to her partner, who smiled and said, "Piss off," which September relayed back to Auggie. "You're turning this information over to the feds, right?" she added.

"Yeeessss . . ." Auggie answered at the same moment Gretchen said loudly, "Don't do it. Keep it from the feds as long as you can. I hate it when they take over."

"I'll bear that in mind," Auggie said with a smile in his voice. "But I may need some help."

"George is at his desk," September told him. "I'm busy."

"What about Pelligree? Or, that guy from Robbery who helped you out last fall?"

"Wes is out in the field, reinterviewing witnesses on that shooting at the Tri-Met station that's about to go to trial, and Maharis is back on Robbery, but he'd help you if it helped him. He wants to move permanently to Homicide. But playing fast and loose with the feds . . ." She trailed off dubiously.

Auggie grunted. "Okay. Stay safe."

"You, too."

Chapter Twelve

Jordanna parked across the street from City Hall, a three-story building on the south side of town near the falls that took function over form to a new level. Composed of cinder blocks painted white sometime during the past millennium, it was now a dusty gray, squatting beside the park that led down to the river, a blight on one of the nicest city views, an eyesore amongst the rebuilt Victorians that backed up to the river.

She pushed through the front door and made her way to the back office that housed the police. It had been a department of five when she'd been a Rock Springs resident and it didn't look much larger now.

The officer wore a crisp blue uniform and sat behind a high counter. She smiled a greeting at Jordanna that didn't quite reach her eyes.

"Hello, I'd like to talk to Officer Drummond," Jordanna said. She didn't know exactly what Peter Drummond's title was, but she figured "officer" would cover it.

It seemed to do the trick. "He's in the field" was the unhelpful answer. "Could someone else help you?"

"Maybe I could just leave my name and number?"

The woman nodded and handed Jordanna a memo slip.

She wrote her name, her number, and then a quick note saying she'd spoken to Rusty Long, who'd suggested she contact Drummond about the "homeless" victim who'd been found on government property, on the side of Summit Ridge Road.

Jordanna had just finished writing the note when she heard voices behind her, two men entering through the front door. "All I'm saying is don't work so hard to ticket every law-abiding citizen," a gravelly and familiar voice was saying.

She felt a shiver start at her nape and dance down to her lower back as she recognized Chief Greer Markum's distinctive tones.

"I don't mean to argue, Chief, but speeding is breaking the law," the younger man with the nasal voice said earnestly. He, too, wore the blue uniform and he was following Chief Markum like a puppy, nearly stepping on his feet he was so anxious to please. "I don't know who I'm supposed to give special treatment to."

"It's not special treatment," Markum said hastily, throwing a glance around the station, looking to see who might overhear. "I'm talking goodwill for the community, you understand?"

Jordanna had turned to look, then quickly shifted her attention away, hoping she wasn't recognized. Her heart was thumping. As Markum and his anxious acolyte moved into her peripheral line of sight, she said, "Thanks," to the receptionist, handing her the slip of paper before turning away from the new arrivals. She'd known there was a chance she might see Markum, but now that the moment was here, she didn't want to have anything to do with him.

"Excuse me, ma'am," he said, and though she kept walking toward the exit, she knew he was addressing her. "Ma'am?" he called again, more loudly.

Caught. Damn. Gritting her teeth, Jordanna slowly turned back around.

He'd aged over the years and not well. His hair was steel gray and there were deep lines cut into his forehead above a pair of beetling, bushy brows. "Can I help you?" he asked, his expression stern. She could tell he was trying to place her.

"I was looking for Officer Drummond," she said.

"Lord above, Jordanna?" he said in wonder.

She couldn't very well deny it, so she nodded briefly.

"Well, what finally brings you back to Rock Springs? We expected to see you at the wedding."

Jordanna let the rebuke slide off her. "Couldn't make it. I did run into Jennie yesterday."

"I haven't talked to her for a few days. Huh. Well, what do you know." He came back to himself and asked, "You know Pete?"

"Not really. I'm . . . exploring a story," she admitted.

"Ahhh . . ." He wagged a finger at her. "That's right. I've seen some of your work. What kind of story you on? I can probably help you as much as Pete. Come on back." He turned toward the half-door at the end of the counter and swung it open, waiting for her. Jordanna reluctantly followed after him, past the reception desk and down a short hall to the office at the back. Markum sank down into the leather chair with a huge sigh, throwing a dark glance at the papers strewn across the desktop.

"You about broke your daddy's heart, not showing up," he remarked.

Jordanna forced a smile she didn't feel. "Well, it's not the first time."

He clucked his tongue. "Still chippy, huh, gal?"

"Still chippy," she agreed, fighting not to snap his head off. Rash behavior had not worked for her in the past. She might not love the police, but there was no reason to let

Markum know it and end up in some kind of wrangle. She recalled he was a man who insisted on having the last word.

"Sit down, sit down." He waved in the general direction of one of the two plain wooden chairs opposite his desk.

She perched gingerly on the edge of one. "I'm interested in the male victim who was found near my father's property about three years ago, the body that was never identified."

"It was found on government land," he clarified.

"That's what I heard, but a lot of that property adjacent to Bureau of Land Management property was owned, at least at one time, by the Benchley family. In fact, the boy who found the body is listed as Zach Benchley."

Markum squeaked back in his chair. "So, what're you gettin' at?"

"I don't know. I just thought it was a story I wanted to explore."

"And you thought Pete would help you?" A smile played at the corners of his mouth, as if he knew a secret.

"I also heard the body was branded. A point you wanted kept under wraps."

His face froze for a moment before he recovered himself. "Who told you that?"

"A number of people. So, it's not much of a secret, from what I can tell."

He touched his fingertips together, giving himself time to think. "Bad publicity for our town. Didn't want Rock Springs splashed all over the news because some nut was defiling corpses."

"So, the branding was done after the man died," Jordanna said. She wanted to reach for her notepad to jot down notes but sensed it wouldn't be wise just yet. She didn't want to inflame him, and she was pretty sure she would unless she trod very carefully.

"Well, of course it was. I would know if somebody was branding live people in my town. And anyway, that's what the ME said when he took the body. Don't start stirring up something scandalous when you don't know what you're talking about."

"Death was from exposure?"

"Yes, ma'am." His eyes narrowed. "Seen your dad yet?"

"Not yet. Could you tell me what the brand looked like?"

"Dayton's probably waiting for you to call," he surmised. "Since you saw Jennie already."

Jordanna thought about Dance, waiting at the house, and suddenly wanted to run to him, throw herself at him, beg to be part of his world and not this one. But in many ways, they were the same world. She had a story to follow, and just because she was uncomfortable in Rock Springs didn't mean she should back away. She'd told Dance she was going to learn what she could about the branded man and she wasn't going to back out now. Switching gears, she asked Markum, "What about Bernadette Fread? I heard she was missing. Are you looking for her? I heard there was a question of possible abuse."

The chief sprang to his feet as if zapped by a cattle prod, his face florid. "Who've you been talking to? It's that kind of rumor that starts real trouble. I don't appreciate you making up stories about upstanding citizens."

"So, Bernadette's father is an upstanding citizen." Jordanna stood, too.

"Yes, ma'am," he said tautly.

"Not a chance of abuse."

"If you want to find out who the dead man is, be my guest. I'll be happy to help in any way I can. But don't think you can come back here and smear reputations. That's not how it works in Rock Springs."

"Especially for members of Green Pastures Church."

She hadn't believed his face could get any redder, but it turned a mottled magenta that made her worry about possible popping blood vessels. "Now you listen. You leave the

Freads alone. Bernadette's taken off before and she'll come back begging for mercy, just like always. She's a good kid, but a bit of a trial to her family. That's all you need to know. Go talk to the ME in Malone, if you want to know about the homeless vic. That's all I've got to say for now."

Jordanna's pulse was pounding, but she met his gaze squarely. "I'd still like to speak to Officer Drummond."

The chief slowly got himself under control, and that whisper of a smile was back. "I'll tell him you're looking for him."

She left, wondering why he seemed so amused by that idea.

The house on Aurora Lane was on the outskirts of Laurelton, barely inside the city limits. Beyond its backyard was a green space with a copse of firs, pines, and oak trees that September knew eventually opened to a small lake that had once had summer cabins ringed around it like a necklace. Over the years, the whole property had devolved into an abandoned outpost, the lake itself having pulled back from its banks into little more than a large, algae-choked pond. She knew this because the Raffertys had once owned property there, which her father had sold when things started going south. Recently, however, September had read that there had been renewed interest in the area, with developers tearing down the rotted cabins and building new ones as the lake waters had returned, fed by underground springs.

But Aurora Lane was not seeing the same rejuvenation. It was a long street with few houses, each residence on a five-plus-acre lot so that your nearest neighbor wasn't within shouting distance. They were in a kind of zoning no-man's-land, not quite farmland, yet not like anything inside the rest of the Laurelton city limits, either. September was well acquainted with the street because she'd had a high school friend who'd lived for a while in her grandparents' house, the first one on the left as you turned onto the broken asphalt road.

The house they pulled up to was near the far end of the lane, just before the road itself petered out. There should have been a cul-de-sac put in for easy turnabout, but the road just came to a stop. Gravel had been strewn over the dirt and grass for the unwary who made a wrong turn and found themselves facing the greenway and copse of trees. September supposed you could make a U-y, but there was a strong chance a tire or two would slip into mud, so the prospect was iffy.

"Who called you to this house?" September asked, looking at the older two-story home. Its shingles were painted dark green, its white trim blistered and rotting. She could see a window below the siding, which indicated there was a basement, where the "skeletons in the closet" had apparently been found. The place looked like a true handyman's delight, the kind that needed a serious overhaul from years of neglect. The only thing new about it was the crime tech's white van parked in front.

"A woman named Carol Jenkins hadn't heard from her sister in a long while so she flew from Florida to see what was wrong, but when she got to the house, she was stalemated by her great-niece and the niece's husband. They wouldn't let her in the door. She set up a clamor, and eventually got a court order to be allowed in, and the niece and husband appear to be minor drug users and dealers. No sign of the sister, until, what do you know . . . a pile of bones in the basement." Gretchen's eyes were bright and glittering at the prospect of what lay ahead. She loved being involved in sick crimes of all sorts, though September was far less eager to delve into the strange, warped, and amoral world that seemed to so fascinate her partner. Literal "skeletons in the closet" definitely appealed to Gretchen.

As September slammed the passenger door shut, her eye on the dilapidated concrete steps that led to the narrow front porch, her cell phone buzzed. Pulling it from her pocket, she looked down at the number and sucked in a breath.

"What?" Gretchen demanded, her head swiveling September's way.

"It's my sister, July. She's past her due date."

"Oh." Babies did not interest Gretchen.

September quickly hit the talk button. "Hey, there," she said, unable to contain the excitement in her voice.

Immediately, July said, "No, no, nothing new. Just wanted to talk to you. I'm blimping around over here, waiting and waiting. Tomorrow I'm going in to see what's what. God knows I'm sick of being pregnant."

July was September's older sister, who'd decided not to let the whim of love or fate decide when she would have a child. Instead, July had gone to the sperm bank and picked out a father. She'd learned a few months earlier that she was having a baby girl in May, and, in keeping with one of the strangest Rafferty traditions—naming a child after the month in which it was born—she'd decided to name her baby girl May.

But now they were getting very close to the end of the month, so September queried, "How do you feel about June?"

"Kinda wanted May, you know."

Their oldest sister, May, had been killed as a teenager and, upon learning the baby was due in May, July had wanted to honor her sister by giving her baby her name. "I know," September agreed. Gretchen was staring at her, making the hand motion that meant for her to wrap it up.

"Oh, who knows . . . maybe I'll name her Gilda," she added impishly.

They both laughed as Gilda was the name their step-mother, who was younger than both of them, had wanted for her own daughter, born the previous January. But of course Rosamund had bent to their father's wishes and the baby had been named for the month she was born as well.

"I gotta go," September said. "But if anything happens—"

"I'm calling you first," July promised.

September had to hurry to catch up to Gretchen, who was eating up the walkway to the porch with ground-devouring strides. As she reached her, her phone rang yet again. Gretchen blew out a raspberry in frustration, but September looked at the screen and said, "Auggie." She clicked on. "Yeah?"

"Jordanna Winters," he said.

"What?"

"Danziger's girlfriend. Jordanna Winters. She's a free-lance reporter. Maybe she's worked with him. I had a still picture of her from the hospital camera and showed it to some of Danziger's colleagues. One of them recognized her. The guy had crossed paths with her in the course of work. Apparently she's written articles for smaller papers."

"Jordanna Winters," September repeated thoughtfully.

"Just wanted to let you know. Oh, and I met with the feds who don't want to share. We both know 'em."

"Donley and Bethwick," September said, recalling the two FBI agents she'd worked with the previous fall.

Hearing the names of the two agents, Gretchen groaned and said, "Frick and Frack." She'd had run-ins with them before, and September had danced around them as well.

"You got it," Auggie said. "They're focused on the Saldanos, so I'm keeping the Winters information to myself for the moment. I'm going to go by her apartment, see if there's any chance she and Danziger are there."

"What about Carmen?" she asked.

"I'm not telling her jack shit, and don't you, either."

"This is your case, not mine."

"For the moment, anyway."

"Stay on it," September advised her brother, and he grunted an assent before she clicked off.

"Are we ready now?" her partner asked her sardonically.

September nodded and followed her inside the house and down the stairs to the basement, where the crime tech crew was just finishing up. "What can you tell us?" Gretchen asked a young man with a pencil-thin mustache and a glittering ruby stud in one ear.

"Looks like the bones from two separate human adults, maybe more," he said.

"More?" Gretchen repeated, but the tech had moved past her on his way out.

Gretchen's curly, black hair seemed to shiver as she growled to September, "Come on. Let's interview the stoners I took to county. They weren't giving up anything about the skeletons before, but maybe they've had a change of heart by now."

"How old are the stoners?"

"Early twenties maybe."

September followed after her into a warming afternoon, where a watery sun gilded the needles of several large Douglas firs. Though she should have been more intrigued by the case, her thoughts had turned to Jordanna Winters, who may or may not be Jay Danziger's girlfriend and who may or may not know a hell of a lot more about the Saldano bombing.

She, like Auggie, wished she could stay on that case.

Dance worked his way into the kitchen and poured himself a glass of water from the tap. He had the vial of painkillers in his pocket and he shook out two tablets, stared at them a moment, then put them back in the bottle and just drank the water. Yeah, his leg hurt. It hurt like hell, and there was a low-grade headache hanging around that was making him testy. Still, it was better than feeling dull and stupid. Jordanna had told him to stay ahead of the pain, and though she was probably right, he wasn't going to listen.

He wasn't particularly hungry, but he hadn't eaten since she'd left, so he opened the box of Triscuits and ate about ten before he couldn't stomach anything further. He hated being an invalid.

He gazed down the scrubbed counters toward the microwave. The refrigerator sat against the adjacent wall, but though Jordanna had plugged it in, its days of usefulness were apparently over. It had irked Jordanna, and she'd growled under her breath about her father, but Dance didn't much care one way or another. The way he saw it, they were camping. They'd both run away from life as they knew it, but soon enough they would be returning, or at least he would. Whether she copped to it, or not, whether she even realized it yet, Jordanna had reconnected with her roots through the unidentified vic who'd been found near her father's property.

He was still standing in the kitchen, leaning on his crutches, when he heard her car approaching. Thumping his way back to the living room, he sank onto the couch, tucking the crutches to one side. He hated the crutches, too. In fact, he pretty much totally hated the situation he was in, except maybe for Jordanna. Sure, she was after a story, and she'd certainly taken advantage of his infirmity to that end, but she was helping him and she was entertaining to boot.

And maybe she could help him in the Saldano investigation. Though he'd told her she was all wet in her theories about them, the audiotape said differently. The same audiotape that had undoubtedly been blown to smithereens. Still, he had a copy. . . .

Footsteps rang on the floorboards of the woodshed. Dance straightened in shock. They were too heavy for Jordanna's. This was a stranger. Quickly, he struggled to his feet, grabbing up the crutches, calculating just how he could use them as a weapon when the kitchen door opened and the footsteps clomped inside. Boots, he realized dimly, lifting one crutch with his right arm and hand to use like a bat, if necessary. His weight was balanced on his right leg as well. Awkward, damn near impossible, but he wasn't going down without a fight.

The man who appeared in the aperture between the kitchen and living room was about six feet tall, somewhere in his fifties, and a complete stranger. He wore cowboy boots and jeans and a leather jacket. He stared at Dance and Dance stared back.

"Where's Jordanna?" he asked.

"Who are you?" Dance responded.

"Dayton Winters. The owner of this property. If you're not with my daughter, you're trespassing, and if you are with her, I'd like to know what you're doing here and where she is."

Jordanna picked up the bag of burgers from the grill counter inside Baxter's Pharmacy and hurried outside to the RAV. She'd wanted to drive straight home after her encounter with Chief Markum, but she'd waited around awhile, lurking inside her car, hoping Peter Drummond would return. In that, she'd failed, but she had seen Rusty Long's cousin, Todd Douglas, entering the pharmacy so she'd hurried up the street to meet him.

"Hey," she'd greeted him, when she realized he was going to the grill counter. It was four o'clock, but he was seating himself on one of the stools and picking up a plastic-covered menu. "Early dinner?"

"Jordanna," he said, smiling. "Yeah, I've gotta head home, but I missed lunch. Heard you met Rusty at the Longhorn last night."

"Yeah, and some ex-classmates as well."

"Where are you staying?"

"Oh . . ." She'd waved toward the north, in the opposite direction of her father's current house, the opposite direction from the homestead. "I just talked to Chief Markum about that branded victim. He wasn't very forthcoming."

"You didn't talk to Pete?"

"He wasn't there. The chief said I should speak to the ME."

"County morgue's in Malone," Todd said.

"Yeah, I know, and that's where you're from."

"You want a ride over there?"

"No, I just was looking for some information, I guess." She hesitated, and that's when Loretta, behind the counter, had asked if she wanted anything to eat, so she'd placed an order for two burgers.

"You're either extra hungry, or you're feeding somebody else," Todd had observed.

"I may be heading back to Portland tonight," she'd lied. "You know, I also ran into Martin Lourde today."

"Don't think I know him."

"He has a dairy farm right next to the Freads' property. Bernadette Fread is the missing girl."

"Oh, yeah."

"Rusty was saying the Freads are members of Green Pastures Church. I know you're not a member of that congregation, but you're . . . more spiritually inclined than Rusty."

Todd snorted. "Nearly anyone's more spiritually inclined than Rusty."

"Do you know much about Green Pastures? I understand it's a very strict congregation . . . a lot of rules?"

"That's about the size of it. What are you looking for?" he questioned.

"I was just at the police station and I mentioned to the chief that I'd heard Bernadette Fread may have run away because her father was too strict. I also brought up Green Pastures, and I questioned whether there was abuse."

Todd signaled Loretta and ordered a grilled cheese sandwich. He then turned to Jordanna. "You should come hiking with me and forget this. I'm serious. You're poking a hornet's nest. The chief's a Green Pasturer."

"I heard that. It was kind of the point of why I brought it up to him. He damn near threw me out."

"Which story are you following? The homeless guy, or the missing girl?"

"Both?" Jordanna said, a bit sheepishly. "I'd like to follow up on Bernadette, as well as the branding victim. I'm thinking about checking in with the pastor at Green Pastures, Reverend Miles."

He shook his head, his gaze admiring as it skated over her. "If you're asking me what I think, I think you should leave it all alone. You go to Green Pastures, you won't be greeted with open arms. They're pretty reclusive."

"My father's a Green Pasturer. I was invited to the wedding, but I didn't go."

"They would have been happy to have you at a wedding, but they won't want you digging into their world, especially if you're trying to find out something they don't want you to know, like why Bernadette Fread ran away."

"You think that's it? She ran away? And some of the parishioners know?"

"What I know is that it's not going to be easy for you to get past their defenses. Don't get me wrong. A lot of 'em are good people, but some of 'em . . . maybe not so much."

That had pretty much been the extent of their conversation and Jordanna had paid for her burgers and left. Now, she was almost back to the homestead, her mind reflecting on everything she'd learned. She was eager to see Dance, too. A part of her had this irrational fear that somehow he was going to get up and leave and go back to Portland and the Saldanos, and she was going to be left in Rock Springs without him.

She pulled around to the garage at the back of the property and gasped when she saw the black Explorer parked in her usual spot. The Saldanos! God, no! No, no, it couldn't be. How would they know?

Oh, God . . . *Dance!*

She ran through the woodshed, not bothering to hide her clattering approach. Her cell phone was in her hand. If he was in danger, she could dial 9-1-1 pretty damn fast.

These thoughts skidded and pinged off each other in her mind, fast as atoms. She'd never thought of herself as brave, but she felt a wild, carnal need to protect. She burst into the kitchen and through it to the living room, where she skidded to a halt upon seeing Dance seated on the couch. He looked up at her, his hands clasped and hanging loosely between his thighs.

Then she whipped around and saw the other man seated on the wooden bench against the opposite wall.

"Holy . . . shit . . ." she whispered.

"Jordanna," her father greeted her carefully, rising to his feet.

"What are you doing here?" she demanded. "What have you been saying?"

"I came to see you, but instead I found Mr. Danziger, who says you two were working on a story together."

Jordanna turning blankly to Dance, who gazed at her calmly and said, "I told your father the truth about you helping me on the Saldano case. He offered up the help of the chief of police here, but I said you had the matter in hand."

"And I told Mr. Danziger that there are only so many places in town that you could be, and that finding you was too easy," her father said. "Once Jennie told me you were in town, it didn't take long to find you. She thought you were just moving through, but I didn't believe you were back just to choose a hiking trail."

He spoke matter-of-factly, but Jordanna was nearly deafened by the pulse thundering in her ears.

"A few days, that's all we need," Dance said to her father, in a tone that suggested he'd made this request already.

"I'm not going to give you away," her father assured him.

"We turned the electricity on. I'll pay you back for all this," Jordanna said tautly, waving an arm to encompass their living arrangements.

"No need. I'm just happy to see you. And I understand that you need discretion. You're lucky you weren't killed by that bomb, son," he added, inclining his head toward Dance.

"Yeah," Dance agreed.

"I'm not stopping by," Jordanna said a trifle too loudly. "Tell Jennie."

"That should be looked at," Dayton said, his gaze zeroed on Dance's bound thigh. "Come into the clinic and I'll—"

"No." Jordanna was emphatic.

"If we're still here early next week, I'll come in," Dance overrode her.

"NO." Jordanna pinned him with angry eyes.

"I don't think that's your call to make," her father told her lightly. "Stay as long as you need, but make sure you're safe and healthy. . . ."

And with that he walked out.

Chapter Thirteen

Across the field from the barn, the house glowed pale yellow in a shaft of afternoon sunlight. He trained his gaze on it, feeling a tightness in his chest. It was a familiar feeling. He took no joy in the job he was facing. Too many of God's children had strayed and the list grew longer each day.

And Boo was a problem. Damn the boy. Why couldn't he stay away from the graveyard? If he kept going out there, someone else was going to learn about it. Boo had to stop feeling sorry for the misguided souls who'd followed Satan instead of the Lord. Just the night before he'd caught him digging up a board in the shed, pulling out a dusty box that held keepsakes. He'd had to wrestle it from the boy, who'd beat at him with both fists, crying that his mother had left it for him.

"I'm doing this for your own good," he'd growled angrily, stuffing the box under his arm and towering over the boy. His fury had sent Boo whimpering into the corner, covering his head.

He'd taken the box away and driven into the hills. He'd driven right past the track that led to the graveyard, which was little more than two flattened lines from his own tires when he'd delivered the latest of Satan's children there.

Didn't want Boo to have another reason to come this way. Instead he'd kept on going and going, right to the lookout above the falls. He'd opened the box with the loud music of the water in his ears, the spray dampening his face. The keepsakes were memories from his own past as well as Boo's: Mama's harsh gifts. Chief among them was the knife that she'd used to gut the deer she'd accidentally run over one starry winter night. He remembered it so clearly. Mama's skill and iron control as she slit open the carcass from neck to hind.

What Boo didn't know was that the knife had been used for other purposes as well and he had the scars to prove it. Mama wasn't the one who'd hid it in the shed, he thought grimly. He'd done that himself, to hide it from her, keep it out of her grasp. Somehow Boo must have seen him tuck it under the boards and, in his jumbled way, thought Mama had left it for him.

He'd thrown the knife, the switch, and other means of Mama's terrifying control over the falls, tossing the box in after them.

Of course Mama was long dead now. She'd been taken by that Treadwell disease. Somewhere in the twists and turns of her family she'd crossed paths with the Afflicted Ones, and when he'd heard the calling from God, he'd made her the first of the saved.

There had been pleasure in it. Mama finally got hers. He worried about what that meant, as it surely wasn't God's intention for him to feel anything but duty. He glanced away from the house, to the stony ground that rose like a hill between the fields, covered with trees. He'd buried Mama over by the hawthorn tree with the prickly needles. His drunken father had wondered what had happened to her, but had accepted that she'd just up and left them. Then he'd died of drink himself not long after, and he'd been taken to that other graveyard and buried there.

For a moment his thoughts got confused. He had a sudden memory of hide-and-seek among the tombstones. Shivering, he dragged his thoughts away from that danger and back to Mama. He'd planned to move her to her special graveyard as well, to be with her own kin, but somehow that had gotten away from him. Now, with Boo traipsing all over the country, looking for his "playground," it seemed best to keep her where she was, though he knew he was running out of time. Besides, there were others he needed to catch, brand and bury there, too.

Jordanna Treadwell . . .

It was a sign, a good sign, that she'd come back to town. He'd always known there were some that had escaped, though he'd always believed that he would be the one to bring them back one by one. That was God's plan. He'd been told it, just like he'd been told what to do with all the tainted ones.

Now, he climbed in his truck and drove toward the main road. Once he reached it, he shot a glance to his left and thought about his neighbors. There was the Wright farm next door, new people he didn't really know, and old lady Fowler next door to them, and then the next one over was the Winters farm. Dr. Winters had taken his young bride away from the old homestead, and it had been empty until the Treadwell girl had returned and taken up residence in her father's home. He hadn't seen her there yet, but he'd been warned she was in town and it seemed right that she'd made for the old homestead.

He turned the truck toward town, rattling along the road with its potholes from last winter's snow. Jordanna Treadwell . . . Jordanna . . . Thinking of her reminded him of Emily Treadwell. Lovely Emily, with those blue eyes like windows into another world. She'd sworn she was on the Lord's path. He'd help put her on the Lord's path, but then she'd kissed him and moved up against him, and he'd wanted her so badly, so . . . badly. It had nearly killed him to thrust her away, cover his ears from her lies.

"It wasn't her fault," he said aloud now. She was cursed. She couldn't help herself.

But she lied, over and over again. The Devil's words had boiled out of her mouth like bats from a cave! Remember? *Remember?*

He shuddered violently and damn near had to pull over to catch his breath. What he remembered was how in the end she'd run away from him, screaming. How she'd driven into the hills and how he'd chased her. How he'd screamed himself as her car slid fully around, three hundred and sixty degrees, and slipped over the edge of the precipice to rumble, crash, and thunder down the cliff, carrying Emily to her death.

He'd cried for her, for the soul he hadn't been able to save. But there were many other sorry souls in need of redemption, and he was ready to answer the call.

"You don't have to accompany me to the clinic, but I need to go," Dance said an hour after they had both watched Dr. Dayton Winters's car disappear back down the long drive. His head had a dull ache and he could feel the incision on his leg, but he damn well wasn't going back to the pain pills. In the meantime, Jordanna had pulled the bench over to use as a table and they'd both eaten the burgers that she'd brought home. Though they'd been stone cold, Dance hadn't cared, and though Jordanna had offered to heat them in the microwave, he'd waved that off. For him, the meal had been damn near perfect, and if the burgers were this good cold, he was going to find where she'd purchased them because they might be spectacular warm.

Jordanna wiped her fingers on a napkin. She'd been tight as a coiled spring since her father had departed, and it was clear that she didn't want to talk about him, ever. But now that they'd finished eating, he wasn't willing to just act like nothing had happened.

"I know," she said. "You should go. You will go. I'll take you and drop you off."

"Tomorrow's Saturday, but he said the clinic was open and he'd be there."

"Yes, he's always available for the residents of Rock Springs."

He tried to navigate her mood, but she'd shut down. He attempted some small talk, but it was never his forte, so eventually he just gave up and asked, "Why'd you shoot him?"

She turned to face him, her hazel eyes brilliant in the last rays of sunlight coming through the living room blinds. "You won't believe me. No one does."

"I've heard a lot of unbelievable stories that were true."

She made a sound in the back of her throat that said he didn't know what he was talking about, but she wiped her mouth with the napkin, then said, "I caught him in bed with my older sister her last year of high school." When he didn't immediately respond, she said, "You're trying to come up with some plausible explanation because he's a wonderful man. Dr. Dayton Winters. Upstanding member of Green Pastures Church. Married to Jennie Markum Winters, daughter of the chief of police. I know. I get it. It's much easier to believe Dayton's middle daughter was crazy, probably as a result of that rogue gene carried through the mother's line."

"What do you mean?" he asked.

For a moment, he thought she wasn't going to answer, but then she heaved a deep sigh and said, "I could use a drink. You want some wine? Oh, wait, no, you're on pain pills."

She headed for the kitchen to get the wine. He could've told her he'd eschewed the analgesic, but what the hell. She was already touchy and seemed eager to shut down the conversation at the earliest opportunity, so he didn't want to piss her off about neglecting to take her advice.

He heard her going through the motions of opening the bottle, then the sound of her pouring liquid into a glass. A few moments later she returned with a half-full plastic cup of red in one hand, the bottle of cabernet in the other.

"I don't trust my father," she said as she sat down beside him on the couch. "He denied everything about Emily. Made us all pretend that I thought there was an intruder. The chief knew, though. But everyone's afraid I'm just like my mother. . . ."

"You going to tell me what that means?"

She took a long sip, then tilted her head. "I don't know yet. Maybe. If I'm liquored up enough."

"Maybe I will have a glass," he said, changing his mind. "I have a confession to make about the pain pills. . . ."

The two stoners in the interrogation room said they were in their late-twenties, but they had the tired, used-up look of chronic drug abusers. If September had needed to peg their ages, she would have thought closer to forty, maybe more.

The man had a scruffy beard that he couldn't stop scratching. The woman was just hangdog limp, nearly falling out of the chair she'd been shepherded into by a stern-faced deputy who uttered no words at all.

Gretchen said, "Are you ready to explain the bones?"

The woman looked at the man, who scratched even more furiously, as if the motion itself would help him concoct a story.

"Uhhhhh . . ." she said, like a record on stall.

The man answered, "Fairy, there, it's her grandparents, I think."

"Fairy?" Gretchen questioned, eyeing the lank-haired woman with the slight overbite.

"It's Frances, and I hate it," she admitted grudgingly. "Everyone calls me Fairy."

"So, what happened to your grandparents?" Gretchen asked her.

"Well, Gramps and Gran didn't really like each other anymore. It happens. My parents didn't last five years. And then, after what happened with Daniel, everything went to hell." She choked a bit and her eyes shone wetly.

September was about to ask her what had happened, but Gretchen was in interrogation mode and didn't want to be sidetracked. Her laser-eyed glare made Fairy shrink back a little, however, and she turned to September. "They really couldn't stand each other," she revealed. "Gramps and Gran. They were dead when we found them. I think she poisoned him, or maybe he poisoned her. We just didn't tell anybody."

"When was this?" Gretchen inquired.

"Oh . . . I dunno." She looked over at Mr. Beard Scratcher, who shrugged and scratched some more."

"How did you find them?" September asked.

Fairy looked to the man and said, "You tell 'em, Craig."

"They were just sitting at the table, kinda slumped over. Like they ate their meal and just died," he revealed.

Gretchen said coolly, "If you don't stop scratching, I'm going to handcuff you." He immediately dropped his hands to the table. To Fairy, she said, "Was this a year ago? Or, two? Those bones have been there a while."

"Umm, maybe three?" she said uncertainly.

"You found the bodies at the kitchen table?" Gretchen queried, and to her quick nod, asked, "And you did what?"

"Huh?" She gazed at Gretchen warily.

September could tell her partner was becoming frustrated, so she clarified, "What did you do after you found them?"

Craig and Fairy shared a look, and he said, "We put 'em in the closet."

"Jesus," Gretchen expelled. "And then what?"

"We said a prayer," Fairy said, her eyes swiveling from Gretchen to September and back again. "Or, two . . . ?"

"The house is owned by Phillip and Jan Singleton," Gretchen said.

"That's them," Fairy said, nodding.

"Did they live with anyone else?" Gretchen pressed.

"Uh . . . just me?" Fairy asked, as if looking for the right answer.

"What if I told you there might be more than the bones of two people in the closet?" Gretchen asked.

Both Craig and Fairy blinked at them blankly.

"Okay, so after you found them, and put the bodies in the closet, and said one or two prayers, what then?" Gretchen asked.

Fairy said, "Umm, Craig moved back in. Gran didn't really want us to be together, on account of the drugs and stuff, but we're married."

"So, Craig moved back in and the two of you stayed there and didn't tell anyone that your grandparents died."

Fairy nodded. "That's right."

"What about the smell?" she asked.

"What?" Fairy asked, and Craig's hands jumped to his beard and began digging again in earnest.

"When those bodies decomposed, it *smelled*," Gretchen explained with extreme patience.

"It sure as hell did!" Craig burst out. "Gagged me all the time! Fuckin' dead bodies! Shoulda buried 'em in the backyard."

"Shoulda called the authorities," September pointed out.

"Yeah, yeah we shoulda," he muttered, shooting a glance at Fairy before looking away.

"Social Security," September said when there was a long

moment of silence, and both Fairy and Craig looked stricken. "That's why you didn't report their deaths. For your grand-parents' Social Security checks."

"Oh, come on," Gretchen said, disbelieving.

"Well, they just kept coming," Fairy defended, going even limper. "Every month. The checks just kept coming. We didn't know who to send 'em back to. And Harry's, too."

"Harry?" September asked.

Craig said grudgingly, "That's kinda how we got the idea. Harry died a long time ago."

"Harry was?" Gretchen asked.

"Gramps's brother," Fairy said. "He just had a heart attack and died one day, and then Gramps said it would be a shame to give up all that money Harry earned, so they just . . ."

"Put him in the closet?" September asked.

"Jesus," Gretchen said again, pacing around the room and shaking her head in disgust.

"Well, they buried him first, but the dog kept digging up the bones." Craig started to scratch, shot a glance at Gretchen, and clasped his hands together as if he were about to pray.

"And no one ever asked about Harry, or Gramps or Gran until Carol Jenkins showed up," Gretchen said on a huge sigh.

"Well . . . yeah . . ." Fairy said.

Gretchen asked a few more questions, but Fairy and Craig were apparently tapped out. September followed her partner out of the county jail, and this time when they stepped out-side, they were greeted by a light rain, which coalesced in Gretchen's tightly curled black hair.

"This is what drugs do. Make everyone a criminal. And the fucking apathy, God help me!" Gretchen stalked through the rain to the Jeep with September ducking her head and hurrying after her. "I thought this was going to be a helluva lot more interesting," she growled as she got into the driver's seat and slammed the door behind her.

Sliding into her own side, September said, "The grandparents might have poisoned each other." In the Jeep's overhead light, raindrops glistened on her ring.

"Doesn't say much for marriage, does it?" Gretchen observed, following September's gaze.

"No . . . it doesn't."

"What are we gonna do with Fairy and Craig?" she muttered, but she really wasn't looking for an answer.

September looked out the window as Gretchen turned around in the gravel. One of the wheels slipped into the mud, but Gretchen pressed her toe to the accelerator and the Jeep lurched back onto the road.

Doesn't say much for marriage at all, September thought.

Jordanna swallowed a healthy gulp of red wine that left her choking. Dance actually reached over and clapped her on the back. "I'm okay," she managed to squeak out, trying to set down her glass on the bench. "Holy moly. I'm going to get some water." She practically sprang to her feet to get one of the water bottles stacked on the kitchen counter, cracking it open and drinking it down between choking coughs.

Finally under control, she took a few more swallows of the water, then returned to the living room. Dance had taken a glass of wine but was drinking it far more slowly. A good idea, she thought ruefully, as she seated herself beside him once more. She topped off her glass and took a deep breath. She'd basically promised to tell him all about her father and her past, and she planned to, she really did . . . she just wasn't sure what depth she wanted to go into.

He was waiting for her, and that annoyed her.

"There are about a million things I'd rather talk about

than my history with my father," she said testily. "I'd rather talk about the Saldanos, or the unidentified body with the branding, or the missing Fread girl, or pretty much anything else."

"Fine," Dance said, and she squinted at him, wondering if he was just humoring her.

"Okay, well, I'm planning to go over to Malone tomorrow and check with the ME. Find out what I can about that body. And I might go to the Green Pastures Church and ask Reverend Miles about Bernadette Fread's relationship with her father, even though Chief Markum would rather cut out my tongue than have me interfere in any way with the good people of the church."

"What did you mean, everyone's afraid you're just like your mother?" he asked when she wound down.

She clenched her teeth and half-smiled. "The Treadwell Curse. She had it, and maybe I have it, too."

"And what's that?" he asked carefully.

Jordanna took another gulp of wine and said, "My mother died of an unknown form of dementia that seems to run in her family, the Treadwells. It manifested when she was in her twenties and she died about ten years later. She had a number of relatives likewise afflicted. It's sort of like Huntington's without being Huntington's. No cure. The victim slowly loses their mental capacity and the body shuts down and then they die. . . . That's the Treadwell Curse. Fortunately, it only has affected a small part of the population, so far. Pretty well contained around here. Unfortunately, that means there hasn't been a lot of testing on it. It's genetic, that's all we know for certain.

"When I shot my father, a lot of people around town thought it was a first sign. I swear Chief Markum wanted to lock me up, but my father stepped in. They settled instead for sending me to a psychologist, Dr. Eggers."

Dance stared into his wineglass. He was listening hard, so she decided to get it all out.

"So far, my sister, Kara, and I seem fine, but there's no telling when that shoe will drop. It could happen anytime, or not at all. My Aunt Evelyn escaped it."

"Who else has it?"

Jordanna considered, then said, "Well, no one, really. We're the last of the Treadwells, so I guess it ends with us. There were some Benchleys that married Treadwells," she remembered.

"Would your dad know?"

Her lips tightened. "Probably."

"You should ask him. Get all the data you can. There might be something you don't know about it."

"Yes, yes . . ." The journalistic approach. Why did it make her feel so weary?

Because you don't want to know. You don't want it confirmed. Because if it's true, you're doomed.

She could feel tears burn at the back of her throat. She'd just told him her big secret, and it was a thousand times worse because it had effectively slammed, bolted, and sealed the door shut on anything lasting between them. Sure, he didn't think of her that way. She understood that. But she'd allowed herself to dream, and now that dream was dust.

"I don't visit Rock Springs all that often," she said unevenly. "My mother's gone, and so's Emily. My other sister's a vagabond, although she did say she would be in the area this weekend—I assume that means Portland—and I don't get along with my father for all the reasons I've just named."

"You brought me here," he pointed out quietly.

She shivered. He was being understanding and that made things a thousand times worse. "I knew the house was empty. I didn't know it was in such bad shape, though." She looked around. "Anyway, now you know," she added lightly.

"You mind a few questions?" he asked.

She laughed silently. "Fire away."

"You said your sister died in a car accident?"

"On Summit Ridge Road, the switchback road that leads to Fool's Falls. You can access it by driving farther south from here on Wilhoit about three or four miles. It leads into the mountains and cuts close to the back of our property."

"Did you think your sister was exhibiting signs of this disease?"

"Emily? No. She was a sleepwalker, but she . . . wasn't sick. She was beautiful. Everyone liked her." Recalling Kara saying Emily was a "ho," she added for honesty's sake, "I think she had a few boyfriends, and there might have been some jealousy from other girls."

"Mind if I play devil's advocate for a minute?" He'd shifted position and she could see his jaw tighten.

"Okay . . ." she said carefully.

"You said your sister was a sleepwalker."

"Yes. She walked into my father's room without realizing it."

"Did she blame your father?"

"No. She was angry with me for accusing him. And for shooting at him," she admitted. "She was right on that, of course. I was reckless, and it was . . . out of control. The big reason people think I have the Treadwell Curse."

"Is there any chance she was telling the truth?"

Another knife to the gut. Jordanna looked away. Why did she keep believing someone would actually hear her, for once? "She called out my father's name when I walked in on them. Screamed it. *Dayton!* She was horrified by what was happening." Something about that bothered Jordanna, just like it always did, some little kernel digging at her brain, but it slipped away before she could figure out what it was.

"She blamed the whole thing on sleepwalking," he repeated.

"That's right."

"And everyone blamed you because you were a Treadwell and Treadwells are crazy."

"Right again," she said bitterly.

"What do you think now?" he asked.

"What do you mean?"

"If it happened the same way, would you do it again? Would you shoot him?"

"Of course not!"

"Why not?"

"Because it was a big mistake. I shouldn't have done it. I should have reported him. I could have hit my sister!"

Jordanna drained her glass of wine and Dance took a long swallow, too. "Well, that sounds pretty sane to me," he pointed out. "Whatever you think about your father, you were a kid and you reacted in the moment. You'd lost your mother and you thought your father was doing something terrible to your family. You wanted to protect your sister."

Jordanna stared at him. It was the first time anyone had ever defended her.

"And I don't know how much I believe in this Treadwell Curse," he added. "Maybe there's a rogue gene . . . something. What I would do if I were you, I'd research the hell out of it, find out every last detail. Don't accept ideas and impressions from a terrible accident to color the truth." His lips quirked. "I'm not telling you anything you don't already know."

Jordanna could scarcely breathe. She felt giddy with relief, in some weird way. She also felt like she should say something. *Thank you*, at the very least, but she was completely bereft of words. She leaned forward and kissed him on the mouth.

She shocked herself and would have pulled back, but his lips pressed back against hers, hot and fierce, at the same moment he slipped a hand around the back of her neck. She could feel his tension, or maybe it was her own. Neither of them moved for a moment. Maybe he was as surprised as she was. Then he slipped his tongue into her mouth, and her body responded as if ignited. She wanted to drag him to her, fall down on the couch and pull him atop her. She might have done just that if she hadn't heard his intake of breath as he shifted position.

His leg . . . his injury . . .

Her eyes fluttered open. He was kissing her throat, not backing off, but she knew they were teetering on a delicate balance. Nothing could happen that wouldn't hurt like hell for him. And well, nothing could happen if she wanted to keep some kind of sane level of existence between them.

"I didn't mean to . . . start this," she gasped.

"You want to quit?"

She paused. "No . . ."

His tongue drew hot circles on the skin beneath her left ear. She was leaning back and he was half atop her. If it weren't for his leg, they would be lying down flat on the couch. A part of her yearned for that so much that she tentatively shifted position.

For a moment she thought he was going to go ahead, whether it pained him or not. But then he simply buried his face in her neck and inhaled deeply, slowly expelling his breath on a hard sigh . . . and silent laughter.

She didn't know what to make of that as he slowly shifted back into a sitting position. Jordanna did the same. His hair had fallen over his forehead and he pushed it back and regarded her ruefully. "I'd like to keep going. I really would."

Her own mouth slowly curved into a smile. "The situation isn't ideal."

"I could go there." There was a challenge in his tone. He was leaving the decision to her.

She was aware how sensitive she felt in her nether regions. Good God. She ached to kiss him, hold him, make love to him. "Maybe we should wait until . . . you're better?"

"Don't look at me that way," he warned.

"Where's that wine bottle?" she expelled.

He reached for it and refilled her glass and his own. "So?" he asked huskily, looking at her intently.

The room had grown dark and only the light from the kitchen threw illumination on them, a square of soft yellow that darkened the planes of his face. She was living her fantasy and it felt dangerous.

"We wait," she said reluctantly.

He drank heavily from his glass. "Okay." Then she saw him sober and he said, "I've wanted to tell you something for a while. I know the Saldanos are dirty, at least some of them. There's smuggling involved. Drugs, maybe. Stolen artifacts? I don't know exactly what, but I have some proof, an audiotape. I don't know which members of the family it implicates."

"You didn't tell me," she said, knowing as she spoke the words that it was because he barely knew her, didn't trust her.

"After I see your father tomorrow, I'll know more about when I can physically face them again. You want to help, you're in."

But he trusted her now, even after everything she'd revealed. "I'm in," she told him, happier than she'd been in a long while.

Chapter Fourteen

On Saturday morning, Auggie met with Agents Bethwick and Donley at a café in downtown Portland near the station. When cases were hot, he worked them all hours. He had no gripe with meeting the two FBI agents, but it was going to be on his terms. They wanted to hash over the case, pick his brain, and that was all fine and good, but he didn't feel like telling them everything. He'd known too many good cops who'd been run over by the feds. He didn't plan on that happening to him.

Bethwick started, taking him through his investigation so far, but offering nothing in return about what they'd learned from the Saldanos. This was no two-way street, but Auggie meant to appear more cooperative than he was. Bethwick was tough and bullying, a bad-cop persona, while Donley tended to step in and smooth over rough spots. Auggie told him his own impressions about Max and Victor Saldano, but kept information about Carmen to himself. As if she were aware of what he was doing, he got a call on his cell from an unidentified number, which he decided to answer as a matter of course to give himself a break from the two agents, only to realize it was Carmen herself. When that happened, he cut the phone conversation short in a hurry, hoping they didn't pick up on the identity of the caller. Luckily, they were more interested in him getting off the phone so that they could ask more questions. He hung up and let them go on awhile until their questions ran in circles, then he made it clear he was tapped out of information.

The two of them reluctantly left him at the café, where he drank black coffee and pretended to peruse a newspaper until they were out of sight. Then he pulled out his cell phone again and looked at Carmen Danziger's number.

A moment later he was out of the café and heading for his Jeep, which he noted could use a wash, the color more light gray than dark beneath the road dust. He climbed behind the wheel, then pulled from his pocket the piece of paper on which he'd jotted down Jordanna Winters's information. Before he talked to Carmen, he wanted to know everything he could about Jordanna. He'd driven into her apartment complex the day before, knocked on her door, but no one had answered. He'd also put in a call to her cell, but when it had gone to voice mail, he'd hung up without leaving a message. He didn't want to give away that he was looking for her unless he had to.

Now he drove back to her apartment complex, but her place seemed just as deserted as it had the day before. Back in the Jeep, he placed a call to Diane, one of the data researchers at the department. "Diane," he said congenially when she answered. "I wondered if you could look something up for me."

"Of course you do." Diane was a smoker and her voice was dry and raspy from years of the habit. Middle-aged, gray-haired, and thin as a reed, she had that "seen it all" attitude like so many other long-term members of the force.

"Some history on a Jordanna Winters. Twenty-six. Freelance reporter. Lives in an apartment on Beverly Drive in Laurelton."

"You want to be her Facebook friend, or something?"

"That would be cool," he said, ignoring her sarcasm. She was a good researcher but there was always a price to pay, as she felt underpaid and overused. "I want to know where she comes from. Anything about her. If you find some intersection with Jay Danziger, also a reporter, mainly for *The Oregonian*, all the better."

"I know Danziger," she said, then, "I'll see what I can do."

"Thanks."

He hung up, drumming his fingers on the steering wheel. He wanted Diane to phone right back, but since this wasn't an emergency, that was supremely unlikely. Biting the bullet, he called Carmen Danziger back, but this time her phone went to voice mail, so he left his name and told her he'd be on his cell. Then, with time on his hands, he aimed the Jeep in the direction of the house he shared with Liv Dugan. Thinking of her, he smiled. Nine was right. Though he could appreciate Carmen Danziger's smoldering sensuality, there was no woman like Liv.

Jordanna drove Dance to her father's clinic and felt herself tighten up more and more as she neared it. She pulled up in front of the gray batten-and-board building with its overhanging porch and split rail fence. It was a block and a half off the main street, but it was clearly constructed with the same architectural design in mind. Western, western, western, and Victorian. Rock Springs had a purposeful quaintness about it that she'd never really appreciated. As she cut the engine, she said, "When I lived here, this clinic was cinder block, like City Hall."

"This is an improvement," Dance said.

"A small one." As he shouldered open the passenger door, she asked, "You want some help?"

"No. Thanks." He wrangled the crutches, sticking them under his arms as he climbed from the RAV.

They'd been very careful with each other since the kiss the night before. Though she'd been happy that he'd admitted the Saldanos weren't the upstanding citizens he'd pretended they were, and that she could help him in his investigation, her brain kept going back to the kiss, and the feel of his hard body pressed to hers, the way her hands had rested on the hard muscles of his arms.

I could go there. . . .

Her heart lurched at the memory. She slammed the driver's door and hurried ahead of him to the clinic's front door, pushing it open to reveal a waiting room with gray carpet and wooden chairs whose cushions were needlepoint depictions of rodeo riders.

"I'm going to run over to the Green Pastures Church and see if I can find the reverend," she said. "If you get done sooner than I think you will, call me from the clinic phone."

"Be careful," he said, and the words seemed ripped out of him as he levered himself into one of the chairs.

It did her heart good to know that he worried for her. "They're churchgoers. I'm not walking alone down a deserted street at two A.M."

"Even a rabbit'll bite you if you corner it." His hair had flopped forward again, giving him an unkempt, rakish air that thrummed something deep inside her.

"You sound like you aren't sure about Green Pastures, either. And I'm not cornering anyone." She drove north out of town a little faster than the speed limit allowed, and after nearly missing a turn, she eased off the accelerator. The road she was driving would take her to Green Pastures Church and beyond. It was the main access to Malone, edging east past Everhardt Cemetery, where both her mother and sister were buried, and then on past the expansive Calverson Ranch with the high, white entry arch at the ranch entrance that bore its name, before dancing through the lower foothills on its way to Rock Springs's sister city of about the same size.

The sign for Green Pastures Church, and a distant steeple she could see over rolling fields of spring green grass, appeared on her left at the same moment her cell phone rang. She slowed to make the turn into the long drive with its painted white fence, reaching a hand into her purse to blindly search for her phone. Getting a grip on it, she gave it a quick glance, half-expecting another strange number, and was a bit shocked to see Kara's name appear. *Screw the rules.* She held the phone to her ear as she continued down the wide asphalt drive that meandered over a slow rise. "Kara," she greeted her sister, smiling.

"I'm at your apartment. Where are you?" her sister asked.

"Umm . . . not home."

"Well, get back. I'm only going to be around for a little while and I still have to go out to Rock Springs to see Dad. Don't be mad," she added quickly. "It's what I do."

"I know," Jordanna said. "It's just that . . . I'm out of town."

"You are? You knew I was coming this weekend." Kara sounded perturbed.

It was so like her sister to blow in and expect everyone to drop everything to be with her. "I sort of knew," she defended herself. "Your plans aren't always rock solid."

"Well, are you coming back? Soon, I mean?"

"Not till next week, I think."

"Jesus, Jordanna."

The asphalt drive looped over the hill and around the side of the church, ending in a parking lot at the back of the building sprinkled with a number of cars. Jordanna weighed whether she wanted Kara to know where she was, but since Dance was already at the clinic, it wasn't like they were staying deeply under the radar. "Kara, you won't believe this, but I'm actually in Rock Springs already."

"*What?* You're kidding. Why? You didn't even go to the wedding!"

If one more person brought that up, Jordanna was pretty sure she would just lose it. "I'm staying at the homestead . . . with a friend. It's a long story."

"Does Dad know?"

"Yes, Dad knows. And my friend's been injured and he's actually at Dad's clinic right now."

"*He?*" she breathed, scandalized. "Dad knows you're staying with a man? He's generally so . . . particular about that kind of thing, y'know."

"Oh, because he's a member of Green Pastures Church? The epitome of propriety?" Jordanna asked coolly.

"Dad's not the bastard you think he is. You have all that stuff about Emily screwed up in your head, but I'm not going to argue about this again," Kara said, sounding weary.

"I'm the last person who wants to go into it again," Jordanna returned.

"Yeah, but you're there. In Rock Springs. Wow. I'll just come that way earlier. I can be there in a few hours, and I'll come straight to the homestead."

"The less people who know about my friend, the better," Jordanna said, feeling a stab of remorse. "So, don't say anything to anyone."

"Who would I say something to?" Kara was faintly amused. "Jordanna, Jordanna . . . you're more like Emily than I thought."

"Huh." Jordanna wasn't certain what to make of Kara's implications. Nothing good.

"I'll see you soon. I'm glad you've talked to Dad."

"Yeah . . ."

She hung up, stepped from the RAV, then bent her head against a sudden wind that slapped her across the face with a wallop of rain. Hurrying, she ran along a pathway that led to the front steps, glad for the shelter of the building. Late May and the weather was turning wet and wild.

Clattering up the front steps, she caught her breath beneath the sharply pitched roof of the porch, staring out across those rolling fields as sweeps of wind-driven rain ran as if being chased.

Shaking her arms to get the water off her black jacket, she let herself inside the church and looked down the rows of empty pews to the grand stage at the far end. A man stood in the center, hands clasped and head bowed in prayer. Then he looked up and stared toward the ceiling, where skylights on either side of a huge wooden cross were streaked with rain. If not for the illumination from the globe lights that hung from overhead crossbeams, the church would have been in darkness.

As if sensing her presence, the man lowered his gaze and looked her way, his gray hair glinting under the lights.

Jordanna guessed that she'd found Reverend Miles.

She headed down the center aisle and he waited for her silently. There was something about being in the church that made her wish she'd brought something to Rock Springs besides jeans. Luckily, the reverend wore casual tan pants and a dark blue sweater over a collared shirt, so her damp black jacket, denim pants, and boots weren't that far off the mark.

"Good morning," he said to her with a friendly smile. "The prayer group doesn't meet till eleven."

"I'm not here for the prayer group. You're Reverend Miles?" she asked, to which he nodded, a bit of puzzlement showing in his dark brown, nearly black, eyes. "I'm Jordanna Winters, Dayton's middle daughter."

His brows lifted a bit. "The reporter?"

"Yee . . . ess." It took her aback a bit to know that he knew that much about her. "I wanted to ask about one of your parishioners, Bernadette Fread. Chief Greer Markum said she was missing and we discussed the possibility that she ran away because of abuse."

Jordanna purposely made it sound like she and the chief were working together. The reverend blinked rapidly several times. "Are you a friend of Bernadette's?"

"I'm on the investigation end," she said. She didn't think it would be to her benefit to say she was a reporter, so she left that part out.

"If you're truly working with Chief Markum, you know that she did not run away from abuse."

Jordanna felt heat rise in her face at being caught in a lie.

But the reverend went on anyway. "Abel's very worried about the choices she's making, but he loves his daughter and she loves him, and that is not the reason she's gone. We're all very concerned she's missing. I'm very glad you're looking for her. It's been over a week, and there's too much apathy. Everyone blaming the family when they should be looking elsewhere. The Freads are good people . . . God's people."

"The chief knows that," she said, hastily. "He's committed to learning the truth and that means following up every rumor."

"And there have been a number," the reverend allowed. "I understand Chase Sazlow is missing as well."

"Bernadette's boyfriend?" Jordanna was surprised. "I didn't know that," she admitted.

"Abel believes they've run off together, and maybe they have. He's worried about Chase's influence on Bernadette. Chase has almost determinedly taken the wrong path all his life. He's deaf to the Lord. One of those rumors is he's cast a spell over Bernadette, which is untrue. No one on earth has that power."

Well, there were casting spells and casting spells. Love, and lust, and revenge were strong emotions that made people sometimes act irrationally, like maybe they were under a spell.

Jordanna nodded gravely. She supposed she should feel bad about lying to the reverend, or at least skipping around the truth, but she wasn't sure yet what she thought of Green Pastures and Reverend Miles. There was something smug there she couldn't put her finger on. Or, maybe that was just her own warped perception when it came to the do-gooders of Rock Springs.

The reverend turned on his benevolent charm. "How are you, my dear? I know of your family troubles with your father."

"I'm okay."

"Dayton's a good man. He took care of your mother, and your sister."

Jordanna almost said, "No, he didn't," but instead she simply nodded and let it go. She thought about asking him about the unidentified body that had been branded, but was afraid she would give away the fact that she was running in the dark. Also, there'd been no mention of Green Pastures connected to that victim.

She left a few minutes later, after assuring the reverend she would say hello to her father for him. Like that was going to happen. Checking the time on her cell phone, she drove back into Rock Springs proper through a light rain, the wind having died down while she was in the church. There wasn't enough time to go to Malone, so she returned to the clinic, waiting outside a while, expecting Dance to call any second. When the phone remained stubbornly silent, she let herself back into the clinic, feeling impatient. The reception room was nearly empty except for a man about her own age slouched in a chair, his booted legs crossed in front of him, a cowboy hat resting low on his head. He had deep-set eyes that seemed to follow her every movement, but then he brought the brim down lower, obscuring his face and leaning back in the chair as if to take a nap. She wished like hell she could feel that relaxed in a doctor's office.

Jordanna walked up to the receptionist, who was young and perky and wore a blue blouse with a bolo. The girl lifted her brows and smiled at Jordanna.

"I dropped someone off here earlier," she said softly, trying not to be overheard. "Mr. Danziger?"

"He's still in the back with Dr. Winters, but I'm sure they'll be finished soon."

"Could you check on that?"

"Sure."

She got to her feet and disappeared through a doorway that led to a corridor beyond. Jordanna thought she heard Dance's deep voice, and then her father's clipped tones. The idea of them together made her feel tense and uncomfortable. Then she heard a familiar female voice chime in and she groaned. Jennie.

Jordanna had just taken a seat when Jennie burst through the door and glanced around the room, her gaze freezing on Jordanna. "Hiking, huh," she said in a tsk-tsk voice. "Come on back. Your father's just finishing up with your *friend*. . . ." She added just enough emphasis on the last word to make it sound like she was in some kind of dirty relationship with Dance.

As Jordanna got to her feet, Jennie went on, "Please come by the house, Jordanna. Bring Mr. Danziger. I didn't realize he was that reporter for the newspaper. He should be on TV. He's so handsome!"

"Yes, well . . ." Dance's whereabouts would hit the Rock Springs grapevine with the speed of light, now that Jennie knew. "I don't think he wants his whereabouts advertised."

"Of course not." Jennie smiled at Jordanna as if they were coconspirators as she turned and led Jordanna into the inner sanctum and down the hallway. "Don't worry. Your father doesn't expect you to be married. He knows we're a little old-fashioned in Rock Springs."

"It's not like that between us. There are reasons Dance doesn't want to advertise his whereabouts, but it's not because of me."

"Well, I just wanted to say your father understands."

Oh, sure.

Jennie showed her to a room where Dance was seated on a chair, a new, snowy bandage surrounding his left thigh. Her father was in the room, wearing his white coat, his arms crossed over his chest, looking for all the world as if he were proud of the new bandage when Jordanna knew it had been applied by one of the nurses, maybe even Jennie. She hovered outside the doorway. She just wanted to get the hell out.

"How're we doing?" she asked.

Her father answered before Dance could speak. "Good. The leg's healing nicely." He flicked her a look, his eyes seeming to search her own. "Jay says you plan to stay a few more days."

Jay seemed awfully friendly, and yet, what was her father supposed to call him? Mr. Danziger? At least he hadn't said "Dance."

Dance got to his feet and tested his left leg, carefully putting his weight on it. He managed to stand without aid, though his jaw was tight. Jennie hurried to hand him the crutches, which he tucked under his arms. He held out a hand to her father and said, "Thank you," as they shook hands.

"The invitation's still open to come stay with us," her father said. "The homestead's pretty rustic. We have a couple of spare rooms."

Jordanna's stomach clenched. "No. Thank you."

"You have to come for dinner," Jennie urged. "You know that Kara's coming? She called your father this morning."

"We wish we could," Dance rescued Jordanna, who was beginning to feel trapped. "But like I said, we've got a lot of work ahead of us. I do really appreciate you letting us stay on."

Her father actually clapped him on the shoulder, and Jordanna had to turn away, walking ahead of them back down the hall. When she entered the reception room, she nearly ran into a woman pushing a stroller, her right arm in a sling.

"Sorry," Jordanna murmured. The cowboy was gone, apparently ushered into an examination room. The woman gave her a tight smile.

When she and Dance were finally outside, climbing into either side of the RAV, she said, "So, you're mending okay?"

"Wish it were faster." He slid the crutches into the backseat and moved carefully into the front. "Pain's diminishing. Your father . . . did a good job."

"Did Jennie wrap you up? That's not my father's job."

"Yeah. Jennie's your stepmother?"

"Yessirree."

"Your sister visit them regularly?"

"Irregularly. I don't really know what their relationship is." Her voice was clipped because she was feeling betrayed. She could tell Dance thought her father was an upstanding citizen, like everyone else. It was in the careful tone of his voice, as if he was afraid of admitting his feelings. Who knew what crazy Jordanna Winters would do next?

"I put my phone back together," he admitted.

"You think that's wise?" Immediately she forgot her family issues, her heart jolting as she thought about the Saldanos.

"Yeah, well, it's out of battery and I don't have a charger with me. I wonder if it would be easier to get a burner in this town," he said, meaning a disposable phone.

"You want to go back now?" she asked reluctantly.

"Still thinking it through. Besides, you've got a few things you're working on here, and I want to help, if I can."

"Sure." Jordanna was relieved. After their closeness the night before, she'd told him about her conversations with Chief Markum, Rusty Long, Pru and Nate Calverson, and Todd Douglas, rattling like a magpie whether he wanted to hear it or not, seeking to smooth over the awkwardness she'd been sure would follow.

"Did you talk to the reverend at Green Pastures?"

"Reverend Miles. Yes, I did." She quickly recapped what had been said, and he listened attentively. She finished with, "I'm planning to go to Malone and talk to the ME about the unidentified body, and I'd like to find out where Chase Sazlow's family lives, maybe talk to them, too."

"You want to go now?" he asked.

"Well, it's Saturday. There's a good chance he won't be there. Depends on what kind of hours he keeps. His name's Dean Ferguson," she added.

"Let's try calling him."

"My phone's in my purse," she told him, and he reached around the back of the seat, grabbed the purse, and brought it to his lap. Plucking out her phone, he looked at her questioningly.

"Have at it," she told him.

Chapter Fifteen

The last part of the highway from Rock Springs to Malone rambled through clusters of farms and ranches, the green fields dotted by rambling farmhouses, silos standing like sentinels, and barns in all states of repair, some bright with brick-red paint and white trim, others graying and listing. The city of Malone itself was a hodgepodge of architecture, some buildings sporting the western style prevalent in Rock Springs, others composed of brick in a variety of shades from tan to carmine, still others built of cinder block and faced with stone. Whereas Rock Springs had one main street, Malone sat on a crossroads whose central businesses were thick with SPACE FOR RENT signs, the main commerce moving from the center of town out each spoke of the road to clusters of strip malls and newer buildings. As Jordanna and Dance approached the town, they passed a car wash, a Jiffy Lube, a Taco Time, and a feed store.

Jordanna's cell rang, and Dance picked it up as she asked, "Would you grab that?" He read the number to her, the same one she hadn't answered earlier. "I don't know who that is," she said.

"You want me to answer?"

"No."

Dance had called the county medical examiner's office and had learned that Dr. Dean Ferguson was indeed the ME on duty that day, which made Jordanna think their trip to Malone was meant to be. Her enthusiasm was dampened a little when Dance had been told Dr. Ferguson would be given his message, but never received a call back.

The county offices were located a half mile out of town, on the road that led north and would eventually lead to Portland. It was a rabbit warren of tan brick, a cluster of buildings that housed the medical examiner's offices, the county jail, and various and sundry government offices. Jordanna waited for Dance to get his crutches in place before she began walking to the front door. She opened it wide and he entered first, though chivalry had him stopping for a moment. "Get over it," she told him on a short laugh, at which he snorted in annoyance.

They were told Dr. Ferguson's offices were in the basement, and the woman manning the phones called but got no answer. A bit reluctantly, she indicated the elevator and Jordanna punched the button for the basement. The doors opened into a linoleum hallway with green walls, and they had to work their way to the office tucked behind a large lab with stainless steel counters, sinks, several large scales, and officious, medieval-looking tools.

When Jordanna knocked on the door, the doctor suddenly opened it as if he'd been standing directly behind it.

"Dr. Ferguson?" she asked. "I'm Jordanna Winters and this is Jay Danziger."

The doctor wore wire-rimmed glasses and he swung his sharp gaze from Jordanna to Dance. "Danziger . . ." he repeated slowly, clearly trying to place why the name sounded familiar.

"I'm a journalist," Dance said.

"Ahhhhh . . ." Ferguson's expression darkened, and for a

moment Jordanna wondered if he was going to throw them out. In the end, he signaled them inside with a curt wave. There was an awkward moment when the doctor didn't know whether to help Dance to a chair, but Dance took care of it with, "I got this," and managed to pull out a chair and seat himself. Jordanna sat next to him while Ferguson walked around the desk and dropped himself into his desk chair with a huge sigh.

"What can I help you with?" he asked, spreading his hands. His long, lined face had a hangdog look that seemed to go well with his job.

The doctor seemed to direct his question at Dance, but Jordanna explained that she'd lived in the area and wanted to know about the branded victim who was found near the Treadwell/Winters property. Ferguson nodded almost immediately. "I remember that one well. Never was identified. Maybe your story will help with that," he said to Dance in a tone that suggested he had little hope for that. "What do you want to know?"

"Everyone I spoke to referred to him as 'homeless,' like it was an understood thing," Jordanna said. "Can you explain that?"

"No. But people around the area always expect to know everybody. Rock Springs is a small community. So's Malone. Someone almost always knows somebody. I'd venture since the body went unclaimed, he was described as homeless. He may well have a home, but it's apparently not around here," he added with a quick grimace that Jordanna thought might have been his version of a smile. To Dance, he said, "You usually write about political and corporate scandals and such." He gazed at Dance's injury and the light clicked on. "There was a bombing at that warehouse. . . ."

"And I was there," Dance said, finishing the thought.

"Is that why you're asking about our John Doe?" he asked.

"Totally unrelated," Dance said.

"Huh," he said, as if he couldn't quite believe him.

Jordanna said, "The body was found on government land by a nine-year-old boy, Zach Benchley."

"He was on an ATV and practically ran over the body. A nine-year-old on a motorized vehicle. People should be more careful." He shook his head. "Victim died of hypothermia. It was January and it was cold. He was found on the east side of Summit Ridge Road, next to the Benchley property. The kid's father was there when we were loading up the body. He stared pretty hard at the victim, but said he didn't recognize him."

"What about the branding mark?" Jordanna asked, making mental notes.

"On his right buttock. Looked like an upside-down cross."

Dance's attention sharpened. "A religious symbol?"

The doctor grimaced again, only this time it looked like a real grimace. "Coulda been, I suppose."

"You have a picture?" Dance pressed.

He inhaled and exhaled heavily. "That would be in the police report. You're going to need to talk to Chief Markum about anything further," he said, almost apologetically. "I'm all for helping close out this case, but it's still active. Talk to the chief."

"Still active, my ass," Jordanna muttered a few minutes later after Ferguson had said his good-byes and closed his door behind them.

"Maybe Markum's ready for some help," Dance said as they worked their way down the hall back toward the elevators.

"I've blown any small chance I had with him. He went apoplectic when I asked about Bernadette Fread."

"He's a friend of your father's. Maybe Dayton could talk to him."

Jordanna didn't respond until they were outside. The rain had stopped, but there was a surprisingly cold, kicky little wind whipping around. It tugged at the hair Jordanna had pulled into a ponytail. "My father wouldn't help me. You know that."

"Maybe he would."

"No. He only wants to absolve himself, and I don't want to play that game." She stalked ahead of him to the car and climbed inside, waiting as he levered himself into the passenger seat.

"You don't know that," Dance said reasonably.

"Oh, but I do. I've been living this life a lot longer than you've been involved with it."

"You're a reporter on a story." He looked at her, as if daring her to argue with him.

"What?" she demanded, though she knew where he was going and it was already pissing her off.

"So, use all your sources. Your father's a friend of Chief Markum's, ask for his help."

"You really don't get it." It killed her that she'd poured out her heart, and now he acted like she should just get the hell over it.

"I get that you think your father sexually abused your sister, and that you reacted violently, whether you meant to or not. I also get that you were a teenager who'd just lost her mother. You may be right about your father. I don't know. But from what you've said, you want to do serious in-depth reporting, and if so, you gotta do the hard work."

She peeled out of the parking lot with a chirp of tires. "Sorry," she said shortly. She didn't want to be at the mercy of her emotions, but he was hitting her in her most vulnerable place, and the worst of it was, he was right.

"Call him up. Tell him what you're doing. You don't have to touch on the rest of it."

"You're not listening. Of course I have to touch on the rest of it. That's what he wants from me!"

"You want me to talk to him?"

"NO."

There was silence as several miles sped by under her tires. Finally, he said in a low, taut voice. "You told me how blind I was about the Saldanos. I denied it, over and over again, even though I knew you were right. I just didn't want to face it because Max is a good friend."

"This isn't the same as that, if that's where you're going," she said stubbornly.

"I had doubts. I just kept pushing them aside and look what happened." He spread his hands and looked down at his left thigh. The material of his sweats pulled tightly where the bandage was.

When she didn't respond, he asked, "What about you? Any doubts? Any at all, that what you saw was your father sexually abusing your sister?"

She wanted to shriek at him that he was wrong, wrong, wrong. But she also knew that those who screamed the loudest oftentimes had the weakest argument.

Could you be wrong? Could you?

"No doubts," she stated firmly.

"Even though your sister denied it. Told you she was sleepwalking, that she made a mistake."

"She was on top of him," she ground out.

"Doesn't that say more about her than your father?"

She slammed on the brakes and pulled over to the side of the road, perilously close to the large ditch that ran on either side of the two-lane highway. Dance met her gaze directly, unmoved by her erratic driving. "Just because you like my father doesn't mean you're right."

"No, it doesn't."

"You . . . don't know . . . anything." She was struggling for words, horrified that her nose was burning and she was close to tears. Swallowing, she put the SUV back in gear and eased out onto the road. Her chest was drum tight. She didn't want to breathe because she thought she might sob.

"I know that your mother died of a terrible disease and your father handled it badly. You saw your sister in a compromising position and you took aim, literally. I know that you might never get past it."

She threw him a hard look. Very slowly, she said, "Don't do this."

"Jordanna, if—"

"DON'T DO THIS. Maybe you're goddamn right. I don't care. You understand? I don't care."

Her cell rang again and she blasted, "Don't answer it," but Dance picked it up and looked at the screen. He turned it her way and she saw KARA. Snatching it from his hand, she clicked on. "Hey," she said in a tight voice.

"Where are you?"

"I'm coming back from Malone."

"Did you see Aunt Evelyn?"

That threw her for a moment. "No. It was something else." She hadn't thought once about her aunt, whom she hadn't seen since her mother's funeral.

"Well, I'm on my way. If you're not there, maybe I should stop and see Dad before coming to the homestead. By the way, how is the place? Livable?"

"Just," Jordanna answered by rote. Her whole being was concentrating on Dance.

"What are you doing in Malone, if you're not visiting Aunt Evelyn? Does it have something to do with your friend?"

"I'll tell you all about it when I see you. I've been looking into things."

"What things?"

"Kara," Jordanna started impatiently, then managed to

stop herself from snapping at her sister. "Just meet me at the house in about an hour or so."

"Okay. I'm going to grab some lunch. God knows, maybe I'll see someone I know around here." She half laughed.

"I've run into a few."

"Oh, yeah? Like who?"

"Martin Lourde, for one. The one you told me about, with Emily? Remember?"

"I'm not likely to forget. What was he like?"

"Not really as interesting as you might think." Jordanna was sorry she'd prolonged the conversation.

"Did you talk about Emily?" she asked curiously.

"A bit. He said he wasn't her boyfriend."

"I know he wasn't." Her voice faded out a little, as if she'd taken the phone away from her mouth. "He was just one of the guys she slept with. The boyfriend was someone else."

"You were only fourteen at the time. How would you know?"

"Because I watched, Jordanna. I followed her. She had this, like, secret life, and I wanted to know about it. The real boyfriend was the one who got her on the path to the Lord."

"Okay, fine. Who is that?"

"I don't know. I just caught a glimpse of him once. He was a big guy."

"They're all big guys around here."

Her attention seemed to be gone, too. "This town . . . it's weird how often you run into someone . . . oh, my God." She made a sound of disbelief. "It's him! HEY!" she suddenly called, and Jordanna could tell she was hailing someone else. "I'll see you later," she said in an aside into the phone.

"Who is it? What do you mean 'it's him'? Who?"

"The dude I was just talkin' about! Oh, my God . . . I'll catch up with you later." She hung up before Jordanna could ask any further questions.

"Your sister ran into someone in Rock Springs?" Dance asked, following her end of the conversation.

"Apparently." She shot him a glance. She'd found Kara's conversation disturbing and couldn't wait to ask her about it. "I don't want to talk about my dad anymore," she said. "Let's pick up some lunch and think about what to do next."

"Find the neighbor kid on the ATV who discovered the body."

Jordanna nodded. It was disconcerting the way he read her mind, but then they thought along the same lines. Another time that would have thrilled her, convinced her that she had what it took to reach his echelon of ability. Today, she just wanted to ignore him . . . because he was making too much sense.

He was coming out of the feed store, hauling bags of grain that he threw into the flatbed of his truck, when the girl called out to him. "HEY!" He looked around, not certain she meant him, but then she came up to him. Pretty gal. Vaguely familiar.

"I know you," she said, and her next words sent him spiraling into a dark past. "You're Emily's old boyfriend."

There was thunder inside his head.

"You're the guy she was seeing," she said in wonder. "I was just talking about you."

The sun came out from behind a cloud and hurt his eyes. Stabbed at him. A message. "Talking about me?"

"I don't know your name, but you're the guy. Who are you?" She was smiling, but it was a smile full of evil intent. "I'm Emily's sister, Kara."

"Kara," he repeated, and the sound vibrated through him, sending waves of panic and disgust. She was one of them. One of the Treadwell sisters. The reporter?

He must have said that aloud, because she answered,

"No, that's Jordanna, my other sister. She's in Rock Springs, too, now. That's who I was talking to. Jesus, it's like we conjured you up." Her grin widened and he thought he saw hot flames beating inside her throat. She'd used the name of the Lord's son in vain. He thought of the branding iron, cold now. But it could seethe with heat quickly.

He looked around. There was no one on the street. A moment in time when everyone was inside the stores. She was standing beside his truck. Her blouse was pale peach and thin, the wind pressing it against her breasts. He could feel his cock rise. Maybe he could have her first, like Emily. Just once. Maybe God would forgive him.

No.

Throat dry, he said, "I'm driving out to feed my horses. Emily loved to feed the horses."

"You have horses?" She sounded delighted. "I'd love to see them, if that's an invitation, but I gotta know your name first."

She was so fucking coy he wanted to slap her. Instead, he pulled his lips into a smile and racked his brain for an answer. It came to him so easily, it sounded perfectly natural when he drawled, "Some people call me Boo."

"Boo? Like, 'oh, my God, you scared me'?"

This time it was the Lord's name. His smile froze on his face. He bent his head, glad for the cowboy hat that obscured his expression. "That's right."

She looked around. "I got a little time to kill."

"You have a car?"

She nodded to a little gray compact next to the curb by Braxton's, some foreign piece of shit, he thought with a sneer.

"Follow me," he told her, then jumped behind the wheel and started the engine.

He watched her sashay across the road, swinging her hips like a mare in heat. He let his hand drift to his crotch and gave himself a few quick strokes through his jeans. *That's all*, he told himself. *That's all. She's Satan's daughter.*

He pulled into the road and kept an eye on her in his rearview. Part of him wanted her to just go away, drive off and disappear. Another part, the hungry part, silently begged her to turn that tin car around and follow after him. But if she did . . . if she did . . .

He thought about Bernie and swallowed hard. He'd managed to keep his cock out of her. He'd kept his mind strong, his mission pure. But he didn't think he'd be able to this time. Kara was too sassy and smart, too much like Emily.

He watched her pull a U-turn and start his way just as he hit the outskirts of town. His mouth was dry, his heart pounding. He wouldn't take her home. He would drive past his property and lead her into the hills, past the Fowler place, past her family's homestead. It was safer that way.

He slid a glance at the glove box. Inside were the drops. Just a couple would knock her out, and then he could administer the eternal sleep.

His inner sight envisioned her hips as she walked across the road. The rhythmic movement. When she was out . . . just before he sent her to a better place. Not heaven—she was too soiled for that—but a purgatory where she could keep away from the devil's clutches . . . Maybe then he could indulge himself, just a little. He wet his lips at the thought. A gift, for being a good soldier in the war against Satan.

No.

"Yes," he growled.

He just hoped Boo would stay inside. If he came out to the graveyard again, he was going to get thrashed. There was no other way to teach him.

He drove a long way, taking the back road that led into the hills, but she stayed right behind him. *She's not the reporter*, he reminded himself. *You need to get rid of Jordanna, the reporter.*

But first . . .

He turned onto the grassy track that led to the graveyard, afraid she might balk at the last moment, but no, she kept on coming. Her car was going to be a problem, but he could get rid of it. It was dense woods around the graveyard, and he could hide the car till dark and then just drive it off the cliff, like when he'd chased after Emily.

A half mile in, he came to a stop, popping open the glove box. He pulled out the bottle with the eyedropper, sucking up just enough liquid to do the trick. Palming the eyedropper, he climbed out of the truck and waited as she slowed to a stop. When she didn't get out of the car, he walked her way.

She rolled down the window. "This can't be your place," she said, frowning. "This is the back side of—"

"This is where I came with Emily," he cut her off.

"In high school?" Her tone said she was having serious second thoughts.

"Your house is just down thataway." He hooked a thumb to his right.

"I thought so. But where's your house? This can't be right." Her eyes swiveled that direction, and quick as a snake he snatched a hank of her hair and slammed her face into the steering wheel. She grunted, blood gushed from her nose and she started gasping and thrashing. Quickly he shoved the eyedropper to the back of her throat and thrust the plunger. She choked and shrieked, and he covered her mouth with his bare hand.

"Shut the fuck up, whore," he cooed softly to her, yanking open the door and dragging her from the car. She started howling as soon as he released her mouth, and he dragged her toward the graveyard, her heels digging into the ground.

But she was no match for him and he flung her down beside the mound that was Bernadette Fread. Immediately he threw himself on her, loving the way she squirmed and squealed beneath him, her movements making him groan with desire, his body pushing against hers until finally she grew quiet.

It took everything he had to keep from sliding into her warmth, feeling her close around him. But if he succumbed, it would be that much longer before he could ascend himself.

Pulling himself together, he stepped back from her. He couldn't leave her here just yet. There was work to be done to salvage what was left of her soul. He bent down and picked her up, hauling her over his shoulder. At his truck, he stowed her into the cab, stuffing her into the footwell as much as possible. He took a blanket from behind the seat and covered her up so she looked like an indiscriminate mound, then he climbed behind the wheel and backed around her car, mashing down grasses, and aimed back for the farm. At the barn he would give her a lethal dose and watch her slip away. Then he would sear her flesh and burn out the devil who was hiding beneath her skin.

Chapter Sixteen

Jordanna went inside the pharmacy again and ordered another two burgers from the grill counter. She looked over the menu but couldn't see anything she would rather have. Besides, she'd told him she was getting burgers, and by God that's what she was going to do.

It took ten minutes and she waited impatiently, not wanting to think about her conversation with Dance about her father, unable to think of anything else. As she walked away from the counter, bag in hand, she half expected to run into someone else she knew, but the only people she saw were strangers. The scent from the burgers made her mouth water.

Climbing back into the RAV, she plunked the bag into Dance's hands and said, "I've got the general idea where the body was found. All the properties off Summit Ridge are part of the old Homestead Act, three hundred and twenty acres, so there aren't that many doors to knock on to find the kid with the ATV."

"Big properties."

She nodded. "The housing tracts near town were put up in the forties, fifties, and sixties, but they're all to the north. The homesteads are south, and then Summit Ridge runs along the back side of about four farms, ours being one of them, and curves up to the falls before heading into the mountains."

"Small town with a lot of land around it," he observed. He lifted the bag. "Thanks for this."

"It was your money," she reminded him. They drove toward the homestead for a few miles, then she said, "About my father, you're right. I should talk to him. Maybe after Kara gets here, I'll give it a try."

He nodded noncommittally. Having said his piece, he apparently was letting her decide. Or maybe he realized he'd said enough to sway her and anything more might piss her off.

That thought made her smile, but then the smile faded. *Do you really remember what you saw that night with Emily? Or, is what you're recalling, what you believe you saw . . . maybe something you turned into fact, whether it is or not?*

Jordanna thought back to that moment when she'd walked in her parents' bedroom, trying to recall every detail of the scene she'd spent so many years trying to forget. What was foremost in her mind was Emily atop her father and the rifle in her own hand. She remembered lifting the gun as Emily looked back and started screaming, and her father sat up straight the millisecond before she fired.

He was damn lucky she was such a terrible shot or she might have killed him.

September yanked up weeds by the fistful in Jake's back-yard. She'd moved into his one-level rambler with him the previous fall, and though he called it their place, she still thought of it very much as his. Sinking back onto her sneakers, she squatted for a moment, reviewing her handiwork. But instead of dandelions and crabgrass, her vision was filled with pictures of Jay Danziger and Jordanna Winters

at the hospital, followed by the image of Carmen Danziger's
set face, and finally a completely fabricated scenario of
the elderly Phillip and Jan Singleton, glaring across a table
from each other, their food poisoned, each hating the other
one. She imagined the Singletons, married for more years
than either had found they wanted, their discontentment nur-
turing a dark, deadly seed that had finally burst open into
out-and-out hate. She'd didn't believe for one minute that the
Singletons had made a suicide pact, the way Fairy and Craig
had suggested. In her experience, it was much more likely
one of them killed the other first, then killed her or himself.

Marriage . . . She shook her head, kind of surprised at her
own dark thoughts.

She'd taken off her ring to do the yard work and now she
looked at her bare finger. Why was she having such a hard
time? It wasn't like her to mull over things too long. The
whole thing was making her half-crazy.

Jake appeared on the back porch. "It's gonna rain again,"
he warned. "Come in and have a glass of wine."

"It isn't five o'clock yet," she said, but she stood up and
picked up the gloves she'd stripped off.

"My family's in the wine business. There are no rules."
He was amused, his smile lazy.

For a moment, she just looked at him, her heart swelling
with emotion. "You know that I love you, right?"

"Yeeesss . . ." he said cautiously.

"We're engaged, and I want to marry you."

"Uh-huh."

"And you want to marry me. That's what we're doing."

"Where are we going with this?" he asked, gazing at
her hard.

"I don't know," she admitted, then rushed out, "I'm just
having a helluva time with the ring!"

"The ring?" He glanced down at her hand and saw it
wasn't on her finger.

"Don't ask me why. It's nuts. I'm nuts. The ring's beautiful. That's not it. I don't want a different one. But when people remark on it, I just want to rip it off and hide it. I'm probably the only woman in the galaxy that feels this way, but it seems like . . . I'm trying to prove something."

They stared at each other a moment; then Jake started to laugh.

"What's so funny?" she demanded.

"Not a damn thing. You don't want to wear the ring, don't wear it. I don't care, if that's all it is, and if it's something more, spit it out."

"No, that's it. I just feel like I'm flaunting it, or something. I know it's what everybody does, but it's not me."

"You still want to get married."

"Yes." She heard the note of uncertainty in her voice and cleared her throat. "Yes."

Jake's gaze narrowed. "You're lying."

"I want to get married," she said positively, walking up to him and slipping her arms around his waist. "I just don't want it to be the first thing somebody sees about me. The ring's like this invitation to talk wedding. And I don't like perps staring at it, either. I don't want them to know anything about me."

He pulled her close and dropped his chin to the top of her head. "Don't wear the ring, then."

"I want to be clear on this. I love you, and I want to marry you, and I kind of want it just to be between us . . . for a while. I don't want the spotlight on me. It drives me crazy every time Pauline Kirby wants to put me on television. She's been chasing me down about this Saldano bombing, even though I'm not anywhere on that case anymore. I just want to be anonymous. If that's a flaw in my character, so be it."

"I kind of like your flaws, among other things," he said, a smile in his voice.

She pulled back and looked up at him. "You're not upset."

"I don't give a damn about the ring. I just want to make sure that's all we're talking about."

"That's all we're talking about," she assured him, pulling his head down to kiss him. He gathered her close and they stumbled back into the house together. September started chuckling and Jake half carried her over to the couch, where they both sank down, still embracing.

She was lying on his chest and she leaned down and pressed her nose to his. "How about we skip the wine and go straight for dessert?"

"What kind of dessert would that be?"

She slipped her hands down his chest and around to the strong curve of his back. "Pineapple upside-down cake?"

He grinned. "Not sure what that means, but I'm all for it."

And then they were both laughing.

Jordanna expected Kara to be waiting for her at the homestead when they got there, but she was nowhere to be seen. "I thought Kara was stopping by here first," she mused, while she put their burgers on paper plates. Then she picked up her phone and placed a call to Kara's cell. After four rings, she was sent to voice mail, so she clicked off. "Maybe she went to my father's, first."

An hour and a half later, she phoned Kara again. This time the call went directly to voice mail. She was sitting on the couch beside Dance, and she tossed the phone on the bench she'd pulled over to use as a table again. They'd eaten their meal and had desultorily talked over the case. She knew he thought she should call her father and now, feeling frustrated, she gave in and grabbed up the cell phone again, scrolling to Jennie's number. After two rings, her stepmother answered in surprise, "Jordanna?"

"Hi, Jennie. I'm calling because I'm looking for Kara."

"She's not here yet, but I've got a place set for you, too, and your friend. Please come by. Your father's looking so forward to it!"

"Okay . . . well . . . I need to talk to Kara. If she shows up, will you have her call me?"

"Okay." She sounded a bit crestfallen, but Jordanna was trying to tamp down a low-grade worry.

"I think I'm going to have to skip dinner," Jordanna said, "but I'll call you again. And I want to talk to Dad, too."

"Oh? Good." Jennie instantly perked up.

"We'll talk later," Jordanna said hurriedly, hanging up. She didn't want Jennie thinking it was going to be any hug fest between them.

Dance asked, "Is it like Kara to go dark like this? Turn off her phone?"

"I don't know. I only see her occasionally. It's surprising we're all in Rock Springs at the same time."

Jordanna managed to wait around for another hour, walking the rooms like a caged lion, while Dance sat on the couch, his eyes closed in thought. Finally, Jordanna said, "I want to go find the kid on the ATV."

He said, "I may need a pain pill."

She quickly got him a pill and a glass of water. "You should have been taking these."

He nodded slowly. "I'd like to go with you."

"Stay here. I won't be long."

She put another text through to Kara, her third, and wished she'd paid more attention to what Kara had said on the phone. And had she really seen the guy she thought was Emily's boyfriend? Why did that chase chills along her spine?

Ten minutes later, she was in her RAV and heading south and then east toward the base of the mountains.

* * *

Todd Douglas liked to hike, and he preferred the rocky tors in the lower Cascades above and around Fool's Falls to the flattened foothills near his hometown of Malone. He'd chosen a Saturday hike, had packed his backpack with a cheese and roast beef sandwich and a water bottle, a first aid kit, a flashlight, and his cell phone. A half-day hike, he'd told himself, and had done just that, starting about 11 AM and ending up above the falls about four. He'd thought about God a lot during his trek. He was religious in a way that his cousin, Rusty, poked fun at, though he struggled with the super-duper religious nuts, the kind that tended toward Green Pastures Church, which he suspected wasn't even enough for the truly fanatical. No, Todd's idea of heaven was nature. In his mind, what lay beyond the Pearly Gates was clear mountain streams, sheer granite cliffs, and verdant foliage gilded by sunlight and refreshed with silvery rain. He would never admit to such thoughts, as Rusty would think there was something seriously wrong with him. If you weren't a carousing, drinking cowboy type with thoughts of screwing women, wrestling livestock, raising crops, and toting firearms, Rusty wasn't completely sure you were a man.

So, Todd didn't let on to his thoughts when it came to his spirituality, though today, even with the beauty of the mountains all around him, his mind had certainly run down a more carnal path. Jordanna Winters had stirred some too-long-dormant sexual interest in him. He'd been reviewing their conversations at the coffee shop and Braxton's counter grill over and over again, every word and every nuance. He understood that she hadn't been thinking about him that way at all, but that was okay. The hike today had cleared his mind, and he'd pretty much decided he was going to ask her on a date. He didn't have her cell number, but he knew she was at the house where she'd grown up, so he thought he might amble on by.

His mind was awash in these pleasant plans, his ears full of the rush of the falls, which tumbled and splashed down to the town below while he stood at the viewpoint parking lot above it, next to his truck. Because of the falls, he didn't hear the car until it was almost in sight, and only then did he turn, waiting for it to come around the hairpin bend where the parking lot sat. Instead, its engine wound down and became indistinguishable over the roar of the water, as if it had been shut off.

Wondering what had happened, Todd walked back around the curve, the late-afternoon sunlight warm on his back. Maybe he'd bring Jordanna to the top of the falls. She'd probably seen the view before many times, but it was still a breathtaking sight. Or, maybe he'd literally ask her to take a hike with him. She was bent on a story, but sometimes taking time off was a great way to gain perspective, charge up the old batteries.

Around the bend from Fool's Falls, Summit Ridge Drive rode a narrow ridge, the spine of a smaller mountain with deep cliffs on either side. It was a bitch to travel this route in the winter, but on a sunny day in May it was scenic, if a bit of a challenge for an inexperienced driver.

The car was a late-model sedan and it was stopped across both lanes, facing toward the edge of the cliff that looked over the ranch and farmland south of Rock Springs. Todd thought it might be aimed over the Sazlow Ranch. Immediately he jogged forward, concerned. "Put the brake on!" he yelled. "You don't want to go forward. You gotta get turned around!"

The driver's door opened slowly and the driver tumbled out onto the ground on the opposite side of the car from Todd.

"Hey, you okay?" he called, worried. He hurried around the rear of the vehicle, not trusting the front, and was surprised when the injured driver suddenly popped up.

"What?" Todd muttered. It was a man, and he suddenly came at him fast. "Whoa, whoa." He was wearing boots, jeans, and a cowboy hat dipped over his face. "What happen—" he got out just before the man's arm came up and smashed a large, jagged rock against Todd's temple. Todd's vision blurred and he went to his knees, crumpling like sand.

Then his backpack was yanked off his back and he was being dragged by his arms, picked up and set in the driver's seat. His head lolled backward. He tried to talk, but his brain couldn't send messages to his tongue. His mouth sagged open.

"Tell the Lord His work is being done," the man said, holding up the huge rock in a gloved hand, the same one he'd smacked against Todd's head, now covered with blood.

Todd wasn't sure, but thought he might have been crying when he said it. Todd thought, *I know you . . .* as the man tossed his backpack into the passenger seat and bent forward into the footwell. Todd heard the engine rev and dimly realized the man had placed the stone on the accelerator. Just as Todd's dulled brain registered he was in real trouble, the stranger reached across his body and shifted the car from park to drive. With a hard jerk the car leapt forward, spun gravel and then charged over the lip of the cliff, plunging downward.

Auggie said into his cell phone, "What did you say?"

Diane sighed dramatically. "I said Jordanna Winters grew up in Rock Springs. Her mother and older sister are deceased. I couldn't find an address for the younger sister, but her father, Dr. Dayton Winters, still resides in town, which is where he has a medical practice. You got it this time?"

"Yeah. Thanks," Auggie said distractedly as he clicked

off. He was staring across the kitchen at Liv, who was bent down, examining the interior of the refrigerator.

"We're going to have to go out," Liv said, her voice muffled as she directed her voice to the sad-looking carrots she'd pulled from the crisper.

"That was Diane. I asked her to dig into some information for me."

"On the Saldano case?" Liv glanced around at him.

She didn't sound like she particularly cared if he answered or not. She was just making conversation. But he answered her anyway. "The woman who left the hospital with Jay Danziger is from Rock Springs."

Now she turned fully and looked at him in surprise. "Really."

"Did you know the Winters family?" he asked.

Liv shook her head. "I think I remember a Dr. Winters, but we didn't go to him. Those were tough years for me."

"I know. Just wanted to ask."

It was as a result of Liv's past that Auggie had first met her. She'd lived in Rock Springs as a young child, but that very childhood held terrible memories for her.

"You think that's where they are?" she asked him now.

"Maybe." He looked at the time. "The feds have taken over, but I set up a meeting with Maxwell and Victor Saldano. Told 'em I had some information for them, which is a bit of a lie."

"Are you going to tell them about Jordanna Winters?"

"Gotta tell Bethwick and Donley first, and I'm not ready to do that, either. The feds," he explained to her questioning look. "Then maybe I'll go out to Rock Springs, nose around. The doctor still has his practice there."

"Hmmm. Okay." She turned back to the crisper and made a sound of disgust. "Never buy something 'in a bag' that you're not going to eat right away."

Auggie walked over to her and put his arms around her. She immediately straightened and turned toward him in surprise. On the counter beside her were papers concerning the real estate exam she was getting ready to take.

"What?" she asked, peering up at him, faintly smiling.

"I was thinking, maybe you want to go with me to Rock Springs?" His cell suddenly started singing its default tone, and he looked over to where he'd left it on the counter.

"Take it," she said.

He reluctantly let her slip out of his embrace as he scooped up the phone, recognizing the number with an inward groan. "Rafferty," he answered.

"Detective, I'm not waiting any longer," Carmen Danziger's cold tones reached his ear. "I've hired a private investigator to find my husband."

Ex-husband, he thought, but let it go. After their telephone tag this morning, Carmen had finally connected with him. The entire conversation had been Carmen firing questions at him that he either couldn't, or wasn't prepared to, answer. His lack of cooperation had infuriated her and she'd hung up in a rage. Now, he said, "Do what you gotta do."

"You people can't even do the job we pay you for," she huffed.

"I'm meeting with your father later," he started, but she cut the connection before he could finish.

"That was . . . ?" Liv asked, this time with more curiosity.

"Carmen Saldano Danziger." He headed back toward the room he used as an office, and the drawer where he kept his gun when he was home. Then he gave her a quick kiss and headed out.

Chapter Seventeen

Auggie's initial talk with Maxwell and Victor Saldano had netted very little information and generated a lot of fear and speculation. This time, when he was led into Victor Saldano's home, he was taking a different tack.

"I don't know why you're here," the patriarch of the family said peevishly. "We're dealing with those G-men. That's enough."

Maxwell Saldano was on his feet, moving around the room behind the wheelchair where his father sat. The first thing he'd asked Auggie was if he knew where Jay Danziger was. "Dance just let himself out of the hospital, and now no one can find him," he said, sounding more bewildered than angry.

"And who's this girl who spirited him away?" Victor demanded. "Carmen told us she pretended to be her."

Auggie said, "The last time we spoke, you believed the perpetrator who left the bomb was a business competitor."

"Sabotage," Max agreed. He'd stopped behind his father's chair, his hands on the handles as if he were getting ready to push the old man away. "Yes, that's what I thought. But who is this girl? Carmen's upset. He didn't tell her anything about where he was going."

"As I recall, you missed the meeting with Mr. Danziger because of a health crisis with your father," Auggie asked him.

Victor answered before Max could. "Heart 'event,' that's what they call it." He harrumphed.

"My father's nurse called me. Dad didn't want an ambulance, and I dropped everything and came back. The ambulance was here by then." He gave his father an exasperated look. "You should have just let them take you."

"No need," he barked.

"Yeah. I know," Max said.

Something in Max's tone suggested this scenario had happened enough times to inure him to his father's condition. "Could I talk to you a moment?" Auggie asked the younger Saldano.

"What don't you want me to hear?" Victor snapped, his face reddening.

"I'll talk to you alone next," Auggie assured him. Max hesitated only a second before leading Auggie out of the study that was now his father's bedroom into the circular entry hall.

"You think your father's exaggerating his condition," Auggie said, watching his face.

"He thinks it's real."

"You don't sound convinced."

"My father wants to come into the office every day. Lots of times he does. And if he feels left out, like we're not listening to him . . ." He compressed his lips a moment, then said, "He's had a few attacks during those times."

"Is he faking it, to get you to drop everything and attend to him?"

"I think he . . . misinterprets the seriousness of every event."

"You think he faked it when the bomb went off," Auggie persisted.

"That's not what I'm saying." Max shook his head.

"There was definite stress on his heart. Raydeen was right there and Dad was struggling. But he wouldn't get in the ambulance, and by the time I got there, the EMTs said he was stable, so . . ." He sighed. "Carmen was already gone, so I stayed with him until he'd calmed down."

"Your father now thinks the bomb was a warning from competitors who believed your company was eating into their profits."

"Maybe he's right. He's a complicated guy. Always planning something."

"Did he know that Danziger and your sister were divorced?" Auggie asked lightly.

Max blinked, started to smile, then asked, "Where'd you get that?"

"Public record."

"Oh, come on."

"You didn't know?"

"No," he ground out.

"Doesn't sound like your father knows, either. Sounds like your sister's deliberately kept that information from both of you."

Max, his eyes sober, his expression full of disbelief, said, "I don't believe you," but he did.

Auggie returned to Victor's room, but the older Saldano had been transferred to a hospital bed and Raydeen tried to keep Auggie from asking questions. Victor, however, had other ideas and waved Auggie to his bedside. "You're spending too much time with us, you and those federal agents, when you should be after the real bombers."

"The investigation is a top priority—"

"Don't give me that double-talk. You want to put it on us somehow. Well, I'm done talking to any of you. Better hope you have job security, son, because I'm calling your boss and ordering him to take you off this case. You should have been looking for Jay Danziger and that woman. It's too late now."

"Did you know your daughter and Jay Danziger are divorced?"

"Lies." He waved a hand and sank back as if exhausted. Raydeen bustled over and this time she showed Auggie out, summarily shutting the door behind him. Auggie looked around the entry hall for Max, but the room was empty. From what he could see of the stairway and other rooms, the younger Saldano was nowhere in sight.

Max might not have known Danziger and Carmen were divorced, but it sure felt like Victor had.

It took Jordanna less time than she'd expected to find the kid who'd discovered the branded body. The farmhouses were separated by miles, and the first one around the bend on the east side of Summit Ridge had a huge fence with a No Trespassing sign that seemed to mean business. The second house turned out to be the one she was looking for, and she bumped down a half-mile-long drive to another Victorian with a wide wraparound porch that extended on the three sides she could see of the home. What was left of the gingerbread had been painted to match the house, a putty color.

It was the two ATVs parked alongside the south side of the porch, both of them looking as if they hadn't been used in a long while, that convinced her she was at the right place even before she heard the loud barking, as a huge, bounding black Lab mix came rushing out to greet her. Jordanna stayed in the car, eyeing the dog, who was then followed by a boy of about twelve who yelled madly, "Dixie, cool it! Dixie! Damn it. Dixie!"

The dog kept barking her fool head off. Only when the

kid had the dog by the collar did Jordanna risk opening her door.

"Shut up, Dixie," he ordered again, slapping his hands together. The dog finally obeyed and sat down on its haunches, panting happily.

"Are you Zach Benchley?" she asked.

He threw Jordanna a suspicious look. "Yeah."

"I'm Jordanna Winters. My father's Dr. Dayton Winters." She had no compunction about using her father's name when it suited her. "I'm a journalist and I'm following up on the male body found near here a few years ago."

"I found him," the boy said quickly, as if expecting someone else to steal his thunder. "I was riding along down the road thataway." He waggled his index finger to the north. "I mean, I wasn't really on the road. I wasn't old enough, y'know." He glanced over his shoulder as if expecting someone to come up behind him. His father, perhaps. "But I can show you right where he was."

"Okay." Jordanna hadn't expected such full-service co-operation.

"I told the cops, y'know. I told 'em where he was and stuff. They thought I came from the field side? Well, I did. I wasn't really on the road . . . much." He scolded the dog, "Now you stay down. DOWN," then released his grip on the Lab's collar. The dog came over and snuffled Jordanna, who stood perfectly still. It seemed friendly enough, but you never knew. Meanwhile, the kid had taken off toward a gate in the fence that surrounded the field on the northern side of the driveway. Dixie, seeing him, wheeled away from Jordanna and raced after him, barking some more.

"Wait. Is it far?" Jordanna yelled.

Zach stopped. "Shush, Dixie. Well, yeah. Kinda."

"Would it be better to take my car?"

He mulled that over, throwing another look toward the house. Jordanna eyed the field he'd been about to cross.

How many acres were they talking about between here and the site where Zach found the body? He'd pretty much alluded to the fact that he'd been on the road at least some of the time. Whatever the case, she was glad she was in her sneakers and jeans, the staples of her wardrobe, in case she was about to be trudging across damp field grass. She threw a look to the heavens. Dark clouds were scudding across the sky, portending more rain.

"It's on the government property." He waved an arm to indicate way, way away. "It would be faster by car."

"Do you want to tell your father that you're taking off with me?"

"Nah. I'll take the ATV and meet you there," he decided.

"How will I know where to stop?"

"Follow the fence line."

She was glad of the enthusiastic help, but wasn't quite certain if this was going to help her. Zach jumped onto one of the ATVs and fiddled for a little while, inciting Dixie to more barking, and then the engine roared to life. He backed out and then bumped toward the field, where he'd already opened the gate. With a quick wave, he churned down a little wallow and up the other side, Dixie bounding beside him, still barking.

Dance settled on Excedrin and aspirin instead of a prescription painkiller. The pain in his head had receded and it was better than feeling drugged and dull. He got up from the couch and put weight on his injured leg, gritting his teeth as his nerves screamed messages to his brain. Not as bad as the headache though. *I am healing*, he thought grimly.

He should have asked Jordanna for her phone. He had some calls to make, some that couldn't be put off any longer. He didn't believe that the bomb had been placed to blow apart the safe and destroy the audiotape, but it was a possibility.

Max had known what was on the tape, and though he hadn't known whose voices he was hearing, and Dance hadn't told him, it was damning stuff.

Worth killing you over?

He pushed his hands through his hair and ran them to the back of his neck, squeezing. Feeling off balance, he walked carefully back to the couch and sank back down. If that were true—definitely a big "If"—then the man who'd recorded the audiotape was in danger, too. *If* Max found out who the speaker was, and *if* Max should decide to take matters into his own hands. Ten days ago, he wouldn't have believed his friend capable of such treachery, but ten days ago he hadn't had possession of the audiotape.

You should go to the police.

He'd resisted alerting the authorities. He'd wanted to believe in Max—and all of the Saldanos, come to that—but that may have been a grave mistake.

He wished he'd gone with Jordanna. He wanted to be with her, talk to her, work out problems with her. She'd wanted someone to be here when Kara showed up and he'd felt punk anyway, but he still wished he was with her. He wasn't good at staying behind and waiting. He needed to be in the vanguard, the first line of offense. Damn his injured leg and weakness.

He also thought about that kiss with Jordanna, those heated moments. He'd wanted nothing more than to bend her backward onto the couch, strip off her clothes, and make love to her. She'd wanted the same thing. He'd seen it in her eyes. Or, maybe not? She'd admitted to following him, an obsession that had more to do with her hunger for the job than for him. Maybe what he'd seen was a carefully orchestrated seduction, a means to an end.

His own cynicism brought him up short. No. Jordanna was too much of an open book to manage that level of deception. It was too easy to push her buttons over her relationship with her father to believe she could hide her true feelings. She'd wanted him, and he'd wanted her. That was a fact.

So, what're you going to do about it?

Absently, he rubbed his left leg. He'd seen the damaged flesh when Jordanna's father had unwrapped the bandage. The march of black stitches across his bruised and battered skin had made his stomach clench. It was a minor miracle that his thigh bone was intact. But he could stand putting weight on it, and he intended to get rid of the crutches ASAP.

The sound of a car approaching brought him to sharp attention. He twisted to look out the window, felt a jab of pain from his leg at the sudden action, but stared out the window, on full alert.

Was this Kara?

Jordanna followed the wire fence line as directed and finally came to the point where it met at a corner and turned ninety degrees east to delineate the end of the Benchley property. *This must be government property, under the Bureau of Land Management*, she thought, surveying the fields north of the Benchley property and along the east side of Summit Ridge, expanses of unfenced land that ran into the Cascades for thousands of acres. To the west were the rear limits of original farms that ended at the road. She'd driven past her father's property long before she'd reached Zach Benchley's house, and now, as she pulled off to the right shoulder, just past the Benchley fence line, she glanced toward the western side of the road, wondering whose farm she was looking at. All of this property had once been owned by Benchleys, she recalled. She'd paid little to no attention to her neighbors when she was growing up; it simply hadn't interested her.

Her right tires were in a low, wide ditch, leaving the car at an angle as she pulled on the emergency brake and cut the engine. Clouds were gathering, darkening the landscape around her. She got out of the car and walked a bit further north, following the line of Summit Ridge. She'd driven this road a number of times when she was young, but there was nothing beyond but fields and fir trees and rocky switchbacks into the mountains, not much of interest to her teenaged self.

She stopped short, wishing she'd brought a jacket with a hood. Up ahead, she saw the way Summit Ridge curved around a cliff. Not that many more miles ahead was where her sister, Emily, had slid off the road into one of the homestead farms, caught up in the stand of firs at the back side of their property. As she gazed north, her eye caught on an area of trampled grass toward the west, as if a vehicle had gone off the road, much like Emily had. She was considering walking up that way and checking it out when she heard the buzz of Zach's ATV, which grew louder as he appeared, coming toward her in a straight line. The dog had fallen behind, apparently, as she was nowhere to be seen.

She waved at him, and he drove right up to the fence line. She tramped over to him and realized there was a gate of sorts, as he undid a section of the wire fencing from a metal post and pulled it back.

"This is where government land starts?" she asked.

"Yup."

"Do you know who owns the land directly across from us?" She pointed west, to land that was undoubtedly one of the homestead farms that couldn't be cut up into smaller sizes, per land use laws. It was a few farms over from the Treadwell homestead.

He followed her finger. "Used to be all Benchley land."

So, he knew that, too. "Are you the last of the Benchleys?"

"Nah. The old people are still there, at least some of 'em. You know them? How crazy they are?" He slid her a glance.

"Not really."

"My dad was adopted. He's not a real Benchley, which is a good thing because they're all nuts. His sister was adopted, too, 'cuz they knew they were going crazy and needed someone to take care of 'em, so that's why they adopted them. That's what Dad thinks."

"I've never heard that."

"Oh, yeah, they're all 'fuckin' lunatics,' my dad says."

"I've heard of the Treadwell Curse," Jordanna responded, wondering if he'd gotten it mixed up.

"What's that?" He was gazing over the area where they were standing, as if getting his bearings.

"It's the unofficial name for an unofficial genetic disease that affects the brain. It sounds kind of like what you're talking about."

He nodded as if they were discussing fact. "The Benchleys for sure. I don't know about any Treadways."

"Treadwells. A lot of Treadwell families settled around here, too."

"All I know is my dad says the Benchleys have brain problems, and he should know, 'cuz his dad, my grandpa, was one of 'em."

Jordanna thought that over. She saw that she was going to have to connect with her father sooner, rather than later. He would know what this kid was talking about. Aunt Evelyn had mentioned the Benchleys, too, she recalled.

Zach had turned off the ATV and now he forged out in a diagonal line from the road. "Over here," he called back to her.

Jordanna followed after him. As she approached, she saw a small, wooden marker shoved into the ground with HM crudely written on it. She doubted it would be seen by the casual motorist driving by.

"What's HM stand for?"

"Homeless man."

"You left the marker here?"

He nodded solemnly. "I almost ran over him," he said, sounding still worried about it. "Dixie found him, so I just missed him."

"What makes you think he was homeless?"

Zach seemed nonplussed for a moment. He blinked at her a few times, then said, "Nobody knew him and we all know everybody around here, pretty much."

"Wonder how he got out here. It's not really near anything. Food, shelter . . ."

"Dad says lots of hobos go out on government land," he said, lifting his shoulders and letting them drop. "Ours is the last farm on this side of Summit Ridge till you get to Fool's Falls. After that it's all public land."

Jordanna squinted toward the trampled grass up ahead on the west side of the road. "What's over there?" she asked.

Zach's face shuttered. "That's Fowler property."

The name rang a distant bell. "I think I remember them," Jordanna said, trying to recall the names of all the families nearby her own. Mostly she recalled the properties had been owned by Benchleys. "Is that access to the Fowler's property?"

"Maybe." His tone was flat.

"What's wrong?" she asked.

"Nothin'." When she kept her gaze on him, he shifted on his feet and said, "Old Lady Fowler is mean, although she's really, really old now. I thought maybe she shot the homeless guy. I wouldn't put it past her, but my dad said no. And anyway, he didn't have any gunshot wounds."

"Where are the old Benchleys that you mentioned?"

He hooked a thumb south. "Right next to us. The only farm on the east side besides us."

"But this land is owned by Mrs. Fowler. Is her husband deceased?"

"Yeah, but I don't think he's in the old cemetery. It isn't used anymore."

"The old cemetery?" Jordanna asked.

Zach sighed, as if having a conversation with her was a trial. "It's a Benchley cemetery, but it's really old, and no one uses it anymore. Now it's on Fowler land, though, so . . ."

"Where exactly is the cemetery?"

He glanced toward the area she'd been looking at. "I don't know."

"Could it be near that flattened grass up ahead?" When Zach didn't answer, Jordanna added, "Maybe someone drove to it. It looks like something heavy was there."

"Nobody uses it."

"You've seen it, though," she guessed.

"My dad would kill me if he thought I was trespassing. I'd better start heading back. Dixie!" he called to the Lab, who was now once again in sight. The dog looked up and came bounding back.

"I'd like to take a look at it," Jordanna said.

"Why? There's nothing there but some old broken-down tombstones. I didn't see anything."

Jordanna was trying to get a bead on him, figure out what was driving him. Clearly he thought the cemetery was anathema, and she'd bet it wasn't just because his father might come down on him for trespassing. She thought about the cemetery, and a distant memory flitted across her mind. Nate Calverson talking with friends in the hall between classes. ". . . so scared she almost peed her pants. I told her it's just a bunch of dead people. They can't hurt you." Jordanna had thought he meant Everhardt Cemetery, though she'd mostly remembered how he'd caught her gaze and held it as she walked by.

But if he'd taken a girl to a cemetery, could it have been to this one, which was far more private?

"Did you see a couple making out at the cemetery?" she called, for Zach was already at the wire fence, yanking the gate into place. When he shook his head, she yelled, "I don't care. I just want to know. Is it kind of a place kids go to be alone?"

"I told the police about it," he hollered back, raising his voice over the revving of the ATV. "They didn't think it had anything to do with the guy I found."

"But it is a make-out spot."

"I haven't seen anybody in a long time," he said. Then the ATV leapt as if it were in a race and Zach, with Dixie running behind, bumped rapidly over the field and raced away from her.

"Well, okay," she muttered, stepping into the road and looking both ways before quickly crossing. She hurried up the road at a jog. She probably should have gotten back in her vehicle and driven, but it wasn't all that far.

When she got there, she saw that the grasses were flattened in all directions and there was a broken-down fence with a rusted gate, the gate having been pushed back into overgrown blackberry brambles. Beyond, she could clearly see where a vehicle or vehicles had driven across a road of sorts that curved to the north and disappeared into a stand of Douglas firs and pines, a small forest that appeared to have grown in all directions over the years.

The branded victim had been older than a teenager, but could he have been at the cemetery for some reason? Some assignation? Zach said he'd told the police about the place having been used as a lover's lane, of sorts, and that they had discounted that as having anything to do with the body. Maybe that was right. Maybe the proximity of the cemetery was completely unrelated. Just because she didn't like Chief Markum didn't mean he and his staff were completely incompetent.

Still . . .

It was a ways up the track, the ground having been trampled down pretty heavily, as if several cars had been down it, or at least one coming and going a few times. The sun was lowering as she turned a corner, entering a thicker grove of fir and pine, and her arms broke out in gooseflesh. The air grew cooler as she went, shadows lingering.

At a last turn, she stopped short. A whiff of something rank reached her nostrils and she recoiled. In front of her was a small plot, not much larger than a twenty-foot-by-twenty-foot plot. Wooden crosses, once painted white and now gray, marked several graves, and there were two granite gravestones, tumbled over and broken. She read some of the names and realized they were all Benchleys, as Zach had said. A cold trickle of fear slid down her spine. The earth of the plot was dark brown, the ground having been recently hoed and raked. Someone had been here tending to the graves.

Something caught at the edge of her vision, and she jerked back, heart pounding. Was someone there?

She stared through the gloom of the copse. No . . . what she'd seen was just a rake leaned up against a tree.

Expelling a deep breath, she realized her hand was at her throat. Creepy. No wonder Zach hadn't wanted to come with her.

. . . so scared she almost peed her pants . . .

If Nate Calverson had brought her here in high school, she would have felt the same way. She would have gone, but she would have felt the same way.

She shook her head. She had a tendency to fall for unattainable men.

But Dance kissed you and wanted more.

"That doesn't mean anything," she whispered. The mood of the place made her keep her voice low. There was something cathedral-like in this ring of towering firs.

She turned to leave, and the scent of rot reached her again. She turned back quickly and gave the whole graveyard a good, last look. At the east end of the plot, the soil was darker, moister, more recently disturbed.

Telling herself to get over her heebie-jeebies, she walked to that side of the plot. With the toe of her sneaker, she pressed into the deeper brown dirt. Was something there? Carefully, she leaned closer. Reluctantly, wishing she had gloves, she reached a hand forward and lightly scraped at the edge of the soil. *Maybe you are as crazy as they say*, she told herself. *Grave digging? What the hell are you doing?*

Shoulders tense, she made a hole about six inches deep and started widening it. There was no marker here. No grave. No casket. But somebody had disturbed the earth and then raked over it, trying to make it appear like the rest. At least that's what she thought.

When the hole was about a foot deep and the size and shape of a large book, she stopped. There was nothing here and it was someone's property. Maybe she was disturbing seeds of some kind, flowers planted for the dead.

Sitting back on her haunches, she dusted her hands. It was then she saw the tiny, pearlescent oval. A fingernail. Horror-struck, she nevertheless reached forward and plucked at the nail. Her hand felt a finger and she jerked back on instinct.

The hand that came free was a young woman's, the painted white fingernails, broken.

A scream bubbled up inside her, but all she did was emit a guttural cry. *Bernadette Fread*, her mind shrieked. Jordanna dropped the hand as if burned. But then she hurriedly scrabbled at the dirt to reveal the right side of a naked female body. It was turned slightly, as if someone had put it down on its side. The branding mark stood out on her hip. A cross. Upside down.

She ran, stumbling away.

Chapter Eighteen

Jordanna burst through the back door of the homestead and pounded across the wooden planks to the back door. "Dance!" she cried. "Dance!"

"What? I'm in the living room."

She ran to him, damn near threw herself into his arms though he was standing without the aid of crutches. Her momentum nearly dropped them both to the couch, but he managed to stay upright, wrapping her in his arms as if he already understood she needed to be held.

"You're trembling. What happened? Are you all right?" he clipped out.

"Yes, yes. It was . . . I'm fine. God . . . my God."

"Did you find the boy?"

"Yes." She nodded over and over again, searching for her voice.

"Sit down," he ordered, letting go of her just enough so she could take a seat.

"There's a body in a cemetery at the back of the Fowler property. It's a few farms over. It's not in a casket. No headstone. It's just buried naked under the surface," she gasped out.

"You found a body in a shallow grave?"

"It's not even a grave, hardly." She heard the half-hysterical

note in her voice and drew a deep breath. She was clinging
to him, feeling the heat of his body. She wanted to wrap herself up with him, run her hands down the hard muscles of his
back, have him drag her to him like she was everything. She
curled up against him, knowing her senses were inflamed,
not caring.

"Jordanna," he said, his voice a rumble as her ear was to
his chest. She could hear the strong beat of his heart.

"Hold me," she whispered.

With that his arms tightened and she squeezed her eyes
closed. She wanted to kiss him. Almost of its own volition,
her mouth lifted to his. He shifted and met the kiss, his lips
hard and wanting.

And then they were kissing madly and she was pulling at
his shirt, drawing it up his chest and dragging it over his
head. She shifted positions, straddling him, and he pulled
her to him, his hands on her thighs.

"Your leg," she murmured, pressing herself to him
through her jeans and his sweats.

"Don't care," he gritted out.

He fumbled between them for the zipper of her jeans. She
squirmed away and stumbled to her feet, yanking off her
jeans, stepping out of them, pulling off her sweater at the
same time. In her bra and panties, she helped pull off his
sweatpants and boxers, half-amused that she recognized
them from her trip to his house. Then she sat on the couch
beside him, and he pulled her atop him.

His hands went around her waist, his mouth at her neck.
His fingers found the clasp of her bra and he pulled it off
her. A thrill of desire shot through her. She'd never been
reckless, but she was now.

The wetness on her skin from his mouth was like an aphrodisiac. Her hands clutched at him, dragging him forward till
he pushed inside her. She was shocked at the sensation, how

fast things were moving, the mewling sounds that escaped her own lips.

His deep groan speared desire through her and she clenched her hands in her hair, her body arching. They strained together and she cried out, her eyes squeezed tightly shut, her body convulsing inside. The release of emotion brought tears to the back of her eyes. No . . . oh, no . . . he couldn't see her crying. That would kill everything!

She held him tightly, refusing to release him even when she collapsed against him, blinking back the evidence of her tears. Good Lord, she needed to pull herself together.

"Good God," he said, dragging in a breath, silently laughing, his mouth nuzzling her ear.

"I should be embarrassed," she said, her eyes still closed, her mouth near his ear.

"Why?"

"It was just so . . . good." She managed a short laugh.

"It was," he agreed.

"I just wanted to close everything out and feel."

"Works for me," he drawled, and by the time he drew back to stare down at her, his blue eyes lazy with satisfaction, the extra moisture in her own eyes had been blinked away.

"You probably won't believe me since you know I was practically stalking you, but I don't do this kind of thing."

"I think I'm happy you were stalking me for a job."

"Me, too," she said, smiling. Then she came back to the present and shivered again.

"Tell me about this body in the cemetery," he said, as they pulled away from each other and found their clothes.

Dressed, she hugged herself and half laughed. "Maybe I am crazy. I feel crazy right now."

"You're not crazy," he assured her, leaning forward and pressing his mouth to hers, kissing her hard.

She wanted to lose herself in him again, but she settled

for sitting close beside him. "How'd the leg fare through that?"

"I'll live," he said, waiting.

She shook her head and drew a breath. "It was a woman's body, and it had been branded on the right hip with an upside-down cross."

"You're kidding," he said in surprise.

"It was just like what Dr. Ferguson described. I don't know what she looks like, but maybe this is the missing girl, Bernadette Fread. Maybe she didn't run off with her boyfriend."

"How did you find this cemetery?" All of the sudden, he was all business.

"Zach Benchley showed me. I'd found his house. He showed me where he nearly ran over the body on his ATV. It wasn't that far from the track to the cemetery, which is why I went there. Two brandings, in proximity . . . it can't be coincidence."

He nodded, serious. "The bottle of wine's open. I'm getting us both a drink."

"Okay."

Dance headed to the kitchen and in a distant part of her mind she saw that he was walking without crutches, albeit limping stiffly and carefully, but without any other aid. He returned a few moments later, balancing the bottle and two empty glasses. She stood up to help, but he shook his head. "I got this," he said, handing her an empty glass, then seating himself down beside her again and filling both their glasses. "Start at the beginning."

She took a gulp of wine, then went back through the events, laying out how she'd met Zach, gone to the site where the body had been found, then become intrigued by the cemetery, thereby subsequently discovering the body.

"You think it's a homicide," he said.

"Yes. Yes, I do."

"Then it's time to go to the police."

"I know. I just needed to tell you first. I wish there were someone besides Markum. Maybe . . . maybe this Pete Drummond. I'll call the station, ask for him."

She started to get up and head back to the kitchen, where she'd dropped her purse and cell phone, but he stopped her with "Before you do, there's something I need to tell you."

She didn't like the sound of that. "What?"

"Your father came by, looking for Kara. He wanted to talk to you. I told him you were investigating the unidentified body that was found a few years ago and that I didn't know when you'd be back."

"Okay," she said carefully. Then: "He doesn't know where Kara is, either?"

"No."

She drew a breath and shook her head. "She should've been here by now."

"Could you tell how long the body had been there?" he asked cautiously.

It took her a moment to read his mind. "Oh, no. No . . . no . . . it wasn't Kara!" She jumped to her feet.

"I'm sure it isn't."

"I've got to call Drummond." She practically ran for her cell phone. No. It wasn't Kara. It wasn't!

"Let's go to the station," Dance said, coming into the kitchen. "Tell whoever's on duty rather than leave a message. "Yes."

It took forty minutes to make it to the police station and by the time they arrived it was full dark. Jordanna walked in and asked for Officer Drummond or Chief Markum and learned, to no surprise, that neither was on duty. She then said she wanted to report finding a body in a shallow grave, and that finally got the receptionist paging Drummond, who apparently said he'd be right there.

"Right there" turned out to be another twenty minutes,

and when Officer Peter Drummond strode into the station, Jordanna fleetingly thought she knew why Rusty called him Mr. Shitface. It had nothing to do with his looks. He was about Jordanna's age, tall, muscular, and in good shape. But there wasn't a bit of humor in his face, and he walked with military precision. His uniform was pressed within an inch of its life. His hair was clipped short, and his eyes were a cold gray.

"Ms. Winters?" he greeted her.

"Yes." When he thrust out his hand, she shook it. Then he turned to Dance, taking his measure as he shook his hand. Dance introduced himself, looking him right in the eye, both men being about six foot two. Jordanna wanted to find a place for Dance to sit down, but he gave her a look, telling her silently that he was okay.

Drummond, however, asked them to come back to an empty room. When they were settled, he took down her cell number and said, "Okay, tell me about this body you found."

Jordanna heard the note of tolerance in his voice but chose to ignore it. She didn't go into her whole meeting with Zach, just how she'd gone to the cemetery and stumbled upon the shallow grave. "It's a private cemetery on what I believe is the Fowler property. There was no casket. Just a body in the ground with barely enough soil to cover it."

Drummond asked, "You didn't contact Mrs. Fowler."

"I came straight here," she said, studiously avoiding Dance's gaze at the lie, her cheeks heating at the memory.

"You understand you were trespassing," he pointed out.

"Oh, for God's sake," Jordanna expelled. "I was looking into the branding victim. The homeless man? I didn't expect to run across another body."

"Who told you about the branding victim?" he asked, his brows raised.

"What does it matter? We talked to the ME," she snapped

back. "It shouldn't be a secret any longer. The public should know. Maybe you'd learn something about the victim, then."

"Now, calm down," he said, which pissed Jordanna off all the more.

Dance stepped in, with "Don't you have a missing girl around here?"

Drummond gave him a sharp look. "What's your stake in this?"

"I'm a journalist," he said. "Like Jordanna."

"Danziger," he said, in a way that suggested he'd just connected the dots. "You write for the newspapers . . . *The Oregonian* . . . in-depth stuff."

Dance nodded.

"Are you going to go check out the body? It's a young woman. It could be Bernadette Fread," Jordanna urged.

Drummond turned back to her, giving her a long, assessing look. "You've been gone a long time, Jordanna Winters. You don't know this town as well as those of us who stayed."

"What does that mean?" she demanded.

"Bernadette's run away with her boyfriend before. Chase Sazlow's been gone just as long as she has." He spread his hands. "They're teenagers in lust, and they don't listen to anyone."

"Well, if it's not Bernadette, it's still somebody," Jordanna stated, growing hot. "Is the chief here?"

"The chief has days off, too." Drummond looked at her with all the warmth of a reptile. "I'll give him the information."

When I'm damn good and ready, his tone said.

Jordanna stared at him for a long moment. "You know Rusty Long?" she asked.

"Yeah, I know Rusty," he allowed.

"He told me I could talk to you."

"And a lot more, I'll bet."

"Are you going to look into this or not?" she demanded.

"Yes, I'm going to look into it," he said, as if it were a foregone conclusion, which couldn't be further from the truth, from Jordanna's point of view.

"We'll go with you," Dance said.

"You go on back to wherever you came from," Drummond ordered, ruffled. "We'll let you know what we find."

"You will?" Jordanna challenged.

"I have your number."

Jordanna would have argued further, but she caught Dance's eye and the almost imperceptible shake of his head. She capitulated with ill grace, nodding shortly to Drummond, who walked them back to the front doors.

"I knew your sister, y'know," he said, as she and Dance stepped outside.

She glanced back. "Emily. I heard that you were seeing her in high school."

He wagged his head back and forth, frowning.

"I heard you dated her senior year of high school," Jordanna manufactured. She knew no such thing. It had been innuendo from Pru Calverson. And right now it didn't even matter, because worry over Kara sat like a stone in the pit of her stomach. If Drummond had been the least bit more helpful, she would have mentioned that her younger sister seemed to be missing now, too, and asked for aid in finding her.

"Emily was good people" was all he said, though his tone suggested he felt differently.

Jordanna turned away from him, hurrying down the steps as Drummond let himself back inside. "Sorry," she said to Dance when he caught up to her. "I just had to leave."

"You brought up Drummond's boss, the chief, intimating that you want to go over Drummond's head and that you think he's incompetent."

"Your point?" She squinted at him.

He was smiling. "You're tweaking his tail." Then, "Should we go to that bar? The Longhorn?"

"You've given up hiding completely?" She wasn't sure how she felt about that.

"Yeah, I gotta take care of things. I need to make some phone calls. Mind if I use your cell?"

"No, go ahead. We'll get you a burner tomorrow. Unless you're ready to leave . . . ?" The thought seized her with anxiety, for him, and because it meant their time together would end.

"Not yet."

Jordanna drove them to the Longhorn and they headed inside. She kept wanting to offer an arm for support, but she already knew that would go over like a lead balloon. She opened the door, however, and remarked, "You could use a cane."

"And a beer," he said, as they headed to one of the booths.

She sank down across from him, aware of him even more than she had been before their impromptu lovemaking. "A lot of things are rotten in Rock Springs and nobody seems to give a damn. Talking to Mr. Shitface was like fingernails on a blackboard."

"Mr. Shitface?"

"That's what Rusty called him. Now I get it."

"I noticed you didn't tell Shitface about the branding you saw on the girl's body."

"I'll tell Markum. I don't like him much, but he's a helluva lot better choice than Drummond, as it turns out."

They each ordered a beer, but when Jordanna's came she turned the glass mug around on the table, smoothing drops of condensation with the bottom of her mug against the lacquered wood top, watching the patterns form and reform. "I don't even know if Drummond, Shitface, will tell the chief. And where the hell's Kara? Why hasn't she called me? Sure, she runs on her own time clock, but she specifically said she was going to be at the homestead and it's been hours."

"Maybe she's there now."

He didn't believe it, she could tell. He was only humoring her. "Something happened to her between here and there. When she was on the phone, she saw someone she thought she knew." She made a sound of impatience and ran her hands through her hair.

"Drummond'll look into it," he said. "He's the kind of guy who loves to be obstinate, but he won't let himself look bad by ignoring you and having it all blow up in his face."

"Good." She thought some more. "If it's Bernadette, somebody branded her, and that somebody probably killed her, too. She didn't die of some accident."

"Probably not."

She lifted the mug to her lips, held it a minute, visualizing the mark on the girl's thigh. "An upside-down cross . . ."

He grimaced. "Think of the mind-set of someone branding human beings. Gotta be some compelling reason."

"Anti-religion?" she mused.

"Maybe just the opposite."

She looked at him across the table. His beard had deepened over the past few days and it gave him a rakish look she found even more attractive. "Think I should talk to Reverend Miles again?"

"Someone in the religion game," he agreed.

"Don't call it a game around this town," she warned, smiling. "Blasphemy. Everyone takes their own religion seriously, at least those at that end of the spectrum. On the other end, the tavern-dwellers have their own form of religion." She lifted her glass and this time she drank lustily, until she started coughing.

"Do I need to clap you on the back?" Dance asked mildly.

Jordanna managed a chuckle, coughed a few more times, then got herself under control. "No, I'm good."

Her cell phone rang and she grabbed for her purse. "There's no way it can be Drummond yet," she muttered, reminding herself. Then she remembered, "You wanted to use my phone."

"Later," he said, as she plucked it from her purse.

"Jennie," she said, disappointed, staring at the screen. She was probably calling for Jordanna's father. She thought about not answering, then decided that would only put off the inevitable. Was that progress? she wondered. Probably. She clicked on. "Hi, Jennie."

"Oh, Jordanna. Thank the Lord. We're so relieved! Kara just texted my phone. She said she had to turn right around and go back to Portland, and that's why she couldn't meet us. I guess something came up."

"I guess so," Jordanna said, also relieved but nonplussed. It was odd Kara had texted Jennie and not her, but then her sister was never one for convention. "Thanks for calling."

"Oh, no problem. We were all so worried. You know, Dayton stopped by the homestead and talked to your boyfriend."

Boyfriend . . . The term brought back their earlier lovemaking and she had to push the memory aside. "Uh, yes, that's right." She could feel Dance's gaze on her and knew what he was thinking. Yes, she should use her father as a source, and no, she wasn't ready to quite yet. Maybe tomorrow.

"Well, I'd still like to host a dinner while you're here," Jennie said. "Life's short, y'know? That's all. You never know what could happen next. Sometimes there isn't enough time for all the forgiveness you need."

"What?" Dance asked, after Jordanna had hung up.

"I think my stepmother just made awfully good sense."

He smiled at her rueful tone. "Do you want to order something?" he asked.

"Do you?"

"I saw a pastrami sandwich with coleslaw on the menu."

"Perfect," Jordanna said.

They ordered and just as their sandwiches arrived, Rusty Long strolled through the saloon doors. He looked around and his eyes passed over her, then yanked back. She lifted a hand in hello, and he strode on over.

"Jordanna, hey." His eyes were focused on Dance and he thrust out a hand. "Rusty Long."

Dance shook the proffered hand. "Jay Danziger."

"Something tells me you're not from Rock Springs. You came with Jordanna?" he asked.

Dance nodded.

Rusty's attention swung back to Jordanna. "Don't be surprised if my cousin calls you. We didn't know you were with somebody." He sounded slightly miffed, but Jordanna just shrugged. She'd kept the information from him on purpose, but she didn't feel like going into why.

"Been calling Todd all afternoon, but can't raise him," Rusty admitted, looking restlessly around the room once more. "Hikes all over the goddamned country and half the time there's no cell service. But we were supposed to meet here, and where the hell is he?"

"You told me Bernadette Fread's boyfriend is named Chase . . . ?" Jordanna asked.

"Chase Sazlow, yep."

"And he's missing, too."

"Is he?" Rusty asked. "Thought he was just bunking at the Calverson Ranch. It's close by the Freads, and he kind of works there and stays with them. We all used to kind of hang out at the ranch, when we were kids, you remember."

Jordanna shook her head. "Chase doesn't live at home?"

"What home? His parents are gone, and Dutton's just gotten stranger over the years."

"Who's Dutton?" Jordanna asked. Dance was following

the conversation closely, but staying out of it, probably correctly interpreting that Rusty would shut down if questioned by someone he considered a stranger.

"Chase's older brother. You know him."

"I don't know him," she said. "And I don't remember you all hanging out at the ranch."

"It was just a bunch of us guys, when we were kids," he said. "We kind of worked around the ranch. Goofin' off. Back before old man Calverson pounded religion into Nate and Pru got a hold of him. But Nate's got Chase working for him hard, so yeah, he probably did run off with Bernadette." He glanced from Jordanna to Dance, and back again. "You writing up that story?"

"You never know. I did meet up with Pete Drummond finally. Just tonight," she admitted.

"What'd you think?" Rusty's grin appeared.

"Aptly named by you."

He chortled, his good mood restored. "Yep, that's right."

The saloon doors swung open and Nate Calverson appeared, alone. He looked around and caught Rusty's eye.

"Where's the better half?" Rusty hollered.

Nate saw Jordanna and smiled, heading their way. He flicked a glance at Dance, then looked harder. "Pru's back at the ranch. Who've we got here?"

"This is Jay Danziger, a friend of Jordanna's," Rusty introduced equably.

"Huh." The name didn't mean anything to Nate.

"Rusty was just telling us about being kids around your ranch, growing up," Jordanna said.

"Rusty talks a lot. We on for poker?" Nate asked him. "Where's Todd?"

"Don't know. Late." Rusty glanced toward the door.

"Well, I don't have that much time," Nate complained. He threw a glance toward Dance. "You play poker?"

"Some," Dance admitted.

"Hell, Nate, we're not starting a game without Todd," Rusty said, annoyed. "Sorry, man," he said to Dance, then to Nate, "Not our fault Pru's got you on a short leash."

"No problem," Dance said.

"Well, I'm gonna get started," Nate muttered.

"Who'd you take to the old cemetery?" Jordanna burst out as he was stalking off toward the back room. Nate threw her a look, but didn't answer. "In high school," she added, raising her voice so he could hear. A couple of people at a nearby table looked over, then turned away.

"The playground," Rusty said, grinning. "Everhardt Cemetery. That's what we called it. Just across from the ranch."

"I meant a different cemetery," Jordanna said.

Rusty looked perplexed. Then Nate demanded, "You coming?" pointing to an imaginary watch on his arm.

Rusty snorted. "Marriage, huh?" he said to them with a smile, drifting away.

Dance waited till they were out of earshot, then said, "You met these guys the other night when you were here."

"Yeah, they're frenemies. I had a crush on Nate in high school," she admitted a bit sheepishly. "I couldn't tell you why now. There's nothing about him that interests me."

"You don't have to explain yourself to me," he said, draining the last swallow of his beer. "I married Carmen Saldano."

Chapter Nineteen

"I can't stand it," Jordanna muttered as she was driving them back to the homestead. "Drummond isn't going to call. He may not have even told the chief."

"You want to go back to the cemetery?" Dance asked.

"Yes," she said.

They drove past the homestead and kept going till they connected with Summit Ridge Road and wound their way toward Zach Benchley's house and the entry to the cemetery. Jordanna's headlights caught the NO TRESPASSING sign across the first property, and she remarked, "That's where the last of the Benchleys live, according to Zach. The family that once owned the greater part of these properties. Not the Treadwells, but most of the others that run almost all the way to Rock Springs, farms and developed land alike."

As they turned a slow curve before the spot where Zach had discovered the body, they ran into a carnival of flashing lights. "Whoa," Jordanna said, braking.

"Drummond brought the cavalry," Dance observed drily.

"He did hear me," Jordanna said. "Woulda been nice of him to let me know."

She drove past the cemetery entrance and pulled to the side of Summit Ridge, wary of the ditch on either side of the road. She and Dance climbed out into a chilly night with fog climbing into the foothills in a wispy blanket.

"Go on," he told her. "I'll get there."

"Bullshit. Hang on." She looped an arm around him and reluctantly, he leaned on her, limping forward.

A young officer stood stiffly at the trampled entrance. "You can't enter. This is police business," he told them crisply.

"I'm the one that reported the body," Jordanna told him, just as crisply.

"Sorry, ma'am."

"Let me talk to Peter Drummond."

"No, ma'am."

Dance inserted, "Has the chief been informed?"

"It's not for me to say, sir."

Dance glanced around at the three vehicles, all with their lights revolving, blue and red strobes coloring the countryside. "I'm going to say yes," he said to Jordanna. "I mean, how many officers and police cars does Rock Springs have?"

"I want to talk to the chief," Jordanna ordered the young officer. "Chief Markum knows me. He's good friends with my father, Dr. Winters."

"I'm sorry, ma'am," the young officer said again, though he sounded a trifle less officious.

"You need to tell him I'm here," she warned. "He'll want to know."

The officer looked at her a moment, then reluctantly moved to his walkie. Dance pulled Jordanna out of earshot. "Try to get him to tell you whose body it is. He's going to want to shut you down, so be ready."

"Oh, I know Markum," she said.

It was about ten minutes later she saw the chief come from the direction of the cemetery into the glare of the revolving lights. She would have hurried forward to meet him, but the young officer held out his arms, as if she were a bronco that needed corralling.

"Jordanna," the chief greeted her as he trudged her way. "Pete says you're the one who called this in."

"That's right," she said. "Who is it? Do you know?"

"Well, that's the thing." He grimaced and threw a glance back the way he'd come, then focused on Jordanna. "There is no body."

She almost laughed. "Yes, there is. I touched it. I could smell it, even before I found it."

The chief shook his head. "There was some soil disturbance, but the only bodies in that graveyard have been there a long, long time."

"That's not possible," Jordanna insisted. "It's only been a few hours since I was here!"

"The ground's been raked. That's about all I can tell you."

"Well, then someone moved her." Jordanna was positive, and growing angry. "And she was branded, just like the male vic whose body was found right over there." She threw an arm out to encompass the whole area. "And there was an upside-down cross burned into her skin."

That took him aback for a moment, but he recovered quickly. "I talked to Doc Ferguson. He told you about the cross."

"Yes, he did," she agreed. "And now I'm telling you it has to be the same marking." When he didn't say anything, she asked, "What?"

"He thinks you're making up seeing the cross to match the facts of the original male branding victim," Dance said drily.

"I'm not!" Jordanna was outraged, and suddenly aware that she was in a very precarious predicament. They all thought she was crazy already, and here she was, damn near giving them proof positive of that fact because someone had moved the body. "Who got here first?" she asked.

"Pete was here, with two other officers. All we had. Because we believed you, but there was nothing here."

"I want to see for myself."

"Jordanna, you're trying my patience," he said tiredly. "I came out here in deference to your father, who deserves a lot more respect than you give him. But there's no body there. Maybe you should think about returning to Portland, or wherever you came from."

"I'm not leaving," she warned him. "Something's going on here, even if you won't let yourself believe anything bad can happen in Rock Springs."

"I know bad things happen," the chief barked out, then turned sharply to trudge on back.

Jordanna looked at Dance. She was so frustrated she could hardly speak. "Do you believe me?" she asked.

She'd let go of him for her encounter with the young officer and Markum, but now he slid his arm around her, pulling her close. "Yes. And even if there's no body, the police know something's going on. They're not just sitting out there in the fog, waiting for spirits to rise."

"Who moved her?" she asked.

He shook his head. "Someone who knew you found it."

"But there was no one around."

"Maybe there was," he said.

A shiver started at the base of her spine and slid upward, cold as a finger drawing a line along her back. Her gaze darted in all directions, trying to pierce through the gray fog and dark night.

Maybe there was.

The shovel rang against the stony ground like a bell in the thick night. He was sweating freely and he had a long way to go before he was done. He'd had to jog back to his truck, after moving the Treadwell girl's car to the cliffs near Fool's

Falls, diving down into the steep slopes of fir and brush along the ditches whenever a car drove by, then had been shocked, stupefied, to see a man suddenly appear at the turnout above the falls. Todd Douglas. Lord above. He'd been ill with remorse when he'd realized who it was he'd had to smack senseless with the rock.

But God had reasons for his plans, he reminded himself. Todd had been there for a reason. His mind touched on the barred door in the barn. He'd had to do many things in His name that hurt him.

He dug some more, his muscles aching at the hard work. It was the appearance of the other Treadwell bitch that had nearly done him in, however. Where had she come from? How had she found the cemetery? *How?*

She's a daughter of Lucifer.

Seeing her there, he'd been jangled with fear. He'd driven the other Treadwell bitch to his barn, stuffed down in the footwell, covered by a blanket. Luckily he'd only encountered one other car on the road, one of the old Benchleys, he thought. Half-blind and barely herding her ancient Ford truck down the road. He'd purposely kept his speed down as she drove past, even though he wanted to tear to safety. The fear of being caught was a rush. At the barn, he'd wanted to pleasure himself with her, but had managed to refrain, though when he'd dumped her in front of the cold brazier, he'd stretched out upon her again and thrust against her twice before pulling himself back. She was dead. One of the lost ready to come home.

He'd just been congratulating himself on a job well done when he'd realized he was missing her cell phone. *How?* He'd been so meticulous, making sure the phone was tucked in her purse and that the purse and her overnight bag were stowed in the cab behind his seat. But when he'd hauled her body and belongings out, no cell phone.

Short panic. But he knew the phone wasn't in the car he'd

shoved down the mountain. He'd made certain of that before Douglas appeared. So, it had to be at the cemetery. He'd been forced to return and it was God's will he arrived when he did, because that's when he saw a woman traipsing down the road. She was turning toward the cemetery as Zach Benchley's ATV zoomed the opposite direction back toward his family's farm. *Who?* He'd thought, slowing the truck.

And then he'd seen the black RAV and he'd known. It was her vehicle. The Treadwell girl. He'd seen it outside the clinic that very morning.

He waited in his car, his breath coming fast. Waited until she'd had enough time to be far enough down the lane not to see his truck when he passed by. He drove several miles farther in the direction of the lookout, but then turned back, whipping the wheel around. That's when the missing cell phone had skittered from under the seat and damn near jammed under his brake. He'd had to stop to remove it, and when he'd seen what it was, he pocketed it and said a small prayer. He almost chuckled at the miracle of timing. Instead of chancing running into her, he'd waited for nearly forty minutes, and by the time he drove back to that stretch of road, her vehicle was gone.

Had she found Bernadette? He couldn't take the chance, so he bumped down the road to the cemetery again, jamming on the brake, the engine still running.

He had to move Bernie's body. Couldn't have Jordanna Treadwell call in the police, and that's what she was bound to do. He was sorry she couldn't stay there with the other lost souls. He needed to bring the afflicted ones to their family's final resting place. That's what God wanted. But the Treadwell bitch had foiled that plan, he thought, baring his teeth. He couldn't let Satan win.

Now, in the stretch of woods east of the barn and between the fields on his own property, he dug past the pebbles and small rocks to the hard earth underneath, digging, digging,

digging. It was temporary, just until he took care of Jordanna. Then he could move the sick ones away from the others.

You have to move them all. They're coming for you. They'll know.

Shuttering his mind to the edict, he kept digging and digging. Finally, he tossed down the shovel, threw back his head, and stared at the heavens, his heart thundering from exertion. He'd thrown off his shirt and perspiration slicked his skin. He took a look at the black holes he'd carved out of the stony ground. They were deep enough for now.

Trudging back to the truck, he pulled Bernie from the cab. Ten days dead, she smelled as putrid as her soul. He flung her into one of the pits and covered her up, dirt and pebbles raining down on her. The other pit yawned. The one for that other sorry, stinking bitch, Jordanna's sister Kara.

Thinking of them, his mind flickered to the other sister, Emily, even though he'd told himself never, never, never to think about her again. He'd loved her like a soul mate. He'd saved her, as much as he could. But she'd been afflicted and nothing could have been between them. She hadn't been responsible for her actions with other men. He knew that, but it had been so hard to witness her downfall.

Pulling his shirt back over his head, he reached down for the jacket he'd tossed on the ground, flinging it over one shoulder. He threw it onto the passenger seat as he climbed into the truck, then drove the short distance back to the barn. There were horses in the north field, just the few left from when the ranch had been in his father's hands. The cows were in the south field and he glanced over where their dark humps studded the landscape. He heard one lowing in the dark as he reached the barn.

It suddenly started pouring rain, dispelling the last wisps of drifting fog, and he turned the truck around in a downpour, backing up to the yawning black hole of the open doorway. He'd hadn't shut the door because he'd known he would be right back.

Once he was back in, he jumped out of the cab and strode straight to the brazier, lighting it up. He'd tossed a tarp over Kara's body and left her on the barn floor. Now he eased the tarp back, looking down at her as he waited for the iron to heat. It took some time, but he was patient, staring into the oven heat of Satan's furnace, watching the branding iron's tip turn from black to molten orange.

He felt mesmerized, but was jarred out of his reverie by the merry ring of a cell phone. Her phone. In her purse still inside his cab. He loped back for it and waited for it to stop ringing, one eye on the flood of rain outside the open barn door. He hoped the hole he'd dug wasn't filling up with water.

Picking up the phone, he carefully fingered the keys, pleased when the screen lit up and he realized it had no automatic locking mechanism. He read the name of the recent caller: JORDANNA.

"Poor sick bitch," he whispered. Though he'd known it wasn't Emily's fault she was such a slut, he'd also known she was doomed. Her family had made a pact with the devil long before and there was no coming back from that.

He scrolled through Kara's last texts. Jennie had been asking her to come to dinner tonight . . . must be Jennie Markum. A downright shame that Jennie, whose soul was pure, wanted to keep in contact with the Treadwell whores. She should know better.

The idea took form slowly and he let it percolate. He'd been accused of being a slow thinker more than once, and he knew he had to think things through carefully or he could make a mistake. Finally, he decided it was a good idea and he texted Jennie back: sory cant make it gotta go to porland

Smiling, he then ripped the phone apart. He removed the battery, then threw the phone on the floor and stomped on it, cracking the plastic and metal pieces beneath the heel of his boot. Gathering them up, he threw what was left of the phone into the brazier. The fire might not be hot enough to melt metal, but it would destroy any part that mattered.

He started when his own cell phone began to ring. He'd zipped it into a pocket of his jacket and had pretty much forgotten about it. Now he went back to the cab again, pulled out his coat, and searched around till he had the phone in hand. He looked at the number, already knowing it would be her. "Yeah," he answered flatly.

"Is it done?" she asked.

"Not completely."

"What do you mean?" Sharp tone.

"I need to sear her flesh."

"You didn't touch her, did you?"

He thought back to those moments at the cemetery and then here in the barn, her body beneath him. To lie would be a sin, but he hadn't done anything, not really. "I kept myself pure."

"Your work is nearly done. You will be rewarded in heaven. There are so few left now."

He licked his lips. "This one isn't the reporter, but she's a Treadwell."

"What? What do you mean?" Even sharper yet.

"This one's the youngest sister. She came to town and she recognized me."

"Lord in heaven," she whispered.

"It's God's will. He looks out for us."

"He certainly does. But you need to take care of the other one. You need to hurry!"

He felt anger bubble inside him and he had to fight it back. He knew what to do. His next words were difficult, ripped from his heart. "Something needs to be done about Boo."

"Stop talking about him." Short and furious.

"He knows about the cemetery. And he might know about the burial grounds on our land."

"Stop talking! Keep your mind off Boo and on our mission. Finish what you started with the youngest sister. Sear her clean."

The phone went dead. He slipped it back in his jacket pocket, then turned to the dead girl. He knew he should be careful of touching her, careful to keep her sickness away from him, but she was too much like Emily for him to feel any repulsion.

The brazier threw orange shadows on her white skin. Slowly, he pulled the glowing iron from the fire. Propping up her hip with his hand, he pressed the cross upside down against her flesh, smelling the sweet, burned scent of seared meat.

Saying a quick prayer, he heaved her over his shoulder, tossed her limp body into the passenger seat, then drove back to the plot where Bernadette was, her temporary resting spot. Pulling her from the back of the truck, he carried her to the pit and rolled her into the muddy water with a splash. Rain came steadily down, running off the brim of his cowboy hat and onto her dirt-splattered body. He felt a weight on his soul. It was easier to kill men, even ones he liked.

Picking up the shovel, he covered Kara with dirt, making her disappear from view as he had Bernadette. He wanted to pat down his work and toss some branches over the makeshift grave, but the rain was making it difficult. There were three bodies here. Bernie, Kara, and the mean bitch who'd sired him. There should have been four, but when he was moving the fool who'd wandered onto their property, his body had fallen out of the back of the truck, landing on the side of the road outside the old cemetery, where he'd meant to bury him with his kin. When he'd realized what happened, he'd started to reverse, but then he'd seen headlights flash on through the trees that surrounded the cemetery. Someone had been there.

Instead, he'd moved his truck farther up the road and had sneaked back on foot. He'd been disgusted to see their car rock and hear their muffled groans and giggles as they giggled and fornicated like rabid vermin. He'd planned to pick up the body when he left, but all of a sudden their car engine was revving and he had to dive into the underbrush, smacking his head on a limb. As soon as they were gone he staggered back to his vehicle, dizzy and nauseous, and drove home. He vomited twice and slept like the dead and didn't remember the body. Later, when he told her about it, she told him he'd had a concussion and was infuriated with him, but by that time Zach Benchley had discovered the body.

He'd worried that maybe the kids in the car had seen him, but that wasn't the case. And then no one remembered who the body was anyway. Called him homeless. God's will again, protecting him. She said they were lucky that the chief had decided to keep the branding a secret, though it kinda got out anyway. Didn't matter. He'd done God's work, and unburdened the souls of the afflicted.

Bernie, young Bernadette, had been much harder for him. But he'd seen her wild rolling eyes and known of her promiscuous ways. She'd been fucking Chase for months before he finally understood that she was another of Lucifer's children. He'd caught them in the act, and that's when he'd had to burn the devil out of her and save her soul. Someday, he would put her corporal remains back with her kin, where they needed to be, and he would add the Treadwells, too.

Throwing the shovel in the back of the truck, he then jumped back inside. The youngest Treadwell woman had been a bonus, but he needed to concentrate on the last sister now. He'd seen her with that man with the limp. She was probably fucking him, among others. That's what Treadwells were like.

He hadn't liked being told what to do, but she was right: Jordanna Treadwell needed to be saved and soon. With her younger sister gone, Jordanna was the last of child-bearing age, and above all else, Treadwells could not be allowed to procreate.

It had to end with Jordanna.

Chapter Twenty

Dance lay on the blow-up bed, tucked up against Jordanna, one arm wrapped around her naked body. It was early, still dark, but he could make out the line of her nape. It was strange. He felt like he'd been sleeping with her forever, and he sure as hell didn't want it to stop.

She'd been quiet when they'd returned the night before, her eyes looking bruised. She'd hung in there at the Long-horn, but then he could practically see her energy wash away. He'd understood completely, even before she'd said, "There *was* a woman's body there."

"Write it down," he'd told her.

"Somebody knew I was there, and they moved it."

"You've got a story. The missing body, the reluctant police force, your own history with this town . . . write it up."

"My own history," she repeated with an ironic twist of her lips.

For a moment he'd thought she was going to ignore him, but then she'd seemed to catch fire. She'd switched on her laptop, opened a Word document, and started writing. Her style was more descriptive than his own straight, terse journalism, so initially he offered editing changes. Her steel spine returned, however, and she started fighting for her words, which he took as a good sign.

He'd left her to it, knowing how often writing had helped organize his own thoughts, forcing him to list events and information in a logical progression. He'd headed to the kitchen and heated up some instant coffee in the microwave, his thoughts turning to the Saldanos, knowing it was time to go to the police with the audiotape. Not the cops here in Rock Springs—like Jordanna, he didn't truly trust their efficiency, maybe even their honesty. No, it was time to go back to Portland.

He'd returned to the living room, aware this could be his last night, struck by a feeling of loss already as he looked at Jordanna, her face illuminated by the light coming off her laptop screen. Aware of him, she'd glanced up, meeting his gaze, and said, "It's rough, but I've got a lot of it down. Somebody saw me and moved the body. I don't know why it was there in the first place, but I disturbed them. How did he see me?"

"He was there and you didn't know it?" he'd suggested. "Nearby, anyway."

She hadn't liked the sound of that. "Does he live around there? Zach said Mrs. Fowler was old. He didn't act like anyone lived with her."

"One of the neighbors?"

"We're one of the neighbors," she'd reminded him. "But I don't know the rest of them. This land was all Benchley land once, and they were the ones who built the cemetery. I saw some of the names on the crosses."

"You need to talk to Mrs. Fowler," he'd told her, seating himself down beside her on the couch.

She'd written a few more words, but he could tell his proximity distracted her. "What are you doing?" she'd asked slowly, but he'd quelled the smile in her voice by saying, "I'm going to take the audiotape to the police."

"You do think it's why Saldano Industries was bombed, then?" She'd sounded faintly surprised, because he'd dismissed that notion from the outset.

"I haven't changed my mind. The tape only alludes to possible smuggling of an unnamed something. It may not be the Saldanos behind the smuggling. That's why I gave a copy to Max, so he could figure it out internally."

"Thought you'd started to believe they weren't on the up-and-up."

"I was doing some checking behind the scenes," he'd admitted. "I knew something was off. Then the bombing, the hospital . . . and you showed up. I probably should have gone to the police immediately, but I have a tendency to not trust them."

"We have that in common," she'd said, and he'd leaned in and kissed her, wanting her in a way he hadn't wanted anything in a long time. After that, they'd fallen into each other's arms and stumbled their way to his room, making love twice before falling asleep.

Now, he wanted to make love to her again. It was crazy. Too many years with Carmen, who was all heat and fire and anger and not enough true connection. He hadn't even realized what he was missing until yesterday.

Jordanna stirred in his arms, slowly turning to face him. He couldn't see her expression in the dark.

"When do you want me to drive you back to Portland?" she asked.

"Tomorrow's fine."

"So that gives us today."

He heard the echo of his own feelings, of not wanting their time together to end. "Yeah."

"You're going to let them all know where you are."

He didn't know how to tell her he felt less vulnerable now, less out of control. She'd extracted him from a volatile situation that he hadn't been strong enough to handle, but it went against his nature to hide out for long.

"I need to show my face to the Saldanos" was his answer. Hers was to wrap herself around him one more time and make love to him with a thread of desperation that he answered in kind.

Auggie rolled over in bed and reached an arm out for Liv, but she was already out of bed. He groaned and buried his head beneath his pillow. He was working a case that wasn't really his anymore, and he'd already been told that he couldn't "harass" the Saldanos any longer.

His lieutenant had called him late Saturday evening. A weekend phone call was unlikely to be about something positive, and when he answered and heard, "What are you doing, Rafferty?" he knew it was about the Saldanos.

He'd tried to plead his case. Yes, the feds had taken over, but he was following another lead. He just needed a little more time.

"I'd like you to go undercover on another case," Lieutenant Cawthorne had answered when he finished.

"I'd like to stay on this one," he'd stubbornly replied.

And that's when Cawthorne said, "Victor Saldano called Captain Jarvis and complained about you. Agent Bethwick had some things to say, too, and the words 'budget cuts' were tossed about. Your record's good, but it's getting political around here. If you want me to go to bat for you, you gotta stop being a maverick."

Auggie hadn't known quite how to answer. He'd worked undercover for the Portland PD on a number of cases. He'd been recruited from Laurelton PD for just that kind of work. But meeting Liv had changed what he wanted to do. Undercover work meant all hours, all the time. Taking on a new persona. Living a double life. Always the threat of danger. Being outside of so-called normal life.

What he really wanted to do now was straight homicide investigation. He wanted to go after the Saldanos. Something was off there. And the fact that they'd called and complained about him said he was on the right track.

"I kinda like being a maverick," he told his boss, whose answer was a sigh and then, "Be ready for a new assignment on Monday."

Now, he heard his cell phone ring and ignored it. He had all day today to decide just how he was going to play this. Let 'em leave a voice mail.

A moment later, Liv's phone began playing a tune that he knew was the ring she'd chosen for his sister. He didn't have special ring tones for anyone, so it was a good bet Nine had called him first, then phoned Liv when he hadn't answered.

He heard a muffled cry of delight, then Liv's footsteps as she flew into the bedroom. He pulled the pillow off his head and looked at her expectantly.

"That was Nine. July's in labor," she said. "Nine's already on her way, so get up and let's go."

"To the hospital?" Auggie asked.

"Yes, sir. We gotta move."

He watched as the woman he loved hurried around the bedroom, on a kind of natural high. Though it was his older sister who was delivering, he wasn't experiencing the same excitement. Now, if it had been Nine, he supposed he would feel differently, but in truth, he was detached and fairly certain he was going to feel like a caged lion if he was forced to stand around a hospital and wait for his niece's birth.

If he were following a suspect, he could exhibit the patience of Job, but when it came to family . . .

"How about I drop you off?" he suggested.

Liv turned and gave him a long look. She had challenges within her own family: her mother had died when she was a child, and her brother had long-term mental issues that caused him to fade in and out of reality. Liv, herself, had spent a chunk of her youth being scrutinized by mental health professionals and had learned never to trust anyone in authority.

"You don't want to go," she said.

"Doesn't this take hours?" He thought about it a moment and said, "It's the thirty-first."

Liv registered that and said, "If she doesn't have the baby today, then maybe she'll be named June instead of May?"

"Or, maybe July'll break tradition and pick some other name for the poor kid. Like Bertha, or Gertrude. That would be the sane thing to do." Auggie threw back the covers.

"So, are we going?" She turned toward the closet, but then squeaked with surprise when he grabbed her around the waist. He began gnawing at her neck and she started laughing and swatted at the arms surrounding her. "Stop it!"

"I'm going to eat you alive."

"Let go of me."

"No." He pressed his face into her neck and said, "I'll go. We'll do the baby thing."

"You don't—"

"Shhh." He moved to the curve of her collarbone, nibbling gently. "But if it takes hours and hours, I'm out of there."

She turned in his arms and pressed her nose to his. "Are you still thinking of going to Rock Springs?"

"Only if I want to commit professional suicide. So, maybe."

"You haven't been able to get through to them?"

She meant Jordanna Winters and Jay Danziger, whom he'd called on both their cells. "No. I could call Winters's father and play my hand. I get the feeling they're hiding out."

She pulled back to look at him. "What do you want to do?"

The Saldano case. But it might mean the end of his job if

he pursued it. "I'm dying to get to the hospital and hang out in the waiting room. That's what I want to do, so stop trying to hold me back."

Jordanna met Dance in the hallway, her hair still wet from her shower. Light was just filtering in through the sheer curtains, the sun having crested the mountains moments before. Dance, too, had damp hair, and he'd shaved the scruffy beard that had been building over the last few days, much to her regret. He looked more like a stranger now. She'd dressed in clean jeans, a black, lightweight sweater, and sneakers. He wore black sweatpants and a gray, long-sleeved T-shirt with a Nike swoosh stitched in white, and he was just putting on a darker gray hoodie.

"I'll buy you breakfast if you drive into town," he said. "I want to return the crutches."

"Maybe exchange them for a cane?"

"I'd go for that," he said.

They'd been rather circumspect with each other since reluctantly getting out of bed an hour earlier. She hardly knew how to act. On the one hand, they'd been ultimately intimate with each other, treating each other like longtime lovers; on the other, there was so much unresolved *stuff* surrounding them that it felt like she was living in an extended daydream.

"We could have breakfast at Braxton's and turn in the crutches," she suggested.

"Good idea."

The drive into town was mostly silent. She couldn't think of anything to say and apparently neither could he. It was weird, almost like a breakup, and it was a relief when he asked about the Benchleys, though she suspected it was just to make conversation.

"The Benchleys are apparently shirttail relatives of mine.

They still have some property. That drive with the big, rusted 'No Trespassing' sign leads to their house. As I recall, they were all old when I was in high school, and I think Zach's father is related. His adoptive parents, maybe? At least one of 'em?"

"You want to talk to them after Mrs. Fowler. See what they have to say about the cemetery."

"Sure."

Jordanna could feel the effects of a sleepless night, a lot of it spent in lovemaking. Her mind kept tripping back to those moments with remembered joy, but then she would think about the body in the grave, and then move on to memories of her father, and Emily, and Kara, and then finally end with her fear of what would happen when Dance encountered the Saldanos again. Then she would circle back around to the missing body, and start all over again, recalling the way Dance had moved above her, the soft sound of his breathing, the male scent of his skin that worked like an aphrodisiac even now.

Wrapping her hands tightly around the wheel, she concentrated hard on the road, forgetting hot, wet kisses and groans of desire, and the feel of hard muscles moving fluidly.

"What?" he asked to the growl she'd unconsciously emitted, low in her throat.

"Nothing."

Margaret Bicknell was behind the pharmacy counter when they turned in the crutches. She stared hard at both of them, her eyes especially raking over Dance. Jordanna didn't doubt that she would report back to her father at the earliest opportunity. *Your crazy daughter was with a man very early in the morning. . . .* Well, her father already knew about Dance, so what of it? She bit back the snarky remark and instead asked if they had a selection of canes.

Margaret pointed them toward the front of the pharmacy, and as Jordanna thanked her, she said pointedly, "I'll be seeing your father at the late morning service today."

Bully for you.

"Reverend Miles likes to start around eleven," she added.

"Let's look over the canes on the way out," Dance suggested, moving Jordanna to the grill counter. Jordanna could feel Margaret's eyes follow her, but then Loretta stepped forward and took their order. Ten minutes later, Dance was tucking into sunny-side-up eggs, three strips of crispy bacon, wheat toast, and orange juice, while Jordanna had one egg over easy and an English muffin. Both of them had coffee, black.

As they finished up, Jordanna inclined her head in Margaret's direction. "I think I'm in trouble for being a) with you, and b) clearly not dressed for church."

"Were you a churchgoer when you were in high school?"

She shook her head. "My father wasn't all that gung-ho about religion back then. That happened afterward, maybe when he hooked up with Jennie. Maybe before, although I don't remember my mother being much for organized religion, either. Emily, my oldest sister, found the Lord the last year she was alive."

"What about Kara?"

"She didn't seem too religious, either." She pushed her food aside, half-eaten, and reached for her coffee. Whenever Kara's name was mentioned, she got an anxious feeling in the pit of her stomach. "How about you?"

"Last time I was in a church was when I got married. Carmen had to have the whole nine yards. I just wanted to get through it. You'd think I would have known then it wasn't going to work, but mistakes were made."

They finished their breakfasts, decided on a cane for Dance, then headed back to the RAV. It was still barely after nine. "Think it's too early to meet Mrs. Fowler?" she asked.

"One way to find out."

She nodded and they climbed into the RAV and headed out of town. "Where do you think Chase Sazlow is in all this? He was supposedly with Bernadette, but if that's her body, where's he? Reverend Miles said he was missing, and everybody else acted like that was fact, except for Rusty, but it sounded like he just didn't know."

"Rusty said Chase's parents were gone and that he thought he was living at the Calversons' ranch," Dance reminded her.

"Then Nate should know whether he's been around or missing." Jordanna thought that over. "You know, they're all members of Green Pastures Church: Nate and Pru Calverson, Bernadette's parents, my father . . . and the service is at eleven."

"You thinking about getting yourself some religion?"

She glanced over at him, loving his rakish smile. "Maybe. What about yourself?"

"We might just have enough time to check in with Mrs. Fowler and then head over there. What's the dress code?"

"Who the hell cares."

He laughed.

Chapter Twenty-One

Jordanna's cell phone rang on the way to the Fowlers', and once again Dance picked it up. "No name," he said, holding the phone her way to reveal the phone number. It was the same one that had been calling her.

"Whoever they are, they don't give up easy."

"Want me to answer it?" he asked.

"Go ahead," she said with a shrug.

"Hello," he answered, purposely giving no other information.

There was a slight hesitation, then a male voice responded, "This is Detective Rafferty with the Portland Police. I'm trying to reach Jordanna Winters." It was Dance's turn to hesitate, but in that moment, the voice asked him, "Is this Jay Danziger?"

He blinked in surprise. So, they knew where he was and whom he was with. "I've met a Detective Rafferty, and she was a woman," he said by way of an answer.

"That's my sister. Detective September Rafferty. I'm August Rafferty, her twin." Dance didn't have any time to process that before he went on, "I've been looking for you, Mr. Danziger, ever since you and Ms. Winters left last week. We found her image on a videotape from one of the cameras

that captured the bombing. Are you in Rock Springs, by any
chance? Because that's the direction I'm heading. . . ."

Auggie had been slouched in a chair in the waiting room
next to Liv, who was looking nearly as uncomfortable as he
felt. The reason: his father and stepmother had decided to
join the entourage at the hospital, and even baby January, his
four-month-old half sister, was at the party. He'd always
thought hospitals had rules about children being allowed in,
especially infants, but apparently there was no such law like
that at Laurelton General.

His father had been throwing him stony looks from the
moment he appeared, which hadn't helped. It wasn't that
Braden Rafferty disliked him; it was quite the opposite in
fact. His father's disapproval was aimed solely at his profes-
sion. Police work? Uh-uh. It was far, far beneath the type of
occupation fit for a Rafferty. Both he and Nine had been
silently rebuked by their father at any and all occasions ever
since they'd not only chosen law enforcement, but stuck with
it. Auggie tended to skip family gatherings entirely, or stay
the minimum amount of time possible. He hadn't expected
this to be such a clan gathering, however, so he'd gotten
caught in this one. The rueful look Liv sent him said she was
sorry she'd talked him into coming. The slight shrug he sent
back to her said it was okay.

But he was itching to leave, and had pretty much decided
to get the hell out when Nine finally arrived. Immediately,
he got to his feet and came toward her, muttering in her ear,
"You're late."

She came to a halt when her gaze fell on their father,
Rosamund, and baby January. "What's going on here?"

"Yeah, well, our father can't ever resist a chance for a
family reunion."

Nine harrumphed, and then there was much oohing and

ahhing over January, who started crying when too many faces crowded around her. Rosamund put her in Braden's stiff arms, and the crying turned into an out-and-out wail until the baby was quickly scooped back up by his mother. Everyone but Auggie, who hung by the open door, crowded in to see July, who was in the midst of labor and had lost her sense of humor. Auggie could see over their heads to her sweating, grim face, and when Rosamund said, "Oh, you're doing so great. So great! Remember, just keep breathing and soon you'll have one of these," squeezing little January to the point the poor kid spit up. July rolled her eyes toward Nine and him, silently begging for help. It was Liv who hustled Rosamund, January, and Braden out of the room, with Nine bringing up the rear.

Back in the waiting room, January started fussing like mad and Rosamund kept walking her around, growing a bit frazzled. Catching his twin's eye, Auggie crooked his head in the direction of the hallway. Nine nodded and followed him into the hospital corridor.

"Anything new on the Saldano case?" she asked him.

"I've been closed out of it." He brought her up to date on what had transpired, adding as an afterthought that Carmen had threatened to find a private investigator to locate her "husband."

"What about this Jordanna Winters?" Nine asked.

"Been calling her, but no answer."

"Gretchen and I got tapped for a new case, though it looks like a Social Security scam." She then told him about the older couple who'd supposedly poisoned each other and the stoner granddaughter who, along with her husband, had been capitalizing on their unreported deaths by using their Social Security money. "Supposedly they got the idea because Gramps and Gran were already doing the same thing with Uncle Harry's money." She then explained about the extra bones in the basement closet.

"How enterprising," Auggie said drily. "How long have they gotten away with it?"

"A lot of years for Harry, it sounds like. About three for the grandparents. I just keep thinking how these people just sat there and poisoned each other. Tox hasn't come through yet to confirm, but I've got this image of them, staring each other down while the poison eats through their systems. Till death do us part and all that."

"Gruesome." And that's when he noticed she wasn't wearing her engagement ring. "What happened here?" he asked, frowning at her hand.

"We're still engaged," she said. "I just can't wear the damn thing."

"Why not?"

"I don't know. Gets in the way."

"Bullshit," he said, growing amused. He knew his twin better than anyone. "You just don't trust your own happiness."

"Look who's talking."

He shrugged. "You're the one screwing with your fiancé's feelings, not me. What does Jake think about this?"

"He's okay with it," she said, a trifle defensively.

"Yeah, right."

"He is," she insisted.

"The old people who poisoned each other bothering you? Making you think there's no perfect ever after?"

"There is no perfect ever after."

"Or our father, with his bad marriage karma?"

"Yeah, well, yes, as a matter of fact. Don't you ever worry about getting married?" she asked.

"Sure, but I don't want to be alone, either," he admitted. "Your problem is, you're overthinking it. Our sister's in there having a baby. No husband. No father. She just up and decided it was time for her, or it wasn't going to happen. It might not be the choice that you want, or I want, but July goes all balls out, and doesn't second-guess herself too much. What the hell. We could all take a lesson."

She stared at him in mock horror. "Who are you, and what have you done with my brother?"

"I'm having a personal crisis," he said, only half kidding. "I don't want to give up the Saldano case. It's become my white whale. They can fire my ass, if they want. I've got a few more pieces I'm working on."

"Jordanna Winters?"

"Yep."

With that, he pulled out his cell phone and dialed her number again. And that's when Jay Danziger answered himself, and Auggie said he was on his way to Rock Springs, throwing a look to his twin, who gave him the okay sign, meaning she would take care of Liv and the rest of the family.

Jordanna immediately pulled over to the side of the road when she heard "Detective Rafferty." Her heart was pounding out of control. If the police knew where they were, then maybe other people did, too. She didn't care what Dance thought. She worried he was still a target, and her primary suspects were the Saldanos.

"I was just thinking of calling the police," Dance was saying into her cell. "My phone isn't working, so that's why I'm on Jordanna's."

She couldn't hear what was being said on the other end of the line, but then Dance said, "There's a place called the Longhorn in Rock Springs, a western restaurant and bar." Then: "Oh, you know it. . . . You know Rock Springs. When do you think you'll be here?" He shot a look to Jordanna. "We'll be there."

"What?" she asked when he hung up.

"Detective August Rafferty, brother to Detective September

Rafferty, is coming to Rock Springs to talk to me, and you," he added.

She thought about the female detective who'd interviewed her at the hospital. She'd seemed better than most of the cops Jordanna had encountered. Maybe her brother would be the same. "Okay," she said.

"If he wants the audiotape, I'll have to go back and get it out of the safe deposit box. I'll call Maxwell. . . ." He trailed off, thinking. "Might as well get my car while I'm there. Good thing we got this." He hefted up the utilitarian metal cane.

"So, what now? Mrs. Fowler?"

"Sure. We're going to miss church, though, since that's about when the detective's showing up."

"Ah, well."

It took them half an hour to reach the Fowler property, which was the adjoining property to Jordanna's family's. The entrance to the three-hundred-twenty-acre farm was similar to that of the Treadwell property: a quarter-mile-long rutted drive that led to a Victorian style house. As they approached the high windows, peeling gingerbread and listing front porch came into view. Some weeds were working their way through the gravel, but overall the place seemed fairly well-tended, certainly better than the way her father had left their homestead.

Jordanna walked up to the front porch and waited for Dance, who wasn't far behind. The utilitarian metal cane gave him stability and more ease of movement.

She tried the ancient bell, but no sound emanated, so she rapped with her knuckles. When that brought no response, she slapped her palm loudly against the door frame.

"Not here," she said.

"Want to interview the Benchleys?"

"Yeah." She checked her cell phone for the time. "When's that detective getting here?"

"We're bound to still have a couple hours."

Suddenly a wisp of lacy curtain was pulled back and an elderly female face stared out at them through a wavy windowpane. Faded blue eyes raked over them.

Jordanna called loudly through the closed door, "I'm Jordanna Winters. I grew up next door?" She swept an arm toward the south. She was pretty sure Mrs. Fowler wouldn't remember her, as they'd hardly ever seen each other and it had been years. It took an inordinately long time for the door to be opened. When it finally was pulled inward, a stooped woman with white hair and a soft face covered in wrinkles stood leaning in the doorway, one gnarled hand gripping the ivory handle of a polished mahogany cane. "Winters," she repeated in a voice that sounded as if it hadn't been used for years. She eyed Jordanna as if she were some specimen under glass. "You're one of Dr. Winters's daughters."

"The middle one."

"Your mother was a Treadwell."

"That's right."

She pushed the door open farther and shuffled back, a tacit invitation. As Jordanna entered the shadowy environs, followed by Dance, the older woman said to him, "What's wrong with your leg?"

"Wrong place at the wrong time," he said easily. "Nice cane."

She looked at his and frowned but didn't comment. She moved slowly into a parlor off the hall entry, and Jordanna and Dance followed her inside. It took her a few moments to settle herself into a chair next to a fieldstone fireplace with an oversized firebox, now fitted with an electric heater. Glowing red filaments created the illusion of flames. Though it wasn't quite midday, the shades were drawn and the room was dark. A floor lamp offered weak yellow light. "I'm Virginia Fowler," she stated, waving a finger at Dance. "Sit down. You make me nervous. You a farmer? That happen to you on the job? You don't look like a farmer."

Dance took an overstuffed chair that looked as if it might be difficult for him to get out of, and Jordanna perched on the edge of a love seat that offered up a whiff of dust. Looking faintly amused, Dance said, "No, I'm not a farmer. I got too close to a bomb."

"Bomb." Her brows shot up. "Well, how did that happen?" Then, before either of them could answer, she asked, "You with those police fellows?"

"The police came here?" Jordanna asked.

"Said someone was trespassing on my property. Defiling the cemetery."

Jordanna started. "I was at the cemetery," she admitted. "Someone had recently buried a woman's body there, just covered it with dirt. I reported it, but the body was moved before the police got there."

Virginia's eyes pinned Jordanna where she sat. "That officer said there was nothing there. He apologized and said he would make sure to keep people out."

"Drummond?"

"Think that was his name, yes." She pursed her lips, then said, "I don't know who'd be messing around out there." Turning to Dance, she asked, "This bomb, was it meant for you?"

"I don't know yet," Dance answered honestly.

"Does it have anything to do with my cemetery?"

"Nope. Separate issue," he said. Then: "Do you live alone?"

"Yes. Why? You planning to rob me?"

She glared at Dance, who asked casually, "You got anything worth taking?"

Jordanna hid a smile as Virginia sized him up for a long, long moment. She was half certain they were about to be flung out on the porch. Then the older woman's lips quirked, and she turned away from him and focused in on Jordanna.

"So, how come you were looking for a body on my property?"

"I was actually following directions to where an unidentified man's body was discovered a few years ago, just across Summit Ridge from your property. Do you know Zach Benchley? He's the boy who found the body."

"I know Zach," she said shortly. "Driving that contraption all over hell and gone. Probably ran over the poor devil and killed him himself."

Not exactly a mutual admiration society, since Zach had tried to blame Mrs. Fowler for the deed as well. "According to the ME, he died of exposure," Jordanna said.

She huffed at that. "Zach's no real Benchley, y'know. His father sure wants everyone to know that he was adopted, so's the whole family's not tainted. Doesn't want anyone to really think he's a Benchley. Being part-Treadwell yourself, you gotta know about that."

"The Treadwell Curse," Jordanna confirmed.

Virginia frowned, her brows forming a silvery caterpillar above her eyes. "What's that? There's no Treadwell Curse."

"It's just what everyone calls it," Jordanna said, wanting to move back to the issue of the missing body.

Virginia Fowler waved a bony finger at her. "Well, I think you've got that mixed up, dear," she said briskly. "The Benchleys . . . now they had troubles. All this land was theirs once, you know. Yours, too. Used to be owned by Danners and Garretts at the turn of the last century, but most of them moved on or maybe Ukiah Benchley pushed them out. My late husband knew all the history, but I'm not as clear on the details.

"But I do know Old Ukiah was from a railway family," she hurried to say, sensing Jordanna was about to interrupt. "Lots of money that he spent on drink, gambling, and women of ill repute. Mean as a poked snake, from all accounts, but mighty attractive. That's another Benchley trait. Good looks." Her eyes glittered. "But then Ukiah married a woman who couldn't produce an heir, so he adopted back his illegitimate son, who was as wild as his old man. Started having children when he was barely into his teens, but those kids started dying young. That's when it became evident something was wrong. You want to name it, you should call it the Benchley Curse. Why do you think they have that old cemetery?" She hitched a thumb toward the back of her house. "Started putting the afflicted there. To keep 'em away from the ones going to heaven." She snorted, as if she thought that was a bunch of rot.

"My mother suffered from the disease, and she was a Treadwell," Jordanna said. "I didn't name it the Treadwell Curse. That's just what people call it."

"Who does?" the old lady demanded.

"Everyone I've talked to," Jordanna responded, faintly impatient.

"That's rot. The Treadwells tried to help the Benchleys. That's all, dear. They tended to the sick when everyone else shunned them. The true Benchleys sold off all their property to the Treadwells, like your mother, and my husband, and those adopted Benchleys, Zach's family. There are three or four of them left, that's all. A few brothers and a sister, Agnes. I don't recall the brothers' names . . . Oswald and . . ." She shook her head. "Anyway, Agnes is the only one that drives and she goes into town now and again and gets supplies. The Treadwells are about all gone, except for you and your sisters, so the Benchleys have to do it for themselves now." She eyed Jordanna. "How many Treadwells are there left?"

"I only know of my sister, Kara. And I have an aunt who never married and lives in Malone. Evelyn Treadwell."

"Oh, that's right. I remember her. She have any children?"

"No," Jordanna said.

"Well, it's too bad for the Benchleys that the Treadwells died off. But you only get that particular affliction by being a Benchley. That's a fact. And there are only a handful of them left, too."

"The Benchleys you mean are the ones living at the curve of the road, the place with the 'No Trespassing' sign," Dance put in.

She nodded. "They don't much like socializing, that's for certain. Never married and had children. Their way of ending the disease."

Jordanna was torn between frustration and amusement. She'd come here for information about the cemetery, but Virginia Fowler was intent on giving her her own faulty family history. Jordanna knew her mother had been sick with the Treadwell Curse. Her father knew it, Kara knew it, and Emily had known it. "My mother died of the Curse."

"Eh?"

"My mother died of the Treadwell Curse." She hesitated, then added reluctantly, saying what she'd sometimes thought, but had never wanted to voice. "And my older sister started acting erratically just before she died in a car accident her senior year of high school. She may have had it, too."

Virginia's eyes bored into Jordanna's. "I don't mean to upset you, dear, but you should look into your family history a little closer."

"If the Benchleys and Treadwells were so interconnected, maybe there was an undocumented liaison between the families," Dance offered up.

Virginia said stubbornly, "It all goes back to the Benchleys. That's who's buried out in the cemetery. Benchleys. My husband's with his family at Everhardt Cemetery out north of town, and that's where I'm going, too." She waved a dismissive hand. "The state can figure out what to do with this property and that cemetery."

They talked for a while more, but Virginia never budged from her insistence that the Benchleys were to blame for the disease, not the Treadwells. As their conversation wound down, Jordanna asked, "Do you know the Freads?"

"I don't believe so. Who are they?"

"Their daughter, Bernadette, is missing, and when I saw the body last night, I wondered if it might be her."

Virginia wagged her head from side to side, then returned to her favorite topic with a relentlessness that made Jordanna want to scream. "If your mama really died of that disease, you ask your doctor father about her," Virginia Fowler said, staring her down. "Bet you'll find out she's a Benchley. And if that's true, my dear, you'd best be practicing that 'safe sex' because you don't want to be having any children. . . ."

Boo sat in the pew, his eyes on Reverend Miles, who was talking, and talking, and talking . . . sermonizing . . . in front of the congregation. Normally Boo liked church. It was soothing, and it reminded him of when Mama was alive. She could sing like a nightingale, Pops would say. Boo had never seen a nightingale, but he heard they sang at night, and that reminded him of Mama, too, because she'd disappeared into the night.

But today he was just scared. He'd heard Buddy on the phone and he knew he'd done something bad again. When Buddy had gone to the barn, Boo had been with him, staying in the shadows, watching. When he'd seen the hot tip of the branding iron, he'd been mesmerized, almost overpowered with the desire to trace his own scar with his index finger. But he'd stopped himself, told himself that God wouldn't want him to dwell. Then Buddy had fallen to his knees and begged God's forgiveness for killing another who wasn't supposed to die. It had been a necessity, he'd sworn, his forehead pressed to the rough boards of the barn floor. He'd had to do it . . . just like the last time. . . .

Boo's eyes had drifted to the door with the bar. Something terrible had happened in there. He wanted to look, but Buddy had been so angry over his special treasure box, he was afraid what he would do if he caught Boo sneaking around some more, looking at things he wasn't supposed to. Instead, Boo had gone back to his bed, tossing and turning all night, wondering if he should tell someone, confess Buddy's sins so that both he and Buddy could be cleansed. Boo had been so angry with Buddy for taking Mama's special treasures from him that he'd stayed in his room for days, lying on his bunk, face turned to the wall. Buddy had railed at him, telling him he needed to grow up, to stop waiting for Mama, who wasn't coming back. Boo had slowly fought back his anger and forgiven him. Buddy was all he had left, unless you counted *her*, which Boo didn't.

But maybe someone needed to know that Buddy had done something unforgivable. He looked at the reverend. He was a good man. A pious man. He would know what to do, wouldn't he?

He leaned forward, half in a trance, ready to walk up the aisle in front of God and everybody, right in the middle of Reverend Miles's sermon, when a hand darted out and grabbed him by the wrist.

"What are you doing?" she hissed, a harsh whisper that sent a cold shiver down his back. Buddy might look up to her, but she scared Boo.

"Nothing," he muttered.

"Don't bother the reverend. What's wrong with you?"

Her hand was curved around his forearm, hard fingers holding him in place. In the pew in front of them, an older woman turned and gave them a *look*. Boo wanted to yell at her to turn around, but he didn't. He was in church, and he knew better.

"Let us pray," Reverend Miles intoned and everyone bowed their heads.

Boo had a moment of panic. He hadn't been paying attention to what they were praying for, and he needed to know. Maybe prayer was all that was needed to cleanse their souls, so he squeezed his eyes shut and fervently prayed with all his being.

"Stop moving your lips," *she* muttered, her grip tightening.

Boo felt embarrassed, but he blocked out her voice and kept right on praying. And why did she have her eyes open anyway?

"Amen," the reverend said at last, and they all repeated "Amen" back to him. Boo opened his eyes. The first person he saw was Nate Calverson, the second, his wife. He didn't like Nate much. He pretended to care about the Lord, but he really didn't. That was his wife's doing, Buddy had said.

"Calverson's as much of a prick as his father was," Buddy had added. "They own practically everything around here. They're locusts. Gobbling up farms and ranches."

"Aren't you friends?" Boo had asked, then shrank back because Buddy glared at him so furiously his eyes glowed like blue fire.

"They're a pestilence, and pretty soon, all of the good families will be gone and only the Calversons and the putrid ones will remain."

"The Treadwell Curse," Boo whispered. Buddy had nodded gravely, and Boo was relieved that he'd said the right thing.

But that was before Buddy had made the bad mistakes.

Looking at Calverson, Boo once more had the overpowering urge to trace his scar through his pants, but *she* would see and so would Buddy. He stirred in his seat and the hand that had started to relax clamped hard on his arm again.

"There's Abel Fread. You see him?" she hissed.

Boo looked toward the front pews. The gray-haired Mr. Fread was seated in the second row, on the right-hand side. He was with his wife and two boys. His daughter wasn't with him. She'd been drinking and whoring around with Chase and was damn lucky she hadn't got herself knocked up, Buddy had said. "She's one of the tainted ones," Buddy had confided to Boo.

"I see him," Boo said now, focused on Mr. Fread, whose hair looked silver under the lights.

Her voice lowered. "Now, listen to me. Bernadette was clean. Do you understand?"

Boo felt a stab of fear. Had Buddy made *another* mistake? No, he couldn't have! "She had the putrid—"

"No! She didn't have it."

He tried to stall. "It?"

"*It.* You know what I mean." Her mouth was practically touching his ear. Her anger was like hot fire. He wanted to squirm away, but she wouldn't let him. "We all have to atone, but whatever you're thinking, stop it. You can't tell the reverend anything now."

Did she know about the man whom Buddy had called collateral damage? Was she just mind-fucking with him about Bernadette Fread? Trying to learn what he knew about Buddy? Digging, digging, digging. Well, she'd learn nothing from him. He would prove to Buddy what a good soldier he could be.

"I'm not saying anything." He was firm on that.

"Good," she said. "Keep your mouth shut about every-thing." She moved away from him, and he could concentrate on the organ music that had swelled up and was making him feel calmer. Church was good.

He looked at Buddy, who'd moved to some remote place in his head. Boo willed him to stay away from her. They didn't need her. They didn't. If Buddy would just break from her, then maybe he wouldn't be making any mistakes.

He thought about that long and hard. He wished, wished, wished she would just disappear.

And then she said, "And where's Chase?"

Chapter Twenty-Two

Dance and Jordanna walked into the Longhorn a little after eleven and found the place nearly deserted. Danny, at the bar, seemed to know exactly what they were thinking because he said, "Most people who come in here pretend they don't go to church, but most of 'em do."

They took the same booth they'd had the night before. Dance picked up a menu, but he wasn't really looking at it. Jordanna didn't know what he was thinking about, probably the detective who was on his way, but her mind kept turning over everything Virginia Fowler had said and intimated. That last line about making sure she didn't have any children was stuck in her brain like a needle in a groove.

She stuck her nose inside the menu, the words an indistinct blur. She and Dance had made love a number of times in the last twenty-four hours with no regard for protection. She was fairly confident that it wasn't a time she could get pregnant, but she was a bit astonished at the way she'd thrown caution to the wind. Hell, she hadn't even really thought about it, which was . . . well, crazy.

"I've been thinking about the bombing," Dance said, after the waitress had come by and taken their order for a beer and a Diet Coke. "I'm going to give this detective the audiotape, but I don't think that's why Saldano Industries was hit. I gave Max the tape. He was concerned about what was on it, worried something was going on through the warehouse they knew nothing about. I'm sure he told Victor about it, and maybe the word got out . . . but for someone to deliver a bomb? That's hard-core. And let's say they knew the tape was in the safe in Max's office, which is where Max said he put it, would they really bomb the building for it?"

Jordanna shook her head, dispelling the remnants of her own thoughts. "I've never thought the bombing was about the audiotape," she told him. "You didn't, either, in the hospital."

He smiled faintly. "What I knew in the hospital was that Max wasn't there when he was supposed to be. That's about as far as I got."

"But you felt threatened. That's why you came with me. Maybe it was at a gut level, but you knew something was wrong."

Dance reached across the table and clasped her hands. "Maybe I was just weak . . . injured."

"I think the bomb was meant for you," Jordanna told him. "That hasn't changed."

"But why? I didn't have anything on the Saldanos. I was looking into their operation, but it was low-key. No big investigation."

"Yet. You were going to be ramping up, because that's what you do," she reminded him, "once you have some evidence."

"But the audiotape doesn't really give anything. It's two guys maybe planning to smuggle in some illegal product, or maybe it's just two guys bullshitting. The point is, it was never enough evidence of a crime on its own. That's why I gave it to Max."

The waitress appeared with their drinks. Dance let go of

her hands and sat back. When they were alone again, he said, "Logically, an attack on me doesn't make sense."

"But you felt it, too. The danger. And it wasn't just because you were hurt."

"Yeah . . ." He frowned.

At that moment, a tall, dark-haired man pushed through the saloon doors. Lean and rugged in jeans and boots, he looked like he fit right in to the Rock Springs cowboy crowd. Spying them, he came straight over. His eyes were blue, a bit grayer than Dance's, and he thrust out a hand to him, which Dance shook.

"August Rafferty," he said, pulling out his ID for them both to examine. As he tucked it back, he shook Jordanna's hand as well, and said, "You're Jay Danziger and Jordanna Winters."

"Yes, we are," Dance said, as Jordanna slid her Coke to Dance's side of the table, then took a seat beside him, inviting the detective to sit down across from them.

"Let me start by saying I'm not on the Saldano case any longer," the detective jumped right in. "The feds have taken it over, and starting tomorrow, I'll likely be assigned to something else. As far as I know, the feds are concentrating on the Saldanos and their business." He looked at Jordanna. "They haven't focused on you yet, but they will. Camera footage from Saldano Industries puts you there at the time of the bombing. They're going to want to know what you were doing."

"I was following Dance," she said.

"My nickname," Dance supplied.

"Why were you following him?" he asked Jordanna.

"Because I'm a reporter, and I guess you'd say an admirer," she admitted, after a brief hesitation, "and I thought he was in danger."

"You thought he was in danger prior to the bombing?" he asked, brows lifting.

"Just an intuition. Maybe a wrong one." She shrugged.

"Did you feel like you were in danger?" he asked Dance.

"Some, maybe. There's always a level of danger when you're investigating a possible smuggling operation. . . ." Quickly, he explained about the audiotape and the fact that he'd given a copy to Max but another was in his safe deposit box. He finished with, "The man who made the tape had already left Saldano Industries by the time he gave it to me. He didn't want the repercussions of being a whistleblower."

"You should have told us this immediately," he said.

"Yes, I should've," Dance conceded. "But, I don't think it's the reason for the bombing." He then related to Rafferty what he and Jordanna had just discussed.

"I'd like to listen to the tape," he said.

"I'll give you my copy, once I get it from the safe deposit box. I can get it to you tomorrow, after my bank opens."

"I'm driving him back," Jordanna put in. "He doesn't have a car here."

Rafferty mulled that over and said to Dance, "I thought the reason you hightailed out of the hospital so fast was because you thought you were in danger."

"I'm ready to get some things straight with Maxwell," Dance said, by way of an answer.

"If part of getting things straight includes telling him that you and Carmen are legally divorced, he and Victor already know," the detective admitted. "I told them."

"Carmen was the one who wanted to keep that a secret. Wonder how it went over." Dance was faintly amused. "She's back now, I take it."

"Yep. And in case you're wondering, she had your vehicle towed back to your house. She's unhappy with how we've handled the investigation, specifically that we didn't put out an APB on you. The last I spoke to her, she said she was hiring a private investigator."

"Well, I guess I've got to do some straightening out with

her, too," Dance said, his long-suffering tone drawing a smile to Rafferty's lips.

He sobered rapidly, however. "You'll have to talk to the feds, too."

Dance nodded slowly, accepting the inevitable.

"Is there anything else you can tell us about the investigation into the bombing?" Jordanna asked.

He said carefully, "I can only tell you what's already been reported."

"We haven't really been keeping up with the news," Jordanna said, thinking of their rustic living arrangements.

If Rafferty wondered why, he didn't ask. "The investigation's proceeding. Progress is being made. I can tell you that the bomb was simple, but effective, and triggered by a remote."

"Remote," Dance repeated. "There was no timing mechanism?"

"Whoever deployed it, did it wirelessly. It still may have been set up for a certain time, or it may have happened instantly, at the push of a button. We don't know that yet."

"It wasn't the audiotape," Jordanna broke in. "Dance could have made ten copies, a hundred, *thousands* . . . so what good would that do to bomb the building to remove the tape? Dance said there wasn't that much on it anyway." She looked at him for corroboration, and he shrugged and nodded, so she plowed on. "You want to know what I think?" she asked the detective. "This is about Dance. I've said it all along, and I'm saying it now." She turned to Dance once again. "This is about you. You're the threat. The investigator who won't give. The terrier with a reputation for uncovering deep corporate secrets. Whoever it is isn't trying to get rid of evidence. They're trying to get rid of the man who seeks that evidence."

There was a moment of silence as the waitress came to

take their food order. As soon as she was gone, Rafferty gave Jordanna a long look.

"I'm kinda thinking you're right," he said.

Rafferty ordered the Longhorn's Sunday breakfast—bacon, eggs, hash browns, and toast—while Dance had another Reuben and Jordanna picked at a green salad with limp-looking vegetables. They went over the case for another hour, with Rafferty still careful to give them only what had already been reported, and Dance only half-convinced he was the bomber's ultimate target. The more they talked, the less comfortable Jordanna became.

"I don't want you to go," she finally said to Dance, when Rafferty took a trip to the men's room.

"I don't intend to stay long. After I get Rafferty the audiotape and meet with Max, I could be back by tomorrow night."

"What's all this 'I' stuff? I'm going with you."

"I thought I might catch a ride with Rafferty. Bring back my own car."

She was taken aback. "That's what you want to do?"

"I want to stay with you," he said. "But I want to take care of this, too."

"You're going to run into Carmen," she said, then was shocked and slightly embarrassed that she'd mentioned that fear aloud.

"She's my ex for a reason," he assured her.

Yeah, but does she really feel that way? Jordanna had no claim on him, and these past few days had been unreal, fraught with tension and danger. She didn't want to have him face the Saldanos without her, but she also sensed he'd already made up his mind.

"You've got a lot going on here," he said, "and I intend to be a part of it, when I get back. Somebody moved that body, and if the police are dragging their feet, I want to get on it and find out who."

She nodded. He was right. She knew he was right.

"Don't take any chances, while I'm gone," he said suddenly.

"That's my line."

He smiled. "Hey, I'm going back with the law."

"Yeah, but Rafferty's not going to be with you the whole time." She drew a quick breath. "How will I get hold of you?"

For an answer, he pulled his phone, wallet, and keys from his pocket. "I've kept all my stuff together. I'll pick up a charger at the house and call you as soon as the phone's up again. We'll get Rafferty's cell number. You can call him if you need to reach me."

"He called my cell, so it's on my phone already."

"Good."

Again, she'd barely touched her meal, but she had no appetite. "While you're gone, I'll talk to my father," she told him. "I should've before, but after what Mrs. Fowler said, I've got a ton more questions."

"Think of him as a source," Dance said softly, sliding his arm around her, his chin on the top of her head.

She leaned into him and closed her eyes. What was happening between them felt so fragile. She was afraid this separation would break it. "You're coming back." It was said as a statement, but she heard the pleading in her voice, whether he did or not.

"Yes," Dance said firmly, as the detective returned to the booth.

Her cell phone rang and she thought about ignoring it, but she plucked it from her purse and looked at the caller. Rusty. She let it go to voice mail, not wanting to miss a moment of Dance and Rafferty's conversation. When Dance asked him if he could cadge a ride back to Portland with him, Rafferty was more than willing. As she processed the fact that he was really leaving, she heard the *ping* that announced she had a text. She ignored the text, but it hardly mattered as Dance and Rafferty's conversation had moved right on by, decisions made, the deal set. She felt left out, and it frustrated her, especially when it looked like Dance was planning to take off immediately, not even go back to the homestead. "I'll pick up some more clothes at home and come straight back," he assured her.

Jordanna nodded, but a cold feeling had settled in her gut. A sense of impending doom. Everything was happening too fast, and she was powerless to change anything. As they walked out of the restaurant in a group, she forced herself to swallow back her fears and misgivings.

"I guess this is it," she said, then was surprised, gratified, and half embarrassed when Dance suddenly gathered her close and gave her a long kiss by the hitching post outside the Longhorn's entryway.

"Don't sound so final," he told her. "See you tomorrow. . . ."

He watched the kiss from across the street, feeling both disgusted and sexually thrilled in a way he knew he shouldn't. Temptation. That's what the Treadwell women were. Satan's little joke. But he wasn't going to give in again. With curiosity, he watched the two men climb into a Jeep and head one way, and Jordanna move to her own vehicle and go the other. The Jeep was aimed north, but Jordanna was heading south, the same direction as the Treadwell homestead. She and her lover were separating? Now what was this about?

Opportunity, he realized.

He eased his truck onto the main street and began following her. Had to be careful. Couldn't let anyone see. God loved the patient man.

* * *

Jordanna was halfway back to the house, her energy on a slow downward spiral, when she concluded she needed to go back to town. She'd put off talking to her father for most of her adult life, and now that she'd told Dance she was going to speak with him, she wanted it done. She wanted closure on her past.

She turned around, her face set. The truth was, she'd balked about facing her father because deep down, she felt guilty. Guilty about firing at him, blaming him for everything, including her mother's death. After all this time, she didn't know what she'd really seen between Emily and her father. Maybe in truth she'd just wanted someone to blame for everything bad that had happened in those years.

Wasn't that what Dr. Eggers tried to tell you? Transference, she said. Shifting blame to someone or something unrelated because you can't blame the responsible party.

She was heading down Rock Springs's main street, toward the housing development where she knew her father and Jennie had moved, but when she passed the Garrett Hotel, she spied her father himself, his hand on the small of Jennie's back, holding the door open for his bride. They were undoubtedly having lunch at the hotel restaurant.

Well, okay. She'd meet them there. She took a left at the next intersection, which put her on the street that ran right in front of the offices of the *Pioneer.* Turning through their lot, she drove back to the center of town, sliding into a parking spot across from the hotel. The street was near empty, as most of the shops on either side of the street were closed on Sunday.

She was conscious of the fact that her father had been in slacks, a dress shirt, and a navy blazer while Jennie had been put together in a white dress with a matching bolero, piped in scarlet, her heels the exact shade of red as the piping. She glanced down at her own jeans, sweater, and boots. What the hell. This was a cowboy town, right?

"Welcome to the Garrett Hotel," a young woman with a ponytail and perfect white teeth greeted her from the maître d' stand. In her arms was a stack of leather-bound menus, the little tassels sticking out from their bottom edges swinging jauntily. "Do you have a reservation?"

"Um, no, I'm joining Dr. Winters's party," Jordanna said.

That threw her. "We have Dr. and Mrs. Winters at a table for two, but we could move them to that one?" She pointed to a table nestled in the bowed space created by three windows.

"Sounds great."

The Garrett Hotel was modeled after the original structure, which was built circa 1890-ish. It had been demolished nearly a century ago and rebuilt at least twice since. Jordanna had been inside the main-floor restaurant several times, and though she suspected the brown short-pile carpet was new, the white gauzy curtains, the bell-shaped light fixtures, the gatherings of oak tables and chairs, and the cabbage rose mauve wallpaper were just as she remembered.

She followed after the maître d' to the rear corner of the room, where her father and Jennie had just been served champagne glasses filled with orange juice. Knowing their tastes, she doubted there was any champagne involved.

"Jordanna," her father said in surprise, half rising from his seat.

The girl with the menus said, "We have a table for three in the front, if that's okay?"

Her father blinked once, and Jennie's mouth dropped open in silent query.

"Sorry I'm late," Jordanna put in.

"Thank you," Dayton said to the girl, recovering quickly. He held out a hand to his wife, who gathered up her glass of orange juice and his, and then moved ahead of them to the new table, shooting an anxious look back at Jordanna.

Once they were all seated and the girl had deposited new menus, Jennie asked, "Where's your friend, Mr. Danziger?"

"Dance was called back to Portland," Jordanna said.

Jennie looked from Jordanna to Dayton, clearly thrown by Jordanna barging in, but she said, "I'm so glad you joined us."

"Yes," her father said, his blue eyes a bit careful, as if he was afraid of what might be coming next. She could hardly blame him.

"We just came from church," Jennie said, trying hard not to stare too pointedly at Jordanna's clothes.

"I figured." Now that she was here, Jordanna hardly knew where to start.

Her father took the reins. "I talked to Greer at church this morning. He said you found a woman's body in the old Benchley Cemetery, but that the body was later missing."

Greer Markum. Jennie's father. "That's true, but he didn't believe me." Jordanna was curt.

Jennie fussed with her napkin, and her father said, "He questions your judgment, Jordanna. But he did say something had been buried there that was removed."

"Well, goody."

"Daddy's very thorough," Jennie murmured.

Jordanna addressed her father. "Did he also tell you I think it might be Bernadette Fread, and that she had an upside-down cross branded onto her buttock, just like the 'homeless' victim three years ago?"

Lines formed between her father's brows. "Branded?"

"Oh, that's right. The chief kept that little tidbit back, although it's an open secret, so I'm surprised you haven't heard. I went out to Summit Ridge to find where the first victim was located, and I practically stumbled on the cemetery. You call it the old Benchley Cemetery. Virginia

Fowler, whose property it's on, said it was for the Benchleys too."

"You met with Virginia?" he asked.

"Dance and I talked to her this morning. Here's the thing. She said she's never heard of the Treadwell Curse. She blamed Mom's disease on the Benchleys. Pretty much blamed everything on the Benchleys, as a matter of fact."

In a whisper, Jennie said, "Could we talk a little softer?"

Jordanna gritted her teeth. She didn't really give a damn who heard, but she dropped her volume. "I feel like people are talking in circles. I can't get a straight answer out of anyone."

"Well, I've never heard of the Treadwell Curse, either," her father admitted. "I know the Benchleys have had their share of physical ailments, in what acts like a genetic disease, though it's never been proven. Sometimes mental illness is inexplicable."

Jordanna stared at him. "You've never heard of the Treadwell Curse."

"No."

"Mom's disease," she said again.

"Your mother had seizures from a car accident when she was young. Her father always blamed himself, but it was really the other driver's fault. Gayle didn't have what the Benchleys had. You knew this," he reminded her, looking at her as if he wasn't certain she was all there.

"No, I didn't. I've never heard this." Jordanna was flabbergasted.

"Well, I've never heard of this Treadwell Curse." He regarded her patiently. "Where did you hear that?"

"From practically everyone. It's . . . a saying," Jordanna insisted.

"Who's everyone?" he asked.

Jordanna looked to Jennie, who was staring at Dayton, as

if mesmerized. "You know it," Jordanna accused. "When we were in high school, I got teased about it. People would talk behind my back."

"I don't know," she murmured, tucking in her shoulders as if she were going to fold in on herself.

Jordanna felt a flash of anger. The little liar. "We all talked about it," Jordanna said. "I just talked to Rusty Long about it. And Kara knows. Emily knew," she added flatly.

Her father glanced around, his expression pained. He leaned closer to her. "I've got something to say, that I've wanted to say for a long time. This isn't the place for this conversation, but since you've chosen the venue, I'm going to take my opportunity."

All of a sudden Jordanna wanted to bolt. If he was going to talk about Emily . . .

"Don't look at me that way," her father said heavily. "You're a reporter now. You look for facts, right?" When she didn't respond, he went on, "Something I've never told you, something your mother and I didn't want advertised, is that Emily was part Benchley. She was abandoned, and we adopted her. We didn't sincerely believe the Benchleys had this debilitating disease, and it wouldn't have mattered anyway. She was a beautiful baby, a beautiful girl. Gayle and I didn't think we could have children, but after Emily, we had both you and Kara."

"You're saying Emily was adopted?"

"That's exactly what I'm saying." He drew a breath. "I know what you think happened between us, but it's not the truth. That night wasn't the first time Emily had come into my bedroom. She was always a sleepwalker. She climbed in bed with us all the time when your mother was alive. It wasn't anything . . . inappropriate."

"I don't believe you," Jordanna said tonelessly.

He lifted a hand, silently asking her to wait until he was

finished. "It's true that Emily became more sexual as she got older. I don't think she could help herself. I wasn't paying enough attention after your mother died. We were all grieving for her. You, especially," he said, shooting her a quick look. "Emily's deterioration got away from me. She was having hallucinations, acting out. I prescribed her antipsychotics, but she wouldn't take them regularly." He hesitated. "I told you all this before, but you wouldn't hear me."

Transference. "I heard you. I just didn't believe you."

"I don't know where this Treadwell Curse came from. Maybe because of Emily? It was clear something was wrong those last few months before she died."

This was too much information. A shift in perception that was almost too hard to make. No Treadwell Curse? How could that be? She'd lived with the term most of her life. But where had she heard it first? Emily . . .? Kara . . . ? Rusty? Nate Calverson? Martin Lourde? She realized distantly that everyone she was naming had been a high school kid at the time, open to suggestion and innuendo, ready to believe the worst of their fellow man in a way that adulthood generally washes away. Had she completely misunderstood? *How could that be?*

"I've got to go," she said, jumping to her feet just as the waiter came by to take their order.

Her father waved the girl away and said urgently to Jordanna, "Stay," reaching out a hand to her.

She pulled back slowly until he was forced to let her go. "No, thank you." She was being inordinately polite. Sick with guilt and unsure in a way that made her feel nauseous. Was this the truth, then? There was no Treadwell Curse? No sexual abuse against her sister? Had she shot her father in error?

"Dayton!" Emily had screamed. Was that because she'd been shocked awake from her sleepwalking? As surprised as Jordanna had been to find herself in her father's bed?

Jennie said, "Oh, don't run off."

But Jordanna needed to leave, time to process. She turned abruptly, nearly knocking over Jennie's almost-empty glass of orange juice. "I've got to go."

"Jordanna . . ." Her father's resigned voice reached her ears, but she was already to the vestibule, her lungs feeling as though they would burst if she didn't get air. She ran outside into late-May sunshine and half stumbled down the front steps.

Chapter Twenty-Three

She caught herself on the porch rail before she fell onto the sidewalk. She felt as if she were sinking, like those few seconds when an elevator drops before your body catches up. She'd prided herself for so long on being right in a world that was wrong. It was dizzying. It was like having an out-of-body experience, she was so inwardly focused.

Drawing a breath, she managed to look both ways before crossing the street. Her RAV was directly across from her. She took two steps forward before it came to her in a rush.

Immediately, she stumbled back up the steps, grabbing the rail, telling herself to calm down, get a grip. Then she headed back inside and swept past the smiling and surprised menu-girl and back to the table where her father and Jennie were staring glumly at one another.

"Aunt Evelyn," Jordanna said, when her father saw her, his eyes brightening.

Instantly, his expression grew wary. "Evelyn?"

"She didn't have any children because she was a Treadwell. She didn't want to pass on the rogue gene. I've heard her say that."

Her father just stared at her, so frozen that even Jennie

grew worried and reached across the table. "Dayton?" she asked in a quavering voice. "Are you all right?"

"I'm fine," he said brusquely, coming to himself.

"Aunt Evelyn knew about the Treadwell Curse," Jordanna stated firmly.

He bent his head, seemed to want to say something, but in the end he merely pressed his lips together and stayed silent. Jordanna took that as an affirmation and turned to leave, but her father's voice caught up with her, "You should really talk to your aunt."

She turned back. "Why? What's she going to tell me? That I'm wrong? She said she didn't want children because she was a Treadwell."

"I don't believe you heard her correctly."

She was sick of his careful tone. "Why?" When he hesitated, she said, "Just say it!"

"She did have a child, Jordanna. Emily is her daughter."

"Hey."

He whipped around, surprised by the voice almost in his ear. He'd been parked down the street, waiting for Jordanna to come out of the hotel. Suddenly she had, but as soon as he'd started his engine, she'd gone back in and he'd had to switch it off again.

He turned now to look at the man who'd come up to the driver's side of the truck. Abel Fread. "Yes, sir?" he asked politely, his heart thudding. Had Abel seen what he was doing? Did he know he was watching Jordanna?

"You seen Chase around?" he growled.

He had to remind himself that Abel was a good man, a God-fearing man, because he suddenly wanted to choke the living shit out of him.

"Nope."

"You see him, you tell him to bring my daughter back, or I'm gonna castrate him."

He had nothing to say to that.

Abel's eyes narrowed. "I'm coming up to your place. Want to see that stallion you put out to stud. Heard you might be sellin' it."

"Who told you that?"

He shrugged. "Don't matter. Stands to reason. Your place in foreclosure, and all. Gotta be lookin' for income somehow."

A knot built in his chest. *Abel's a good man. He's in God's favor.*

"You goin' back now?"

"Not yet."

"Okay, I'll stop in and wait for ya, then. Got some time. Meet 'cha there." He ambled away toward his own truck, a new black Ford F-150.

He felt a roar building in his chest. He gazed at the front door of the hotel in blank fury, then switched on the ignition and headed back to the farm.

With her father's bald announcement still ringing in her ears, Jordanna drove back to the homestead. She'd left almost as soon as he'd told her Emily was Aunt Evelyn's, completely discombobulated all over again. How many more secrets did her father have in store?

As she walked along the wooden planks to the back door, she texted Kara again. Call me. I really want to talk to you. Inside the house she went straight to her laptop, switching it on, waiting for it to flicker through its wake-up routine.

Emily was abandoned. . . .

What was the truth about the Treadwells and the Bench-leys? So many half-truths and tantalizing glimpses, but nothing of substance. Why hadn't anyone been straight with her?

Would you have listened? When you were just trying to

survive after Mom's death? Would you have believed anything anyone told you?

She stared at the computer screen. The cursor flashed at her like a warning. She was tired. She hadn't had enough sleep, but she wouldn't change the way the night before had spun out for the world.

You're in love with him.

"Fat lot of good it'll do me," she said aloud, though a part of her wanted to believe that everything was going to work out beautifully . . . that they would plan a life together . . . work together . . . spend endless days together.

Shoving the laptop onto the bench, she sank down on the couch and covered her face with her hands. The next twenty-four hours were going to be hell . . . and that was if he made good on his promise to return as fast as possible.

Dance leaned back against the headrest and closed his eyes. His head faintly throbbed, but it was nothing like before. He'd taken some more aspirin this morning, but he was through with the pain pills.

He and Rafferty had made desultory conversation for most of the ride to Portland, but the last twenty miles they'd fallen into companionable silence. He hadn't wanted to leave Rock Springs, but he was tired of his own dependency. He needed his car, and his phone, and to set things right with the Saldanos, as much as he could.

"I'll pick you up tomorrow and we'll go to the bank," the detective said when he dropped Dance off at his house.

Dance nodded. He expected to be driving himself, but he would figure that out in the next few hours. Rafferty seemed reluctant to let him go, possibly thinking he'd disappear on him again, but he waved and walked toward the front door.

He had a hot moment of memory about making love to Jordanna, and he smiled faintly. In the hospital all he'd wanted was to get out and figure out who'd bombed the Saldanos and why. He hadn't expected to actually meet someone. He couldn't remember the last time he'd had a truly romantic thought, and this kind of sexual jolt of recall.

He was inserting the key in the lock when the door flew inward. Carmen glared at him, a virago in a tight black dress, her hair swept into a messy bun, dark eyes flashing. Her hair reminded him of Jordanna, but that was where the similarity ended.

"So, you're alive," she said, as if the idea offended her.

"You're back from Europe," he answered mildly.

"We've been worried *sick* about you, and you just waltz in here like nothing's happened."

"I'm not waltzing," he pointed out, lifting his cane.

She looked like she wanted to rip it from his hands. "You owe me an explanation. I hired a goddamn private eye to look for you! Where have you been for the last week? And who is *she*?"

Her fury was like a blast of heat and it made him feel tired. The thought of trying to get past her and work his way up the stairs was a daunting one. "I'm going to sit down," he told her, brushing past her to the living room. The headache that had been a minor annoyance was now starting to pound. She followed after him, shivering with some suppressed emotion. "Go ahead," he invited, giving her a rolling wave. "Get it all out."

"Bastard," she spat.

It was funny how quickly he didn't like himself when he was around her. They'd fallen into such an ugly relationship.

He waited, but she couldn't seem to come up with anything further. He'd hoped he would have a little time before this showdown, but this was her house, too. These uncomfortable moments just made it even clearer that it was time to move on. Past time, really.

"Who is she?" she asked again, having pulled herself back from the brink of out-and-out fury.

"I assume you're referring to Jordanna. She's someone I'm working with," he said carefully. The last thing he wanted was to drag Jordanna into his problems with Carmen.

But Carmen was already there. "She was in this house. In our bedroom. Wasn't she?"

"You and I don't have a bedroom anymore. This is why I should have moved out. Come on, we've been divorced since—"

"She was in your closet. I looked through your things because I didn't know where the hell you'd gone! She got you those clothes!" She threw a disparaging arm out, encompassing his sweats and Nike shirt. "I recognize them. Was she in your bed, too? How many times, Jay, or can't you remember?"

He stared at her, doing an internal check on what was really going on, a tactic he automatically employed when he was faced with an angry interviewee. People say one thing and mean another. "The first time I met her was at the hospital."

"Bullshit, honey," she said, falsely sweet. "You sent her here and she went straight up to your bedroom closet and packed for you. She didn't even bother with any other bedroom. Just beelined for yours. She had to have been here before."

"How do you know she went straight up to the bedroom?" he asked slowly.

Color ran up her neck to her face. "I guessed, okay? Stands to reason, since it wasn't the first time she was here. The point is, how many times did you bring her here? How long have you been fucking her?"

His own temper flared, and he climbed back to his feet, walking toward the kitchen.

"Where are you going?" she demanded. "Where are you going!"

He hoped to hell Rafferty was right and she'd had his SUV returned. He wasn't going to bother with his clothes. Ten minutes of Carmen was more than he felt like dealing with, and it was a relief when he found his Highlander parked in the garage, side by side with her Mercedes.

"You're just going to leave?" She'd followed him to the garage and stood in the doorway, wild with disbelief.

"You wanted us to pretend we were still married while you figured out how to tell your family. Now they know, so there's no reason for us to live together one more minute."

"My father doesn't know," she said quickly.

"Yeah, I think he does." He climbed into the vehicle, inserted the key in the ignition, and revved the motor. She was still talking, trying to be heard above the engine, but he'd closed his ears. He pushed the button for the garage door. In the time it took for it to raise, she was at his driver's window, banging on it with her palm.

"Jesus, Carmen," he said, rolling it down.

"You told him?! You *told him.*" She was damn near hyperventilating.

"The police told him. Now step back. I don't want to run over your Christian whatever-the-hells."

"Louboutins, you asshole."

But she drew back and he reversed into the alley, then aimed for the road in front of their house. He could feel the strain on his injury, but it was his left thigh and the pain was tolerable. Her dark gaze followed him as he drove off. It was a relief when he turned the next corner and he was out of sight completely. Looked like a hotel was in order for tonight.

As he drove, he dug out the car charger from the glove box and plugged it in. Then he finagled the wire into his phone. It took a moment or two, but then he saw the screen light up. Hallelujah. Now he could contact Jordanna and Max.

Boo stared at Abel Fread with fear. Why had he come to their farm? Why was he staying and staying and staying?

Buddy had pulled in behind Abel and stomped out of the car. He was really, really mad, but Abel didn't care.

"Somethin' dead around here," Abel said, almost the moment he angled out of his shiny new truck.

Boo didn't want to look, but he did. His eyes just slid toward the barn and Abel saw it.

"What the hell you got there, boy?" Abel asked Buddy.

Boy? Boo knew Buddy was about to become a volcano. That's what happened if you didn't treat him right. But Buddy smiled at the older man and said, "Thought you wanted to see Jericho."

"That's the stud you been braggin' about?"

Buddy's eyes narrowed. Boo knew he hadn't been bragging about the stallion. That wasn't the way to act. *Blessed are the meek. . . .*

Buddy said, "Come on in the barn, then. . . ."

No! Don't take him to the barn. . . . And besides, Boo knew Jericho was out in the fields because the weather was good. He glanced to where the horse liked to be, afraid the stallion might just come up to the fence and toss his head, looking for an apple. Jericho could be a handful, but sometimes he was downright playful.

But luckily the horse was nowhere in sight and Buddy was striding determinedly toward the barn.

He's going to know, Boo wanted to cry. *He'll tell. You shouldn't have done it. You shouldn't have done it!*

Buddy slid back the barn door and the powerful stench reached out like a hand.

"Whoa, Lordy," Abel said. "You got some dead animal in here."

Boo's .22 rifle was propped against the wall. He was supposed to shoot at squirrels with it, but he liked squirrels and left them alone. A .22 really didn't do much damage, Buddy had said, unless you were right up on the person.

His stomach dropped as Buddy idly picked up the gun.

"Had to put him down," Buddy said.

"Doesn't smell right," Abel said. "You should call the knacker, get the carcass taken away. Woowee, boy."

"I'll do that," Buddy said. He looked ready to explode. Boo imagined ash and fiery rain, lava, falling down on them, as Buddy walked toward the closed door with the wooden bar.

No . . . Boo hung back. He didn't want to look. Didn't want to see, but his eyes wouldn't turn away.

Abel made a face and said, "Now, we can play games all day, but you know I'm looking for your brother. You hidin' him around here? He ain't been at the Calversons since Bernadette disappeared."

Buddy threw back the bar and shoved the door open with his shoulder. Boo started to whimper and Abel gave him a hard look.

"What's the matter?" the old man asked suspiciously.

Buddy said, "Chase is right here. Take a look."

Alarm lit the old man's eyes and he hesitated.

Boo was breathing hard. The smell nearly knocked him over.

When Abel wouldn't move, Buddy aimed the rifle at him. "I said take a look."

"Great God in heaven . . ." Abel whispered.

"TAKE A LOOK."

On leaden feet, Abel moved forward, peering into the darkened stall. Chase was sitting naked in the corner, the flesh peeling off his skull, his eyes sunken and melting, running down his face. His jaw was slack and he still looked surprised. Like he had when Buddy had blasted him with the rifle, straight through his heart. He'd caught him fornicating with Bernadette and had shot him as soon as he stood up. Chase had sunk back down in shock and Bernadette had gone into hysterics, but Buddy had squirted the juice in her mouth and held her close till she'd gone limp.

Boo knew all this, but had tried to block it out.

Now, Abel's keening cry sounded like a dying animal. The old man flapped his hands and backed up, stumbling in the straw, panicked.

"No," Boo whispered, as Buddy raised the rifle, took two steps closer, and shot the old man once through the heart.

Chapter Twenty-Four

Her cell ringing woke Jordanna with a start. She'd been lying on the couch, lost in exhausted sleep, but she scrambled for her phone, wondering what time it was. "Hello?"

"Hey," Dance's slow drawl reached her. "I've got a cell again."

"Oh, good." She was thrilled to hear from him. She glanced out the window, where late-afternoon sun slanted across the drive. "Are you back in Portland?"

"Yeah, I'm calling Max next. Tomorrow Rafferty and I are going to go to the bank and get the audiotape. Then I'm driving your way. You sound like you've been sleeping."

"I just passed out for a while. Guess I was tired." She could hear the smile in her own voice as she recalled moments of their lovemaking. What that man could do with his tongue . . .

"I'm a little tired myself." His voice held a smile as well.

"I talked to my dad earlier, and he said some interesting things."

"Yeah?"

"I'll tell you about it after you meet with Maxwell."

"You okay?" His radar had apparently picked up messages she hadn't meant to send.

"It's just difficult with my dad, you know. A lot of layers to peel back. Some of it my fault," she admitted with an effort.

"Take it easy. I'll be back tomorrow."

Will you? She sure as hell hoped so. "Okay." There was a moment of awkward silence, and Jordanna called on her courage and said, "I kinda miss you."

"I kinda miss you, too. I'll call you later."

"Okay."

More energized, she got up and headed to the kitchen, running the conversation through her mind several times. She glanced around, searching for something to eat. She probably should have stayed and had a meal with her father and Jennie; then at least she'd be fed. But there'd been no way.

She cut up an apple and ate the slices one by one as she stared out the kitchen window to the fields beyond. The afternoon sunshine had a paleness about it, as if it were too weak to hang on for long. There were high clouds on the far horizon, but the rain and fog had disappeared overnight and it seemed like the good weather might hang around the rest of the day.

As she stood there, she went over all the events of the past day and a half. It felt as if she had more questions than answers, but she hardly knew which direction to take first. After a couple of moments, she picked up her phone and stared at her last text to Kara. She dialed her number, but once more it went to voice mail and she hung up. Frustrated, she texted: Are you coming back?

She waited a few minutes, her eyes on the phone, but Kara didn't respond. It bothered her, the way her sister had just disappeared. And she really needed to talk to her, compare notes about everything their father had said.

Emily was Aunt Evelyn's daughter. . . . She shook her head. She was really having difficulty computing that one.

Phone in hand, she scrolled through her numbers, looking to see if she had Aunt Evelyn's. Nope. No surprise there, as it wasn't like she kept in contact with her aunt, either. She supposed she could call her father and get the number, but she really didn't want to. She was still processing everything he'd said, running it through her own bullshit meter, sifting through the words, looking for verisimilitude. It had certainly sounded like the truth, but she'd distrusted him for so long it was difficult to shift gears and head in a completely different direction.

She supposed she could go visit her aunt. Unless she'd moved, and Jordanna had never heard a peep to that effect, Aunt Evelyn was probably in the same small house on the same street. She'd been a schoolteacher, recently retired, and had lived alone her whole life. She was a difficult personality, and the few times their mother had taken them to visit, their aunt had been cordial but stiff, making complaints right and left. Aunt Evelyn had never come to their home in Rock Springs, as far as Jordanna could remember. If what Dayton had said was true, it made a certain amount of sense.

The drive took forty minutes, and Jordanna swept an eye over Green Pastures Church, Everhardt Cemetery, and the Calverson Ranch as she retraced the route she and Dance had taken yesterday to Malone. Had it really been just twenty-four hours ago? Dr. Ferguson had wasted no time in telling Chief Markum that they had visited him, and that he'd told them about the scar. Jordanna felt as if her every move was monitored around here, and maybe it was.

Aunt Evelyn's house was small but tidy. A two-bedroom cottage with a white picket fence, the front walk lined by roses. Jordanna parked in front and glanced down at the robust red row of Mr. Lincolns, the predominant rose that lined the exposed aggregate walk. The air was redolent with the flowers' sweet scent, as she walked to the dark green door.

Jordanna rang the bell. If someone else lived here now, maybe they could direct her to her aunt, she thought, but when the door opened, the sixtysomething woman with the dyed red-brown hair and hazel eyes, so much like Jordanna's own, was nearly as she'd remembered her.

"Hi, Aunt Evelyn. It's Jordanna. Your sister's middle daughter."

There was a moment of consideration, as if she was thinking of some reason to keep Jordanna out. She wore a white blouse, gray skirt, nude nylons, and black medium heels. In the end, she eased the door open a bit and said, "Well, my, my. Isn't this a surprise? What are you doing in Malone, Jordanna? Come on in, but I have to say, I'm leaving in just a little bit."

"Thanks. I was just stopping in anyway."

Jordanna stepped across a polished oak floor. The living room was to her left, and there was a grouping of two overstuffed chairs and a love seat in a puce shade arranged in front of a brick fireplace. A tan area rug, bordered with a pinkish frondlike design, covered a big chunk of the oak floor, and a brass screen with a similar frond design stood in front of the firebox, which looked like it hadn't been used in years.

Evelyn gestured to one of the chairs. "I could offer you tea, or a glass of water?"

"I'm fine, really." She perched on a chair and Evelyn stood by the couch, one hand resting on its back. She looked as if she were ready to fly away at the first opportunity. Maybe she suspected what was coming.

"I haven't been around, and I rarely talk to my father," Jordanna began. "But I'm trying to put some things straight in my life."

Evelyn's fingers plucked at the piping on the edge of a soft cushion. "Oh?"

"Do you mind if I ask you a few questions?"

"I don't know how I can help you, dear."

"Have you ever heard of the term the Treadwell Curse?"

"Treadwell," she repeated, startled. "No."

"I just remember a time when you said you wouldn't have children, because of the curse."

"What? Heavens no." She plucked almost spasmodically at the piping, then, realizing what she was doing, curled her fingers into a ball. "I just wasn't made for motherhood, that's all."

"But you had a daughter. . . ." Jordanna said. "My father told me Emily was your child."

Her hand flew to her throat. "Oh, my goodness! Why would Dayton say such a thing?" She sputtered and looked around wildly, then focused on the jeweled watch on her arm. "I'm having drinks and dinner with a friend, and I don't want to be late," she murmured.

That might be true, but Jordanna kind of suspected her aunt might just be trying to get rid of her. Well, fine. No need to pussyfoot around. "I thought you were the one who called it the Treadwell Curse, but apparently not. From what I hear, it's the Benchleys who suffered from that debilitating, hereditary disease. The Treadwells just somehow became associated with them."

"Oh, yes, yes," she said distractedly. "Treadwells and Benchleys have lived near each other since the homesteading days. Some of the Benchleys did seem to have a genetic disorder, but they're all gone now. Dayton must have told you this."

"I always thought it was the Treadwells."

She shook her head. "No. It wasn't the Treadwells." She swallowed and the hand that had flown to her neck stayed where it was, a kind of protection.

"Was Emily a Benchley?" Jordanna suddenly asked.

"Oh, my Lord. I don't know why your father would say

these things! Actually, I do. He's never liked me. I just can't imagine what would make him come up with such stories!"

"Yeah," Jordanna said, watching her closely. "To what purpose?"

"None that I can see, but he's a hard man, isn't he?" Her lashes fluttered and she looked down a moment, then glanced up. "You surely know," she said, a sly glint entering her eye. "You shot him. I know Dayton was adamant that it was an accident, but I always thought maybe you had a good reason."

"Well, I thought he was having sex with Emily," Jordanna answered, surprising her aunt with her honesty. "But I'm starting to wonder about that. Apparently, Emily was sleep-walking. Maybe she thought she was with one of her boyfriends."

"One of her boyfriends."

"I'm learning she was . . . indiscriminate," Jordanna said, purposely pushing her aunt.

"Emily was a good girl," Evelyn came right back. "She had a nice boyfriend from the church."

"You kept tabs on her?"

"I . . . paid attention to what all of you girls were doing. You were like my own daughters." She lifted her chin in a challenge.

"Do you remember the name of this boyfriend?"

"No."

Jordanna heard the finality of Evelyn's tone and tried another tack. "Emily was adopted. My father said he and my mother took the baby because she was abandoned."

Her face suffused with sudden color. "She was not abandoned! She was . . . not abandoned," she repeated, realizing she'd already given away more than she'd meant to.

"Was she a Benchley?" Jordanna pressed. Her aunt was holding back, but it felt like the dam might break if she pushed in the right spot.

"Emily was a beautiful girl." She was suddenly fighting emotion.

"I've always thought I was destined to lose my mind like the rest of the Treadwells," Jordanna said.

"It wasn't the Treadwells! How many times do I have to say it?"

"I thought it was. I was told it was. For years. Maybe it wasn't by you, although I know you said you wouldn't have children because you were a Treadwell."

"That's not what I said." She looked like she was about to burst into tears. "I said Benchleys and Treadwells couldn't have children . . . together."

Jordanna looked at her aunt, whose composure was disappearing in front of her. "Emily's father was a Benchley, and that's why you gave her up. You didn't intend for my parents to adopt her."

She could tell Evelyn wanted to deny it. Maybe years of hiding the truth had made her half believe the story she'd told herself. But the urge to unburden herself seemed to win out and after a moment of silence, she sank onto the love seat, her gaze on the tan carpet. "She was such a beautiful, beautiful baby. I didn't want anyone to know she was mine. I moved to Malone and gave her up to an adoption agency, but your mother intervened. She wanted the baby. Didn't think she could have any of her own. I was against it from the start, but then I thought maybe it would work, that I could be a part of her life, but it turned out I didn't want to be. It was too hard. But I did keep track." She lifted her gaze to meet Jordanna's.

"What happened to her father?"

"Liam." She swallowed. "He got ill shortly after Emily's birth. His family took over his care and I understand he didn't last long. It often happened that way with them, although some of them lived a lot longer than anyone expected. Before he got sick, Liam used to say it was a prison at their farm, laughing about it, but I think it was true, in a way. Agnes kept the world out, and them safe."

"Agnes . . . ?" Mrs. Fowler had mentioned that name.

"Agnes Benchley. She's the matriarch of what's left of their property."

"The farm on Summit Ridge."

"I haven't paid attention for years. I don't know about them, and I don't want to know. If you have questions, people in Rock Springs should know more than I do."

Jordanna opened her mouth to ask another question, but with a return of starch her aunt abruptly straightened, wiped her hands together as if dusting off their entire conversation, and said, "Now, I've really got to run. I was devastated about losing your mother, and then Emily. It was terrible. I know you had your troubles, too, dear. But I have a life here, and it's not for public view. I've talked to you as a member of your family, you understand?"

"You don't want to see your name in any newspaper article."

"That's exactly right. Or, a television report, or anywhere. I'm already sorry I talked to you. I should've made sure this was off the record straight from the start."

"Don't worry. I'm only looking for answers for myself," Jordanna said, getting to her feet.

"Good. Let's keep it that way. I know you consider yourself a reporter. Just don't report on me."

Jordanna was hustled out the door with very little further fanfare after that. She heard the lock click behind her, and she walked back down the rose-lined walkway, armed with a lot more family information and a feeling of entering someone else's life. Lost in thought, she climbed into her SUV and turned back toward Rock Springs, glancing toward the sun now hanging low over the western horizon.

She sighed. Was it wrong that she was already counting the hours until Dance returned?

* * *

Dance checked into a Marriott Residence Inn off I-5 near Laurelton. He could shoot up Sunset Highway into Portland and across the Marquam Bridge, or he could go west toward Laurelton and Saldano Industries. He was near his own house, right where he was, but he had no intention of going back there, though he had neither extra clothes nor his phone charger. The car charger would have to suffice.

He'd shown up at Max's house, but Max hadn't been home. He'd then broken down and phoned his friend, though he'd wanted to meet him in person first. Max had been amazed to hear from him, and then pissed off that it had taken him so long to get in contact.

"What the hell happened to you, man?" Max demanded. "Jesus, Dance. The bomb and then you're just *gone?* No one would let me talk to you, and I about went crazy. I thought you were dead and they just weren't telling me."

"I'm sorry," he apologized.

"Well, *where were you?* Why'd you leave?"

"I want to talk to you about that. I stopped by your house, but you weren't there."

"I'm at Dad's. He had another heart event yesterday. Jesus. Everything's so fucked up. Come over here and you can tell me what happened to you."

Maxwell hung up before Dance could respond, and Dance had almost called him back and turned him down. He preferred to talk to Maxwell by himself. But in the end he'd texted and said he would be there in a couple of hours. In the meantime, he'd booked himself into the hotel, wondering if he had time to buy himself some more clothes. He still needed sweats or loose pants to get past the bandage, so there wouldn't be much improvement there. He tried to imagine working his way through a mall to a store and, with a growl, gave up the idea. He'd meet Maxwell and Victor as is.

He called Jordanna on the ride over. "Hey, there."

"Hey, yourself. I can't tell you how glad I am to hear your voice."

"What happened?" he asked, hearing the relief in her voice.

"Nothing, really. Actually, I'm just leaving Malone. I met with my aunt Evelyn. She cleared some things up for me, kind of."

"What do you mean?"

She laughed without humor. "My whole past, everything I've believed in, seems to be a mirage. I'm just thinking it through."

"You don't sound happy."

"No, no, it's probably all good, for me anyway. It appears, like Virginia Fowler said, there is no Treadwell Curse. Practically everyone I've talked to since says the same thing: the Benchleys had the genetic illness, not the Treadwells. I've been trying to figure out where this got started, but maybe it doesn't matter. It's strange. I've always worried about what could happen to me and Kara, and now I should be jumping for joy, but I'm having some trouble believing it." In a bemused voice, she added, "Like Aunt Evelyn, I always kind of thought I'd never have children. It's weird to open that door and think it might be possible."

Dance's mind moved ahead. In all his time with Carmen, he'd never thought about having a child. She didn't want one, and he'd never really cared one way or the other. He hadn't even touched on that idea with Jordanna yet. The relationship was too new, but suddenly he had an image of a little boy, and a girl, and a life that had been impossible until now. "It's a good door to open," he said softly.

"Yeah?"

"Yeah."

"Where are you?" she said after a moment.

"On my way to meet Max and his father. Hey, how are you talking to me?" he asked. "You don't have Bluetooth."

"I know. I'm living dangerously. I'll probably get picked up by the chief or Mr. Shitface."

He grinned at her tone. "I'll call after I talk with the Saldanos."

"Okay."

He almost said, "I miss you," but they'd already gone through that earlier, and it made him feel a little silly, like he was going through a first crush again. Instead he said, "Take care," and clicked off.

Jordanna had a smile on her face for a dozen miles, thinking about Dance. His allusion to it being good to be able to have children felt like it portended something more. Maybe there would be some longevity to the relationship. God, she hoped so.

As she neared Rock Springs, she came to the twin entrances to Everhardt Cemetery and the Calverson Ranch, directly across the road from each other. A green Dodge Ram truck was coming from the direction of Rock Springs, slowing and waiting for her to pass so it could turn beneath the arch that marked the entrance to Calverson Ranch. On a whim, she switched on her left blinker to indicate she was heading to the cemetery. She glanced at the driver as she turned and realized it was Martin Lourde. He lifted a hand at her and she did the same.

The entrance road to the cemetery was little more than parallel graveled tracks. Even though the access was rudimentary, the cemetery itself was manicured with clipped grass and headstones that marched in a line over a sloping knoll. One lone oak stood like a sentinel at the far corner.

She pulled into a gravel area near the oak and got out of

the car. She was the only person at the cemetery. She knew where her mother's grave was, and that Emily's was next to it. As she headed toward them, along the path through the headstones, she heard an engine approaching. When she looked up she saw the green Dodge Ram rumbling along the periphery road. It pulled in beside her RAV and Martin climbed out of the cab. He hailed her again, then started her way.

By the time he reached her, she was at her mother's grave, but his eyes had already drifted toward Emily's. Modest granite markers, flat on the ground, designated which was which. "Figured this is what you were doing," Martin said.

"I haven't been here in years," Jordanna said, though he probably knew since she'd taken off right after high school.

"I come here sometimes," he admitted.

"It looked like you were turning into Calverson Ranch."

"I was, but then I saw you, and well, Pru's having one of her Sunday get-togethers and I'd just as soon blow it off. She does them all the time. Tries to fix everybody up with everybody." He made a sound between a snort and a laugh. "Nate's branding cattle, though. He won't come in till after dark. Just his way of kinda pissing her off, I guess. She's a little needy," he added, by way of explanation.

"I kinda saw that."

His gaze slid to Jordanna's mother's grave. "Too bad she got sick."

"Yeah . . ." She regarded him speculatively. "I just learned it wasn't the Treadwell Curse. In fact, I learned there is no such thing as the Treadwell Curse. What do you think of that?"

He regarded her as if she'd said the moon was made of green cheese. "Well, it would be nice if there was no such thing."

"It's the Benchleys who passed on the bad gene," Jordanna said. "Not the Treadwells."

His brows drew together. "Okay . . ." he said dubiously.

"I heard it from several different sources. Do you remember when you first heard the term?"

"All my life, I guess."

"From someone at school?"

"Maybe. I don't know. Does it matter?"

"Maybe not." She let it go, gazing across the cemetery, thinking of all the people in Rock Springs who were buried here. "Did you hear about the woman's body I saw at the old Benchley graveyard, the one on the Fowler property?"

"Yeah . . . kinda."

"I did see it," she assured him. "I was just wondering, why was it moved? Maybe they were afraid of what her body might reveal."

"Like what?"

"I think it was Bernadette Fread. And I hear her boyfriend, Chase Sazlow, went missing about the same time. I don't know how fast the police are going to get on this. They don't quite believe there was a body even there. But I want to find Chase Sazlow and hear his story."

Martin turned his head in the direction of the entrance to the cemetery. Beyond, the arch that led to Calverson Ranch was visible, backlit by the descending sun. "He was bunking at the Calverson Ranch. That's where he works."

"Has anyone seen him since Bernadette disappeared?"

"You'd have to ask Nate."

"Maybe I will." She followed his gaze, but her interest in stopping by while Pru was holding a soiree of some kind was close to nil.

"We used to play out here at night," Martin said reflectively, a small smile touching his lips. "Scare the shit out of each other."

"Rusty mentioned that."

"You'd just be sneaking around and somebody would jump out from behind a headstone and yell 'Boo!' and it damn near gave you a heart attack. We practically peed our pants. Some of us did, actually. Not me, of course," he added quickly.

Jordanna had an inward smile. "Of course."

"I remember one time, this was when Nate's dad was still alive and we were really young, maybe nine or ten. Anyway, Mr. Calverson realized we'd all snuck out and he came in the truck and was hollering like the crazy asshole he was. He grabbed Nate by the arm and shook him like a dog with a rat. And then he went after Rusty, and of course, he was always mean to the guys who worked on the ranch." He suddenly bent down and examined Emily's grave, his nose nearly to the ground. Near the headstone there was a bumped-up mound of grass. He dug his fingers into the mound and dragged out a tarnished chain. He had to give it a hard tug to get it to come free of the dirt and grass, but when it finally released, it swung in his fingers, a long chain with a tiny, once-silver cross swaying back and forth. "God Almighty, I put this here," he said, choking up.

"You did?"

"Yeah." He shook his head in disbelief. "She'd gone so religious and I thought she might like it."

The sun was at the very edge of the horizon. If they tarried much longer, the place was going to be in total darkness.

Martin placed the cross lovingly atop Emily's headstone. "Rest in peace," he said gently.

Jordanna looked from Emily's grave to her mother's and silently thought, *Yes, rest in peace.*

Maxwell looked at Dance with cool, gray eyes. Since the phone call, he'd recovered his composure and now acted like he couldn't care less about where Dance had been and what he'd been doing. The friendship that had been between them had taken a great hit, and maybe was even over. Dance felt a pang of regret, but knew he wouldn't change things. Not if it meant going backward.

"Sit down, sit down." Victor flapped an age-spotted hand at him. "Break my neck looking up at you."

"Carmen told us you wanted out, so she granted you the divorce," Maxwell said shortly.

There was truth there, but it wasn't all of it. "Actually, she suggested the divorce."

"Because you wanted it," Max reiterated.

"So, now you can be with your girlfriend," Victor said, eyes glittering. "Fine. Go. You've always been suspicious of this family, anyway. Always checking to make sure we're on the up-and-up."

"Dad," Max said, shooting his father a quelling look.

Victor ignored him. "So, who bombed us? That's what I want to know."

"I don't know," Dance answered. He looked at Max, thinking of the audiotape he'd given to his friend. Max gazed steadily back at him. Though Dance couldn't believe what was on the tape warranted the bombing, he wondered what Max felt about it. Had he even told his father about it?

"You have some kind of theory," Victor accused him, then grumbled, "Cops and G-men all over the place. Everybody asking questions, no one giving any answers. They act like we're criminals, like we're the culprits."

"They think we are," Max said coolly.

"They're trying to get at the truth," Dance said.

"So, you're on their side now, huh?" Victor was annoyed. "Tell us where you've been."

Dance carefully recounted that he'd been in Rock Springs and had been working on another story there. He didn't want to give too much away, but they seemed to feel he'd been plotting against them, and that wasn't true. Max didn't even appear to be listening, but Victor was all ears. When Dance finished talking, there was a protracted silence.

It was Victor who roused himself first. "So, who gets the house?" he asked, going back to the divorce. "You or my daughter?"

"Carmen can have the house."

Max snorted. "Always the magnanimous one."

"You were divorced, but still living there, together?" Victor questioned.

Again, Carmen's idea. "I'm moving out" was all Dance said.

"Are you looking for who bombed us? I mean, for anyone other than us? You're the man of the people, aren't you?" Max accused. "After the big, bad corporations."

"Only when they do big, bad things," Dance returned coldly. There was only so much he was willing to take, only so long he would play the whipping boy. "Any evidence I find, I'm turning over to the police."

"So, you are working with them," Victor said in disgust.

Dance lasted about ten minutes longer, but then curtly told them he had to leave. As soon as he was outside he sucked in a long breath. He limped as fast as he could toward his car, slamming the door behind him. They wanted to make him the bad guy, so let 'em. Pulling out his cell phone, he called Jordanna again. The screen quivered a little before it held firm, which made him wonder about the phone itself. Maybe he'd damaged it when he'd taken it apart.

It was great to hear Jordanna's voice warm when she realized it was him. "What are you doing?" he asked her.

"Driving to the homestead. I'm going to go inside and go straight to bed. I don't care what time it is. I'm going to bolt all the doors and crash on the blow-up bed."

"I wish I was there," he said with feeling.

"Tomorrow?" she asked.

"Tomorrow," he assured her, meaning it.

* * *

Headlights approached the house. Boo looked at Buddy, who stood in the driveway, making sure the approaching car stopped and didn't get any closer to the barn. Boo shuddered. Abel Fread lay under a tarp, but Boo still could see the old man's face staring up at him, mouth open as if he had something to say that he just couldn't get out. Buddy had covered him up almost immediately, angry that he had another body to get rid of.

"That bitch ruined the homestead cemetery for me," he muttered. "She did it on purpose."

Boo wished she hadn't done that. She was just making it harder. All Buddy wanted to do was save her.

The headlights were cut and they were plunged into darkness once more. No moon was visible, but though he couldn't see it from where he stood in the driveway, Boo knew the brazier was lit. Buddy had closed the barn door, but he could see it in his mind, glowing hot.

The driver's door opened, throwing on a dim interior light. It was *her*, he thought, his chin dropping to his chest. He never liked it when she came.

She stepped out of the car, still in her clothes from church. In her hand was a small white bag. He knew what that was.

"What's Abel's truck doing here?" she asked sharply.

Boo's eyes automatically went to the black truck. Buddy had parked it around the back of the house, so only its rear end was visible. He was surprised she could see it in the dark. She was like an animal, the way she could sense things.

"Abel's truck?" Buddy repeated, trying to play it off. Boo coulda told him that wouldn't work with her.

"Yes, Abel's truck, you idiot. Where is he? Why did he come here? Oh, no. He was looking for Chase?"

"He wanted to see Jericho," Buddy denied. "Use him for stud, maybe."

"Jericho," she sneered. "That horse isn't worth dog meat. If you believe that's why he's here, you're dumber than I thought. Where is he?"

"I dunno," Buddy said.

She sniffed and Boo blinked with fear. "Something's dead," she said.

Boo couldn't smell it from here. That's why Buddy decided to stand in the driveway, to keep whoever was coming by from smelling the bad smell.

"What is that?" she demanded.

"I dunno," Buddy muttered again.

"Should I ask Boo?" she queried, smiling, but it was a really mean smile. "He'll tell me the truth."

"You bringing me that?" Buddy pointed to the bag.

"I'm bringing you this, but I want to know where Abel is, and I want to know where Chase is!" A wisp of a breeze flipped at her tightly curled hair. "What's that *smell*?"

Boo looked fearfully at Buddy, whose face had gotten all tight and mean. "Come with me," he said, reaching for the bag. Reluctantly, she handed it over, but then she marched right alongside Buddy as they headed toward the barn.

Inside, the brazier turned the area orangey-brown. Buddy pulled down the chain for the overhead light, then walked up to Abel and threw back the tarp with the toe of his boot. "There he is," he said.

She was coughing, her hand over her nose and mouth. "Whad'you do?" Her words were garbled, her eyes bugging.

"He wanted to see Chase," Buddy said, turning to the door with the wooden bar. He slapped it open, and pulled on the handle.

Nooooooo. . . . Boo swallowed back the scream in his throat, as he, too, stared into the murky corners.

She walked forward gingerly and shot a quick look inside. Immediately, she rocked backward, staggering a bit. "You killed him? You . . . shot Chase?"

"Him and Abel," Buddy said.

"Oh, my Lord. Oh, Lord . . ." She stumbled toward the barn door, then stopped and stared at Buddy. "What's wrong with you?" she practically screamed. "You have to get these bodies out of here, and forget about that Benchley grave-yard. Do you know how soon they're going to be here to take this farm from you? Do you know the bank is taking this land? Do you understand? You lost this place. You don't know a thing about *anything*. You don't have the sense God gave a worm!"

"Stop it." Boo slammed his hands over his ears, but he couldn't hold her out.

"Your mama would be ashamed," she said.

"My mama beat the living snot out of me," Buddy growled.

Boo's eyes felt they were going to pop right out of his head. *No, she didn't! Mama was good.*

"Your mama tried to knock some sense into you," she argued. "Your dad was a drunk, but even he did a better job of running this farm. Where are Abel's keys? We gotta move that fine new truck before someone sees it."

"No one ever comes here," Buddy said. He reached in his pocket for Abel's keys, looking down at them.

"Liam Benchley did," she reminded him, snatching the keys from his grasp.

"He's dead now, too."

"I'm moving the truck," she said. "I'll take it into town. Leave it on a side street. You come get me, and then we'll all go to our homes. When the cops come looking for him, we don't know anything. You'd better get rid of both of those bodies tonight. I don't care how. But get them off this property."

And then she stomped over to Abel's truck

Chapter Twenty-Five

Monday morning, Auggie sat in Lieutenant Cawthorne's office, one eye on the clock that sat on his boss's desk. He'd been called in early, but he was bound and determined to meet Danziger at ten at his local Bank of America. He'd planned on picking him up, but Danziger had called and said he had his own vehicle and would rather meet him there. Auggie had to agree, but he wanted Danziger and the audiotape wrapped up before he spilled what he knew to the lieutenant.

Cawthorne strode into the room. "Good, you're here," he said. He was the youngest lieutenant on the force, and there was something rough-and-tumble about him that had remained from his days as a detective. On the whole, he and Auggie got on well. They shared some of the same sensibilities, and political pressure from above, like what was coming down on the Saldano case, pissed them both off.

"The feds think they've found the man who made the bomb," Cawthorne said without preamble. He stood behind his desk and threw a glance out his office window, not being the kind to sit down and have a long tete-a-tete.

"Good," Auggie said. "Maybe we'll get some traction on the case."

"This guy's known to them. No ideological issues here, he's strictly for hire."

"So, who hired him?" Since Auggie was ostensibly no longer on the case, he had to tread carefully.

"That is the next question to be answered." He glanced Auggie's way. "I have another job for you. Undercover. Looks like insurance fraud. Arson."

Auggie nodded slowly. "Can you give me today on the Saldano case?"

"And have you piss them off some more? Get another call from the captain?"

He decided to lay his cards on the table after all. "I met with Jay Danziger over the weekend. He has an audiotape that he's getting me today. A conversation between two or three people in the warehouse, discussing some kind of smuggling operation apparently."

Cawthorne turned from the window and crossed his arms over his chest. "Have you heard this tape?"

"Not yet."

"Nobody's going to be happy you got this on your own."

"Danziger was apparently doing some . . . soft . . . investigation into the Saldanos before the bombing. That's how he got this tape. He gave a copy of it to Maxwell Saldano a couple weeks before the bomb went off."

"He should have given it directly to us."

"He's not convinced it's the reason for the bombing."

Cawthorne harrumphed. "When are you getting a copy?"

"I'm meeting Danziger at his bank. It's in the safe deposit box."

The lieutenant made a face. Auggie waited on tenterhooks. He knew how unpopular Cawthorne was going to be if he allowed him back on the case.

"Okay, one day," he said. "As soon as you get the tape, bring it back here. And bring Danziger, too."

"I'll ask," Auggie said dubiously.

"Bethwick and Donley will want to talk to him."

"I know."

"Where's the man been the past few days?" Cawthorne asked.

Though the question sounded rhetorical, Auggie freely answered. "Rock Springs. And it sounds like he's heading right back there."

"What's in Rock Springs?" he asked curiously.

"A woman."

"Ah. Well, I'll take the heat for you today, but that's all we got."

Auggie was already out of his chair, cell in hand. Head down, he strode out of the office, scrolling through his stored numbers. As he pulled up Danziger's, he damn near ran into someone in the hall. "Sorry," he muttered as he punched in the number.

"Rafferty?"

Auggie glanced around and saw it was Geoffrey Stevens, the tech who'd shown him the videotape collected from the cameras on the buildings opposite Saldano Industries. "Oh, hey, Geoff."

"You're off the Saldano case, right?"

"Got reprieved for a few more hours."

"Really?"

His tone of interest caught up Auggie, who was walking away. He shot a look back at the tech and asked, "What?"

"I'd rather give this to you than the feds."

Auggie slowed to a stop. "What have you got?"

"Camera footage from that building that's for lease on the opposite end of the block from where the Winters woman was. I don't have to tell you how hard it's been to find who was in charge of those cameras. Leasing agent wouldn't help us. Corporate kept passing the ball from exec to exec."

"What did you get?" Auggie interrupted.

"The tapes came through this morning, so I did a preliminary check. About three hours before detonation, someone in a trench coat, hat, wig, the works, walked into the lobby. The front of the building's open during the day, per the leasing agent. The only cameras they've got are set up in the lobby and outside the building. Well, the elevators have cameras, too, but the elevators aren't operational right now. She had to take the stairs."

"She?" Auggie asked carefully.

"I can't say for certain, but it's the way she walks," he said. "Even with men's shoes. Kind of a hip sway. When I take a closer look, I think we'll find it's a woman."

A woman. "Son of a bitch."

"Come on and take a look," Geoffrey invited, but Auggie had already fallen in step beside him. He had just enough time before he was due to meet Danziger.

Jordanna was writing down notes as fast as her fingers could fly across the keyboard. Her thoughts were in no chronological order, but it didn't matter. All she needed to do was put something down to remind herself later.

She thought she might be getting used to instant coffee. Some of the stuff on the market wasn't half bad.

Dance had phoned her this morning on his way to the bank. "Rafferty called and wants me stop by the station afterward. I said no, but he was insistent. Said that I'd want to be there. For all the times I've tried to get law enforcement to talk to me and hit a brick wall, I think I'd better go."

"Okay."

"I'll be there soon," he promised. "Be safe."

"You, too."

She settled back to her computer, but had barely dragged

her mind off Dance and back to her notes, when her cell rang again. She picked up the phone, looked at the screen, and said, "Rusty." This time she answered. "Hey, there, Rusty. I'm sorry I didn't call back. I did get your text. I haven't seen Todd."

"Todd's dead," he stated flatly.

"*What?*" She nearly knocked over her coffee cup.

"Found his truck at Fool's Falls lookout this morning, but he wasn't in it. There was blood on the ground, just on the other side of the curve. Right about where Emily went over, y'know?" He choked, sounding like he was breaking down for a moment, then pulled himself together. "I looked over the edge and there was a car down there. A gray sedan. I called the cops and they found out it's a rental. Rented to Kara Winters."

"What?" she repeated herself, more faintly. "What do you mean? Where's Kara?"

"Don't know. Todd was in the driver's seat. He's dead, Jordanna." Rusty sounded dazed.

"What cops found the car? Where's Kara?"

"Drummond and a couple others . . . they took Todd by ambulance, but he's dead. He's gone. There's no doubt about it." He was chattering. "They're pulling the car out now. I think Drummond called your father, but I knew you'd want to know."

"Yes, yes . . . I'll be right there." She was already in motion, checking for her purse, turning back to switch off her laptop.

"I'll see you here."

She moved so fast that the phone slipped out of her hand and crashed to the floor. "Shit, oh, shit." She swept it up, relieved to see it was still working. As she grabbed her jacket, she belatedly listened to the message Rusty had left on her voice mail, which said he'd just found the truck, he was going to look around for his friend and that he hoped Todd had called Jordanna.

She ran down the wooden walkway to the back door, her feet clattering loudly. She was sick with renewed fear. How could Todd be dead? Where was Kara? And why was Todd in her rental car? How had she gotten to Portland? *Had* she gotten to Portland? Jesus. Had she really even called Jennie . . . ?

Jordanna punched in Jennie's cell number as she jumped in her RAV. She counted her heartbeats, waiting for her step-mother to answer. "Come on, come on."

Finally Jennie picked up. "Jordanna," she said. And in that one word Jordanna knew she was already thinking along the same lines as she was. "You know about the car over the cliff? That they think it's Kara's car?"

"Yes. What about the text, Jennie? When did that actually come in? And what did it say? I mean, exactly. What did it say?"

"I—can't look at it when I'm on the phone," she said tearfully. "I don't know how."

"I'll hang up. Look at it, and call me," she ordered. "Do you hear me? Call me back. Where's Dad?"

"He's at the clinic, maybe on his way home now."

"Okay . . . okay. Call me back," she said again. She wasn't quite sure Jennie was really hearing her.

"I will," Jennie promised.

Jordanna clicked off and drove with studied concentration. She counted in her head until Jennie called back. Though it was mere minutes, it felt like forever before Jennie rang through again to say that Kara's message had come in directly before Jennie had phoned Jordanna with the information. She repeated the message, then spelled it out just as it was written.

Jordanna said, "She got 'Portland' wrong and 'sorry'?"

"Well, it is a text."

"Yeah, but . . ." Kara's most common form of communication was texting, and Jordanna always noticed how correct it was.

"Maybe she was driving," Jennie suggested.

"Yeah, maybe. Okay, thanks." With that, she tossed her phone onto the passenger seat and pressed her toe to the accelerator, driving as fast as she dared up Wilhoit to Summit Ridge, past the older Benchley's farm with their NO TRESPASSING sign, and past the drive to Zach Benchley's farm. She flew by the entrance to the old cemetery, then slowed for the curves before Fool's Falls. Suddenly she had to stand on the brakes because there were vehicles parked haphazardly all along the road. One of the cop cars had its light bar flashing. A winch was just pulling the gray sedan over the lip of the cliff.

She slid to a stop and leapt from her SUV. "No sign of Kara?" she asked to the crowd at large.

"You're going to have to move your car," the same young officer from the night before warned her.

"Fuck that." Rusty was hurrying toward her, his strawberry-blond hair disheveled. He swept her into a full-body hug. Jordanna hugged him back, aware his whole body was trembling.

"Kara?" she asked again, when Rusty released her.

He shook his head, looking lost. "They took Todd to the hospital morgue in Malone. I can't believe he's gone. Why was he in that car?"

She felt terrible about Todd, but her worry about Kara was in the forefront of her mind. "Do they have an idea when this happened?"

"Yesterday sometime."

"My sister supposedly texted that she was heading into

Portland yesterday. But if this was her car, it doesn't make sense. You said Todd was found behind the wheel?"

"Yes."

"Could they have met up with each other?"

Rusty's eyes moved to the edge of the road, where tire tracks ran over the edge. "Here's Shitface," he muttered.

Peter Drummond's head could just be seen clearing the lip of the road as he trudged up from the crash site. The rest of his body appeared step by step, and then he reached the asphalt, dusting dirt from his hands. He looked at Jordanna, his expression hard to read, then he strode over to her, lifting a chin at the gray sedan that was being moved onto the flatbed of a tow truck. "Your sister's vehicle."

"That's what I heard. But you haven't seen her?"

"Nope. Did she know Douglas?" Drummond had turned his attention to Rusty.

Rusty shook his head. "Todd just met Jordanna the other day, and he was . . . he liked her. If he knew Kara, he woulda said something to me, or her."

"He liked you?" Now Drummond was looking at Jordanna again.

"I barely knew him," she said.

Drummond said, "You seem to have a few admirers. Where's Mr. Danziger?"

She didn't want to tell him that Dance was out of town, so she just said, "Working on a story."

"The story about the missing body in the cemetery?" His tone suggested he thought her account was a total fabrication.

"Among others," she said shortly.

"What happened to Todd?" Rusty broke in. "He didn't just run off the road."

Drummond wasn't ready to give it up. "This body in the cemetery that you say you saw—"

"That I did see," she corrected.

"A woman's body. If that's true, you think there's a chance it could have been your sister?"

Jordanna's heart jolted before reason reasserted itself. "The body in the grave had been dead for some time. I talked to my sister on Saturday."

"Huh. Well, it's a mystery then, isn't it?" He glanced around, their conversation apparently over.

"Someone did this to Todd, Pete," Rusty said, his voice raspy. "You need to find out who."

"Oh, I will," Drummond said, all business again. He strode back to his car, the one with the light bar still circulating with red and blue, and got on his walkie, though Jordanna wondered if he was really doing anything more than posturing. She didn't trust him to help her.

Where was Kara?

Grabbing her cell phone from her purse, she texted her sister once more. Found your car over a cliff. Looks like an accident. She purposely left out that Todd was behind the wheel. Please tell me you're okay.

She waited for nearly an hour, but Kara never returned her text.

The person on camera moved with a slight hitch to her hips. Even with the layers of clothes, the wig, the sunglasses that looked more male style than female, the chin tucked into the overcoat, covering up the lower part of her face, Dance would bet it was Carmen.

"You're saying she pushed the remote," he said.

Rafferty said, "Seems likely."

They were in a video room at the station. Dance couldn't take his eyes off the image on the screen. Carmen was just stepping into the building's lobby.

"Can you think of a reason your ex would want to kill you?" Rafferty asked.

He almost laughed. "She's Carmen Saldano."

"Meaning?"

"She's been trained to get what she wants at all cost. If she can't achieve it, she's just as likely to destroy it."

"She didn't want the divorce."

He shook his head, his throat dry. Though she was the one who'd initiated divorce proceedings, he'd always known she hadn't really wanted it. He'd just thought she'd finally recognized there was nothing worth saving in their marriage.

Rafferty cleared his throat and said, "Maxwell Saldano was called away from the bomb site because of his father's illness."

Dance ripped his gaze away to meet the detective's eyes. "Carmen wouldn't have told him. You think Victor knew and faked it."

"It's a possibility. Maybe Maxwell knew, too."

Dance struggled with all of it. He'd considered them his family.

"Federal agents Bethwick and Donley are on their way," the detective said. "They're already pissed that I'm involved. Seeing this isn't going to improve their moods. They're going to want to talk to you."

"They've got ten minutes, then I'm out of here." He hesitated. "What about Carmen?"

"We're picking her up," he said. "Don't go home."

"Don't worry."

Jordanna tried calling Dance, but the phone went straight to voice mail for the third time. She knew he and Rafferty had probably picked up the audiotape from the bank and were at the police station by now. She needed to talk to him, but he'd probably turned his phone off. It's what she would do when facing the police, not to mention the FBI or any other federal agents.

She texted him, also for the third time, saying the same thing she'd said the first two times. Cops found my sisters car at the bottom of a cliff. Todd Douglas was in the drivers seat, dead. Kara's not answering texts or calls. Don't think she ever left for Portland.

When he turned on his phone, he would see that and call her.

The crime tech team was scouring Summit Ridge Road. She realized they were collecting bits of blood. Todd's blood . . . or Kara's. She inhaled sharply. She couldn't think like that.

"I'm going to go," she said to Rusty, who'd wound down into silence.

"Where?" he asked, as if there was nowhere he could think of to be.

"I don't know yet."

She walked back to her car. She kept going back to her last conversation with Kara. Who had her sister seen in town? She'd recognized someone . . . Emily's old boyfriend? That had been the thrust of the conversation. But who was that? Not Martin Lourde. According to him, Emily had broken up with him, not the other way around, and he was still affected by her death. Not Rusty. He was Jordanna's age and Emily wouldn't have looked at someone younger, and even if she did, Jordanna would find it hard to believe she'd choose goofy, freckled Rusty. There were tons of guys from Emily's class who could fill the bill, guys Jordanna scarcely remembered. She'd only had eyes really for Nate.

Nate.

Jordanna swallowed hard, making herself think back. She'd been entranced with Nate Calverson. A really deep crush. He'd been the handsome, wealthy, everything guy, whereas she was the doomed, half-crazy Treadwell girl, not even the prettiest one. That had been Emily.

Someone had said how attractive the Benchleys were . . .

Virginia Fowler? Well, that was certainly true in Emily's case. And something had switched inside her mentally toward the end. She'd become promiscuous, and she never had been before, as far as Jordanna knew. Was that a function of the disease? And would Nate Calverson, Mr. All That, have decided to take advantage of her? Maybe helping her onto the righteous path of the Lord, something Emily might have needed to hear at that point in her life?

Jordanna headed back into town. It was noon and the skies were threatening rain. Would Nate be at the ranch now, or would he be at lunch? She supposed she could call Rusty and get his number, but she liked the idea of surprising him.

She drove past Green Pastures Church and then under the arch to the Calverson property. The driveway curved around, flanked by magenta rhododendrons on either side, their blooms just past their zenith. Several dogs began baying at her arrival—beagles, she saw, as they darted out of the main ranch house, both brown and white splotched, their tails wagging rapidly in eager greeting.

Pru came to the door. "Down," she ordered, snapping her fingers at the dogs, who wanted to put their muddy paws on Jordanna's jeans. They sniffed her and sniffed her, and then suddenly tore around the outside of the house, baying madly some more. "Well, hi, there," Pru said. "What a surprise. Come on in."

"Is Nate here?" Jordanna asked tensely.

"Well . . . nooooo . . . he's down at the barns with some of the workers." She looked slightly alarmed that Jordanna wanted her husband.

Jordanna didn't plan on telling her about Todd Douglas and Kara. She wanted to see Nate's reaction firsthand. "I need to ask him some questions. I won't stay long."

"What kind of questions?" Now she was fully alarmed,

either for some reason she wasn't saying, or just because she was so afraid of any woman getting near him.

"I see the barns," she said, looking into the fields. "Why don't I just hike over there?"

"They could be out a ways away branding cattle," Pru tried to discourage her.

"I'll find him." Jordanna picked up her pace, practically race-walking away. She didn't want to give Pru too much time to think about it, and she didn't want her accompanying her, either.

The barns were a little farther away than she'd initially thought, the distance deceptive. By the time Jordanna reached them, she was out of breath from hurrying.

Nate was right inside the doors, leaning against a stall door, looking lazily at a young man who was cleaning the straw and horse dung from another stall. "Put your back into it," he said. "There are ten more of these, and if you don't get going, it'll be midnight before we're done."

He spied Jordanna and straightened up, looking surprised to be caught idle while the young man was working hard. "Well, how do you do, Ms. Winters."

"I've been up at Summit Ridge. Todd Douglas is dead. His car went over the cliff, right where my sister did years ago."

"Holy shit," he said. He came out of the barn, grabbed Jordanna's arm, and walked her out of earshot of the younger man. "Douglas is *dead*?"

"Rusty called me. He thought I might have talked to Todd, but I didn't. Todd's truck is at the lookout at the top of the falls, but he was found behind the wheel of the car my sister, Kara, rented. We haven't heard from Kara since Saturday."

Nate was blown away. "Wow . . . that's terrible."

"Kara supposedly left Rock Springs and went to Portland. She left a text to that effect. But she saw someone in town the last time I talked to her. Someone she thought was familiar, and she acted like it was Emily's boyfriend from her last year of high school."

"Emily dated a lot of guys," he said carefully.

"I know." Jordanna didn't have time for pussyfooting. "That's the last time I talked to Kara, when she met up with this guy. No one's seen her since, and now her car's been found."

"But she texted you that she was leaving?"

"Someone texted Jennie," Jordanna corrected. "I'm not sure it was Kara."

"What are you saying?"

"I wondered if it was you she saw in town. I thought Kara might not really remember you from high school. Maybe she saw you, and you looked familiar."

"Oh, Kara knows me. Rock Springs had the best basketball team in its history when I was a senior, and I was the captain. Of course she knows me." He sounded affronted that Jordanna could suggest otherwise. "And I remember her. Kinda cute. She was a freshman or maybe sophomore?"

"You didn't run into her in town the other day?"

"No."

"Did you take Emily to the old homestead cemetery in high school? I remember you talking about some girl you'd taken there."

"Now, wait a minute. I mighta taken somebody, maybe Emily, to the cemetery across the road, but I never went to that one. A lot of people did, but not me. I was here." He was positive. "What are you really getting at?"

"I want to know who Emily was seeing at the end of her senior year. Her boyfriend. Because that's who I think Kara ran into on Saturday, and now she's missing."

He stared at her a long moment, then his mouth turned down at the corners. "I don't know how to say this much plainer, but Emily was kind of a slut. She'd make out with anybody. Hell, she was with *Lourde*. Did you ever meet his wife? She was as homely as a mule, and even she divorced him."

Jordanna held her temper with an effort. "Emily was with someone after Martin. She broke up with him around Christmas."

"You'd have to go through the yearbook. It'd be easier to know the ones she didn't sleep with."

"You're a real peach." She had to work herself out of her anger. "It was someone religious, who got her on the path to righteousness. Give me a few names. I'll take it from there."

He glowered at her. "Most of the real Bible thumpers stayed away from you Treadwells, no offense."

"Who told you there was a Treadwell Curse?" she asked.

"What's that got to do with . . ." He stopped himself and answered flatly, "Everybody told me."

"Think back. Try to remember who was adamant that the Treadwells were genetically doomed." Nate held up his hands and shook his head, as if he thought she'd really gone around the bend. "It's all a lie," she told him. "A falsehood. Somebody made it up, and we all believed it."

"Maybe you ought to talk to Reverend Miles," he suggested.

"Why? Would he know?"

"I'm thinking that you're pretty upset. Say what you will about Green Pastures, there's a lot of good that comes out of talking things over in church." Then he hurried back to the barn just as the rain began to fall in fat drops.

"Thanks," Jordanna said drily. He was no help at all.

She left him standing outside the barn and hurried back to her car. She had no plans to talk to Reverend Miles. What could he help her with?

Her wipers were going like mad by the time she reached the road, and then shortly thereafter she came to the entrance to the church. What the hell, she thought, turning in. Nate wanted her to see Reverend Miles because he thought she needed help, and it was true the man knew all the people in town that she did. And church was a good place to find someone who was deep into their religion.

A sheet of rain was pouring as she turned into the long drive that led to the church. She pulled around to the back parking lot and parked next to a battered truck, the only other vehicle in the lot.

While the rain pounded onto her windshield, she sent another text to Dance: Want to know who kara saw in town. Emilys boyfriend?? At gree

She jumped when someone tapped on her window, sending the text too early. "Damn," she muttered. He made motions for her to roll down the window and she cracked it open a teeny bit, mindful of the rain splashing inside. A man in a cowboy hat was standing beside her car. He'd apparently come from the other vehicle

"Fancy meeting you here," he said.

"Do I know you?"

"Don't you?" He smiled.

He looked somewhat familiar, but she wasn't placing him. "Not really," she said. He was good-looking with a lean, hard build, and when he tilted the hat back, she saw he had penetrating blue eyes. "It's raining hard," she said, wanting to roll the window back up.

"You going to church? Get out and make a run for it."

She rolled up the window, tossed her cell in her purse, then slid out of the car, ducking her head. She was going to look like a wet dog. "I'm looking for Reverend Miles," she said, glancing toward the church. The entrance was toward the front. "Do you know if—"

Suddenly he was on her, grabbing her, slamming her body against her car. She squeaked in surprise and slipped against the wet fender. She had no time to react before he was shoving something between her teeth—a vial?—and squeezing something down the back of her throat.

"Uh—uh," she gasped. What the hell was that?

When he suddenly shifted to pull her away from the car, she doubled over and shoved her fingers down her throat, throwing up bile and coffee into the rivulets of water running across the lot.

Before she knew what was happening, he smacked her hard across the face, hard enough that she saw stars. Then he hit her again, a demon in a cowboy hat with rain pouring off the brim.

That was the last thing she remembered.

Chapter Twenty-Six

Jordanna woke slowly, mouth dry, feeling as if her limbs were weighted down. There was a god-awful smell of rotting flesh that brought up her gag reflex again, and she coughed twice. She was in a barn, seated on the wood floor, wisps of straw here and there. Across the way was a fireplace of sorts with a branding iron sticking out of its depths. There was a faint orange glow within, like dying embers.

Somewhere, almost out of earshot, there was shouting going on. Angry tones that faded in and out.

A woman was yelling. ". . . shouldn't have . . . able . . . and Bernadette was *clean* . . . happens when they foreclose? . . . you dumb bunny, you . . . the law down on all of us!"

A man interrupted. ". . . know what I'm doing . . . not listening to you anymore, you filthy, fucking . . ."

She started screaming back, words Jordanna couldn't make out.

He said clearly, "Boo was right about you."

More shrieking from her. "The Treadwell girls! That's all you were supposed to do! The Treadwells!"

Smack.

Jordanna shivered, recoiling, squeezing her eyes closed.

He'd hit her, too, if it was the same man, and who else would it be? Her head hurt and she felt dizzy, but maybe that was from whatever he'd given her, too.

Smack. Smack.

The woman was sobbing. ". . . God will never forgive . . ."

Then the sudden report of a rifle.

Jordanna's eyes bolted open. *Oh, God. Oh, no. Oh, my God.* Tears seeped down her cheeks, from fear, from the rank smell that was something dead, something large. . . .

He came striding into the barn, his blue eyes so bright in the slanting afternoon light that they looked lit from within. "Sometimes God sends us exactly what we're looking for," he said.

Jordanna had closed her eyes again, but her breathing was rapid. He'd probably seen that she was awake. He came over and she sensed that he'd squatted down in front of her.

"You just stay quiet," he whispered. "Let the juice do what it's supposed to."

The juice? What he'd given her?

Then he walked away and she heard something being dragged. She squinted her eyes open just a thread and saw that he was hauling a body from beneath a tan tarp. Gray-haired, lined face, eyes open and staring, a spread of red across the front of his shirt. Was this his victim, then? She'd heard a woman's voice.

He hauled up the body and threw it over his shoulders, fireman-carry style. She heard what sounded like a body thrown into a metal container and realized he'd probably tossed it into the back of his truck.

He was out of earshot for a time, but then she heard him again, approaching. She shut her eyes again, waiting, and after a minute he snorted in derision and moved away. Once again she barely lifted her lids and saw that he had a woman's body over his shoulders. Someone with tight, curly dark hair. Middle-aged.

Her head flopped back and Jordanna jerked as if stung. Margaret Bicknell! What the hell had happened?

He strode out of view again and she heard him grunt as he must've tossed her body in the truck as well. Then the engine fired up and it rumbled away.

As soon as she was certain she was alone, she tried to struggle to her feet. Her hands were caught and she realized they were tied behind her back with twine. A short piece of rope extended from a post and was tied to the twine. She wrenched herself around to see the rope was pulled through a hole in the post and back to her hands. The only way to untie herself was at the point where her hands were held together, and her captor had secured her tight enough that her hands were numb from restricted blood flow.

Shit. Who was he? Was he the one Kara had seen? He must be. *The Treadwell girls*, the woman—Margaret?—had screamed. *That's all you were supposed to do! The Treadwell girls*.

She moaned with fear. What had he done?

And then her cell phone started ringing from inside her purse. It was sitting on a bale near a door shut with a wooden bar. *Dance*, she thought, struggling against her bonds. *Dance!*

Dance listened to his cell phone ring on and on. He'd really wanted to hear Jordanna's voice, but she wasn't picking up. As soon as he'd been free of the federal agents and police, he'd grabbed up his phone to call, but the phone had hesitated. Swearing, he'd jumped into the Highlander and plugged in the car charger. He switched on the engine, but the phone had remained dark and stayed that way until he was about an hour from Rock Springs, when it suddenly flashed on. Immediately, he'd put through the call, but now she wasn't answering.

He saw there were several texts. Three times she'd written: Cops found my sisters car at the bottom of a cliff. Todd Douglas died in the drivers seat Kara's not answering texts or calls. Don't think she ever left for Portland

And the other one read: Want to know who kara saw in town. Emilys boyfriend?? At gree

"Jesus." He called her number again. It rang about four times, and when her voice mail came on, inviting him to leave a message, he hit speakerphone and yelled, "Jordanna. Pick up! Todd Douglas is the missing friend of Rusty? The one he and Calverson were waiting to play pool with? Are the police sure it was Kara's car? Call me." He clicked off, his nerves on edge. Jordanna had said Kara texted Jennie . . . but how had she gotten to Portland if her car was in Rock Springs?

A lot of questions, none with any answers. He settled in to drive, one eye on the rearview mirror because he didn't give a damn about the speed limit.

He was gone a long time and Jordanna tried everything in her power to get her hands free. She looked around the barn wildly, searching for a tool to aid in her escape, and though she could see a pitchfork, a scythe, and a rifle, none of them were close enough to reach. The scythe was nearest, and it was the tool she wanted most, but it was still out of range.

Who was he? Where was this barn? Oh, God. Why had he killed Margaret and that other man?

Her gaze traveled to the branding iron heating in the fire and she felt ill. She would bet it was a cross, one he could turn upside down.

And then she heard the truck's engine and the splash of water as the tires bumped through rain puddles. Could she feign more sleep? He seemed to think the juice would help her relax. She felt foggy, but she was fighting it for all she was worth.

He strode into the barn, and she watched him through the haze of her lashes. His denim shirt was damp and mud-spattered now. She shut her eyes completely as he came her way. She could hear the stretch of fabric and his own close breathing, and she was pretty sure he'd crouched in front of her again.

"You're awake," he said, sounding a little excited about it. "You hawked it up, you bitch. And now you're awake." She gasped when he grabbed her head and dug his thumbs in her eyes. "Open up," he sang.

"Stop . . . please . . . stop! I'm awake."

He pulled his thumbs away and Jordanna opened her eyes. They ached but apart from renewed tears, she could see fine. She stared at him. His blue eyes were bright and vacant. She'd always worried she'd lose her mind, but this was what real crazy looked like.

He seemed to be content to watch her.

She licked her lips. "I don't know who you are," she said.

"You should. Your sister did."

"Which sister?" Jordanna asked with dread.

He came even closer, to look her directly in the eye. "Both," he said, confirming her worst fears. "But I only loved Emily."

Her cell phone started ringing again and his head whipped around. *No*, she thought, sick with fear. He went over to her purse and dug around for her phone, pulling it out to look at the screen.

"This your crippled boyfriend?" he asked, turning the phone around so she could see it, walking back her way.

"No," she lied, reading Dance's name.

"Another one of your studs?"

"I think you have the wrong impression of me."

He threw the cell on the floor, stomping it with the heel

of his boot with a fury that frightened her. "I know you Treadwell girls," he declared breathing heavily. "She told me." He threw a dark look back toward the barn door. "You're all filthy whores."

She must be Margaret Bicknell. But she asked, "She?"

"She's dead now, which means I can do whatever I want now. God sent you to me."

Jordanna's heart thudded so hard she could see it. She was in real peril. *Keep him talking. Keep him talking.* The only weapon she had was time. If Dance couldn't reach her, he would find someone who could. She had to believe that.

"If you loved Emily, how can you call her a whore?"

There was a sudden transformation. His eyes suddenly rolled heavenward and his body jerked like it had been shocked. A moment later, he observed her with an entirely different expression, almost a pleading one.

"Buddy's sorry about Todd. He liked him," he said.

She drew a shallow breath. What was this? "Did Buddy put Todd in Kara's car?" she asked carefully.

"Uh-huh. He had to."

"Do you know what happened to Kara?"

"Buddy saved her. Sent her soul to heaven. Seared out the devil."

Jordanna's jaw started to quiver. "Is she dead?"

Tears filled his eyes. "Yes, but she's with God now. She was Lucifer's daughter, but Buddy saved her."

Jordanna's shoulders sank. Grief filled her so completely she felt like she was going under. She believed him. She didn't want to, but she did. *Kara was dead.*

With an effort, she asked, "Who are you?"

"I'm Boo."

"Boo?"

"Yeah, like BOO, you're it!" He suddenly laughed uproariously, causing Jordanna to flinch. "Buddy won't let me play in the playground anymore. But now you're here. You can help me talk him into it, okay?"

Jordanna stared blankly at him. *Find me, Dance. Hurry. Please, find me!*

Dance reached the outskirts of Rock Springs at four and planned to plow through town directly to the Treadwell homestead, but as soon as that thought coalesced, it seemed wrong. He took his foot off the gas. She wasn't answering her phone. Something was wrong, and he didn't think she was at the homestead. What had the last text said? She was at "gree." Was that some kind of garbled word?

He drove straight to the police station and limped through the rain, pushing through the front door. He spied Rusty almost immediately, waiting near the reception desk. He looked wrung out and half wild, his hair straggling, as if he'd been standing outside for hours. He was demanding the police do something, but no one was paying much attention to him, though they appeared sympathetic. It was grief talking more than anything.

"Rusty," Dance said.

He turned around, his eyes hollow. "Where's Jordanna?" he asked.

"That's what I was going to ask you. I just got back. She's not answering her phone."

He shook his head dolefully. "I don't know, man. I don't know."

"Is the chief around?" Dance looked toward the front desk, where two officers were talking in low tones.

"I think he's with the doc . . . Jordanna's father."

"At the clinic?"

"Nah, I think he went home because of Kara."

Dance looked around, thinking hard. He didn't have

Dayton Winters's number in his phone. "You know where Dr. Winters's house is?"

"Sure." He gave Dance directions, pointing down the street in the direction he'd come. "You can't miss it. It's got a red birdhouse on a stick out in the yard, and if the chief's there, you'll see his car."

"Can I ask you a favor? Would you go out to the Winterses' homestead and see if Jordanna's there? I don't think she is, but if she is . . ."

"Sure, man. I'm not doing any good here." He seemed almost relieved to have a call to action.

"Thanks."

Dance headed back to his Highlander and waved a goodbye to Rusty as he walked toward a blue truck. He then made a three-point turn in the center of the street to reverse direction, drawing a honk from an incensed driver who flipped him off as he tore back the way he'd come. He wound through a housing development and, per Rusty's directions, found the Winters house with ease. There was no black-and-white prowler out in front, so he assumed the chief had already left.

He grabbed his cane and hurried, half hopping, up the walk. A porch light was on against the dark afternoon. It was June first, he realized. It had been less than a week since last Tuesday's bombing.

He knocked rapidly on the door, waiting impatiently until sharp footsteps came his way. The door swung inward and Jennie Winters stood in the aperture. "Oh, hi, um . . . Mr. Danziger."

"Call me Dance."

"Jordanna's not here."

"You have any idea where she might be? I've been out of town and I'm looking for her."

She shook her head. "Maybe Dayton knows something.

Have you heard that they found Kara's rental car?" she asked as she stepped back inside. "And about Todd Douglas? It's just terrible."

He nodded. "Jordanna left me a message about it. Kara hasn't turned up?"

"Nobody knows where she is. I thought she texted me, but Jordanna seems to think it wasn't her."

She led Dance across an oak entryway, down a step to a sunken living room that turned a corner into a dining room, kitchen, and a family room, where Dance could see the flickering pictures of a television, the sound turned down. Dayton Winters was sitting in an easy chair, his eyes focused on the TV, but Dance could tell he wasn't seeing anything. As soon as he saw Dance, he got to his feet.

"Have they found her?" he asked anxiously.

"Kara? I don't know. I'm looking for Jordanna."

He said, "We haven't seen her since she left the restaurant yesterday." He ran a hand through his silvered hair. "I thought maybe you had news about Kara."

"Jordanna sent me a text, three texts, actually, about one o'clock with the message about Kara. That's the last I heard from her." He quickly brought Dayton up to speed on what he knew. "She's not answering her phone."

Dayton's worry meter inched upward. "Well, where is she, now?" he asked tensely. "Greer said Officer Drummond saw her at the crash site, but that she left."

"Do you have any idea where she was going?"

Both of them hesitated, looking at each other as if willing the other to speak first. Jennie finally shook her head, and Dayton did the same.

They were no help. "Let me show you her last text." He pulled out his phone and showed Dayton what she'd written: **Want to know who kara saw in town. Emilys boyfriend?? At gree**

"Is that supposed to be 'agree'?" Dayton asked.

"She never finished the thought. Maybe she got interrupted."

"What does she mean by Emily's boyfriend?" Dayton asked.

"The last time Jordanna was on the phone with Kara, Kara ran into someone she recognized. She was in Rock Springs, and she said something to Jordanna that led her to believe it was Emily's boyfriend."

"Emily's boyfriend . . ." Worry had carved deep lines in Dayton's face. "Kara knew all the boys she dated."

Jennie suddenly spoke up. "Well, maybe not all of them." When Dayton turned to look at her, a blush crept up her neck. "She dated quite a few, for a while. She was kind of secretive about it all."

"She started going to church," Dayton said, trying to deny what Jennie was telling him, yet he was clearly aware enough of Emily's indiscriminate dating. "She was putting her life together. It's really what helped me turn to God and become a member of Green Pastures."

Dance's pulse leapt, and he quickly turned on his phone again, sliding his finger across the screen and finding the message button, drawing up Jordanna's last text. "She's at Green Pastures," he said.

"Are you sure?" Dayton's disbelief would have been comical if Dance weren't so worried.

Dance was already in motion, hurriedly making his way back through the house. "Emily's boyfriend was a churchgoer," he said over his shoulder.

"Let me get my jacket," Dayton said, moving toward an alcove at the back of the kitchen where there was a coatrack. "I'm going with you."

Dance opened his mouth to tell him no, when Dayton's face suddenly took on a baffled look.

"You don't mean Dutton Sazlow, do you?" he said.

"Who's Dutton Sazlow?" Dance asked quickly.

"Emily spent a lot of time with him that last spring. I always credited him for helping her discover her spirituality and the Lord."

Dance was thinking fast. "He's related to Chase Sazlow, Bernadette Fread's boyfriend?"

"They're brothers."

"Where does he live?" Dance demanded.

"Just south of town, the second homestead from Rock Springs."

If he could have run, Dance would have already been out the door. As it was, he limped, hopped, and half ran out the door and to the Highlander. Dayton had grabbed his coat and was on his heels.

Chapter Twenty-Seven

They were trekking through the rain, following the ruts that were now filled with water from the barn to where he'd taken the two bodies. "Haven't had time to bury them yet," he told her conversationally. Boo had wanted to show her the playground, but Buddy had returned with a rolling of the whites of his eyes and a hitch of shoulder muscles. He'd released her from her bonds, but was now walking behind her, the .22 pressed into her lower back. If she ran for it, she might escape, or he might hit her in the spine.

"You shouldn't have found Bernie," he said. "She's supposed to be at the Benchley cemetery. That's where they're all supposed to be. Now, what am I gonna do, huh? Where can I put 'em?" He nudged her hard with the rifle and she stumbled and nearly fell into the puddles of dirt.

She wished she was still with the "Boo" persona. Buddy was far more dangerous.

"Who was the man that was under the tarp?" she asked, searching for conversation.

"Abel."

"Abel Fread?"

"I like talking to you," he said on a note of discovery.

"I never got to talk to the others, except for Emily . . . and Mama . . ."

Jordanna wiped rain off her lips. "Is Mama somewhere here, too?"

"I killed Mama first," he said, his voice chilling in its lack of emotion. "I didn't want to, but she was a sick bitch, like you. Not a Treadwell, but she had it, too."

"You mean, she was a Benchley?"

He was silent for a moment. She sensed that she'd given him something hard to think about. "What's it to you?" he finally demanded.

"Benchleys have the disease, not Treadwells," she told him.

He grabbed her shoulder and whirled her around, glaring down at her, his face shadowed by his cowboy hat and the softly falling rain. She braced herself for another hit, but then he laid a palm against her cheek and started to chuckle. "You're a good liar. Satan taught you well."

"I'm not lying. Margaret told you to get the Treadwell girls, but she was wrong. It's not us. We're not the ones who got sick."

"Yes, you are."

"No."

"You're all whores. And Bernadette was fucking Chase. She wasn't clean!"

Jordanna reheard Margaret's voice in her argument with Buddy. *That's all you were supposed to do, the Treadwell girls!*

"You killed Bernadette," she said, trying to keep the fear out of her voice. "What happened to Chase?"

"Caught them fornicating. Shot him in the stall."

"In the barn?"

"You smelled him, didn't you?" he stated.

Her stomach revolted at the remembered scent. She

visualized the door with the wooden bar. Chase Sazlow was rotting in the barn.

He pushed her hard with his hand, and she stumbled and trudged toward a copse of trees, the ground rising a bit, becoming stonier.

"Over there," he said, stopping her, then grabbing her head and turning her to her right. He nudged her in the new direction and she could scarcely make her legs propel her forward.

"Where's Boo?" she asked, her steps slowing as she saw the mounds of dirt ahead. He was digging graves, she realized. She could see a rain-damped, denim-clad leg. Abel Fread.

"Boo's not here," he snapped. "He's back at the house, where he should stay."

Jordanna wondered what would happen if she told him that he and Boo were one and the same. Her jaw was quivering and to keep her teeth from chattering, she said, "I don't remember you. I don't remember anyone called Buddy in high school."

"That's not my name." He made a sound of disgust. "That was Mama's name for Boo. She liked Boo, but he hid from her, so she hit me with the strap. Sent me to Calverson's place to work. Old man Calverson. What a fucker. Hit me with the hot branding iron once. Said it was a mistake, but it wasn't. He meant it. Got the scar to prove it."

They were at a makeshift graveyard. The rain was diminishing and a mist was rising from the ground. She could see the new dirt over what she assumed were several bodies. Was one of them Kara? she wondered, bile rising up her throat. Margaret Bicknell and Abel Fread were lying on the ground. He'd started several new holes, but had apparently grown tired and come back for her.

"See?" he said. Then, "They'll be okay for tonight."

"How many . . . are here?"

"Mama, Bernie, *Kara*," he said, deliberately stressing her name, "and now Aunt Margaret and Abel. Liam fell out of the truck before I could bury him. Don't worry. . . . There's room for you."

Jordanna felt dizzy. Liam? Liam Benchley? He was long dead, wasn't he? She wondered if she was going to pass out, from whatever drug he'd given her, from grief, from fear. "Margaret Bicknell's your aunt?" she asked, hearing her voice as if from a long ways away.

"She's the one that told me about you Treadwells," he said. "She said you had the putrid disease and it was up to me to save you all."

It started with Margaret, Jordanna realized dully. Margaret, the pharmacist, who'd known her father for years, and who had access to all kinds of drugs. In a vague corner of her mind, she remembered her mother saying to her father, "If Maggie Bicknell had her way, the girls and I would disappear. Poof!" And she snapped her fingers, and added, "Then she could have you all to herself."

"You've seen 'em. Time to go back," he said, grabbing her and physically turning her around.

She gazed at the barn. Thought of the branding iron. "Boo said he wanted to go to the playground."

"Don't listen to Boo!"

"He said I could talk you into it."

"Noooooo!" And then he went through that peculiar hitch and he threw his head back and she saw the eye roll. And then Boo was back, looking at her from under the hat with sadness, she thought.

Jordanna took off running for the barn.

The gun . . . the gun . . . she thought wildly. She zigged to the left. Racing full out. She stumbled a little against rain-slick grass and mud, but kept barreling forward. It was still light out, but fog was starting to roll in. Her ears were full of noise: Her stuttered, gasping breathing. The rush of air. The silence behind her. Was he aiming?

She bent forward, then had to catch herself, her strides shortening, becoming uneven. She listened for the report. Expected it. But what she heard were pounding footsteps. He was chasing her.

She doubled her speed, avoiding the ruts from the tires, staying on the grass. The barn was ahead to her left. *No, don't go there!* Death waited. Torture. The house, then?

Her eyes shot to the right, where the farmhouse stood. Dilapidated, gutters overflowing, back porch roof sagging. Foreclose, Margaret had said.

. . . you dumb bunny, you . . .

She made it halfway to the house before he tackled her. Her breath rushed out with an *oof.* Her face plowed into the wet grass.

"Bitch! I'll kill you."

He was rolling on her, turning her over. She hauled back a fist and hit him in the face, but it only served to infuriate him. His hands were around her throat.

"Succubus!" he screamed.

The light around her narrowed to a tiny white bead.

"Dance," she said softly, then the light was gone.

The Highlander screamed through Rock Springs and onto Wilhoit Road. Dance hoped he'd pick up a police car. "Call the chief," he ordered Dayton, who was hanging on to his seat and staring grimly through the windshield.

Dance had left his phone charging in the car and Dayton picked it up. He punched in the number from memory. Too slowly, Dance thought, his teeth grinding.

But he got through and said succinctly enough that he

and Jay Danziger were heading to the Sazlow farm in the belief Jordanna was in danger at the hands of Dutton Sazlow.

"Who's this Dutton?" Dance demanded as soon as Jordanna's father broke the connection.

"His father was an alcoholic. Died when Dutton turned eighteen. His mother left when Dutton and Chase were in grade school. That farm was one of the last pieces the Benchleys hung on to, but they were losing it, and Kate Benchley married John Sazlow to keep it in the family. Now, I think . . . she may have suffered from the disease. She was beautiful. We all had a crush on her. It was a shock when she married Sazlow, but I think now he was malleable." He threw Dance a look. "Dutton's ten years older than Chase and there was a rumor that Kate was pregnant when she married Sazlow. Probably no truth in it. What is true is there was no money. They had the land and John Sazlow's skill as a farmer, but it was hard. Kate shoulda just let the land go. She grew unhappy . . . antisocial. There were stories about her acting out in the grocery store, at church, wherever, though I never saw any of that. She became a recluse and then she was just gone."

"You think she had the curse." He said it as a statement, eyes glued to the road.

"Well, there's something that runs through the Benchley family," he admitted reluctantly. "Emily showed symptoms. It was heartbreaking."

"Emily was a Benchley?" he asked in surprise.

"Jordanna hasn't told you?"

"I haven't really had a chance to talk to her."

Briefly, the doctor explained the history surrounding his eldest daughter and Dance realized what Jordanna had been processing when she'd returned from her aunt's and sounded so unhappy.

"I thought Dutton was good for her. He took her to

church. They were friends, not lovers," Dayton said. "At least that's what I thought."

"And now he has Jordanna." *And what did he do with Kara?*

"I hope I'm wrong about this," the older man said tautly, but the look on his face said he didn't believe it for a minute.

Dance concentrated on the road. Ten more minutes. It couldn't be more than that.

"Wake up," he growled in her ear. He slapped her cheek. "Wake up. Your lover's not here, so quit calling his name! WAKE UP."

He was shouting in her face when she came to, but this time it was easier to pretend she was still out. She was covered in mud, as was he. He'd tossed her down where she'd been before but hadn't tied her up again. He was shaking her like a rag doll, her head flopping loosely on her neck. He threw her down in disgust.

And then there was crying. Was Boo back? Or, was it an elaborate ruse on Buddy's part?

She kept her eyes closed, not daring to crack them open this time.

"Old man Calverson hurt me," Boo said, sniveling. "Did it to Buddy, too."

Don't open your eyes! But it was like they had a will of their own, slitting open. Boo was standing a few feet from her, his hands at his belt buckle.

Alarm licked through her, but she stayed still. What was he planning to do with his belt? Whip her?

But instead of yanking the belt free, he pulled down his pants and she saw the "C" scar on his thigh. *"See,"* he said. "LOOK." Vaguely, she realized he meant C, the letter. "You know what it's for? Calverson." A jerk and an eye roll and

Buddy was back. "Stop faking it, or I'll burn you while you're awake."

She slowly opened her eyes. He'd lost his cowboy hat in the tussle, but he had the .22 in one hand. As if realizing it, he propped it against the wall.

"You said you loved Emily," she said, seeking to appeal to some human part of himself, maybe the part reserved for Boo. "But you killed her."

"No." He shook his head vehemently. "I was chasing her. She lost control. That was before I knew what I had to do."

"Before Margaret told you to kill the Treadwell girls." What time was it? Where was Dance? Oh, God, she wished she still had her phone. If there was just some way to call him.

Another swift change, and then Boo cried, "It wasn't Buddy's fault! She was mean. And . . . and . . . they needed to be sent back to God."

"They. I'm one, too," she reminded, trying to appeal to him. Boo was childlike in comparison to Buddy. "Buddy made a mistake about that."

"Noooooo . . . !"

And then Buddy was back again. His gaze dropped to Jordanna's breasts and he licked his lips. "You wanna see Chase?"

"No."

"He's right behind the door. Wanna see?"

"No . . . no . . ."

But he was on his feet and hurrying to the stall door with the wooden bar. She braced herself as he suddenly stopped and trembled. Boo's higher voice cried, "She doesn't want it! Don't open it."

But even as he was talking, he was lifting the bar. The door swung outward and she caught a glimpse of a nightmare corpse, the mouth dragging downward, the eyes sunken and liquid, receding into a skull of darkly rotting flesh.

"You're Chase's older brother," she said, searching for the name. *Dutton . . . Dutton Sazlow.* She didn't remember his face, yet he had to have been at school about the same time she was. And he'd known Emily. "You didn't go to Rock Springs High?"

"Mama taught me everything."

And suddenly she remembered Emily straightening up from straddling their father, shrieking, "Dutton!" Not Dayton. She'd been shaken awake from sleepwalking and had called out to her boyfriend.

"You were the one who got Emily on the righteous path to the Lord," she realized dully.

"I loved her," he said again. "But if she'd lived, she would have had to die. Like you . . ." His eyes were hot as they looked her over. Jordanna shrank back, aware that he was lusting for her, uncertain whether he had any self-control left. Then he pulled a small white bag from the pocket of his jacket and opened it up to reveal a small vial. He stuck the eyedropper inside and filled it to the top.

Dance missed the turnoff to the Sazlow property. It flashed by on his left and he stood on the brakes. The Highlander fishtailed, shuddered, and stopped. Quickly, he threw it into reverse. Dayton got a new hold on the chicken bar and then they were plowing down a rutted lane filled with muddy, rain-filled potholes.

"I don't need that," Jordanna told him.

"Yes, you do. I have to sear out the bad," he said.

"I can take it."

He was very near. She'd tucked her hands behind her as

if they were still tied, hoping he would forget she was free. He didn't seem to be tracking very well. The switch between Dutton and Boo took a toll.

"It will be too painful," he said.

"You won't hurt me, will you?" She gazed at him appealingly. If she stirred his compassion, she might be facing Boo again. That's what she wanted. The weaker persona.

"It will hurt." He frowned. She sensed he was fighting to keep Boo away. Outside, she heard the approach of a racing engine. *Dance!*

With a roar, Dutton pulled away from her, dropping the eyedropper. Jordanna was up in a flash. The scythe? No. The gun!

Dutton had run for the branding iron. What he intended to do, she didn't know, but she guessed he was going to finish what he'd started come hell or high water. She tore for the .22, yanking it into her hands as he whipped around with the red-hot iron. She could see the "t" of the cross.

Car doors slammed. She heard a shout. Dutton was lost for a moment, not sure which threat to attack first. Jordanna lifted the rifle to her shoulder, sighting. "I'll shoot you," she said. "I'm a pretty good shot."

"Jordanna!" Her father's voice was like the crack of a whip. She faltered, but Dutton whirled around with the branding iron, silently charging Dayton. Dance was suddenly in the barn door, hampered by his leg.

"Wait!" he called to Dutton, but it was too late. He thrust the iron at Dayton's chest, searing through his jacket and shirt. Her father cried out in pain.

"Drop it," Jordanna ordered Dutton.

He paid no attention to her, but Dance was on him, trying to knock the iron out of his hand. It went flying toward the hay bale. He got off balance, his leg weak, and Dutton kicked at him.

"Don't do this, son," her father pleaded, reaching toward him. Dutton roared again, glancing around wildly.

"Get out of the way, Dad." Jordanna's finger was on the trigger.

Dance stood up. "Wait."

Dutton hesitated, couldn't decide between Dayton and Dance. But Dayton was closer. He reached for the pitchfork and whipped it at him.

"GET OUT OF THE WAY, DAD."

Dutton grabbed her father's arm, but Dayton pulled back. *Blam!*

Jordanna blasted Dutton Sazlow, who stared down at the hole in his shoulder for a brief moment, then sank to the ground in utter disbelief.

It took hours to straighten everything out. Chief Markum and Peter Drummond came flying up the lane, lights flashing and sirens blaring. Dutton sat for a stunned moment, while Dance ripped off his own jacket and pressed it against the wound; then he turned into Boo and curled into the fetal position, crying softly and saying it wasn't Buddy's fault, over and over again.

Jordanna huddled beneath a blanket beside Dance and let the police take over. An ambulance was ordered and Dutton was taken to Malone, under police custody. Peter Drummond got all officious and demanded statements, even from her father, who refused to go to the hospital as well. His burn, tempered by his clothes, wasn't as severe as it could have been. Markum wanted to forgo questioning Dayton at all, but Jordanna's father insisted he be a part of it, so they all trooped to the station and made their statements. Jennie came rushing in and Dayton held her close. Dance lasted about an hour before dragging Jordanna away, declaring they all could pick it up again the next day, and taking her home.

Home . . . Rustic as it was, the old homestead felt like it welcomed her with open arms. She stood beneath the shower's spray until the hot water ran out. Then Dance came in and wrapped her in a towel. Soon after they made love again, sweetly and tenderly, and she told him she loved him without caring if it was too soon.

"I think I've loved you since you showed up at the hospital" was his heartfelt response, which made her nose burn with unspent tears.

Three weeks later, she was at her laptop, putting the finishing touches on a story that was planned as a weeklong series for *The Oregonian,* an in-depth look at life in a small-town farming and ranching community that also touched on one homesteading family's history with a disease that had devastating consequences for those afflicted, and those who helped take care of them.

Jordanna finally had the opportunity to interview the Benchleys, Agnes Benchley, to be exact, the matriarch of the remaining Benchley family, who let her behind the NO TRESPASSING sign and into her home, filling her in with some missing family history. The older woman was as spry and sharp as Virginia Fowler, though not quite as forthcoming. She hemmed and hawed awhile before trusting Jordanna with her tale. She lived with her two remaining siblings, Oscar and Leonard, still handsome, elderly men who could have been twins. "We all made a pact," Agnes told Jordanna, and the two brothers nodded. "The Benchley disease was going to end with us. We all stuck to it. Leonard and I never married, never had families, and Oscar and his wife, Clarissa, God rest her soul, adopted a boy and a girl."

"Allen and his sister," Jordanna remembered. "I met Zach, Allen's son."

"That's correct. But . . . when I said we stuck to the pact, that isn't completely true. Our sister, Mona, who was stricken, had a child, Liam, and after her death, we took care of him. We'd lost most of our property by then, all we had was what's now the Sazlow place and this last farm. Now, it's just the farm."

"Liam Benchley. I was told he died young," Jordanna said.

"No." Agnes shook her snow-white head. "Sometimes it happens like that. They live a long time." Her smile was reflective, sad. "He was a charming, handsome little boy. We hoped he would be like Oscar, Leonard, and me—not afflicted—but it wasn't the case. When he got ill, we took care of him here for the rest of his life."

"So, my sister, Emily, was the last of the Benchleys?" Jordanna had told her about Aunt Evelyn and Liam, and it had come as a surprise.

The older woman looked down at her hands, almost in prayer. "We didn't know Liam had a daughter until you told us. And we also didn't know that my father had another child, Henry, until much later when Henry showed up in Rock Springs with his wife. He'd taken the Benchley name, even though our father never acknowledged him while he was alive. Henry had the disease, it was clear, but it was a milder case. And he'd already had two daughters, Kate and Margaret, who both kept the Bicknell name. We were all praying that everything would work out with them, but . . ." She wagged her head. "Now they're both gone."

Jordanna had nodded. Kate's bones and Margaret's body had been transferred from the Sazlow property to Everhardt Cemetery. Chase, Bernadette, and Kara had been interred there as well. The community had held a joint service for all of them, and Jordanna had stood beside her father at the ceremony. When he'd reached for her hand, she'd held on tightly.

Agnes had initially worried about Dutton and Chase. "I knew they were Kate's, but it always seemed like they were fine. Margaret never had children and she led a normal life, so it was just Dutton and Chase. Well, and Liam."

Liam had never left the house until just before his death, when he'd started to wander back to the old property. Twice, Allen had gone in search of him and had brought him back. It embarrassed him, Agnes revealed, and he and his adoptive father, Oscar, had fought about it, but then Liam was gone and Allen said he couldn't find him.

Liam was the homeless man, discovered three years earlier. She'd already figured out as much from what Dutton had said. Agnes and her brothers hadn't told the authorities that Liam was missing, and when, and if, they'd been apprised of the death of a "homeless" man, they apparently never made the connection. It was Jordanna who gave Agnes the information that the man was her brother, Liam, to which Agnes simply nodded and said they'd figured he was gone. Jordanna didn't mention the branding. It would do more harm than good at this point, she felt. If someone else told the family matriarch, fine, but if Agnes never knew the extent of Dutton's downward mental spiral, so much the better. All she'd been told was that several bodies had been found on the Sazlow property. She probably had to suspect foul play was involved, but she didn't ask, and Jordanna didn't tell. When her series came out, some of that would be revealed, but Dutton's craziness wasn't the thrust of her story and she'd downplayed it.

But, in the telling, Jordanna had written about Margaret's mission to purge the Treadwells from Rock Springs. Margaret must have truly believed the Treadwells carried the rogue gene as she'd clearly beaten that information into Dutton's head. Jordanna had quizzed her father about Margaret, wanting to know if she had ever been interested in him romantically. He'd shaken his head in disbelief, but finally admitted, yes, she'd once chased him down with a persistence that had been both irksome and slightly scary. Though Margaret's laserlike focus on Dayton had bothered Jordanna's mother, he'd personally dismissed it. He found it horrifying that she'd since focused on his children as the targets of her campaign to purge the disease forever.

Jordanna also kept Dutton's regression into the persona of Boo from Agnes, though she touched on it in her series as well. That division had apparently started when his mother had begun to fail and taken out her aggressions physically on her oldest son. To get him out of her sight, Kate Sazlow had sent Dutton to work at the Calverson farm at a very young age. There, he'd encountered Gerald Calverson, a rigid taskmaster with a sadistic streak, who had branded the boy, all under the guise of an accident that Jordanna just didn't believe. It seemed like Nate might share in some of his father's traits, she thought, recalling how he'd ordered around the poor kid cleaning out the stalls. Though the Calversons were no relations to the Benchleys, they certainly had their own dark family history.

She was just closing her computer when she heard Dance open the back door. Dayton had blessed them with a working refrigerator, and though they'd both protested that they were only at the homestead temporarily, neither had made any serious effort to leave yet.

"How'd it go?" she asked, when he appeared in the doorway, holding a bag from Braxton's Pharmacy. His injury was well on the way to being completely healed and he'd given up the cane shortly after the debacle at the Sazlow farm. Dutton was also healing, she'd heard, and was awaiting his fate in a jail cell. Everyone suspected he would never be pronounced fit for trial.

"Okay," he said. "Max apologized to me."

Jordanna's brows lifted. "What happened?"

"Guess he finally realized none of it was my fault."

He came and sat down beside her on the couch.

Dance had been driving back and forth from Rock Springs to Portland and back again, dealing with the aftermath of the bombing and the involvement of the Saldanos. Carmen had been arrested and had immediately hired a high-powered attorney, loudly insisting that she was innocent, and it was all a setup. Victor's health had taken a steep nosedive, and until today, apparently, Maxwell had given Dance the cold shoulder, especially when it appeared that the two men on the audiotape had been under Victor's personal employ. Apparently, Victor had sporadically smuggled in stolen artifacts from other countries, intending them for his personal collection. He'd learned of Carmen's plan and had faked his heart "attack" to make certain his son was safe. Dance was working with the police to bring all the evidence to light.

"How's the writing going?" he asked, throwing an arm over her shoulder.

"I'm kind of tired of it." She glanced at the bag. "What's in the bag? Lunch?"

"Well . . . it's almost edible." He pulled out a bottle of lime-pomegranate body wash.

Jordanna grinned. Since their first night together, she'd been thinking about his body pressed to hers, slick and wet. "Think your injury can handle it?"

His snort of derision said it all. She kissed him hard on the mouth, laughing, as he pulled her to her feet.

Epilogue

The late-June day was warm and bright with none of the "June gloom" so often associated with the month along the West Coast. September walked along the beach with her cell phone pressed to her ear, her sister, July, strolling beside her, baby Junie strapped into a Baby Bjorn across her front.

"You seriously get enough signal here?" July asked skeptically.

September nodded, listening to her brother recount what had gone down with the Saldano case.

". . . lawyers are trying to get her off," Auggie was saying, "but I don't think all her father's money is going to help. The videotape's damning, and with the audiotape Danziger provided, Victor Saldano's goose is cooked, too."

"What about Maxwell?" she asked.

"So far he's in the clear. Maybe he knew something about the smuggling, but if he had a clue about the bombing, he should get an Academy Award, because that was some acting. I think he always thought it was sabotage, and that's what it looked like."

"Danziger's lucky, then, that Jordanna Winters got him out of the hospital, because Carmen doesn't seem like the kind of woman to give up." She heard beeping in her ear and pulled the phone away to see who was calling. "Auggie, I gotta go, it's Gretchen," she said when the cell was to her mouth again.

"Even when you're on vacation," he tut-tutted. "You're as bad as I am."

"You got that right." She said good-bye and clicked over. "This better be good, Sanders, because I'm walking on the beach with my sister and my new niece, and Jake's back at the cottage we rented, getting his three favorite women appetizers and wine from both the Westerly and Rafferty vineyards, though of course July's drinking grape juice and, well, Junie's on breast milk."

July blew a raspberry, but she was smiling, looking down at her sleeping baby with tenderness.

"You're gonna want to cut that vacation short," her partner predicted. "Remember Fairy and Craig and the skeletons in the closet?"

"I'm not likely to forget."

"Finally got all the forensic work back. Remember there was Gramps and Gran and Uncle Harry, too. Lots of stealing money from the government. But wait, there's more. A new guy, too. This one's about our age, so no one's hiding him in order to cash his Social Security check."

"Really?" September said.

"Bones are pretty clean, so he's been there awhile. Looks like we got ourselves a bona fide case, Detective Rafferty. When can you get back?"

September looked at her sister, then out across the restless gray ocean, the frothy white waves rushing up the beach and nearly touching her sneakers, then down at her bare finger, the one she'd decided probably needed that ring after all. Nothing like a newborn baby to put things in perspective. And no, she wasn't ready for motherhood yet, but geez Louise, time had a way of running faster and faster, and putting off marriage to the man she loved because she felt conspicuous about wearing a ring? What the hell was the matter with her?

"Oh, no, what's she saying?" July asked, reading September's expression correctly. "You promised a whole week, remember?"

September nodded to July, and said, "I'll be back on Monday," to Gretchen.

"Come on, Nine. I could have this thing solved by then," Gretchen protested. "Come back tomorrow."

"Monday," she reiterated, clicking off as Gretchen swore pungently. Then she leaned over and kissed Junie's clean little brow, her mind traveling along pathways she tried to ignore.

"You're not going to make it till Monday," July predicted.

"Sure I will."

"Wanna put a hundred dollars on that?"

September started to protest, to tell her sister she was all wet. She wasn't nearly as gung-ho as her partner about these kinds of weird cases. But, she could admit a little tickle of interest growing, a desire to know the truth. Extra bones? Someone around her age dumped into the mix at the house on Aurora Lane? A possible homicide?

July had thrust out her hand, waiting for September to shake on the bet. September curled her fingers into her palms, ignoring the request, and July laughed out loud, an "I told you so" evident in her amused eyes.

Romantic Suspense from
Lisa Jackson

Absolute Fear	0-8217-7936-2	$7.99US/$9.99CAN
Afraid to Die	1-4201-1850-1	$7.99US/$9.99CAN
Almost Dead	0-8217-7579-0	$7.99US/$10.99CAN
Born to Die	1-4201-0278-8	$7.99US/$9.99CAN
Chosen to Die	1-4201-0277-X	$7.99US/$10.99CAN
Cold Blooded	1-4201-2581-8	$7.99US/$8.99CAN
Deep Freeze	0-8217-7296-1	$7.99US/$10.99CAN
Devious	1-4201-0275-3	$7.99US/$9.99CAN
Fatal Burn	0-8217-7577-4	$7.99US/$10.99CAN
Final Scream	0-8217-7712-2	$7.99US/$10.99CAN
Hot Blooded	1-4201-0678-3	$7.99US/$9.49CAN
If She Only Knew	1-4201-3241-5	$7.99US/$9.99CAN
Left to Die	1-4201-0276-1	$7.99US/$10.99CAN
Lost Souls	0-8217-7938-9	$7.99US/$10.99CAN
Malice	0-8217-7940-0	$7.99US/$10.99CAN
The Morning After	1-4201-3370-5	$7.99US/$9.99CAN
The Night Before	1-4201-3371-3	$7.99US/$9.99CAN
Ready to Die	1-4201-1851-X	$7.99US/$9.99CAN
Running Scared	1-4201-0182-X	$7.99US/$10.99CAN
See How She Dies	1-4201-2584-2	$7.99US/$8.99CAN
Shiver	0-8217-7578-2	$7.99US/$10.99CAN
Tell Me	1-4201-1854-4	$7.99US/$9.99CAN
Twice Kissed	0-8217-7944-3	$7.99US/$9.99CAN
Unspoken	1-4201-0093-9	$7.99US/$9.99CAN
Whispers	1-4201-5158-4	$7.99US/$9.99CAN
Wicked Game	1-4201-0338-5	$7.99US/$9.99CAN
Wicked Lies	1-4201-0339-3	$7.99US/$9.99CAN
Without Mercy	1-4201-0274-5	$7.99US/$10.99CAN
You Don't Want to Know	1-4201-1853-6	$7.99US/$9.99CAN

Available Wherever Books Are Sold!
Visit our website at **www.kensingtonbooks.com**

Books by Bestselling Author
Fern Michaels

___The Jury	0-8217-7878-1	$6.99US/$9.99CAN
___Sweet Revenge	0-8217-7879-X	$6.99US/$9.99CAN
___Lethal Justice	0-8217-7880-3	$6.99US/$9.99CAN
___Free Fall	0-8217-7881-1	$6.99US/$9.99CAN
___Fool Me Once	0-8217-8071-9	$7.99US/$10.99CAN
___Vegas Rich	0-8217-8112-X	$7.99US/$10.99CAN
___Hide and Seek	1-4201-0184-6	$6.99US/$9.99CAN
___Hokus Pokus	1-4201-0185-4	$6.99US/$9.99CAN
___Fast Track	1-4201-0186-2	$6.99US/$9.99CAN
___Collateral Damage	1-4201-0187-0	$6.99US/$9.99CAN
___Final Justice	1-4201-0188-9	$6.99US/$9.99CAN
___Up Close and Personal	0-8217-7956-7	$7.99US/$9.99CAN
___Under the Radar	1-4201-0683-X	$6.99US/$9.99CAN
___Razor Sharp	1-4201-0684-8	$7.99US/$10.99CAN
___Yesterday	1-4201-1494-8	$5.99US/$6.99CAN
___Vanishing Act	1-4201-0685-6	$7.99US/$10.99CAN
___Sara's Song	1-4201-1493-X	$5.99US/$6.99CAN
___Deadly Deals	1-4201-0686-4	$7.99US/$10.99CAN
___Game Over	1-4201-0687-2	$7.99US/$10.99CAN
___Sins of Omission	1-4201-1153-1	$7.99US/$10.99CAN
___Sins of the Flesh	1-4201-1154-X	$7.99US/$10.99CAN
___Cross Roads	1-4201-1192-2	$7.99US/$10.99CAN

Available Wherever Books Are Sold!
Check out our website at **www.kensingtonbooks.com**